Estelle

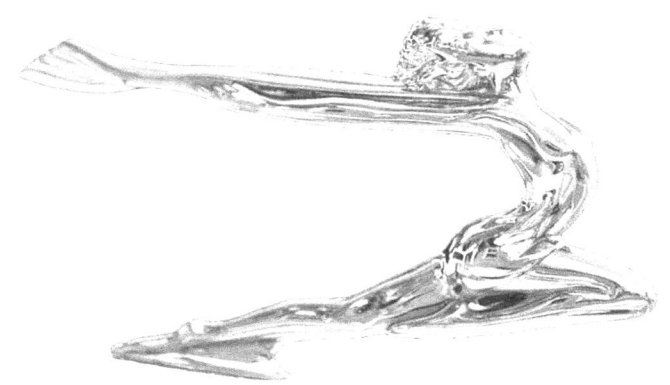

H. P. OLIVER

HPO Productions
8698 Elk Grove Boulevard, Suite 1-271
Elk Grove, California 95624

Cover art and book design by Steve Eitzen

Printed in the United States of America

MYSTERIES IN HISTORY

ISBN-10: 0-9994150-0-X
ISBN-13: 978-0-9994150-0-9

DEDICATION

This novel is respectfully dedicated to the custodians of our planet's information, the Librarians. Without the men and women who catalogue, store, and protect our books, electronic media, and other informational documents, we would be dumber than dirt.

AUTHOR WEBSITE

You are cordially invited to visit the author's website at http://www.hpoliver.com for many free features related to this and other H. P. Oliver books. These include a unique visualization section providing illustrated quotes from ESTELLE that will increase your reading enjoyment by allowing you to "see" parts of the story (use link below).

http://www.HPOliver.com/BOOKS/ESTELLE/VISUALIZATIONS/INDEX.html

ACKNOWLEDGMENTS

The author gratefully acknowledges the following research sources used in the writing of this novel: Los Angeles Public Library, City of Santa Barbara, Santa Barbara County, California Department of Parks and Recreation, Pierpont Inn, Los Angeles Millennium Biltmore Hotel, Ascent Real Estate, Montecito Inn, American Gas & Oil Historical Society, The Old Motor Webzine, and Ventura Community Memorial Health System (Big Sisters Hospital). Also, special thanks to Gary Weisenberger for keeping me honest.

PLEASE NOTE

This novel occasionally refers to individuals and groups with terms that are considered disrespectful and inappropriate in today's society. These terms, however, were in common usage during the historical period in which this story is set and are included here solely for the purpose of accurately depicting the attitudes and customs of the day.

Map of Metropolitan Los Angeles
courtesy of
YOUR NEARBY GILMORE GASOLINE DEALER

You can't afford to buy gasoline with your eyes closed! Get the lion's share of motor performance with GILMORE Blu-Green Gasoline!

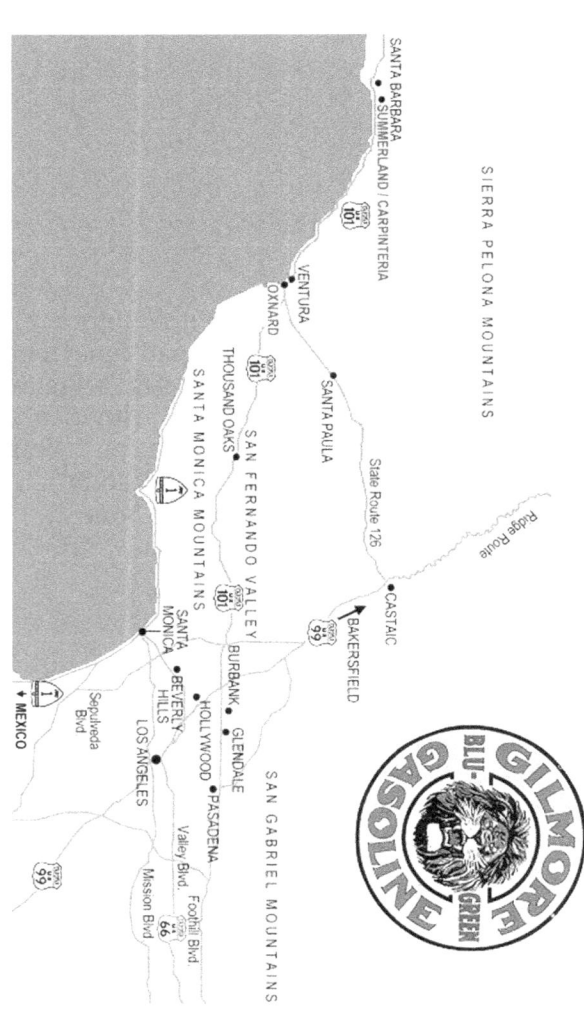

ONE

Tuesday - September 4, 1928

I was struggling mightily to conceal my aggravation, but apparently failing miserably in that endeavor. Mister Hamm seemed quite capable of reading my countenance just as he read the copy we reporters submitted for articles in the *Santa Barbara Tribune*, which he edited.

"I have no doubt you would much prefer a front page assignment, such as Lieutenant Commander Byrd's expedition to Antarctica; however, Mister Kinney, you are still new to our community and the assignment I have given you provides an excellent opportunity to become acquainted with the most influential people in Santa Barbara, acquaintances that will serve you well in the future."

Frederick Hamm, a robust man in his upper forties, and I were seated opposite one another at a cluttered desk crowded into a small space designated as the editor's office. This was only the second occasion on which I found myself in Mister Hamm's domain, the first being one week earlier when I was hired to fill a vacant reporting position.

The editor's office was at the center of a busy beehive known as the newsroom. The office was also furnished with windows in all four walls, presumably so Mister Hamm could keep an eye on his staff—experienced reporters busily typing the sort of hard news stories I longed to write. Swallowing my exasperation along with a good deal of pride, I said, "Yes, Mister Hamm, I will do my best to write a comprehensive story about Missus . . . ah . . . Abernathy's donation to Saint Andria's orphanage."

"Better make that Miss Abernathy. She has never married." Then surprising me with a friendly smile, Mister Hamm added, "Do not despair, Mister Kinney. If I am any judge of journalistic talent, you will be moving on to bigger and better assignments before we know it."

"Thank you for your encouragement, Mister Hamm."

Ignoring my small gesture to remain in the boss's good graces,

Mister Hamm said, "Estelle Abernathy will present her donation during a ceremony at the County Courthouse next Saturday. We need an announcement article for Friday's edition and a report on the event for Monday."

While I wrote these instructions on the stenographer's pad I use for notetaking, Hamm added, "That gives you plenty of lead time, so I suggest you do some research in our morgue and at the city library. See what you can learn about Estelle Abernathy. Then, with what you glean from those sources in hand, go see the grande dame, herself, and get a few quotes to liven up your announcement article. I want that article by noon on Thursday, so hop to it."

A few minutes later I was back at the small desk provided for my use in a remote corner of the newsroom thinking about the best way to proceed with my new assignment and deciding I would begin with the library. The *Tribune's* archive—or morgue as news people call it—was just downstairs in the basement, but I felt a need to go out and about in the real world. That decision made, I rolled down my shirt sleeves, straightened my snazzy blue and white polka dot tie, donned my suit jacket, and out I went.

The *Santa Barbara Tribune* offices and presses are located on Anacapa Street across from city hall and around the corner from our competition, the *Santa Barbara Post-Dispatch*. The library is situated about five blocks to the north, where Anacapa intersects Anapamu Street. Being that it was a pleasant afternoon, I left my automobile parked at the curb and set out afoot.

The downtown commercial area of my new hometown began beyond the city hall, a block to my left. The area through which I walked was called the civic center because it was home to most of Santa Barbara's municipal buildings—the city hall, the courthouse, the county clerk and recorder's building, and my destination, the city library.

In 1916 the city received a Carnegie grant to construct a new library, and the resulting three-story mission revival edifice was completed the following year. I knew these historic facts not because I possessed any great knowledge of Santa Barbara history, but because I stopped to read the text of a bronze plaque located next to the library's tympanum-topped main entrance.

A great deal of Mister Carnegie's money was spent on creating a colorful woodcarving of the city's coat of arms for the semicircular recess above the entrance, and I had to wonder if there was anything left in the budget for books. I was promptly relieved of this concern, however, upon entering the enormous high-ceilinged main reading room. Shelves on all of the walls were lined with tomes galore and freestanding shelving filled the expansive space with even more volumes. Surely I had stumbled into Bibliophilic Heaven.

As this was my first visit to the Santa Barbara Public Library, I had no idea where the local history section might be, so with my footsteps on the tile floor echoing off the high ceiling, I walked toward a large desk bearing a sign that spelled out "REFERENCE." Presiding over this desk was an attractive young woman of about my same age. At that moment she was engrossed in a large dark green, cloth-bound book that, from my vantage point, looked as if it might be an encyclopedia volume.

While standing patiently at the desk waiting to be acknowledged, I admired the young woman. Her eyes were large and brown. Her short dark hair was done up in what I believe is called a finger wave bob similar to the styles made popular by several well-known motion picture actresses. She was attired in a long navy blouse with a white collar and featuring bold white stripes in a geometric pattern. While the rest of her outfit was concealed by the desk, I judged her style of dress to be conservatively flapper-ish.

While ogling lovely women is a pleasant pastime, it was not accomplishing the task for which I traveled to the Santa Barbara Public Library. When it seemed I had waited more than long enough to warrant some sort of acknowledgement, I quietly cleared my throat. That gesture earned me a glare from the large brown eyes and a verbal acknowledgement somewhat different from what I was expecting.

"Sir, will you kindly wait your turn? I am currently researching another patron's reference question."

As she turned back to her reading, I looked around for the other "patron." There was no one else anywhere near the desk and I was about to comment on this when I noticed the telephone on her desk. It was the older candlestick variety with a dial affixed to the round base and the earpiece was off its hook. Apparently one could call in to have a reference question answered. Now, if that isn't the cat's pajamas, I don't know what is.

I strolled to a nearby bookcase and perused the titles with one eye while watching the reference woman with the other, lest I miss my turn and have to wait even longer. Eventually, she spoke briefly into the telephone, hung the earpiece back on its hook, and swiveled her chair around to replace the volume she was using on a shelf behind the desk. When she turned around, I was standing front and center at the desk.

She looked up, glowered, and said in a cold tone of voice, "Yes, sir, how may I help you?"

"I've come in search of background information about Estelle Abernathy and I'm new to your library. Would you please direct me to your local history section?"

Standing, she said, "I would be happy to do so, but it would help me narrow the search if you told me what sort of information you need about Miss Abernathy."

Nodding my understanding, I said, "I am a reporter for the *Tribune* and . . . ."

The young woman's complexion suddenly turned an embarrassed shade of red. "Oh, my! You must be father's new reporter. If I had known, I would not have spoken so . . . curtly . . . earlier."

I wondered if reserving courtesy for employees' families was library policy, but kept the thought to myself and smiled to put her mind at ease. "Do not concern yourself. I am quite willing to wait my turn, I just did not realize you were serving a patron on the telephone. That is something unique in my experience with libraries."

She returned my smile in a way that caused her face to light up just as a sunrise brightens the darkest night. "Santa Barbara is a town of progressive citizens who expect innovative services in exchange for the taxes they pay." After a momentary pause, she offered me her hand to shake mine as emancipated women tend to do since they were given the vote and added, "By the way, my name is Eliza Hamm."

Gently shaking the hand she offered, I said, "Lester Kinney. It's a pleasure to make your acquaintance."

Eliza's small warm hand felt quite pleasant in mine and I held it a brief moment longer than Emily Post would deem appropriate. If Miss Hamm noticed, and it was unlikely she did not, she made no comment. Instead she said, "I think we'll find the information about Estelle Abernathy you need in the nine-seven-nines. Please follow me."

Miss Hamm led the way to a large group of bookshelves against the back wall labeled in accordance with Mister Dewey's decimal system: "900 – 999/History." There, she selected a volume entitled *Pioneers of Santa Barbara* and, from another part of the history section, Eliza pulled down a much thicker tome called *A Comprehensive History of U.S. Maritime Shipping in the Pacific Region*.

Handing me the books, she said, "These should give you some of the background you need." Miss Hamm must have noticed me looking questioningly at the second book because she quickly added, "Miss Abernathy's father founded a shipping line which she inherited and managed for many years. That's where the family wealth originated."

I settled down at a nearby table with the books and my notepad to begin searching the indexes and tables of contents for references to "Abernathy." There was an abundance of such references. In less than an hour I had accumulated several pages of notes.

In brief, what I learned was that Estelle Abernathy is the daughter of Duncan and Gillian Abernathy, who arrived on our eastern seaboard from their previous home in Aberdeen, Scotland in the 1870s. After landing on American shores, the Abernathys traveled west to San Francisco, where Duncan invested his last dollar in a steamship, which he planned to be the first vessel of the Caledonian Lion Steamship Line. He named that ship *The Highland Unicorn.*

Duncan Abernathy's intention was to establish cargo service to the Orient, which he did with considerable success. Within five years of its founding, the Caledonian Lion Steamship Line added more ships and expanded its routes to become one of the major shipping enterprises on the west coast. In 1876 Duncan and Gillian also expanded their family with the birth of their only child, Estelle.

Skipping ahead to the turn of the century, I learned that Duncan died in 1900 and Estelle did something virtually unheard of at that time. At the young age of twenty-four she assumed complete management of the steamship line. Apparently she was quite adept at that undertaking because, when she sold the Caledonian Lion Steamship Line lock, stock, and barrel a decade later, it was the most profitable shipping company in the Pacific trade.

Estelle's mother, Gillian, passed away the next year, 1911, at which time Estelle promptly up and moved south to Santa Barbara, whether by coincidence or not *Pioneers of Santa Barbara's* author did not say. He did explain that, once settled in her new home, Estelle began investing her already rather considerable fortune in a variety of enterprises including, in 1920, the Summerland oil fields along the Pacific coast just a few miles south of Santa Barbara.

This last fact was of particular interest from a reporter's point of view because I had already learned that oil production in Summerland was becoming a subject of controversy. Lovers of nature were raising their voices in protest over the unsightly muddle of derricks, spilled oil, and railroad tracks on the beach along the coast highway leading into Santa Barbara from Los Angeles. Having driven my automobile along that route many times, I could certainly understand the concern, and I wondered what Miss Abernathy's thoughts on that subject might be.

It was at this point that Eliza Hamm returned to my table and asked, "Mister Kinney, the library will be closing soon. How is your research progressing?"

I looked up into her charming face and silently wished we were on a first name basis. "Quite well, Miss Hamm. In fact, I think I have all I need for the historical background. I will pull more recent items from the *Tribune's* archive."

Eliza lit up our corner of the room with her smile again and said, "Wonderful. I'm so glad I could help."

Returning her smile, I replied, "And I am very grateful to you for that help. Without it, I would still be wandering the shelves." The large Regulator clock mounted on a column near the library entrance indicated the time was four-forty-two, and I decided to take a shot in the dark. Turning to Eliza, I said, "Miss Hamm, would you consider joining me for a cup of coffee or tea when you leave here?"

She tilted her head a little to one side, gave me a smile that some might have labeled "coy," and said, "As a rule I don't socialize with library patrons, but you are very nearly family, working for father and all, so we should get better acquainted. I would be delighted to join you for a cup of tea."

Sounding a little more enthusiastic than I intended, I said, "Swell!"

She chuckled at my response. "There is a pleasant little tea room across Anapamu Street. I could meet you there in about twenty minutes. Would that be acceptable to you?"

Making an effort to refrain from appearing so eager, I said, "That would be fine. See you then."

Strolling across the street toward Auntie Alicia's Tea Room, a storefront establishment in the Odd Fellows Building, it occurred to me that dating the boss's daughter could be unwise, but I quickly shrugged that thought away. After all, a cup of tea hardly qualified as a date.

Since I couldn't recall ever actually being in a tea room before, I wasn't entirely sure what to expect before I walked into the establishment. What I found was a relatively small space resembling, more than anything else, a residential parlor. The room was filled with eight tables, each covered by a white linen cloth and displaying a small arrangement of flowers in a vase. Three of the tables were occupied by groups of two and three women who appeared as if they might be enjoying tea at the end of a day spent shopping.

Prints of famous paintings by European artists hung on side walls covered with flowered wallpaper above dark wood wainscoting. Windows in the front wall looked out on the traffic along Anapamu Street and a long sideboard filled most of the rear wall, leaving space for a door I guessed led to a kitchen where the tea and its accompaniments were prepared. Otherwise the décor included only a few fern plants in decorative pots scattered here and there.

As I stood just inside the door taking in my surroundings, a woman who may or may not have been Auntie Alicia approached. She wore a full-length flowered bib apron over a plain black dress and her words were colored with what sounded to me like an authentic British accent,

"Good afternoon, sir. One for tea?"

"No, we will be a party of two."

"Very good, sir. Please follow me."

Our hostess escorted me to a table near the front windows and asked, "Would this be satisfactory, sir?"

I said it would be quite satisfactory, and after seating myself, I set about studying a neatly hand printed menu to see what is served in tea rooms. Auntie Alicia's Special Afternoon Tea, for example, offered my choice from seven varieties of tea, as well as coffee, chocolate, or cocoa. The teas were available hot or cold.

Included with the tea were marmalades on muffins or assorted sandwiches and a French pastry or ice cream. Other treats, the likes of Charlotte Russe and custard caramel were available ala carte. Even though I was certain the quantities would be small, the special tea sounded like too much food to be eaten this close to the dinner hour. I resolved to skip the special and simply have a cup of coffee.

A few minutes later the tea room's front door opened, tinkling a small bell as it did so, and in walked Eliza Hamm. She and our hostess exchanged a few words in such a manner as to make me think Miss Hamm was no stranger to Auntie Alicia's. Then Eliza Hamm turned toward our table and I stood to greet her.

After holding Miss Hamm's chair, I sat opposite her and said,

"I trust the city's books are all in order and locked up safely?"

As I had hoped, my comment brought a smile to Miss Hamm's face as she said, "The books are, indeed, secure; however, they aren't necessarily in their proper places. Our Pages take care of that chore first thing every morning."

Grinning, I said, "Just think of that, a library with pages. Many of them have covers, too, I imagine."

That elicited another smile. "Not the pages in the books, silly. These Pages are employees and volunteers who shelve our books in the proper places when patrons return them."

Even though I was quite familiar with the duties of Library Pages, I donned my most studious expression. "Clearly, I have a great deal to learn about the library business."

"As long as you know how to use a card catalogue, you'll get by."

I nodded. "That I do know. In fact, Mister Dewey and I are well acquainted."

On that note our hostess arrived to take our orders. Miss Hamm said she would have a cup of Orange Pekoe tea and I asked for coffee, black.

That chore out of the way, Miss Hamm asked, "Tell me, Mister Kinney, how long have you lived in Santa Barbara now?"

"Almost a week to the day. When your father offered me a reporting position, I resigned my job at the *Glendale New Press* and came a' running."

"Oh, my. You really are new to our town then. Have you been able to find a place to live on such short notice?"

"Yes, I rented a cottage in a garden court sort of place on Micheltorena Street. It will serve my needs well for the near future and the monthly rent is within my budget."

"Oh, good. That's quite a nice neighborhood, too."

Our tea and coffee were served and I raised my coffee cup in a toast. "Here's to my lovely newfound friend, Miss Eliza Hamm, the Librarian."

She raised her teacup and said, "What a kind thing to say. I'm sure I must be blushing."

At least a hundred clever responses raced through my mind at that moment, but I chose not to push my luck and, instead, said, "I hope you don't think me too forward, addressing you by your first name in that manner."

Her smile lit up the room again. "Not at all, if you don't mind me calling you Lester. As I said earlier, we are almost family."

Achieving a first name basis so quickly was more than I

expected, and the prospect of spending more time with this wonderful young woman in the future left me feeling something akin to intoxication. This was the first time I ever reached that state drinking coffee.

We spent the next fifteen or so minutes chatting about this and that and everything else, and then Eliza looked at the tiny round gold wristwatch she wore on her left wrist. "Oh, my goodness! Look at the time. Mother will be fretting if I am not home soon."

"We certainly don't want that to happen. May I give you a ride? My car is back at the *Tribune*."

"It is kind of you to offer, Lester, but I ride my bicycle to work. Our home is only six blocks from the library."

I left a quarter on the table to pay for our drinks and a tip, and then escorted Eliza to the bicycle rack in front of the Library. There, we shook hands, and she said, "Lester, thank you so much for a lovely after-work treat. I'm just sad that our time was so short today."

Eliza's words sounded like an opening to me, so I took advantage of it. "Perhaps we could get together again sometime. Maybe we could take in a motion picture or something."

She tilted her head again and gave me that look I thought verged on coyness and said, "That would be lovely, Lester. The new Al Jolson talkie is playing at the Granada. I have been hoping to see that one before it leaves."

I smiled. "Friday night?"

She lit up her smile again and said, "It's a date. Would you mind looking up the showing times and calling me on Thursday to make our final arrangements? The library's number in the central telephone exchange is three-one-two."

I said I wouldn't mind at all, and we shook hands again before she climbed aboard her bright blue bicycle and pedaled off in a northwesterly direction on Anacapa Street. I, in turn, began walking in the opposite direction toward the *Tribune's* office to retrieve my automobile. Along the way, I found myself humming a popular little ditty called *The Girlfriend* by Rogers and Hart from the Broadway musical of the same name. It fit my mood quite nicely.

TWO

Wednesday - September 5, 1928

My Wednesday work day began well before the big clock in the County Courthouse bell tower rang in the seven o'clock hour. Fortunately, Mabel Stafford, the woman who oversees the *Tribune's* archives, is also an early riser. Missus Stafford was not only at her desk, she was also brewing a pot of her well-known coffee on an electric hotplate.

That last point is why I arrived in the *Tribune's* basement with my notepad in one hand and my coffee mug in the other. Missus Stafford noted this and said, "The coffee will be ready in just a few minutes, Mister Kinney. In the meantime, you may look through this folder. It contains the news articles you requested yesterday afternoon on Miss Estelle Abernathy."

There was something in her tone of voice when she said "Miss Estelle Abernathy" that sounded to my ear like animosity. Since Missus Stafford and Miss Abernathy were of similar ages, I wondered if the two women had a skeleton or two in a mutual closet. I made a mental note to pursue the subject with Mabel Stafford at some future meeting.

I accepted the folder and thanked her for having the articles ready. Then I slid a chair up to a work table and opened the folder. Running an efficient newspaper morgue, I have learned, requires the diligent cataloguing of articles about people, places, and events. The articles then become a valuable research archive for future stories on the same or related people, places, and events.

Missus Stafford's diligence as an archivist was apparent to me immediately upon opening the folder. It contained six articles from past issues of the *Tribune* spanning a period from about five years in the past to a few weeks ago. I knew from experience there were certainly more articles about the woman in the files, but Missus Stafford had, in effect, cut to the core of the matter by choosing the clippings that were most relevant to the articles I was writing.

I started with the oldest article and added to my library notes about Estelle Abernathy. Moments later Missus Stafford arrived at my table, coffee pot in hand, and poured a generous measure of the brew into my mug, saying, "Now you will be careful not to spill on those clippings, won't you?"

Tasting the hearty brew she poured, I said, "I will, indeed."

"Are you finding what you need, Mister Kinney?"

"Yes, I am. I can now clearly see why the fellows in the newsroom upstairs hold you in such high regard."

With modesty and a smile she said, "Oh, go on with you, Mister Kinney. Those scallywags only use the archives as an excuse to come down here for coffee."

We both had a laugh about that and I took another swig of coffee as I returned to my reading. The coffee was worthy of any excuse it took to obtain a cup, and I was very careful not to spill on Missus Stafford's articles.

As expected, there was some duplication of what I learned at the library, but there were also more recent facts, including an estimate that placed Miss Abernathy's worth in the neighborhood of twenty million dollars. A fortune in that particular neighborhood made Estelle Abernathy one of the richest women in the world.

I also discovered that, in addition to her investments in the Summerland oil fields, she speculated heavily in the entertainment industry. According to an article from the financial section, Miss Abernathy's holdings included shares in the Paramount Famous Lasky Corporation and Charles Chaplin Productions. Those investments told me she was not afraid of risky ventures.

As to her style of living, I learned the Abernathy residence was a four-thousand-square-foot hilltop mansion in the fashionable Riviera district. I took a drive through the Riviera on one of my first trips to Santa Barbara, and I can say from firsthand experience the coastal views there are beyond compare.

The final article in the folder was dated August twenty-four of this year and contained the significant details of Miss Abernathy's anticipated donation to Saint Andria's orphanage. The charity's origins in Santa Barbara dated back to the 1850s.

Estelle Abernathy's donation on Saturday was intended to provide funds for a major modernization of the charity's facility on La Colina Road in the downtown area. The project is expected to cost approximately fifty-thousand-dollars.

I leaned back in my chair and reread the recent additions to my notebook while finishing my coffee. From all indications Miss Abernathy was quite a gal, a woman well equipped to succeed in a "man's world," a fact she had demonstrated beyond any doubt. Thinking that interviewing her would be an interesting experience reminded me I needed to schedule an appointment with the "grande dame," as Mister Hamm had described her.

Borrowing Mabel Stafford's Santa Barbara directory of telephone numbers, I looked in the A section. There I found two Abernathys, neither of which with the first name of Estelle. That did not surprise me. People of Estelle Abernathy's status valued their privacy. I had her street address, but there was not time to set up an appointment by mail, and since arriving unannounced seemed a surefire way to get the door slammed in my face, I needed a telephone number. I thought if anyone was privy to that information, it would be my boss, Frederick Hamm.

After thanking Mabel Stafford for her diligence on my behalf and for her hospitality, I made my way upstairs to my desk in the newsroom. Most of the other desks were now occupied and the uproar of typewriter clacking and chatter was already approaching a cacophonous level.

An advantage of the editor's office windows was they offered a view in as well as out. Thus, I could see Mister Hamm at his desk and he was alone at the moment. I made tracks in that direction and knocked on his door.

Through the window in the door I saw Mister Hamm make a gesture indicating that I should come in. I did so and stood at his desk patiently waiting for him to finish reading whatever he was editing. Waiting patiently for members of the Hamm family was a skill at which I was becoming quite adept.

Finally, Mister Hamm dropped the red pencil with which he was making editing marks on a story and looked up at me, saying, "Good morning, Mister Kinney. How are you coming with your Abernathy stories?"

"I'm making progress, sir. I just came from reading clippings in the basement and I did some research at the library yesterday afternoon."

"So I heard."

I thought I saw the trace of a smile on his face, which I took to be a good sign. "Yes, sir. Your daughter was most helpful."

"I'm glad to hear she's earning her salary. Now, how can I help you?"

"I need to interview Miss Abernathy next, and I was wondering if perchance you know of a telephone number where I can reach her or her secretary to arrange my interview."

"I do and I will give it to you, but you must treat the number as privileged information. Miss Estelle Abernathy's residence telephone number is a closely guarded secret. If we abuse it, she will have it changed and we'll be back out on the street."

"Yes, sir."

Mister Hamm removed a small black address book from his bottom desk drawer and opened it to one of the first pages. "The number is four-four-four."

"Thank you, sir. I will call her a little later so as not to disturb her too early."

Frederick Hamm shook his head. "No need to wait. I assure you Miss Abernathy is already up and well along with her day. You'll soon learn that she is not among the idle rich in this town."

I said, "Yes, sir," and turned to leave, but Mister Hamm stopped in my tracks.

"Kinney, I understand you plan to see Eliza socially Friday night. Is that correct?"

Suddenly a knot began forming in the pit of my stomach, as I turned back to face him. "Yes, sir. We discussed taking in a motion picture Friday night."

He leaned back in his swivel chair and stared at me with a thoughtful expression. Not knowing what thoughts were behind that expression made me a little nervous. I had no idea how he felt about an employee seeing his daughter socially, but I got the idea I was about to find out.

Mister Hamm, it turned out was also something of a mind reader. "Relax, son. Eliza's friends are her business and I trust her judgement. I was just surprised when she said you were going to the motion picture show together."

"Why does that surprise you, sir? I'm just honored Eliza thinks I'm worthy of her time and attention."

Frederick Hamm shook his head as if that physical action would clear his thoughts. "I've already spoken out of turn here, Mister Kinney. I am simply suggesting you not let your expectations with regard to Eliza rise too high. Now go interview Miss Abernathy and let me get back to work."

I decided to make my telephone call from the basement to escape the newsroom racket. On my way downstairs, I pondered Frederick Hamm's advice. It seemed his comment was intended more for my benefit than his daughter's. That thought made me wonder why he thought I needed such a warning, and it was definitely a warning. There could be no doubt of that.

A woman answered my telephone call. I said, "Good morning. My name is Lester Kinney. I am a reporter for the Santa Barbara

Tribune writing a feature article about Miss Abernathy's donation to Saint Andria's orphanage. I'm calling in hope of arranging a meeting with her today for an interview on the subject."

A long pause followed my request. Finally whomever I was speaking with said, "Miss Abernathy is terribly busy at this time. I doubt very much she has time for an interview on such short notice."

"I understand and apologize for the short notice. I only received the assignment yesterday afternoon."

"I see. What did you say your name is?"

"Lester Kinney."

After another pause she said, "I don't seem to recall seeing your byline in the *Tribune*."

"That would be because I just joined the staff a few days ago."

"Oh. Is this possibly your first assignment for the *Tribune*?"

Mentally sighing, I said honestly, "Yes, it is."

I was growing weary of the woman's third degree interrogation. Either Miss Abernathy had time to see me or she did not. None of what she was asking me could change that either way. Or could it?

"Mister Kinney, can you be here in thirty minutes?"

Trying not to sound overly excited about the woman's apparent change of heart, I said, "I most certainly can."

"Very well. Miss Abernathy will see you for a short interview at precisely nine o'clock. The address is 1919 Las Tunas Road."

I was about to say I'd be there, but the telephone line clicked dead before I got the words out. Then it occurred to me to wonder how Miss Abernathy's employee could make commitments for her without the boss's approval. Well, I would soon find out.

By eight-forty-five I was heading across town past old Santa Barbara Mission and up the hill to Santa Barbara's Riviera district. What I found at 1919 Las Tunas Road was a long winding drive through a grove of large oak trees to a sizeable two-story mansion in a Mediterranean style of architecture that included a red tile roof, balconies, and a substantial oak entrance door equipped with a large black iron knocker. I used this device for its intended purpose.

A slender Latin fellow dressed impeccably in a dark suit answered my knock. I told him who I was and, after a glance at his wristwatch, he invited me in, saying, "Madam is expecting you, Señor Kinney. You may wait for her in the library."

I followed him to a sunny room on the south side of the mansion. The rough texture of its lath and plaster walls gave the library a rustic feeling while their white paint reflected light from a large window and a French door overlooking the garden area surrounding a gently burbling stone fountain.

In addition to built-in shelving niches around the room, the library was furnished with three comfortable overstuffed chairs upholstered with suede leather, one with a matching ottoman, and a large rough oak desk. This last item was not the sort of ornate writing desk one finds in well-to-do households, but a hefty business-like desk of the kind that would be at home in an office where substantial deals are consummated. These furnishings stood on a rust and pale blue carpet of geometric shapes covering the same dark red floor tiles used throughout the mansion.

Looking at the bookshelves directly behind the desk, I spotted a remarkable brass ship's clock with large black numerals on a white face. The clock was cradled in an ornately carved wooden chest that bore the inscription, "Highland Unicorn 1875." I was apparently looking at the ship's clock from Duncan Abernathy's first ship. Judging by the clock's prominent position in the room, I concluded it was a cherished memento of Estelle Abernathy's maritime upbringing.

I was glancing at the titles of the books in one of the built-in bookcases, mostly subjects of a maritime nature, when the Highland Unicorn's clock chimed twice. I was thinking, "nine a.m. and all is well," when a woman's voice I recognized from my earlier telephone conversation interrupted my nautical musings, "Good morning, Mister Kinney."

Turning, I saw a large-framed, white-haired woman dressed in a dark blue skirt, white blouse, and the female version of a reefer jacket, or blazer, as they are sometimes called. In either case, it was also dark blue and featured two rows of brass buttons in the traditional nautical style. She wore the jacket unbuttoned. I recognized her face because I had just seen it in photos accompanying the news articles Mabel Stafford had collected for me.

I took all this in as Estelle Abernathy walked briskly across the room with her arm extended in a gesture I took to mean she intended to shake my hand, which she did with a strong, forceful grip. This new fashion of shaking women's hands was taking some adjustment on my part.

As I shook the hand she offered, I said, "Good morning, Miss Abernathy. Thank you for agreeing to see me on such short notice."

"You're welcome, young man. Now, please have a seat and ask your questions. I must leave for another appointment in fifteen minutes."

We sat in two of the overstuffed chairs that more or less faced each other. Then, opening my notepad to a fresh page, I asked, "As I understand it, you are making a rather substantial donation to the Saint Andria orphanage. What is there about that particular charity that prompts such generosity on your part?"

She studied my face for a long moment. "First, let me say I am not Catholic. I was raised Presbyterian; however, I choose not to affiliate myself with any organized religion these days.

"I support Saint Andria's orphanage because of the fine work they do in helping displaced youngsters. I had the great good fortune to be the daughter of loving parents who strongly influenced who I am today. It is my intention that the Sisters of Saint Andria's should have every help they require to place the children in their care with the same sort of loving parents."

Making my notes hastily, I said, "According to everything I've read about you, Miss Abernathy, you have done quite well for yourself in the world of high finance, both in managing your family's shipping company and later with wise investments in a variety of enterprises. To what do you attribute your business acumen?"

Miss Abernathy again studied my face for several seconds before speaking, and I wondered if these pauses gave her time to frame her answers or if she was being cautious of any negative undercurrents such as those so typical of muckraking yellow journalism, particularly that of the Hearst newspapers.

Finally, she said, "I am successful for two reasons. First, my father schooled me well in the practices of banking and investment, and second, I am thorough.

"Mister Kinney, research is as important to an investor as it is to a newspaper reporter such as yourself. Success depends not upon what one knows, but upon what one knows how to find out. Over the years I have cultivated a grapevine, so to speak, of sources from which I regularly harvest reliable information regarding potential investments and other matters.

"I might add as a piece of personal advice that you would do well to adopt this approach to your reporting. You will reap benefits in ways you cannot begin to imagine at this juncture."

I recalled Frederick Hamm emphasizing the importance of learning all I could about Estelle Abernathy before I interviewed her. It would seem they shared at least that bit of philosophy.

Catching up with my notes, I said, "Miss Abernathy, when you left San Francisco in 1911, you had virtually the entire world in which to choose your new home. Why did you choose Santa Barbara?"

For the third time Estelle Abernathy studied me before answering. "I selected Santa Barbara as my permanent home for many reasons, some of which are obvious, such as the wonderful climate and delightful views of the sea and hills. The less apparent reasons concern the sort of people who reside here.

"As you pointed out, I had the world from which to choose, but a good deal of that world is populated by people with whom I share nothing in common. It was my desire to live among intelligent people of my own race—people of high moral principles and ethical standards. By the simple expedient of what it costs to live here, those who lack such qualities are excluded. Put another way, Santa Barbara is an exclusive town built for and by the elite."

Standing, Miss Abernathy brought an abrupt end to our meeting. "Now I must leave for the other appointment I mentioned." Offering her hand again, she added, "It has been a unique experience meeting you, Mister Kinney. While not entirely aligned with the expressed subject of our interview, your questions were thoughtful and interesting. I intend to tell Frederick Hamm I am impressed with his new young reporter."

As we shook hands again, I said, "Thank you, Miss Abernathy. I appreciate the time you've given me and your hospitality."

Then, almost as if by magic, Estelle Abernathy disappeared and her Latin manservant, or butler, appeared in her place. He escorted me to the front door, and as I walked along the wide, curved driveway to where I parked my car, a shiny new Cadillac Phaeton—the kind with dual cowls—passed me. It was a dark red in color and its rear doors bore gold crests surrounding the initials E and A. Three people rode in the automobile. A liveried chauffeur was driving and an attractive young woman with black hair shared the rear seat with Estelle Abernathy.

On my way back to the *Tribune* office to begin writing my articles I reviewed the past half-hour in my mind. Meeting the grande dame, Estelle Abernathy, was quite an experience. Perhaps the most curious aspect of the meeting was Miss Abernathy's conduct during my initial telephone conversation with her. It was not that she lied about with whom I was speaking, she just avoided mentioning that detail. Naturally, I wondered what was behind such unusual behavior.

THREE

Wednesday - September 5, 1928

According to the electric clock on the newsroom wall it was a few minutes past one o'clock when I rolled the last page of my first story on Estelle Abernathy's donation to Saint Andria's out of my typewriter. After reading through the article again to be certain of my grammar, syntax, and spelling, I assembled its three double-spaced pages in their proper order and dropped them into the wooden tray designated for completed copy.

Then deciding that finishing the story a full twenty-four hours ahead of the deadline entitled me to a small reward, I retrieved my old childhood lunch pail from the bottom desk drawer. Doing so reminded me of my school days when the lunchtime ritual included eagerly exploring the pail's contents to discover what my mother had included in my midday meal. Her oatmeal cookies were my favorite lunch pail treasure.

Since I prepared my own lunches nowadays, the surprise element was long gone. Hunger, however, still provided ample enthusiasm for opening the pail. The midday repast I'd assembled was not as creative as mother's lunches and certainly did not include her wonderful cookies, but it still looked tasty to my eyes. On this day my lunch included a thick slice of whole grain bakery bread, a block of Cheddar cheese imported all the way from Tillamook, Oregon, and several stalks of celery. Mother always insisted vegetables were a necessity in every meal.

I was savoring my last stalk of celery—if indeed celery can be savored—when Edna, the young woman who oversees the *Tribune's* reception area, approached my desk. She offered me an envelope, saying, "This must be very important. It was delivered by a uniformed messenger."

Looking down at the newly arrived envelope I saw that it bore my name writ in a bold and flowing script. Below my name another line read, "*Santa Barbara Tribune.*" Curious though I was, I restrained myself from ripping the envelope open because Edna was also curious. She was standing next to my desk apparently waiting on pins and needles for me to open the missive. Since it was unlikely that whatever the envelope contained was any of her business, I said, "Thank you, Edna. I'll open it when I've finished lunch."

I punctuated the comment by taking a big bite of crunchy celery. Just before Edna stalked off, she gave me a look that said she thought I was nuts for not opening the envelope immediately. Of course, the minute she was out of sight, I carefully unsealed the envelope flap.

The mysterious envelope contained an invitation. It was neatly handwritten on the finest quality white linen paper. At its top the invitation card was embossed with the same gold crest design I'd seen on the doors of Estelle Abernathy's Cadillac Phaeton.

The invitation read as follows:

You and your guest are cordially invited to attend a
Reception
at the residence of
Estelle Abernathy
1919 Las Tunas Road, Santa Barbara, California
At 7:00 P.M.
Saturday, the eighth day of September, 1928.
Libations ~ Dinner ~ Formal Attire
Répondez, s'il vous plait

I sat at my desk staring at the card with my mouth hanging open. Of all the thoughts that might go through one's mind upon receiving such an invitation, the dominant one in my mind was where in heaven's name I was going to get a top hat and tails.

Then my brain settled on a more pertinent question. Why had Estelle Abernathy gone to the effort of inviting a lowly newspaper reporter to her hoity-toity society event? Several possible answers came to mind, and some of them were not at all flattering. Perhaps I was to be there for comic relief. Sensing I needed another opinion, I slid the invitation back into its envelope and went to see Frederick Hamm.

He looked up and before I could speak he said, "Good, Mister Kinney. I was just going to send for you. I have a piece of news I think you ought to hear. First, though, I've read your Estelle Abernathy story and I like it. You wrote it in a style that is more sophisticated than we're used to out here in the hinterlands, but a little culture never hurts, especially when dealing with the upper class."

"Thank you, sir. I came in to ask about . . . ."

"Sit down, Mister Kinney. I have more news for you."

As I sat, Mister Hamm said, "I received a most interesting telephone call from Estelle Abernathy earlier."

That news gave me a tingle of concern. Miss Abernathy told me she was going to call Mister Hamm, but what had she actually said to him?

"Aren't you curious as to what she told me?"

"Oh, yes sir. What did she say?"

With a rather large grin on his face, Frederick Hamm said, "Quoting her words, 'Your young Mister Kinney interviewed me this morning, and I am quite impressed with him. Lester Kinney showed me great respect and put to me some of the most intelligent questions I have ever been asked by a news reporter. You would do well to hire more like him.'"

I guess my relief at hearing what Estelle Abernathy said to my employer must have shown because Mister Hamm asked, "You look startled. Did you expect her to tell me something different?"

"No, sir. Miss Abernathy told me she intended to tell you exactly what she told you. I guess I'm somewhat surprised she actually went to the trouble of doing so."

He smiled again. "In my experience, Miss Estelle Abernathy generally does exactly what she says she is going to do, and the fact that she went to the trouble of contacting me means you conducted yourself in such a way as to cast a good light on the *Tribune*, and equally important, on yourself. Mister Kinney, you have just become this publication's fair haired boy."

Feeling somewhat emboldened by Mister Hamm's comments, I casually flipped the invitation to Estelle Abernathy's reception onto his desk. "Then what does this make me?"

Removing the invitation from its envelope, he said, "What's this?" Then, as he read the words on the card, his eyes widened in surprise. "Great heavens! How did you ever come by this?"

I shook my head. "I haven't the foggiest notion. A messenger apparently delivered it half an hour ago."

Handling the invitation as if it were pure gold, Frederick Hamm said, "Son, what you have here is the most sought-after invitation in Santa Barbara, maybe on the entire west coast. This is . . . well, it's simply incredible!"

"Then you think it is legitimate?"

Cocking his head to one side, he asked, "Do you have any

reason to suspect it is not?"

"No, sir. I just wasn't sure what I should do about it?"

His expression turned to surprise. "Do about it? You will go, of course!"

"I can't, sir."

He frowned. "Why on earth not?"

More than a little embarrassed, I said, "Well, sir, the invitation says the event is formal, and I don't own a tuxedo."

Mister Hamm laughed. "Oh, for heaven's sake! You march right over to Coulter's Men's Clothing on State Street this afternoon and have them outfit you. Tell Tom Coulter to send the bill to me. This is most certainly a business expense."

Feeling as if I were being roped into something I had no desire to do, I asked, "What about the RSVP, sir?"

Looking at the invitation again, he thought for a moment, and then said, "I'll have our society reporter, Ida Madison, prepare a reply on *Tribune* stationary, and we'll send it to Miss Abernathy's home by messenger this afternoon. One thing, though."

"What's that, sir?"

"Your guest. The invitation is for you and your guest. Who is your guest going to be?"

A pleasant idea crossed my mind, but I held it in reserve. "I don't know, sir. Who would you recommend?"

Frederick Hamm returned to a thoughtful state for several seconds before saying. "Certainly not someone from the *Tribune*. That would make it appear to Miss Abernathy that we were trying to exploit the situation. No, it should be a friend of yours, a personal acquaintance."

I trotted out my idea. "Would it be appropriate to ask Eliza? She's one of the few personal acquaintances I've made beyond members of the *Tribune* staff."

He nodded slowly as if contemplating my question. "That's an excellent idea. Eliza knows who's who in this town as well as anyone, and she is well up to date on all the proper etiquette for such occasions." Reaching for the telephone on his desk, Mister Hamm added, "I'll call her."

"Ah . . . excuse me, sir, but if you don't mind, I would prefer to ask her myself."

Slowly returning the telephone instrument to his desk, he said, "I see. I guess that would be more appropriate." With an expression I can only describe as sheepish, Frederick Hamm added, "I apologize if I'm overly eager, but this comes under the headline of a once in a lifetime opportunity. It is, of course, your opportunity. I'm just anxious to see you take the best possible advantage of it."

"I appreciate that, sir. Clearly, I am well out of my element in such matters."

Mister Hamm smiled. "You won't be for long, son. Now, you had best get going. You have a lot to do this afternoon."

Retrieving the invitation and its envelope, I returned to my desk. Donning my suit jacket, I noted the time was two-fifteen. Having no idea how long it would take to be fitted for a tuxedo, I decided Coulter's would have to be my first stop. I also noted the slightly threadbare condition of my jacket cuffs, something the salesmen at Coulter's were certain to notice also.

Coulter's Men's Clothing was located on State Street next to the Arlington Hotel, a distance of about six blocks. Normally I would make such a short trip on foot, but time was of the essence, so I drove my Chevrolet coupé and parked across State Street from my destination.

Inside the store I was approached by a stout fellow impeccably attired in a dark gray pinstripe suit. Before I could say what I came in for, he said, "Might you be Mister Kinney?"

Surprised, I said, "Yes, but how . . . ."

"I'm Tom Coulter. Frederick Hamm just called to say you would be coming in and that we were to fit you for our best quality and most stylish formal attire for an event on Saturday. I believe he said it was a reception with dinner, is that correct?"

"Yes, that . . . ."

"Very well, sir, if you will kindly step this way, we will get started."

The hands on my pocket watch were pointing to four-thirty as I walked out of Coulter's with instructions to return Friday morning for the purpose of picking up a list of items that covered all the lines in two pages of Mister Coulter's receipt book. I did not see the total amount of the order, but judging by the prices I saw of various items Mister Coulter selected in my presence, I calculated the *Tribune* was going to receive a bill of more than one-hundred-dollars, an amount slightly greater than my monthly salary. That realization gave me cause to wonder if shirt studs and cufflinks really must be made of genuine Australian onyx to achieve the height of fashion.

Remembering that the Santa Barbara Public Library closed at five, I hurried in that direction. It occurred to me, however, I failed to ask Mister Hamm if Eliza was working this afternoon. At this point there was only one way to find out.

Parking near the library, I was relieved to see Eliza's shiny blue bicycle in the rack next to the entrance. I sat on a nearby bench and used my remaining time deciding how I was going to ask Eliza to join me in attending what I now understood was tantamount to the social event of the year.

Ten minutes after I heard the Courthouse clock chime five times, beautiful, wonderful, amazing, Eliza Hamm exited the library. I noted, as she walked briskly toward the bicycle rack, that she was all in shades of brown today—not dull browns, but exciting browns assembled in a style that emphasized the grace of her movements.

When she looked up and saw me standing there, Eliza smiled her amazing smile. "Why, Lester, how nice to see you again." Eliza's tone of voice was bright and made me think she truly meant the greeting.

"It's good to see you again, as well, Eliza. I apologize for showing up unannounced like this, but something unforeseen and rather urgent came up this afternoon, and I would like to discuss it with you."

Frowning slightly in puzzlement, Eliza said, "Then by all means, let us sit down and discuss this unforeseen matter."

We sat on the same bench I occupied a few minutes earlier. While sitting there, I had decided the best way to broach the subject of my visit was to simply show Eliza the invitation and let her read it for herself.

Handing her the envelope, I said, "This is the unforeseen matter."

Looking even more mystified, she accepted the envelope and removed the card it contained. She spent a moment reading the invitation and then laughed. Before I could ask what she found so funny, Eliza said, "Forgive me, Lester. When you said something urgent had come up, I was afraid you were here to tell me you wouldn't be able to attend the motion picture show with me Friday night."

She momentarily leaned against my shoulder as she said, "I am so relieved to learn that your unforeseen matter is something else entirely. You really had me worried!"

Wishing she had leaned on my shoulder a little longer, I said, "I certainly didn't mean to worry you."

Eliza held up the invitation. "This is really quite something, Lester. Thank you for showing it to me. Now, what is so urgent?"

There was a hint of that now familiar coyness in her tone and expression that suggested she was already anticipating my answer to her question. I said, "The urgent parts are the third and fourth words of the invitation's first line."

She looked back at the card, read it, and smiled. "Your guest?"

"Quite right. Eliza, would you do me the honor of accompanying me to Miss Estelle Abernathy's ritzy shindig."

Eliza managed a surprised expression despite my suspicion she knew exactly what I was going to ask. "Me? Why, Lester, it would be my pleasure to accompany you to Miss Abernathy's shindig." Then she laughed again, adding, "Although, I believe the word soirée is a more acceptable term in the best circles."

Then her expression changed to one of curiosity. "Tell me, if you don't mind, how you came to be invited to such an event." She quickly added, "Not that there is any reason you should not . . . ."

Interrupting, I said, "I know what you mean."

I spent a few minutes explaining my morning's activities involving Estelle Abernathy. When I finished the tale, Eliza said, "My goodness! Apparently I'm not the only woman in Santa Barbara who finds your charms irresistible." Then her expression took on a shade of suspicion. "Lester, forgive me, but I must ask. Did my father suggest you invite me to be your guest at the reception?"

Shaking my head vehemently, I said, "Not at all. It was entirely my idea and, I might add, an excellent one. I did, however, ask his approval."

Eliza gave me a stern look. "Lester, there is only one instance I can imagine in which you would be required to ask my father's approval concerning any plans you and I might have, and that would be a matter of tradition more than one of actually needing his consent."

Momentarily puzzled, I asked, "What instance . . . oh."

With a smile, she promptly changed the subject. "I see the invitation says formal attire. That means I have preparations to make and precious little time to make them. I hope you will understand if I rush off to begin those preparations."

"Of course, Eliza. I wish I could have given you more notice, but the invitation only arrived this afternoon."

Taking my hand in hers, she looked me in the eye. "Lester, thank you. I truly am honored that you have chosen me as your guest for Miss Abernathy's reception. I promise I will make you proud of that choice."

Before I thought of a response, Eliza gave my hand a squeeze, stood up, and said, "Don't forget to call me tomorrow so we can finalize our plans for Friday night. You may telephone me at home, if you wish. Our number is 525. Goodbye for now, Lester."

As I watched her pedal briskly up Anacapa Street, I briefly wondered what she meant about making me proud of choosing her as my guest. I also wondered what Miss Estelle Abernathy would think of a woman who rode a bicycle to work. For some reason, I had the feeling she would approve.

FOUR

Friday - September 7, 1928

When I spoke with Eliza via the telephone Thursday night we agreed I would call for her Friday night around seven-thirty for an eight o'clock showing of Al Jolson's new talkie, *The Singing Fool.* The film was playing at the Granada Theater, which was just a block from Coulter's Men's Clothing, where I picked up my new tuxedo earlier in the day.

Friday evening was balmy and I drove beneath a sky full of stars as I set out in my Chevrolet to pick Eliza up at her parents' home. Frederick Hamm and family resided in a tidy craftsman style home at the corner of Arrellaga and Laguna Streets about a mile north of town. Their quiet neighborhood was populated by modestly prosperous homes, mostly in the same architectural character as the Hamm's home.

The front door on which I knocked had a pattern of beveled glass inserts allowing visitors a view of the living room while they waited on the porch. A moment later I saw Frederick Hamm walking briskly to answer my knock. In that moment I felt the same silly nervous tingle I remembered from when I was a high school student calling for my date to the prom. That, I decided, had to stop. Eliza and I were adults, for crying out loud.

Mister Hamm invited me in, saying, "Good evening, Mister Kinney. Welcome to our home. Liza will be here momentarily." Smiling, he added, "You know these modern women, they won't set foot out in public if so much as one hair is out of place."

"So I understand."

Eliza's voice came from a door on the other side of the room. "What do you understand, Lester?"

"Ah . . . ."

Hamm grinned at my discomfort and came to the rescue. "Oh, it's nothing, Liza. I was just regaling Mister Kinney with one of my observations on modern women and he was being polite."

Eliza gave us a suspicious look. "I see. Lester is always polite. It's one of his most endearing charms." Taking my arm, she said,

"Shall we go, or would you rather be regaled by more of father's observations?"

"Ah . . . ."

Frederick Hamm laughed. "Get along, you too. And don't stay out too late. You have a busy day tomorrow, Mister Kinney."

"Ah . . . yes, sir."

Walking to my Chevrolet at the curb, Eliza said, "You really ought not to let father buffalo you like that. He doesn't bite."

"But he does sign my paycheck."

Eliza smiled. "Well, there is that, I suppose."

As I opened the passenger door for her and Eliza climbed gracefully onto the front seat, I was again struck by her beauty. On this night Eliza was outfitted in an ensemble consisting a simple short-sleeved dark green dress with narrow pleats below a sash belt at the dress's slightly dropped waist and a mid-knee hem. Around her neck were draped two loops of white pearls, and on her feet were brown leather shoes with button straps and modest heels. At least I thought that might be how a society reporter like the *Tribune's* Ida Madison would describe the outfit. I was paying more attention to such things lately. When one is keeping company with a modern woman of style, one ought to be up on the latest fashions.

On the short drive to the theater I asked a question that occurred to me while in the Hamm's living room. "I noticed your father calls you Liza, without the E. Do you prefer that or is it a pet name only your father has for you?"

"I guess most of my friends know me as Liza, but I would like it if you called me Eliza. Truthfully, I never cared much for the name, but I really like the way it sounds when you say it."

"How do I say Eliza differently from the way anyone else says it?"

Since I was paying attention to the road ahead of us, I sensed, rather than saw, her turn to look at me. Eliza stared at me such a long time I was about to give up on an answer to my question when she finally said, "I think you say it as if it means something . . . as if the word is more than just a name. Does that make any sense?"

Surprisingly, it did make sense. "I think so. Eliza has a kind of old fashioned sweetness about it that befits you, even though you are a thoroughly modern woman."

"What a beautiful thing to say! Obviously being in the frequent company of a writer will take some adjustment."

I smiled at that. "I like the 'frequent company' part of that statement, but I'm not sure I understand the rest of it."

"Lester, I am a reader. I seldom write anything more creative than a shopping list or a note to my cousin in Iowa. In the short time we've known one another, however, I can already see that you think quite differently than I do." She quickly added, "That's not a bad thing! Please don't think that. It's just that you continuously surprise me with the ways in which you express your thoughts. It isn't simply a clearer way of speaking, it's . . . it's . . . it is more complete. When I listen to you, I think I'm feeling as well as hearing what you say."

As I pulled to the curb half a block from the Granada Theater, I thought about what Eliza had just said. My silence worried her.

"Lester, I hope I didn't say something to upset you. I didn't mean anything bad . . . ."

I shut off the Chevrolet's engine and turned in my seat to face her. "No, Eliza, you didn't upset me. You just made me think about myself a little. Believe me, my dear, despite what you say, you are no slouch when it comes to clear communication."

"Oh, there you go again being sweet and kind and . . . ." I guess she couldn't think of how to finish her sentence, so she ended it with a kiss on my cheek. Then Eliza smiled and said, "Now, let's go into the theater while I still have any interest in seeing the film."

The Granada Theater was housed in an eight-story brick and stone building with three sets of double entrance doors below a marquee with "The Granada" spelled out in a large serif font with a Mediterranean feeling about it. On either side of the theater's name, the sections of the marquee that revealed which motion picture was currently playing, said, "Al Jolson in The Singing Fool" and "Vitaphone Sound." The black letters also proclaimed, "Seven Sensational Song Hits!"

After presenting the loge section tickets I purchased that morning, we entered an opulent theater rivaling the splendor of Grauman's Egyptian and Chinese Theaters in Hollywood. The auditorium wasn't just ornate, it was also huge. Upstairs, the balcony featured three rows of loge seating. There were also two columns of regular boxes and private boxes stacked on both sides of the proscenium arch.

Our seats were in the first row of the loge section at the front of the balcony, and from that perspective it was clear that, despite its size, the huge auditorium was filling quickly. I was glad I had the foresight to buy our tickets in advance. The way things were shaping up this showing would be standing room only.

At the time, I wondered if paying fifty cents apiece for loge seats was really necessary, but when we were seated, I was glad I had. The seats were quite comfortable and our view of the screen was perfect. On top of that, everyone with seats in the balcony had to file past one side or the other of the loge, so we got to take a good look at our fellow theater-goers. At first I thought it odd that most of them, particularly the men were also taking a good look at us. Then it dawned on me they weren't looking at us, they were looking at Eliza.

The Singing Fool was a disaster of the first order from the time the theater lights dimmed until they came back on. The only positive thought I had throughout the film was that Jolson played the role of a fool admirably. Ballyhooed as a dramatic love story, *The Singing Fool* was one of those stories clearly written for the sole purpose of tugging at the heartstrings of those willing to pay for the dubious privilege of feeling sad and depressed.

My impression of Jolson's female costars, Betty Bronson and Josephine Dunn, was that they would be hard pressed to act their way out of wet paper sacks. Then, when I was certain things couldn't get any worse, the author scored an emotional coup de' gras by killing off Jolson's five-year-old kid so the fool could hold the dying boy in his arms whilst belting out a heartfelt rendering of *Sonny Boy*.

Honestly, I found it far more entertaining to watch Eliza's reaction to the scenes as they dragged on. It was plain to see she was struggling to keep from laughing out loud at the corny dialogue. Of course it didn't help matters any when I made sad faces and crying gestures to egg her on. Eliza's reactions were doubly amusing to me because the middle-aged woman sitting behind her balled like a baby every time Jolson suffered another emotional setback, of which there were an overabundance.

Adding insult to our injury was that *Singing Fool* was the only motion picture on the bill so there was no second feature or even a short subject to cleanse the dreadful acting from the screen and our memories.

After suffering several giggling fits as we walked to my automobile, we got into my Chevrolet and Eliza said in mock irritation, "You know, Lester, you have a mean streak a mile wide in you."

I feigned surprise. "Me? What have I done?"

"You know perfectly well what you did. You sat there and made silly faces at me when you knew I was barely able to refrain from laughing at that awful melodrama."

I laughed. "That might be considered by some to be just desserts for suggesting we see that dismal attempt at cinematic art."

Unable to maintain her angry act any longer, Eliza broke into uproarious laughter. "Okay, okay. Touché. You get to pick the next movie show we see."

Eliza's laughter was completely genuine because she put her entire heart and soul into it. No dainty giggling into a hanky for this woman, no sir. I would not have minded sitting there listening to Eliza's laughter all night, but she finally regained control and said, "Honestly, Lester, I do apologize for putting you through that appallingly bad experience."

"No apology is required. Spending the evening in your company is well worth enduring *The Singing Fool*."

Eliza grinned in the darkness. "Oh, my. I certainly have you bamboozled, don't I? Where are we off to now?"

"That is sort of up to you. I don't want to get in Dutch with your father for keeping you out too late."

Holding her wrist up to the window so as to read her watch from the light of a streetlamp, Eliza said, "You know, Lester, it isn't even ten o'clock yet. That could hardly be considered too late by even the most overly protective father."

"All right, then, where shall we go? Would you like an ice cream sundae or . . . ."

Interrupting my recital of options, Eliza said, "If you don't mind, what I would like most is to show you a place I go when I want to shut the world out and think about wonderful things."

"Okay, lead on, MacDuff."

"First, make a U-turn. We need to go the other way on State."

After driving as far as one can go on State Street without getting one's tires wet in the Pacific Ocean, Eliza asked me to turn right on Shoreline Drive, which as the name implies, follows the curves of the shoreline southwest of town. During another few minutes of driving, Shoreline climbed the bluffs above the ocean. From there, Eliza directed me to make a left turn onto a short side street. Half a block later the Chevrolet's bumper was nearly hanging out over the beach.

Looking proud of her navigation skills, Eliza said cheerily, "Here we are."

Even in the darkness we could distinguish rows of white breakers rolling onto the beach below us, and while the night air was cooling, it wasn't so cold we couldn't roll down the windows a few inches to better hear the surf. Besides, the slight nip in the air gave Eliza an excellent excuse to slide over closer to me on the seat.

I will admit to being surprised that Eliza steered us to what had to be one of the best petting locations in town. Giving the girl credit, she knew what she wanted and was not shy about going after it. If those were traits common to this new breed of thoroughly modern women, I was all for enlightened womanhood.

Settling into a comfortable position with her head resting lightly on my right shoulder, Eliza said, "Well, what do you think?"

"You are quite right, this is a wonderful place to escape the cares of the world."

"Or to at least put those cares into clearer perspective. Will you tell me something, Lester?"

"If I can, certainly."

"When we left the house father said something about you having a busy day tomorrow. Was he referring to the reception tomorrow night, or is there something else on your schedule?"

"He was referring to Estelle Abernathy's donation ceremony at the County Courthouse tomorrow morning. I'm supposed to cover it for the *Tribune*. Why do you ask?"

"Oh, no particular reason. I was just curious. It certainly wouldn't do for father to know more about the man in my life than I do."

"I see, and am I the man in your life?"

"Lester, if you have to ask that question, I must be losing my touch."

"Oh."

Eliza lifted her head so she could look at my face. "I should not have said that. It makes me sound like some sort of wicked vamp. I'm nothing like that, honestly. Truthfully, I've never been up here with a man before. In fact, I haven't ever been anywhere with a man recently. I was just trying to sound . . . oh . . . I don't know what I was trying to sound like."

"A sophisticated modern woman?"

She returned her head to my shoulder. "I guess. You know, I'm not really."

"You certainly have me fooled. You seem quite cosmopolitan."

"In my beliefs about a woman's rights being equal to those of men I am, but the rest is all an act. If a male patron in the library gives me the onceover, I'm ready to run and hide."

I chuckled. "Don't look now, but I have not only given you the onceover, but the twice- and thrice-over."

"I am quite aware of that. I would have to be blind and deaf not to have noticed, but you are different."

"How am I different, Eliza?"

She was quiet for several moments, apparently thinking about how she found me different. Finally, she said, "You are different because . . . because I think you have more on your mind than . . . sex . . . when you look at me. I know you find me physically attractive, but I feel you appreciate all of me, not just my . . . well, you know what I mean."

Letting her off the hook, I said, "I think so. In my eyes you are a most remarkable woman in every way."

"See? That's what I'm getting at. I really feel those are more than just words said to impress or seduce me. It's like the way you put meaning into my name when you say it."

"Speaking of words," she said, skillfully changing the subject, "I saw your story about Estelle Abernathy in tonight's edition. Your story elevated the *Tribune's* level of reporting about two hundred percent. I know father was pleased. He seldom singles out an article especially for me to read, but he made sure I saw that one."

"Thank you. He told me the article was a little more sophisticated than what *Tribune* readers are used to, but he made no editing changes to my original story."

"I don't think I'm giving away any family secrets by telling you that father is impressed with your skill as a writer. I can tell by the way he speaks about you."

Surprised again, I asked, "He talks about me at home?"

I felt her shift her position on the seat next to me slightly. "Well, yes, but that was largely because he knew you and I were going to see a motion picture tonight. That was before we knew about the reception tomorrow night.

"Anyway, he talked to me about seeing you socially. Father is old fashioned in that way. He wasn't warning me about you or anything like that. I think it was actually his way of telling me he approved of us going out together."

Her comments reminded me of the conversation Mister Hamm and I had on Wednesday when he told me he was surprised that Eliza was going out with me socially and that I should not let my expectations rise too high. I still had no idea what he was getting at, and I considered asking Eliza what she made of it, but decided against revealing something that was perhaps unwisely said in confidence.

Instead, I asked another question. "Eliza, since I have not yet met her, tell me about your mother."

I suspected I'd hit a nerve when she was a little slow in replying. Finally, she said, "I am sorry to say Mother is no longer with us. She was infected by Tuberculosis when I was fifteen and the doctors were unable to save her, so now it is just Father and me."

"I'm so sorry, Eliza. You must miss her terribly."

"I do, but to be completely honest, I have always been closest to Father. He is my hero and protector. He watches out for me."

Again, I was reminded of Frederick Hamm's warning to me about Eliza. Somehow it did not fit with what she had just said about him. When I was slow in responding to what Eliza said, she leaned her head back and looked up at me again. "Did I say something I should not have said?"

Turning to look at her face, I said, "No, not at all. I guess I was just lost in the time and place. It is very pleasant to be here with you."

Eliza cocked her head to one side. "Pleasant? Mister Kinney, you just stopped communicating. Why?"

I grinned. "Miss Hamm you are an astute observer."

"I am swiftly becoming an astute observer of you, your expressions, and your words. I hope that meets with your approval, because I am not sure I can do otherwise."

"I approve most enthusiastically of that pastime."

"Good, then please be honest with me. Why did you suddenly get so quiet?"

I gave her question a moment of thought and decided honesty, at least semi-honesty, was the best policy. I said, "I truly was becoming lost in this time and place with you, but I was also cautioning myself not to let my expectations about our being together rise beyond what is reasonable."

Eliza reached up and held my face in her hands. "Lester, I still have the feeling there is something you are not telling me, but I will say this to you: where I am concerned you need have no reservations about your expectations. To be totally honest, I am falling hopelessly in love with you. It is a completely new experience for me to find myself in love with a man, especially a man I have known for just a few days, but that is the situation. So much so, that if you suggested we run away together right now, I would be sorely tempted to accept the invitation."

With that she leaned toward me, and still holding my face in her hands, kissed me squarely and firmly on the lips. I was so surprised, it took me a moment to react, but when I did, that kiss quickly grew to an intensity I have never before experienced.

When the need to breathe necessitated ending the kiss, Eliza looked into my eyes and just said, "Wow."

Then she quickly leaned back and again rested her head against my shoulder. When I turned to look into her face, she said, "Lester, don't you dare kiss me again. I know I instigated this, and I am sure I will again, as will you, but the way I am feeling right now, I could very easily lose what control I have left, and that could prove disastrous. Do you understand what I mean?"

I nodded. "Yes. I think we are discovering something precious about us tonight. More than anything else, I want to do this right. I mean slowly and thoughtfully."

Even in the darkness I saw something warm and loving in her big brown eyes as she said, "Thank you, Lester. Thank you so much. Gosh, I . . . you mean more to me than I can say."

At that point we both ran out of words, or perhaps we just didn't feel anymore words were necessary, so we just sat there holding hands and relishing the new closeness we were experiencing. If someone had asked at that moment, I would have said we were as close to heaven as two people could be. How that was possible after only having spent time together on just three occasions I could not explain. It just was.

After what seemed all too short a time, Eliza said, "It is the last thing I want to do, but I think we should be starting for home now. Though it could not change things between us, there is no sense to getting off on the wrong foot with Father."

As I retraced our route, Eliza said, "You know, we talked about my name earlier, but I did not ask what you prefer. Would you rather I call you Lester or Les?"

I smiled. "Anything short of 'honey lamb' would be fine."

"Come on, I'm being serious."

"Okay, okay. I guess most of my friends back home know me as Les. I'm kind of used to that version."

Giggling a little, she said, "All right, Les it is, as in I want to see more of Les."

"Ha, ha. You're a regular Fanny Brice. We should sign you up for the *Ziegfeld Follies*."

"You leave my fanny out of . . . oops! I'm sorry. I forgot we are mixed company."

"Too bad. You have such a nice . . . ."

"Lester!"

Pulling to the curb in front of the Hamm residence, I hugged

Eliza and got a short, but sweet kiss in return. "See you tomorrow night, Les darling."

"I'll be here with bells on."

She smiled. "I hope you also have a tuxedo on. I'll bet you are going to look simply swell in tails."

Then I escorted her to the front door, where I got another quick smooch before I saw Frederick Hamm enter the living room wearing a maroon robe and matching slippers.

"How was the motion picture show, kids?"

Almost in unison, we both said, "Don't ask."

Mister Hamm laughed and I said, "Goodnight, sir. I'll be seeing you tomorrow night."

"Goodnight, Lester. Don't forget you owe me another story on Monday."

"I'll have it ready, sir."

As Eliza turned to close the door behind me, she gave me a wink. I winked back, not really caring if her father noticed or not.

FIVE

Saturday - September 8, 1928

If I were required to pick one feature of my rented cottage about which to voice a complaint, that complaint would be in reference to the mirrors, or more accurately, to the lack thereof. Throughout the entire two bedroom bungalow, there is a grand total of one mirror. It hangs over the bathroom sink and is about the size of that photo of your favorite uncle hanging in the hallway.

I would make such a complaint not because I enjoy looking at myself, but because, on occasions such as this, it would be nice to see that my shirt is tucked into my trousers properly and other such details. As it was, about all I could determine from my puny bathroom mirror was that my bowtie appeared to be more or less straight.

The occasion for this sartorial concern was Estelle Abernathy's donation to Saint Andria's orphanage. This grand event was scheduled to occur during an outdoor ceremony on the County Courthouse grounds in about two hours, at ten a.m., and I was expected to attend, take in the proceedings, and write an article to appear in Monday's *Tribune* glorifying Miss Abernathy's extreme generosity. Since I was told by my boss that every government official from the mayor to the dogcatcher would be on hand for the ceremony, it seemed appropriate to show up dressed as well as possible given the meager contents of my closet.

When I was finally satisfied with my attire, I found I had time for another cup of coffee before setting out for the Courthouse. I poured that cup from my dented, secondhand coffee percolator and sat at my kitchen table to enjoy it. Just as I lifted the steaming cup to my lips, however, the telephone rang.

My telephone instrument resides on the table I intend to use as a desk in my spare bedroom. It had rung three rings by the time I grabbed the handset and said, "Hello?"

"Hello, Mister Kinney. Fredrick Hamm at this end. I am glad I caught you before you left for the Courthouse."

I couldn't imagine why Mister Hamm was calling me. "Yes,

sir. What's going on?"

"I wanted to give you a warning about something that is very likely to happen at Estelle Abernathy's donation ceremony this morning."

"Oh? What is that, sir?"

"I am assuming you have not seen our competitor's front page yet this morning."

Wishing he would get to the point I said, "No, I haven't."

"There is a story above the fold on the *Post-Dispatch's* front page about oil washing up on a beach near Summerland, and I am certain Tom Wigand or one of the other *Post-Dispatch* reporters will try to corner Miss Abernathy for a statement, she being one of the larger investors in the Summerland Oil Field Company."

"I see."

"This sort of thing has happened before and the *Post-Dispatch* loves to turn any minor incident into a disaster of biblical proportions because the headlines sell newspapers."

I repeated myself. "I see. Is there anything in particular you want me to do with this information?"

"Yes, a couple of things. First, stay away from Wigand or any other *Post-Dispatch* reporters who show up to the ceremony. I don't want Miss Abernathy to get the idea we are in cahoots with them."

"Got it."

"I also want you to get your story on the ceremony written as quickly as possible, maybe today if you can."

"Why the rush, sir?"

"In the unlikely event there is really anything to the *Post-Dispatch* story, I want to put you on it. If you play your cards right, you could be in a perfect position to dig up the straight dope about what's going on, if anything is actually going on."

"You mean tonight, sir"

"I mean tonight and any other time or place you can take advantage of Estelle Abernathy's fondness for you."

"All right, sir."

"When you get through at the ceremony, come on in to the office. We can discuss this further and you can get going on your ceremony story. In the meantime, I'm sending Joe O'Conner out to photograph whatever he can find at Fernald Point where the spill supposedly occurred. It's only a few miles away, so he can be back and have the photos ready by the time you return from the event. Got it?"

"Yes, sir. I'll see you as soon as the ceremony ends."

"Good. And one more thing."

"Yes, sir?"

"I don't know what you did to my daughter last night, but keep it up. Liza is brighter and more cheerful than I've seen her in some time. Oh, and she says to tell you good morning."

"Thank you, sir."

I found myself smiling on the way back to the kitchen. It seemed even a secondhand greeting from Eliza had the power to raise my spirits, and at that moment they needed some elevation. That Fredrick Hamm wanted to put me on the oil spill story because some rich old dame was fond of me rather than because of my journalistic skills did nothing for my self-confidence.

I sighed, took two quick gulps of my coffee, and pointed my Chevrolet toward the Santa Barbara County Courthouse. My route took me northeast on Micheltorena Street to Anacapa, where I turned right and drove three blocks to the Courthouse, which is located across Anacapa Street from the library.

The three-story Courthouse occupies a full city block of Santa Barbara real estate, but the building itself takes up less than half of that space. The rest of the block is filled by a park-like garden planted with lush lawns on raised and sunken levels, towering palm trees, and all manner of exotic greenery I could not identify if my life depended on it.

To this setting city employees were busy adding a speaker's podium, rows of wooden folding chairs, colorful bunting, and tables that were probably intended for refreshments to be served following the presentation. Fortunately, there was no wind to disturb the decorations. In fact, it was such a beautiful sunny morning I wondered if Saint Andria himself had put in a request for the exceptional weather.

The Courthouse building is L-shaped and borders the southwest and southeast sides of the block. I, however, parked on Anapamu Street to the northwest, a spot which allowed me to observe the preparations relatively inconspicuously. By nine-thirty people began arriving for the event, but I remained where I was a while longer. I wanted to wait until Tom Wigand or anyone else from the *Post-Dispatch* showed up so I could choose my viewing spot for the ceremonies without running into them.

I met Wigand on one of my first job hunting trips to Santa Barbara and his appearance made him easy to remember. He was short and slender with pinched features and a perpetual sneer on his face. Another feature making Tom Wigand easy to recognize is the oversized fedora he wears, most likely because he thinks it makes him appear larger in stature. In truth, all he needs is a press card stuck in the wide band of his hat to become a caricature worthy of the *Tribune's* funny pages.

A few minutes after Wigand arrived I learned that the first rows of chairs were reserved for honored dignitaries. I learned this because Wigand was promptly shooed away by a Santa Barbara policeman when he tried to seat himself in the front row. Instead he took up a standing position at the far end of the first dignitary row. I, in turn, stood about halfway back on the opposite side of the general seating area.

Unlike most civic events I've attended over the years, this one began on time. The Courthouse clock tower chimes struck the ten o'clock hour, and as the last chime faded away, Mayor Theodore Finley stepped up to the podium and opened the festivities by introducing the attending dignitaries. Of course each of them received an ovation.

Next came Estelle Abernathy, who presented her fifty-thousand-dollar check to a representative of the Daughters of the Charity of Saint Andria. The recipient of the check in turn thanked Miss Abernathy profusely for the good Christian deed she was performing by helping Saint Andria's continue to care for the orphaned children of Santa Barbara. Then the pastor of the Mission Parish blessed the assembly and that was that.

The dignitaries and spectators broke into small groups near the refreshment tables and Estelle Abernathy spent a few minutes speaking with a group of nuns, while her entourage—the young dark-haired woman I'd seen riding with Miss Abernathy in her Cadillac and the tall Latin fellow I'd met at the Abernathy mansion—waited impatiently on one foot and then the other for Estelle Abernathy to finish her conversations.

While all this was going on, I was watching Tom Wigand. He reminded me of a jungle cat stalking his prey for the kill. At the precise moment when Estelle Abernathy and her entourage turned toward Anapamu Street to depart the event, Wigand sprang.

Stepping directly in front of Estelle Abernathy to block her departure, I heard him say in a loud nasal voice, "Miss Abernathy, would you care to make a statement about the oil spill disaster at Summerland that was reported in this morning's *Post-Dispatch?*"

The glare Estelle Abernathy directed at Tom Wigand would have caused most civilized men to cower in a corner, but Tom Wigand showed no signs of cowering. He firmly stood his ground, giving Miss Abernathy little choice but to answer his question.

"No, I would not care to make a statement because I have not read the article to which you refer, but if it appears in the *Post-Dispatch,* the odds of there being any truth to it are slim."

With that, Estelle Abernathy and her group resumed their departure from the Courthouse grounds. Wigand, however, was not so easily put off the scent of a scoop. Again he stepped into their path, this time shouting, "Some experts are claiming the spillage is due to haphazard procedures in use at the Summerland Oil Field, in which you are heavily invested. Would you care to comment on that?"

Suddenly, a large man I recognized as Estelle Abernathy's driver materialized out of nowhere and, with the slender Latin man at his side, began advancing on Wigand in what I can only describe as a threatening manner. At that juncture Tom Wigand showed his true colors and beat a hasty retreat.

At this point two police officers finally realized the event's guest of honor was being accosted and quickly moved in to discourage the *Post-Dispatch* reporter from continuing what thus far had been a decidedly one-sided interview.

A moment later Estelle Abernathy's entourage passed and she recognized me. In a voice I'm certain Tom Wigand could not help but hear, she said, "Mister Kinney, I was quite pleased to learn you will be attending our reception this evening."

Smiling, I said, "Thank you for inviting me, Miss Abernathy. I am very much looking forward to the event."

When I turned to glance at Tom Wigand, he was, as they say in the pulp fiction magazines, looking daggers at me. While his displeasure initially pleased me, further thought gave me to wonder if angering Wigand was smart.

Smart or not, Wigand was angered and there was nothing I could do about it, so I shrugged and walked to my automobile. From there I drove five blocks to the *Tribune* offices. Frederick Hamm's four-door Buick sedan was parked at the curb. I parked behind it.

Inside, I went straight to my desk in the newsroom and hung up my coat. The big space was empty and quiet as a tomb until Mister Hamm's voice broke the silence.

"Mister Kinney, come in here, please."

As I entered his windowed office, Frederick Hamm asked, "How did the ceremony go?"

"The presentation of Estelle Abernathy's check was short and sweet. After that, though, things got a little more exciting."

"Wigand?"

I nodded. "Wigand. As you anticipated, he confronted Miss

Abernathy about the spill at Summerland."

"Tell me about it."

I described Tom Wigand's two unsuccessful attempts to wheedle a statement out of Estelle Abernathy. I concluded my account with Miss Abernathy's greeting to me and Wigand's response.

Mister Hamm gave my report a moment's consideration before saying, "Mister Kinney, when I telephoned you this morning, I should have included an additional warning."

"About Wigand?"

"Yes. As you have witnessed firsthand, he is a wicked little man and not one who suffers indignations lightly. When it comes to dealing with Tom Wigand, you would be wise to exercise caution."

"I'll bear that in mind, sir. Has the photographer returned from Summerland with his photographs yet?"

He looked at me for several seconds, his expression of concern over my encounter with Tom Wigand still on his face. Finally, he nodded. "Yes, he rolled in just minutes before you got here. Apparently he found a lot to photograph."

"Oh, oh."

"We'll see. It's going to take him a while to develop the film and make contact prints, so you might make use of the wait by starting on your presentation article."

"Yes, sir."

At my desk, I removed a few sheets of paper from the bottom drawer and rolled one of them into my typewriter. Since I had written most of the article in my mind during the ceremony, finishing it required only that I get the words on paper and smooth out a few rough spots.

The black hands of the big white electric clock on the newsroom wall were indicating eleven-thirty when I rolled the final double-spaced page of my story from the typewriter. I was reviewing the article for typographical errors and making a few minor changes when a movement at the center of the newsroom caught my eye. A man carrying a sheaf of what looked like photographs strolled into the editor's office.

I was already on my feet and moving when Frederick Hamm shouted my name. The third man in the room when I got there was a stocky gray-haired fellow with a ruddy complexion and pale blue eyes. Mister Hamm said, "Joe, meet Lester Kinney, our new reporter. Mister Kinney, Joe O'Conner, the *Tribune's* Senior Photographer."

As I shook his hand, O'Conner said, "Welcome aboard, Lester."

"Thank you, Mister O'Conner."

O'Conner's eyes had what might have been a twinkle in them as he said, "Call me Joe. Save that 'mister' business for the big shots, like the boss here."

While O'Conner and I were shaking hands, Frederick Hamm was busily spreading four-by-five sheets of photo paper out on his desk. From the way the paper drooped as he set the sheets down, I got the idea the contact prints were still damp from the water bath.

Joe said, "I made twenty exposures in all, but these tell the story best."

Mister Hamm agreed. "They sure do. Good work."

"Thank you, Mister Hamm. You'll notice I included a footprint in some of the photos for scale."

"I see that. Mister Kinney, take a look at your new assignment."

I moved closer to the desk and stared at thick black globs of something on the sand in the photographs. The globs looked to range in diameter from about an inch to five or six inches and had a slight sheen to them, indicating a reflective surface.

Frederick Hamm said, "Joe, tell Lester what he's looking at."

Nodding, O'Conner said, "I made these images on the beach at Fernald Point, which is just this side of the Summerland Oil Field. Those black globs are what you get when waves wash crude oil up on a beach and it congeals."

"I see."

"The stuff is not as solid as it looks. You can easily squish it with the toe of your shoe."

I picked up a wider shot that showed a long stretch of beach. The globs were distributed more or less evenly over the sand. They made an otherwise pristine beach appear dirty and littered.

"Where did this stuff come from?"

Mister Hamm responded to my question. "That's what you need to find out. Similar spills in the past have been attributed to one of two sources. One is a well that has somehow developed a leak, and the other is a natural seep."

Joe picked up the explanation from there. "A natural seep occurs when small amounts of crude oil work their way up through the ocean floor due to gas pressure from below. If these globs come from a natural seep, there's nothing to be done about it, but clean the oil off the beach. Eventually natural seeps usually cork themselves, but not always."

Frederick Hamm said, "If the oil on Fernald Beach comes from a leaking well, we could have a big problem on our hands. Small well leaks can become very large leaks. If that happens, the oil can affect large stretches of coastline and cause a lot of damage to seabirds and marine animals."

I made the connection between what I was seeing and Tom Wigand's questions to Estelle Abernathy. "So the *News-Press* is trying to pin the blame for this on a leaking well?"

Mister Hamm said, "Exactly right, but their article offers no proof or scientific evidence for their claim the oil is coming from a leaking well. That's pure conjecture on their part."

"What do they gain by doing that?"

Frederick Hamm said, "They gain newspaper sales. A mismanaged well gives people someone to blame and creates controversy. A natural seep is nobody's fault. Putting the blame on nature doesn't sell newspapers."

"I can see that, but how do we go about learning the truth?"

"You talk to the experts—the geologists and managers of Summerland Oil Field. When it comes to oil production, they don't miss much. You can be sure that by now they know exactly where the oil on Fernald Beach is coming from."

"Yes, sir, but will they tell me if it is coming from a leaking well? That seems like information they would rather keep to themselves."

Frederick Hamm's expression and tone of voice were tinged with exasperation. "Mister Kinney, that is precisely why you are getting this assignment. Estelle Abernathy is your key to getting in the door at Summerland. Find out what you can by keeping your ears open tonight, but do not let her know you are interested in the oil spill. Sunday I want you out at Fernald Point to get the lay of the land. First thing Monday morning we will decide how we can use your friendship with Estelle to determine what's really going on out there.

At that point it became clear to me that Frederick Hamm did not really know Estelle Abernathy. He had her sized up entirely wrong. If he knew her, he would also know she will not allow herself to be "used" for any purpose other than one of which she approves. Estelle Abernathy was one sharp cookie, and what Frederick Hamm wanted me to do could end in no way other than badly.

I could see no purpose to be served by trying to set him straight. Instead, I said I understood my assignment and excused myself to finish the presentation ceremony story. I was just signing my initials at the top of the first page when Joe O'Conner arrived at my desk.

I looked up and was surprised to see him shaking his head. With a quick glance toward the editor's office, he said in a quiet tone, "I understand your predicament, son. Now is the time for you to play things very cagey, and if there's any way I can help, let me know."

Then, before I could say anything, O'Conner said in a louder voice, "Mister Hamm thought you ought to take these contact prints with you when you go out to Fernald Point tomorrow. I will run them through the print drier again and leave them in an envelope on your desk. I'll also write my telephone number on the envelope in case you need more photos or anything. Okay?"

I nodded. "Okay, Joe. Thank you."

SIX

Saturday - September 8, 1928

When I arrived at the Hamm residence around six-thirty, Mister Hamm had already left for a dinner engagement which meant there was no one around to object if Eliza and I misbehaved a little. She greeted me with a warm kiss and hug followed by a fashion model turn to show off her ensemble for the evening.

To say that Eliza took my breath away in the evening dress she chose for Estelle Abernathy's reception might be an exaggeration, but only a slight one. I expected her to be stunning. She is always stunning, but the way Eliza looked Saturday night was well beyond any expectation I could have imagined.

Her dress was a shimmering silver-gray. I discovered that the shimmer was due to silver beadwork and iridescent sequins stitched in simple geometric patterns accenting the shape of the gown. Sleeveless, the dress featured V-shaped necklines front and back that were just deep enough to be a little spicy without seeming indecent. The hem was sort of scallop-shaped and ended at a point just below her knees.

To my eyes, the best part was the way the dress fit. It was tight enough to flatter Eliza's trim figure, but still loose enough to allow a little shimmery movement when she walked. The outfit was finished off with matching silver-gray T-strap leather shoes with slim heels, black gloves that reached to her elbows, a small black beaded bag, and a long rope of faux pearls that looped around her neck three times with enough length left for a flattering drape.

When Eliza completed her turn, she looked at me for my appraisal. "What do you think? Am I suitably bedecked to fit in with the swells at Estelle Abernathy's soirée?"

"To heck with the swells. I want to keep you all to myself."

Eliza grinned. "I wouldn't mind that at all, but father paid for this extravagant frock, so we'd better put in an appearance."

It struck me as ironic that we were both dressed in clothes paid for by Frederick Hamm and the *Tribune*. While I didn't mention that the paper bought my tuxedo, she was right, we owed the *Tribune* a night's work.

In a disappointed tone of voice I said, "Oh, all right. I'll share you, but I'm not happy about it."

Picking up a light filmy gray wrap from the arm of a chair, she walked to the door, saying, "Don't be disappointed, Mister Kinney. We are not expected back until the wee small hours of the morning, so we might squeeze in a little time just for us."

I started the Chevrolet's engine and turned to look at Eliza again. I didn't say anything, I just looked. After a moment, Eliza said, "What is it? Is my eye makeup smudged?"

"No. You are just unbelievably beautiful, that's all."

It was hard to tell for sure in the darkness, but I think she might have blushed. "I'm really glad you think so, darling. You make me feel like a movie star or something. You really do, and by the way, Mister Kinney, you look pretty spiffy, yourself. You should wear tails more often."

Smiling, I said, "Don't count on that too much. I feel like an overstuffed penguin in this outfit."

"Well, you do not look at all penguin-ish."

As I pulled away from the curb and pointed my Chevrolet east toward the hills of the Riviera, Eliza said, "Before we get to Miss Abernathy's, there are two subjects I would like to discuss with you. Is that all right?"

"Of course it is. Go ahead."

"Okay. The first is sort of silly, but it's important, too. I just can't get used to calling you Les. Would you mind if I went back to calling you Lester?"

Relieved that the subject of this discussion was more of a frivolous nature than something of great consequence, I said, "Not at all. I told you, short of honey lamb, you can call me anything you like."

"Thank you. It's just that Lester somehow better fits the picture I carry of you in my mind. It's more . . . I don't know . . . more dignified I guess."

Chuckling, I said, "We certainly do not want to be undignified!"

"No, we do not. Now, the second subject I need to discuss with you is a little more involved, so be patient with me while I try to say this right."

That did not sound good to my ears. I felt a little twinge in the pit of my stomach. "Okay, tell me."

"Mind you, I'm not entirely sure about this, but I have a

strong feeling that Father's opinion of you has changed in some way. Everything was fine when he went to the paper this morning, but when he got home in the afternoon, something had changed. Now he seems . . . annoyed, I guess is the word, with you. Can you think of some reason why that might be?"

I knew exactly why Frederick Hamm was annoyed with his new cub reporter. I thought about brushing Eliza's question off, but that didn't seem right. Hoping my mother was right about honesty always being the best policy, I said, "Yes, Eliza, I think I know exactly why your father is upset with me. We had a conversation this afternoon during which he instructed me to do some things, I don't feel right about doing. I didn't say that to him, but I don't think I hid my feelings on the subject very well."

There was a lot of concern in Eliza's voice when she said, "Oh, my. Can you tell me what the conversation was about?"

I said I could and gave her as exact a report as I could on what transpired in the editor's office that afternoon. We were almost to Estelle Abernathy's mansion when I finished my tale.

Eliza said, "Lester, can you pull over for a minute? I want to say something before we get to the reception."

I pulled the Chevrolet off onto an empty spot alongside the road. "Okay, what are you thinking?"

"If I am understanding this correctly. You feel it isn't right to use Miss Abernathy's fondness for you as an advantage to get inside information about this oil spill. Is that right?"

"Yes, but there's more to it. Your father's approach to this simply will not work."

Putting on what I took to be a thoughtful expression in the dim light, Eliza said, "I don't disagree with that, Lester, but tell me why you think it won't work."

"Because Estelle Abernathy is sharp as a tack. In that regard she reminds me a little of you. She doesn't miss a trick, so no matter how tactfully I broached the subject of the oil spill, she would immediately realize what I was up to and that would put an end to my friendship with her on the spot. I'm pretty sure Miss Abernathy brooks no disloyalty among her friends and associates."

Eliza nodded slowly. "Everything I know about Estelle Abernathy tells me you are right about that, and I'm sorry Father has put you in such a bind. I think he's wrong, and what's more, I think he knows he's wrong."

"You certainly know him better than I do, but he seemed quite definite about this."

"Sometimes he changes his mind after he has some time to

think about a situation. So what are you going to do?"

"Tonight I'm going to keep my eyes and ears open in hope of finding a better approach to the Summerland Oil Field Company, and tomorrow I'll drive down to Fernald Point and see what I can learn on my own."

"Lester, for what it is worth, I too will keep my eyes and ears open tonight, and I think tomorrow would be a lovely day for a short drive down the coast, that is, if you'll allow me to come along."

"Eliza, I don't want to put you on the spot with your father. This is between him and me."

"No, Lester. This is between my father and the man I like . . . no, damn it, I'm not afraid to say it . . . the man I love. That makes it my business, too."

Eliza leaned over, and holding my face in her hands as she had the night before, she kissed me. "Now, dearest Lester, let's go mingle with the swells."

Pulling through the gates onto Estelle Abernathy's estate, we could see the long drive was already lined with cars. An attendant at the gate, however, told us to continue on to the house and someone there would take care of the car for us.

Driving past a long line of Cadillacs, Packards, and even two sporty Duesenbergs, it occurred to me that, if automobiles had feelings, my humble, but loyal little Chevrolet was probably feeling quite out of place among such automotive luminaries. For that matter, I was having some of the same feelings about myself, so I gave it a pat on the dashboard. Eliza gave me a strange look, but did not ask.

We pulled up in front of the mansion's entrance where valets in black and gray striped vests opened the car doors for us. The fellow on my side of the car handed me a small ticket stub with which he said I could reclaim my automobile when we were ready to leave.

The festive illumination for the party was almost garish. There were large, colorful bulbs strung overhead and carefully placed spotlights lit up the house, itself, making the mansion appear to float like Xanadu against the dark hillside. We could hear music, too, and it was definitely not Victrola music. It sounded as if a small orchestra had taken up residence in the backyard. They were playing *Mountain Greenery*.

Eliza's eyes were wide. "Heavens, look at this place! My parents took me to the Venice amusement pier when I was ten years old and it had nothing on this."

We were met at the mansion's entrance by Miss Abernathy's Latin butler. "Good evening Señorita Hamm and Señor Kinney. Welcome to Miss Abernathy's reception. Dinner is to be served in the grand hall at eight o'clock. Libations and hors d'oeuvres are available in the garden by the swimming pool. If you should desire anything else, feel free to ask any member of the staff. Please enjoy yourselves."

As we walked inside, Eliza leaned toward me and said softly, "Wow, they know you by name around here. You must be special."

"Not that special. I was just here Wednesday. I will admit, though, his attitude toward me seems much friendlier than it did last time."

Eliza lit up her smile. "How could anyone not be friendly to such a charming and witty fellow?"

"I can't imagine. This way."

Wondering how it was that Estelle's butler also knew Eliza at a glance, I led her into the library where I interviewed Miss Abernathy. From there we went out the door to the side garden with the fountain. Outside, we walked around toward the crowd in the backyard. This maneuver allowed us to see the party in full swing without being in the middle of it.

"Gee, you sure know your way around this place. You sure you were only here once before?"

Looking the crowd over, I said, "Positive. Tell me, who is that dark-haired woman in the red gown over there dancing with the bald fellow?"

Trying to sound indignant, Eliza said, "Well, that beats all! We haven't been here five minutes and you're already looking at another woman."

"She's not my type. I just saw her with Miss Abernathy this morning and I thought it might be a good idea to know her role in this spectacle."

"If you must know, that is Aurora Abernathy, Estelle Abernathy's daughter."

"Daughter? I thought Miss Abernathy never married."

Eliza gave me a pitying look. "Just so it doesn't come as a big surprise to you someday, darling, one does not have to be married to have a child. In this case, however, Aurora is Estelle Abernathy's adopted daughter. Miss Abernathy adopted her from Saint Andria's a while back. Maybe five years ago."

My arm was around Eliza's waist and I gave her a squeeze. "Thank you, and thanks for the biology lesson. I'll be sure to keep it in mind."

Giving me a nudge with her hip, she said, "See that you do."

"Would you care for a libation, Miss Hamm?"

"I would. Just a Coca-Cola, please."

Grinning, I said, "What? No booze?"

She gave me a stern look. "That would be a violation of the Volstead Act. Lips that touch liquor shall not touch mine!"

I look heavenward and muttered, "Oh brother," as I walked off to the bar.

Returning with two Coca-Colas over ice, I handed one to Eliza. "Thank you, darling. While you were gone I did some celebrity spotting. Would you like a rundown on the Who's Who of who's here?"

"That would be most helpful."

"All right, the most recognizable celebrities I've spotted are Gloria Swanson and Harold Lloyd. He's here with his wife, Mildred. As for local bigwigs, Mayor Finley is here, as is Laselle Thornburgh, the esteemed president of the City Council."

"Very useful, but you missed one of the biggest names here."

Surprised, Eliza said, "I did? Who did I miss?"

"Charles Chaplin."

I had succeeded in surprising her. "He's here?"

"Right over there, the fellow talking with the redheaded woman in the green dress."

"That's Chaplin? I didn't recognize him without his moustache and derby. Goodness, he's quite a handsome fellow without his tramp makeup."

Giving Eliza a small dose of her own medicine, I said, "He's a louse."

"Darling! How can you say such a thing about the poor little tramp?"

"Poor? Chaplin is one of the richest men in the world. And he's still a louse."

Looking coy, Eliza said, "Don't worry darling, I will remember who brought me to the ball."

At dinner Eliza and I were seated next to one another about halfway down one side of the table. The menu included baked ham, goose, and more than a sufficient number of side dishes to make the sideboards sag under their weight, including a heaping lump of pate de' foie gras.

The conversation at our end of the table, however, was less abundant. I got the idea the people around us were there for a command performance and they were none too happy about it. Despite her "grand dame" stature, Estelle Abernathy was not loved by all.

After dinner we returned to the back garden. The little orchestra was playing again, so Eliza and I took advantage of that fact to have our first dance together. I'm no Vernon Castle, but Eliza's grace on the dancefloor made me look quite accomplished. I was just commenting on that fact when Estelle Abernathy's Latin butler approached us.

"Please excuse my interruption, Señor Kinney, but Miss Abernathy requests a moment of your time."

I glanced at Eliza. She said, "Don't worry, darling, I'll enjoy the music and the view while you are gone."

Nodding and wondering what this turn of events was all about, I followed the butler into the house and to the library. He held the door open as I walked in, and then closed it behind me. Estelle Abernathy was seated behind the massive desk.

"Mister Kinney, are you and Miss Hamm enjoying yourselves at our little party?"

A little surprised that Estelle Abernathy also knew Eliza, I said, "Well, Miss Abernathy, your hospitality is most gracious, but to be honest, I'm feeling a little out of place."

Estelle Abernathy surprised me again by laughing out loud. "Don't let that concern you, Mister Kinney. You are no more out of place here than I. Most of these folks would not give me the time of day if I were not rich enough to buy and sell every one of them."

Her laugh was contagious and I couldn't help smiling. "Oh, I doubt that."

"Believe me, Mister Kinney, it's the gospel truth. That, however, has nothing to do with why I asked to see you. The last time we were in this room together you asked some thoughtful questions, and then you turned my answers into a well-written and precise article. I was quite impressed, so I decided to make myself available in case you had any other particular questions on your mind tonight."

Damn! She knew! I don't know how she knew what Frederick Hamm wanted me to do, but that had to be behind the unusual offer she was making. Maybe she was simply intuitive enough to make a good guess, but however she figured it out, I had only a moment to make a choice. I went with my sense of what was right.

"No, Miss Abernathy, I have no questions at the moment. Of course, I'm interested in hearing more about your life and experiences, but nothing of an urgent nature."

Estelle Abernathy looked into my eyes. Her face was totally

without expression, and she just stared at me for several long moments. Finally, she asked, "Are you quite sure of that, Mister Kinney?"

Without hesitation, I said, "Quite sure, Miss Abernathy."

She smiled. "In that case, Mister Kinney, you may call me Estelle from now on, assuming of course, you don't mind me calling you Lester."

Thinking this was the second time in a few hours my name had been the topic of conversation. I said, "Of course you may call me Lester. I'm honored that you choose to do so."

Still smiling, Estelle said, "I know you must be curious about what just happened here, and you will figure it out in time. For now, however, it is only necessary that you understand I consider you a friend, an important friend.

"Also, there is a good deal more I wish to discuss with you, but that can wait a while. I imagine you will be quite busy tomorrow. Perhaps we can meet Monday evening for a time. Say here around eight o'clock?"

My mind was literally spinning as I tried to figure out what Estelle Abernathy was up to. Cautiously, I said, "I think Monday evening will fit my schedule, Estelle."

"Thank you, Lester, and for now, it might be prudent to keep our discussions between ourselves. You will see why I suggest that on Monday. Now, just one more thing before you go back to the party."

"Yes?"

"I just want you to know I think you made an excellent choice in selecting your date for this evening. Eliza is charming and intelligent, to say nothing of her being a very beautiful woman. I hope your appreciation of her is more than just skin-deep."

Not sure that my feelings for Eliza were any of Estelle's concern, I said, "I assure you it is."

I left the library by the side door again and walked toward the back garden, still wondering what in heaven's name had just happened. I spotted Eliza almost immediately. She was standing with her back to me not far from where we stood when we first arrived. She was, however, not alone.

As I approached, I heard her say, "Mister Chaplin . . ."

"Charlie. Call me Charlie."

"Mister Chaplin, I have already explained to you that I am waiting for someone and I have no desire whatsoever to dance with you."

Chaplin sounded almost desperate. Apparently he was not

used to being turned down and his ego was bruised. "Why not? There isn't another woman here who wouldn't love to dance with me."

"Then go dance with one of them and leave me alone."

"But . . ."

"Mister Chaplin, I have it on good authority that you are a louse. I do not dance with lice. Now leave me alone or I will make a scene."

Chaplin looked ready to take one more try at Eliza when he saw me approaching. He gave me a smirk and beat a hasty retreat.

To Eliza I said, "How about dancing with me instead?"

Without turning, she said, "That is the offer I have been waiting for, Mister Kinney."

The orchestra was playing *Poor Butterfly*, and from the way Eliza held me close and rested her head on my chest, I am certain those who bothered to notice us had no doubt as to the nature of our relationship.

As the song ended, I said, "We have a couple of things to discuss. How much longer would you like to stay?"

Eliza grinned. "I was about to ask you the same question."

Waiting for the valet to bring our chariot, I glanced at my pocket watch. The time was ten-thirty. I hoped Eliza was right about not being expected home until the wee small hours of the morning. Once behind the wheel, I pointed the Chevrolet toward the spot to which Eliza took me the night before.

SEVEN

Saturday - September 8, 1928

As we drove down the hill from Estelle Abernathy's mansion, Eliza brought up the subject of lice. "I'm sorry I had to be so forceful with Mister Chaplin, but he was sorely trying my patience."

Feigning sympathy for the louse, I said, "Gee, all he wanted to do was dance with you."

"Maybe, but when a fellow prefaces his invitation to dance by patting me on the fanny, I tend to think he might have more on his mind than the Charleston."

"He did that to you?"

"He most certainly did. And I didn't imagine it, either."

"No wonder he left in such a hurry when he saw me. He got his comeuppance, though. I think you bruised his ego."

"I doubt it. You couldn't bruise that little jerk's ego with a sledgehammer, but never mind that. What did Miss Abernathy want from you? Or can you say?"

"Well, Estelle asked me to keep our meetings between her and me, but I'm pretty sure that wasn't meant to include you. All in all, it was one of the oddest meetings I have ever attended."

"Oh, oh."

"Nothing bad, just strange."

I was pulling into the parking spot overlooking the beach where we parked Friday night as I began the story. I told her about Miss Abernathy repeatedly asking if I had any questions for her and how I responded. Then I described how I was suddenly on a first name basis with Estelle.

Eliza tilted her head to one side and gave me her curious look. "You think Miss Abernathy knew what father put you up to about the oil at Summerland? How would she know that?"

"After going over the conversation in my mind a few times, I've come to the conclusion she played a hunch. Estelle knows how newspapers work. I think she just put two and two together and guessed your father would have me try to take advantage of the situation by pumping her for information about the oil spill."

Frowning, Eliza said, "She figured it out all on her own?"

"It has to be something like that. The only other person who knows what your father wanted me to do is Joe O'Conner, and I can't convince myself he told anyone about it."

"No, Uncle Joe is not the sort of man to talk out of turn."

"Uncle Joe?"

"He and my father have known each other since I was a little girl. Sometime along the way I started calling him Uncle Joe, and I still do to this day."

"Then there is no one else who could have told her. She had to have figured it out for herself."

"It's not very flattering of her to think my father would take advantage of the situation like that."

"Yes, but he did, or tried to."

Eliza was quiet for a long moment, and then she sighed. "You're right, he certainly did."

"That's less a statement about your father than it is recognition of Estelle's ability to size people up."

Looking less than convinced, she said, "I suppose so. What else can you tell me about your chat with Miss Abernathy?"

"Estelle had some nice things to say about you. She said you were an excellent choice as my date tonight and that you are charming and intelligent as well as being a very beautiful woman. She told me I should appreciate you for all of your qualities, not just your beauty."

When I looked into Eliza's face she was frowning. "And do you . . . still?"

"That's an odd question for you to ask. I hope you know without any doubt that I appreciate everything about you. I've said as much."

She lowered her head and I saw her wipe a tear from her cheek. "What's the matter? Why does that upset you?"

Eliza turned toward me and began sobbing. I put my arms around her and, not knowing what to say, just held her close. After several minutes, she pushed away and sat up. "Lester, I have to tell you something . . . two somethings. You won't like hearing them, but I have to tell you."

Not sure what was coming, I tried to reassure her. "Eliza, there is nothing you could possibly tell me that would change how I feel about you."

She looked up at me with tears on both cheeks. "I hope not, but I won't blame you if . . . ."

While I sat on pins and needles, Eliza was quiet, as if summoning up her courage to say something very difficult. Finally she said, "Lester, Estelle Abernathy is a . . . she likes young women."

For a moment I was relieved. "So what? Women who are involved with other women are not all that uncommon these days. It doesn't matter to me what Estelle Abernathy does in her bedroom."

The tears were flowing again and I realized there was another shoe to be dropped. "No, but how I know she likes young women will matter to you."

"Eliza . . . ."

"No, Lester. Let me say this." She took a deep breath. "I know she likes young women because for a short time, I was one of those young women. It happened just after I graduated from high school. I was looking for work and Estelle ran a help wanted ad in the *Tribune* for a secretary. I applied and she gave me the job.

"After a short time, she began to . . . to make advances. I've never had a lot of self-respect and I was flattered. Besides that, I needed the job. I went along with it for . . . for a few . . . weeks, but then she began demanding . . . things . . . every day . . . she wanted me to move in with her . . . and . . . and I . . . couldn't . . . ."

Eliza ran out of words and the tears came again. I hugged her close, feeling each sob wrack her trembling body. "Eliza, none of that matters to me."

"How can you say that? I did disgusting things."

"I can say that because it's true. I've lost respect for Estelle Abernathy, though. Not because she's a lesbian, but for setting traps to catch young naïve women like you for her use. That . . . ." I searched for the words and all I could come up with is, "That is just wrong."

"But I was wrong, too. I let her . . . ."

"You did something you regret. None of us is without some regrets. That is one of the ways we learn about life."

Eliza pressed her head against my chest. "Oh, Lester."

As we sat there quietly clarity suddenly began arriving in large doses. "Tell me something, Eliza. Is this why you haven't been dating? Have you been afraid some . . . oh hell!"

Eliza jerked her head up. "What?"

In an instant several puzzles solved themselves. "That heart-to-heart chat Estelle and I had earlier suddenly makes perfect sense, and I couldn't have been more wrong about it. She wasn't wondering if I was going to ask her about the oil spill at all. She wanted to know if you told me she was a lesbian. That was the subject she thought I might want to ask her about, and when I didn't tumble to it, Estelle figured you had not told me so she made sure I would find out. She said nice things about you as if she knew you well so I would wonder how she knew you."

Eliza looked completely bewildered. "But why? Why would she want you to know?"

"That's easy. When Estelle saw us at her party together it must have been obvious we are romantically involved. She wanted me to find out about her affair with you hoping it would scare me off. She would see that as a way of getting even with you for walking out on her years ago."

"Oh, no! Do you really think so?"

"I wouldn't put it past her and it makes a lot more sense than anything else we've come up with."

"Oh, Lester. What have I gotten you into?"

I forced a smile I did not feel. "You haven't gotten me into anything we can't handle."

"But what are we going to do if she persists in trying to make trouble for me . . . for us? Estelle owns this town. She can do anything she wants."

"For now, we're going to proceed exactly as planned. We just need some time to think this . . . ." Another big lump of clarity had just arrived.

"What now?"

"Eliza, does your father know about you and Estelle?"

She turned pale as a ghost. "Oh, God! I hope not!"

"I don't want to upset you further, but I think he might know. Either he knows about it or he has a suspicion."

Fear spread over Eliza's face. "Why do you think so?"

"When he learned that you and I were going to see a motion picture, he said he was surprised we were going out together. When I asked why that surprised him, your father said he had already spoken out of turn and told me just not to let my expectations where you were concerned rise too high. Those were his exact words, 'do not let your expectations rise too high.' Can you think of any other reason he would give me that warning?"

Crying again, she sobbed, "He does . . . know! This just keeps getting . . . blacker and blacker."

I pulled Eliza into my arms again and kissed her on the forehead. I followed that with a kiss on her lips. It was an entirely different sort of kiss than the one we shared Friday night. This one was full of tenderness instead of passion. It saddened me to feel the tears on her cheeks.

Then, sensing that she was not thinking as clearly as she would when the shock of our conversation wore off, I offered a suggestion as to how we ought to proceed.

"We've put you through the wringer tonight. I think you need some time to see everything we've talked about more clearly. I suggest we take you home and . . . ."

"No!"

The vehemence with which she spoke that single syllable startled me. "You don't want to go home?"

"I can't, Lester. I can't go home knowing father thinks horrible things about me. I just couldn't face him now."

"Then where do you want to go?"

Her eyes seemed to be pleading with me when she looked up. "Can we . . . can we go to your house?"

"Eliza, that's not a smart thing for us to do. For one thing your father will be worried about you. Regardless of how you are seeing things right now, your father loves you. I'm sure of that, but spending the night at my place is not going to make it any easier for him to understand the situation."

"Lester, how can my father love me when he thinks I'm a . . . when he feels he must warn a man who wants to go out with me that I'm a lesbian for heaven's sake?"

While I didn't entirely agree with Eliza's assessment of her father, I could understand why she felt that way. Still, spending the night with me was certain to complicate matters.

"Eliza, don't you have a girl friend or someone you could . . . ."

She lowered her head again and said softly, "I knew it. You don't want me around now."

"Eliza, I cannot believe you said that. You know better. I'm just trying to prevent the situation from getting even worse. I love you, and you know that's true."

"I'm sorry, Lester. I just need to be with you tonight. It can be purely platonic, but I need to feel close to someone I know cares about me."

I sighed. "All right, darling, we will go to my cottage, but you are going to call your father and tell him where you are and why. If you don't, I will. I don't want him worrying about you any more than he already is."

She nodded her understanding of that, and ten minutes later I pulled to the curb in front of the garden court complex on Micheltorena Street. I unlocked the door to cottage number ten and, hoping my neighbors had gone to bed already, ushered Eliza inside.

"Sorry about the lack of amenities. I rent this place furnished and the owner doesn't believe in over furnishing his rentals."

Holding on to my arm and showing a little perkiness for the first time since we figured out what was going on, Eliza said, "The only furnishing I care about in this apartment is you."

I smiled. "Well, you've got that and you don't even have to dust me."

We went into the spare bedroom and I seated her at my desk-table. "There's the telephone. I can wait outside while you call your father if you'd prefer."

"No. No. Please stay with me."

I sat on the corner of the desk and watched her slowly dial five-two-five. After a short wait, I heard a click and the muffled sound of a man's voice escape from the handset Eliza held to her ear. She was quiet long enough for the man to say 'hello' a second and third time before Eliza spoke.

"Father, this is Liza."

After another long pause, she said, "I called to tell you I am not coming home tonight."

The man's voice said something and Eliza's eyes flooded with tears again. She dropped the handset and ran from the room. For a split-second I debated between running after Eliza and picking up the handset. The handset won.

"Mister Hamm, this is Lester Kinney. I . . . ."

"Kinney, what the hell is going on? Where are you? Why haven't you brought Liza home?"

"Mister Hamm, you'll have to wait until Eliza feels like talking to you for the details, but the salient points are these: Eliza is fine physically, but she is extremely distraught over an incident that occurred at Estelle Abernathy's party and she thinks it would be better for her not to come home until she calms down and can talk the matter over with you calmly. She asked to stay at my cottage tonight, and I can assure you it will be purely platonic."

Hamm was so angry he was sputtering. "Kinney, I'm holding you responsible for my daughter's wellbeing! If you don't bring her home right this minute, I can assure you that you will no longer have a job on Monday!"

"Mister Hamm, in a choice between Eliza's welfare and my employment, Eliza's welfare takes precedence. Besides, the decision as to whether or not Eliza comes home is not mine to make."

"Then you had best begin looking for a new position! And you can tell that little tramp I hope she never comes home. I won't have her living under my roof any longer!"

I was glad he slammed the telephone down at that point because none of the responses to Frederick Hamm's tirade running through my mind were going to improve the situation. Setting the receiver back into its cradle, I looked up and saw Eliza peeking around the doorframe like a child overhearing an adult conversation not meant for her ears. There were more tears on her face along with dark smudges of eye makeup. Even in that disheveled state, Eliza's face was the prettiest I have ever seen.

I beckoned her into the room and she ran into my arms. I noticed she'd lost her pretty silver–gray shoes somewhere along the line.

"I'm so sorry, Lester. I just couldn't do it. Was Father angry?"

"Furious would be a more appropriate adjective."

"I heard the last things he said clear over there in the doorway. I guess Charles Chaplin's character and I have something in common now. We're both homeless tramps."

She stood quietly in my arms for a little while before I heard a small voice ask, "I'm not really a tramp, am I?"

"Not by any definition of the word I know. For that matter, you are not homeless, either. As long as I have a roof, you have a home. Now, let's get busy working out the details here so you can get some sleep."

She nodded and I said, "First of all, we need to find you something to sleep in. Sleeping in beads and sequins might be stylish, but I can't imagine it would be very comfortable."

Eliza looked down at her evening dress. "I guess not. Do you have an old shirt I could borrow? At least I would be decent then."

I reached into the bedroom closet and brought out a pale blue dress shirt that is somewhat threadbare around the cuffs and collar. Holding it up in front of her, I said, "This would make at least two and a half of you decent."

She took the shirt and held it to her face. "Oh, it smells a little like you. That's nice."

"I'm glad you approve. The bathroom is through that door. You'll find a tin of Doctor Lyons toothpowder in the medicine cabinet, but I'm afraid I only have one toothbrush, so you can either use it or, if you are worried about cooties, use your finger.

"I use Boraxo hand soap, but that will be harsh on your soft skin, so you might want to wet my shaving brush and use a little shaving soap instead. It's much milder. Oh, and there are clean towels in the cabinet next to the door."

Holding her impromptu nightgown to her chest with one arm, Eliza hugged me with the other. "You are so dear to think of all these things for me. If tonight wasn't so horrid, this would be fun—sort of like playing house for grown-ups."

I would have agreed with her, but I was doing my best to keep things prim and proper, at least as prim and proper as having a woman in my apartment overnight allowed. Instead, I gave her a gentle push toward the bathroom. "When you're done in there, you can hang your dress in the closet so it won't get wrinkled."

While she made use of the bathroom, I quickly put fresh sheets on the bed. It was a good thing I had not changed the sheets since moving in a week ago because I only own two sets of bedsheets. Then I found her handbag, wrap, gloves, and shoes. I put the shoes next to the bed and her handbag on the nightstand. I hung the other items around a hanger in the closet.

Next I slid my overstuffed chair from the living room to a spot by the bed. Eliza said she wanted me close, but that was as close as I dared get with any reasonable expectation of keeping things platonic. Finally, I hung my tux trousers and jacket in the closet, and put on an everyday shirt and slacks. I looked at the dress shirt before stuffing it into my dirty clothes sack. I would have to ask Eliza how one removes eye makeup from . . . .

BANG . . . BANG . . . BANG! The pounding on my front door was so loud I jumped. Fairly certain I already knew who was doing the pounding, I hurried to answer the knock before he woke up the entire neighborhood.

Frederick Hamm stood on the other side of the door with his fists balled and a face so red I was afraid he might go into convulsions right there on my porch. "Where is my daughter? I'm going to take her home regardless of what you say."

Now that everyone else in the garden court knew I had someone's daughter in my apartment, I said, "Hell, Hamm, fifteen minutes ago you told me you didn't want her under your roof any longer. Either way, you are not taking Eliza anywhere she doesn't want to go."

He took a menacing step toward the door. Pointing my finger an inch from his nose, I said, "Take another step and I swear I will deck you right here and now."

Apparently Frederick Hamm was not spoiling for a fistfight. He stepped back and changed his tone. "At least let me speak with Liza."

"I'll ask her if she wants to talk with you."

Before I could turn around to call her, Eliza's voice came from somewhere behind me. "Go away, Father. You don't really want to be seen talking to a tramp, do you? We'll talk another time when I'm convinced you are worthy of being my father."

Hamm was looking past me and his eyes were as big as saucers. "Kinney, you are fired! I don't want to ever see you at the *Tribune* again. As for you, Liza, you are making the biggest mistake of your life. You will live to regret the decisions you've made tonight."

On that note Frederick Hamm steamed off into the night and I closed the door.

When I turned around I saw why Frederick Hamm looked shocked when he saw Eliza. She was standing there in my shirt, but she had only fastened the bottom buttons and the shirt hung open leaving her small, firm breasts clearly visible.

"Eliza! For crying out loud, what are you doing?"

Putting on a pouty expression, she said, "My father thinks his daughter is a tramp, so I wanted to look the part."

I sighed. "What the heck am I going to do with you?"

She trotted over and threw her arms around me. Pressing her body solidly to mine, she said, "I hope you're going to take me to bed and love me until we fall asleep from sheer exhaustion."

She was gripping me so tightly it took a few moments to push her back so we weren't in such intimate contact and I could look her in the eye. I said harshly, "That is one thing that certainly is not going to happen."

"Why not? I can tell you want to. I could feel you!"

Taking hold of her wrist, I led Eliza to the bedroom and pushed her onto the bed. "Get under those covers. Now."

While she meekly went about adjusting her position on the bed, I walked through the house making sure the doors and windows were locked and the lights were all off. When I returned to the bedroom Eliza was under the covers and looking up at me through wet eyes.

I sat in the overstuffed chair without comment and laid my hand on the edge of the bed. She quickly grabbed it.

"I'm sorry, Lester. I really am. I'm just so upset I don't know what I'm doing."

I nodded, and because I could not think of anything else to say at that moment, I just said, "Things will look better in the morning."

She smiled a little. "I cannot imagine how you could possibly look any better to me than you do right now. You are truly my knight in shining armor."

I stood up, leaned over the bed, and gave her a soft kiss on the lips. "Goodnight, Eliza."

"Goodnight, my love."

I'd been sitting there holding her hand in the darkness and listening to her soft breathing for several minutes when Eliza said in a perfectly normal tone of voice, "Just so you know, darling Lester, I really would have let you make love to me, and if you had, I would never have regretted it, not even for an instant. So thank you for doing the thinking for both of us tonight."

EIGHT

Sunday - September 9, 1928

Sunday morning arrived under a blanket of storm clouds that appeared ready to release a downpour at any moment. I know this because I was awake to see the dawn, or at least what dawn there was to see.

Among the discoveries I made the previous night was the sure and certain knowledge that my overstuffed chair was not designed for sleeping. Moving carefully so as not to awaken Eliza, I stood up and moved my aching muscles into the bathroom.

After standing in a hot shower spray long enough to ease the discomfort some, I dressed and shaved. What little I could see of the fellow in my tiny mirror bore no resemblance to a knight in shining armor whatsoever. My only comfort was that I had kept my promises to Eliza and her father. Eliza's virtue survived a night in my cottage.

Seeing that she was still asleep, my next stop was the kitchen. There, I brewed a pot of coffee and thought about what to make of the day. Being now unemployed, there was no particular reason to follow my original plan of driving down to inspect the oil spill on the beach at Fernald Point. Still, something in my mind was still pushing me in that direction. I wondered why. Maybe I just didn't like to leave a job unfinished.

Another, far more important unfinished job chose that moment to join me in the kitchen. Eliza gave me a hug and asked, "Is coffee included in the price of a room at this establishment?"

"Only for our important guests, of which you happen to be the most important."

I took my only other mug down from the cabinet and filled it with coffee. "I have some sugar, but no cream. Is that okay?"

Eliza looked at me through sleepy eyes and said, "I'll have it black, thanks."

Still wearing my shirt, now buttoned all the way to her neck, she sat opposite me at the small kitchen table and tasted her coffee. I said, "I hope you weren't awakened by all the racket I made when I got up. You only got a few hours' sleep."

Eliza reached out and took my hand. "And you got even less. I could tell you weren't sleeping well. That chair must have been terribly uncomfortable. I'm sorry I put you through a night of complete misery."

"Kiddo, I want you to make me a promise."

She looked up at me. Her eyes seemed a little more awake than they had. "Of course, darling, anything."

"I want you to remove the words 'I'm sorry' from your vocabulary in all conversations we have from hence forth."

"That will be hard to do. I feel as if my behavior has caused you a lot of grief. That is the last thing I ever wanted to do."

"I would also appreciate it if you would stop thinking of all that has happened as your responsibility. Unless you run me off with a stick, we are in this together. That makes it OUR responsibility, not just yours."

Eliza's face reflected a pained expression. "But you didn't ask for any of this. You were just in the wrong place at the wrong time. I almost wish you had never walked into the library last Tuesday."

I cocked my head to one side and looked her in the eye. "Do you really?"

She shook her head vehemently. "No, no I don't really wish that. Tell me, as a kid, did you say your prayers every night when you went to bed?"

Not certain what saying one's prayers had to do with the matter at hand, I said, "Sure. It was part of the nightly ritual . . . brush my teeth and say my prayers."

"Well, I still say my prayers every night, and last night I thanked God for bringing a wonderful blessing into my life. That blessing is you."

Hearing that embarrassed me for some reason and Eliza immediately saw my discomfort. "I'm sorry, Lester. I don't mean to say . . . ."

"Hey, stick to your promise. No more 'I'm sorrys'."

Eliza half smiled. "I told you keeping that promise wouldn't be easy. For example, do you know what thought was on my mind when I woke up a little while ago?"

"No, but I bet you're going to tell me."

"I am. I woke up remembering that you are now unemployed because of me. I behaved like a . . . like a tramp . . . and got you fired last night."

"No you didn't. By the time you performed your sleepwear fashion show your father had already told me during our telephone conversation he was going to fire me if I didn't bring you right home. And I don't want to hear the word 'tramp' anymore, either."

She gave me a full-fledged smile. "You sure are full of rules this morning!"

I smiled back at her. "Yes, I am, and you'd better start obeying them or I'll take my shirt back."

Eliza squeezed my hand and giggled. "I tried to give it back to you last night, but you refused to take it."

"All right, Miss Smarty-Pants, that will be enough of that. We need to be thinking about more productive things, like getting you something a little less fetching to wear in public. I don't suppose there's any chance we could sneak into your father's house and grab some of your clothes."

Eliza shook her head. "If this were a normal Sunday, he would be going to church later, but I don't think we can count on that today. It's okay, though. I have another solution, at least a temporary one."

"What is that solution?"

"The just-in-case clothes I keep at the library."

"Just-in-case clothes?"

"Yes. I keep a skirt and blouse in the employee room just in case I spill something or tear what I wear to work. I also have a pair of comfortable shoes there, and my keys to the library are on the ring in my bag. I'll just get back into my evening dress and, if you'll be so kind as to take me to the library, I can change and we can get on with our plans for the day, whatever they might be."

"It would be my pleasure to provide transportation to your just-in-case stash."

"Good. Finish your coffee. I won't be a minute."

On her way out, Eliza turned in the doorway. "Lester, I love you with all my heart, but may I make the next pot of coffee? Yours is awful."

I snapped a handy kitchen towel at her behind, but she lithely avoided it and escaped into the bedroom. Mostly what I was feeling at that moment was relief at Eliza's recovery from the previous night's torments. I could not fool myself into thinking all was hunky-dory with her, but she seemed to be functioning more normally. I mentally added "resilient" to my list of her admirable traits and concentrated on my own functionality, which was still much too far from normal for my liking.

The storm clouds finally turned loose the downpour they had been threatening all morning. They did so at the precise moment

Eliza returned to the car after changing her clothes at the library. Nearly shouting to be heard over the roar of raindrops pelting the metal roof of my Chevrolet, she said, "Wow that was close!"

I switched on the car's windshield wipers and we cautiously inched our way down the alleyway that provides access to the library's service entrance. I paused where the alley opened onto Anacapa Street.

"Where to next, kiddo?"

Eliza was thoughtful for a moment. "I think what we need most right now is a plan. We've been sort of letting the winds of chance blow us along this morning, but I'm really feeling like we need some definite idea of how we are going to resolve our—notice that I said 'our'—problems."

"I did notice, and I agree. How about we do that planning over breakfast?"

She smiled. "An excellent suggestion."

"Thank you, but this being Sunday morning, finding a place that's open could be a problem."

"No, it won't. Hotel restaurants are open for their guests, and if there is one thing this town has, it is hotels."

"Good thinking. Do you have a particular hotel in mind?"

Eliza thought about my question for a moment, and then said, "Yes. I know just the place. Turn right. This hotel just opened and it is some distance from downtown, so we aren't likely to encounter anyone we don't want to see."

I followed Anacapa all the way to the beach, where Eliza directed me to make a left turn on Cabrillo Boulevard. We followed Cabrillo for quite a while, eventually passing the Montecito Country Club. By the time we reached the little community of Montecito the storm had dwindled into a drizzle and we had no trouble finding the rambling three-story Mediterranean-style Montecito Inn.

I almost laughed when I saw where we were, but I kept a straight face as Eliza took my arm and we entered the Inn's dining room in a single-story wing at the southeast corner of the hotel. The restaurant wasn't at all busy and we were seated right away.

We were studying the menu when I heard Eliza say, "Oh, fiddle."

I looked up. "What's the matter?"

She gave a head nod to her right and said, "Look who just came in."

I looked in the direction she indicated and saw Charles Chaplin sitting in a banquette against the wall. I gave up trying to keep a straight face. Eliza scowled at me. "What's so darn funny?"

"Well, I would be happy to stand up for your honor by throwing that louse out of here, but that louse happens to own this hotel."

"You are kidding me!"

At that point Chaplin looked in our direction and caught us looking at him. I figured that since people were always looking at celebrities he wouldn't pay us any attention, but Chaplin has a good memory for pretty faces and he recognized Eliza's. He gave us an embarrassed nod of recognition, and quickly turned back to his menu.

The Montecito Inn is a first-class hotel and their prices, including those in the dining room, reflect that level of quality. Considering my current employment status, I settled on a poached egg with toast and coffee, which even at Chaplain's snooty joint could be had for fifty-cents. Eliza ordered oatmeal with cream, strawberries, and a cup of coffee that was no doubt superior to the cup she drank earlier.

The business of ordering our breakfasts completed, I asked, "What sort of plans do you think we need in order to solve the dilemma in which we find ourselves?"

Eliza gave my question a moment of thought, and then said, "Well, given the fact that father fired you last night, maybe we should start by inventorying our resources." After a pause, she added, "You know, there is a possibility he might change his mind about firing you. Sometimes he realizes his mistakes and corrects them."

Shaking my head, I said, "I don't think that's very likely in this instance, and even if he did change his mind, I would not work for him again under any circumstances." I had more to say on that subject, but thought better of saying it.

"As for my resources, the rent is paid until October first and I was paid for my first week at work Friday, so putting that with a little money I saved while working at the newspaper in Glendale, I have roughly one-hundred-eighty-dollars in my bank account. I also own the Chevrolet outright, so we are not entirely destitute, just close to it."

The waitress delivered our breakfasts, but neither of us had much interest in eating at that moment. Eliza said, "Well, Mister Kinney, as an equal partner in this venture, I can add to those resources. Despite paying father ten dollars a month for room and board—my idea, not his—I have saved about two-hundred dollars in my bank account. That account is in my name and no one else has access to it. Of course, I have some things of value at my former home, but I don't think we can count those items until we have them in hand."

"Eliza, I appreciate your willingness to contribute to the cause, but I'm not in favor of spending your money unless it becomes absolutely necessary to keep from starving."

She shook her head to indicate something like disgust. "Lester, you beat all! You have been reminding me all morning that we are in this situation together, but when I talk about doing my share to get us out of this mess, you don't want to hear about it. I helped us get into this situation and I want the satisfaction of helping us get out of it. Besides, you know darn well if it hadn't been for me, you would still be sitting pretty with a good job and . . . ."

"Okay, okay. We'll share equally in whatever it takes to survive this situation. Now, tell me what you think that entails."

Eliza looked puzzled. "What do you mean?"

Trying to think of a better way to explain what I was thinking without hurting her, I said, "On the surface, our losses add up to my job and your home, but we have other damages to repair that are not so easy to define."

Now her brow was furrowed in confusion. "I'm still not following you. What damages do we need to repair?"

"One that weighs heavily on my mind is your mental balance."

Eliza looked surprised. "My mental balance? What's wrong with my mental balance?"

"At the moment, kiddo, nothing. But last night you were on the verge of hysteria and you were doing things that are a major departure from your normal behavior."

"That was because I had to face the bad memories Estelle stirred up . . . I needed to tell you intimate details of my past that disgust me. Those things were terribly difficult for me. It's no wonder I was in awful shape last night."

She looked across the table at me with tears in her eyes. "Eliza, stop for just a minute and look inside yourself. What are feeling right now?"

Eliza lowered her head and was quiet for what seemed like a very long time. Finally she looked at me again and quietly said, "I feel . . . I feel confused, and that frightens me. I'm scared, very scared."

I reached across the table and took her hand. It was shaking a little. "What is confusing you, Eliza?"

"Everything. No, that isn't right. I'm very sure about some

things. What confuses me is that I don't know how I can make up for all those disgusting things I did with Estelle. I so wish I had never done . . . done any of that, but I can't just wish those things away. They happened and I have to live with the consequences."

Looking deep into her soft wet eyes, I said "Now tell me some of those things you are very sure about."

"I . . . I know I can be very smart. I know I can be strong. I know . . . I know I can be independent and make my own choices, but I also realize those things aren't enough. I need more than those things to be happy. Most of all, I know for certain that I love you and I need you to be an important part of my life."

Giving Eliza an encouraging smile, I asked, "Why do you need me in your life?"

Her brow furrowed again, this time in what I took to be deep thought. Lowering her head again, she began to draw small circles on the tablecloth with the tip of her index finger. "I need you in my life because I love you. No, that's not it. I mean I do love you with all my heart, but I need you in my life because . . . because . . . ."

Suddenly she lifted her head and looked me straight in the eye. "I need you because I do not want to go through life alone. I want a partner to share it all with, someone I can count on . . . someone who really cares about me . . . about how I feel . . . about . . . about what upsets me and makes me lose my mental balance."

I smiled. "I think you just answered your own question, I mean about why you sometimes lose your mental balance. You have regrets, but you know you can't undo what's been done, so you try to keep all those bad things inside, but sometimes they just get to be too much for your heart to hold and that scares you so much your mind won't work the way you want it to. Does that sound right?"

Still looking me in the eye, she nodded.

"I think you also put your finger on the solution, I mean a partner who doesn't judge you by the past. With someone like that, you don't have to be afraid of your regrets because you have a partner who will face them with you, along with all the good things to come. What do you think?"

Eliza nodded slowly. "Somehow I've known since the moment we met that you were all the things I need . . . and more."

"I think I knew that, too. I mean that you were the partner I need in life. You excite me, inspire me, and make me see things in a different light. So, what do you think we ought to do about these parts of our situation?"

Even though Eliza's big brown eyes were still wet from her tears, a smile appeared on her lips. "I think we need to be together . . . for as long as we both shall live. But even though I may be a thoroughly modern, emancipated woman, I am still old fashioned enough to want my future husband to do the proposing."

"And you aren't afraid we haven't spent enough time together to really know one another?"

Eliza frowned. "No. Are you afraid of that, Lester?"

"No." I took a deep breath and said, "Eliza, these are not the circumstances nor the place I want us to recall years from now as the day I proposed. I don't even have a ring to give you yet. Despite all that, I believe it is very important we make a commitment to one another we can count on until that special day arrives. So, Eliza, I want more than anything besides your happiness to have you for my wife. Do you feel the same about me?"

There were tears on her cheeks again, but to my eyes they looked like tears of happiness. Eliza said, "Yes, Lester. I want you for my husband more than I have ever wanted anything."

Smiling, I said, "Then I believe we are now engaged to become engaged. Agreed?"

Eliza cocked her head to one side and gave me her coy smile. "Lester, I think that is the most unusual proposal in the history of mankind, but those are also the most wonderful words I have ever heard and said. Agreed." Then she quickly added, "But only if you let me make the coffee and don't make me spend anymore nights by myself in that big empty bed. Agreed?"

I couldn't help laughing. "Agreed! And now I think we are really prepared to deal with the rest of the issues we face, like finding me new employment and figuring out how to dissuade Estelle Abernathy from meddling in our lives."

We then turned our attention to the lukewarm oatmeal and poached egg in front of us. By that time we were both hungry enough to eat our breakfasts, regardless. Actually, they tasted pretty good.

Then I asked our waitress for the bill and we got a pleasant surprise. Smiling, our waitress said, "Oh, Mister Chaplin paid for your breakfasts and said he hopes you enjoy your stay at the Montecito Inn."

I turned to look at the booth in which Chaplin had been sitting, but it was empty. Eliza said, "Gosh, maybe he isn't such a louse after all."

"Or maybe the louse just has a guilty conscience."

I left a generous fifteen-cent tip on the table. Then, arm-in-arm, Eliza and I went out to face a cloudy world together.

NINE

Sunday - September 9, 1928

Sitting in my Chevrolet outside the Montecito Inn I turned to Eliza. "You know, I think pre-engagement engagements are supposed to be sealed with a kiss."

She smiled her sunniest smile at me. "Since, as far as I know, we are the first people in the world to become engaged to become engaged, it should be up to us to establish the traditions associated with pre-engagement engagements. I think sealing the deal with a kiss makes it more . . . romantic."

Leaning toward her, I said, "Then a kiss it is, but not just any old kiss. This has to be a special kiss full of love and passion."

"Darling Lester, at this moment in time, I cannot imagine us kissing any kiss that would not be full of love and passion."

Eliza was absolutely right. Our kiss began with love and ended with enough passion to leave us both a little short of breath.

Leaning back to look at the narrow space behind the front seat of my coupé, Eliza said, "Do you know if two people have ever successfully made love in one of these little cars?"

I couldn't help laughing out loud. "Kiddo, I'm not certain parked in front of the Montecito Inn during broad daylight is the right place to determine if that feat is possible."

She leaned back with her head on my shoulder and simply said, "Spoil sport."

As I started the engine, Eliza asked, "Where are we off to now?"

"Well, I originally planned to take a look at the Fernald Point Beach oil spill so I would be prepared to write an article about it for your father. That article is no longer in the cards, but for some reason I have the strong inclination to go there anyway."

"Then let's do it. Have you been Fernald Beach before?"

"No."

"That's okay, I know the way. It's less than a mile from where we are right now. Go straight ahead on this road."

Pulling out onto the street, I said, "The oil spill is right here in this tourist area? That makes it even more serious."

Eliza nodded.   "That's the main issue about Summerland. There is some very expensive property along the coast here. Turning it all into a tar pit would cost some important people a great deal of money."

We ended up traveling southbound on the wide two-lane US Highway 101, but for only a short distance. Eliza pointed to a barely paved road leading off toward the beach on our right. "Take that turn. It goes straight to the beach you want to see."

The road ended just beyond the Southern Pacific's railroad tracks and right at the edge of the beach. We got out to take a look. There was a lot to see.

Less than a mile south of us there were enough oil derricks to make Signal Hill down near Long Beach jealous. In and around the forest of oil wells we could make out a chaotic jumble of rickety piers and railroad sidings. In other words, the Summerland Oil Field did nothing to enhance the beauty of California's coast.

To the north, however, were the pristine white beaches and crystal blue harbors of Santa Barbara. Even on an overcast day it all looked very summery.

And directly in front of us was an odd composite of the other two views—a half-pristine beach and a noisy diesel-powered tractor with a push-blade. The operator of the tractor was using the blade to scrape the top layer of sand, along with thousands of crude oil globs, off the beach and onto large piles paralleling the railroad tracks.

Leaning close to my ear so I could hear her over the racket made by the tractor, Eliza said, "Will you look at that!"

I nodded, but I was looking across the beach to the surf breaking on the sand. To my surprise I could clearly see fresh globs of crude oil being deposited on the beach by the waves. Judging by how far away the surf was, I guessed we had arrived at low-tide. That made sense because it gave the tractor the greatest area of dry beach to work on. The part that didn't make sense was that all the work being done by the tractor was temporary. By high-tide the entire beach would once again be covered with crude oil globs.

Pointing this out to Eliza, I said, "I don't get it. Why bother to clean up the beach before they fix the leak?"

She pointed toward the tractor, which was now heading more or less in our direction. "Maybe the tractor driver can answer that question."

I looked at my pocket watch. It was a few minutes before

noon, so I thought the guy might be about to take a lunch break. "I think I will, but I'm going to try being tricky. Just follow my lead."

As the tractor stopped next to a truck full of tractor parts and fuel barrels about twenty yards away, Eliza grinned. "Oh, boy! I simply adore it when you are tricky."

I made a face at her and walked toward the truck and tractor. As the operator hopped down from his rig, I shouted, "Howdy!"

He looked in our direction and gave us the same greeting. As we got closer, I offered my hand and said, "I'm Lester Kinney."

The operator started to reach for my hand but stopped and held his hand up to show the grease and oil covering it. "I'm kinda dirty."

I pushed my hand at him again and said, "Heck, a little grease never hurt anybody."

He grinned, shook my hand, and said, "Al Stone, Summerland Oil. Glad to meet ya, sonny."

"Likewise. I'm out here this morning because my boss, Estelle Abernathy, wants a firsthand report on how things are going. I see you're getting things cleaned up nicely, but it looks like there's more crude rolling in."

Al glanced seaward and said, "Sure is. I heared they is havin' trouble cappin' the leak. It's a crack in well number sixteen's casing and they can't get to it."

"Yeah, that's what I heard, too. Forgive me, but I'm kind of new at this oil business. How can they fix something like that?"

"Well, there's a couple of ways to go about it, but no matter how they do it, the well has to be shut down. The thing is, sixteen is a big producer and the bosses ain't anxious to stop pumpin' cuz it'll eat into their profit."

I nodded. "And I guess if something goes wrong with the casing repairs they could lose the well all together."

Al smiled. "You catch on quick, sonny. Anyways, in the meantime they got me out here wastin' time cleanin' off the beach just so the crude can mess it up again. Don't hardly make no sense to me."

"Doesn't make any sense to me either. Well, Al, I don't want to keep you from your lunch, so I'll get out of your hair. Thanks for filling me in."

"My pleasure, sonny. Now, you and that pretty little gal of yours have real fine afternoon."

I tossed Al a salute and led Eliza back to the Chevrolet. When we were out of earshot, she said, "Gosh, Lester, you are great at being tricky!"

"Not really. Old timers like Al just naturally love to educate us young'uns. All you have to do is get 'em started. Now, unless word gets back to Estelle that I was out here masquerading as her employee, we're home free."

When we got to the Chevrolet, I stopped at the passenger door. "Eliza, do you know how to drive an automobile?"

"Sure! I drive . . . I've driven father's Buick lots of times. I even have a driver's license."

"Good. You can chauffer us while I write down my notes from this interview before I forget half of what we learned."

Almost gleefully, Eliza hopped in and slid over behind the wheel. I grabbed a rag from behind the seat and wiped off some of the oil and grease I collected while shaking hands with Al. Then I picked up the stenographer's pad I keep in the car and climbed into the passenger seat.

Eliza was a good hand at driving. She handled the clutch and gear shifting like a pro . . . another worthwhile talent discovered.

"Where do you want to go now, darling?"

I looked up from my notes. "I don't have any place in mind, except a stop at a grocery store might be a good idea if we can find one open. My pantry looks like Old Mother Hubbard's Cupboard."

"I think I know where there might be an open market, but do you mind if we make a stop at a sundries store on the way? If I'm going to continue residing in your cottage, I need a few things." After a pause, during which I was busy writing my notes and didn't say anything, some of the previous night's anxiety returned to her voice. "Am I going to continue residing at your cottage?"

"Absolutely. Who will make the coffee if you don't?"

"Thank you, darling. I know just the place to pick up the items I need. It's at the ocean end of State Street and they're always open. Is that okay with you?"

"Hey, lady. You're the driver. I'm just a passenger on this bus."

"Okay, then. Here we go."

I finished writing the notes from my Al Stone interview, and when I set the steno pad on the seat, Eliza asked, "Did we do any good back there?"

"We did far better than I had any right to expect. We now know the oil spill is from a cracked casing in well sixteen, and not from a natural seep. That right there is worth plenty, but we also know Summerland Oil is dragging their feet about fixing it because the repairs will be costly and they could lose one of their top-producing wells in the process. We hit the jackpot with that tidbit. Finally, we learned that Summerland is trying to make things look better by continuously cleaning the beach."

"That's all good to know, but what are you going to do with the information?"

"Eliza, you of all people should know that information is power. Our job is to figure out how we can make the most of that power."

As we pulled to the curb in front of Beachside Sundries, Eliza said, "This may take a few minutes. Do you want to come in or wait out here?"

"I think I'll come in with you. I could use a lesson in the art of sundry purchasing."

"Okay, but I'll bet you will be bored to tears."

Actually, I wasn't bored at all. I watched with interest as the pile of Eliza's selections grew on the store's counter. Among them were a bar of Ivory soap, a bottle of Watkins Mulsified Cocoanut Oil Shampoo, eye makeup, Kissproof lipstick in a pale shade of red, Max Factor Pan-Cake Makeup, and a Doctor West's toothbrush.

Eliza even consulted me on an item. Poking a sample bottle of eau du cologne under my nose, she said, "This is called Emeraude. What do you think?"

"Like you, it's subtly exotic and smells wonderful."

That opinion earned me a kiss on the cheek. Then Eliza subtly told me to get lost.

"Darling, I need to pick up a couple of 'unmentionable' items to tide me over until I can go to a regular department store. Would you mind waiting for me in the car? I'll only be a few more minutes."

I grinned. "Darn, just when we get to the interesting part, you run me off."

"A girl has to have some secrets. Besides, I imagine you'll see everything I pick out sooner or later anyway."

"All right, I'll be in the car. Would you like some help paying for this stuff?"

"No thanks, darling. I already asked, and they will accept my check."

On my way out I noticed a stack of the *Post-Dispatch's* Sunday edition next to the magazine rack. I picked one up and handed the woman behind the counter a nickel.

Eliza was as good as her word and came prancing out to the car with her purchases a few minutes later. Since she had been doing such a good job driving, I was sitting on the passenger side, but she came around to my door and told me slide over.

"Why? You are a terrific driver."

She put on her coy look. "I know, Lester darling, but when you drive I get to sit closer to you."

Since I could not argue with that logic, I slid over and she hopped in. "Now, where is this grocery market you think might be open today?"

It wasn't far, and it was open. A half-hour later I drove through the entrance to my apartment complex and parked at the back. I usually park on the street, but we had a lot of stuff to carry, so I made things easier for us.

Inside apartment ten we stacked everything on the kitchen table and I took a look around. Everything was in order, so I relocked the front door and we set about unpacking our treasures. After hanging her evening dress back in the bedroom closet, Eliza took her packages of sundries into the bathroom while I unpacked the groceries.

From the bathroom, I heard, "Lester, is it okay if I put some of my things in the medicine cabinet?"

"Sure. Just move stuff around if you need more room. Eggs go in the refrigerator, right?"

"Right."

When I finished stocking our larder, I went in to see how Eliza was coming. In the bathroom, I noticed a pale blue soap dish on the sink with a fresh bar of Ivory soap in it. The medicine cabinet now held two toothbrushes, one pink and one blue, and a few makeup items parked next to my shaving mug and safety razor.

Back in the bedroom, Eliza said, "You weren't using the middle drawer of the chest, so I moved into it. Is that all right?"

I grabbed her shoulders in mid-stride between the chest and the closet. "Eliza, you don't need my approval for every little thing you do. This is OUR cottage now and I want you to be comfortable in it. Anything you do short of painting the walls pink with purple stripes is perfectly all right with me."

"Thank you, Lester. I just . . . just don't want to upset your life. I mean, you are used to living alone and suddenly having me here will take some adjustment."

"You make it sound like an ordeal. I couldn't be happier to have you here and . . . ."

Someone knocked on the front door. Eliza instantly turned pale and her eyes went wide. Trying to sound reassuring, I said, "Just go ahead with what you're doing. I'll take care of it."

Opening the door, I realized that taking care of it might not be as easy as I thought. Two Santa Barbara police officers were standing on my porch.

The one with three-stripe chevrons on his uniform sleeves said, "I'm Sergeant Sullivan with the Santa Barbara Police Department." Gesturing toward the big tough looking guy behind him, he said, "And this is Officer Robertson. Would you be Mister Lester Kinney?"

Having no idea why these cops were at my front door, I kept my answer simple. "I am."

Nodding, Sullivan asked, "Would there be a Miss Eliza Hamm here, also?"

Piece by piece the picture was becoming clearer. "Yes."

"Would you please ask her to step to the door?"

"I will."

I yelled over my shoulder, "Eliza, please come in here."

Eliza walked through the hall door and stopped dead in her tracks when she saw the cops. "What's going on?"

Sergeant Sullivan stepped forward, put his hand on my shoulder, and moved me back out of the doorway. I didn't resist.

"Mister Kinney, we are here to return Miss Hamm to her parents and arrest you for kidnapping an underage minor."

That brought a quick end to my cooperation. I broke his grip on my shoulder and stepped back. Holding my hands up to stop his advance in my direction, I said, "Sergeant, I suggest you ask a few more questions before you cost the City of Santa Barbara a great deal of money in a false arrest suit."

He looked confused, but remained calm. I wasn't so sure I could expect the same from Officer Robertson who was now filling the front doorway.

Sullivan looked me in the eye. "What questions would you suggest I ask, and of whom?"

"First, I suggest you ask Miss Hamm how old she is, and then ask her to show you her California driving license as a means of verifying her age."

Suddenly Sergeant Sullivan lost some of his confidence. Turning to Eliza, he asked. Miss Hamm, we were told you are twenty years of age. Is that correct?"

There was fury in her eyes when she said, "No, that is not correct! I am twenty-two. Wait here, Sergeant. I am going into the bedroom to get my purse."

She came back with her black beaded bag and removed a white card. She handed it to Sergeant Sullivan. He looked at it and handed Eliza's driving license back to her.

I said, "Miss Hamm has just proven to you that she is past the legal age of consent. Now ask her if she is here of her own free will. I'll leave the room if you would like."

Sullivan cleared his throat. "Ah, that won't be necessary. Miss Hamm, are you here of your own free will?"

"You're darn right I am!"

Before she could say anything further, I said, "All right, Sergeant Sullivan, have we proven to your satisfaction that no crime is being committed here?"

Looking more than a little sheepish, Sullivan said, "Yes, sir, Mister Kinney. Apparently we were misinformed." Turning toward the door, he said, "I'm sorry we bothered you."

"Not so darned fast, Sullivan. Now it's time for you to save your stripes by answering a few of my questions."

Sullivan stopped. "Yes, sir."

"First, tell that ape lurking in my doorway to go wait in your car. I don't like my neighbors thinking there is a police raid going on here."

Sergeant Sullivan turned to his partner. "Go wait in the car, Ike. I won't be long."

"And close the darn door behind you, Ike."

I glanced at Eliza. She was leaning against the hall doorway frame. The beaded clutch was still in her hand and she was staring at the floor. I did not like the way she looked at all, but I had to deal with Sullivan first.

He said, "Mister Kinney, this was clearly a case of . . . ."

"Sullivan, who told the department Miss Hamm had been kidnapped?"

Sullivan swallowed a dry swallow. "Miss Hamm's father signed the complaint, sir."

"And the department accepted his claim at face value?"

"Well, yes, sir. Mister Hamm is the editor of the *Tribune*. He's an important man in town."

"Mister Hamm is also a damned liar."

Sergeant Sullivan nodded, but not enthusiastically. "I can see that now, Mister Kinney."

"And are you going to arrest him for filing a false police report?"

Sullivan swallowed again. "I guess that would be up to you, sir. If you insist, I will, but I would prefer a different course of action."

I glanced at Eliza again. She looked worse. I said, "Let's hold off on that decision for a while. What I think you should do now is find Mister Hamm and read him the riot act for wasting your time and the taxpayers' money. Drop a hint about the charges that could be brought against him, but leave it at that. Are you willing to follow that course of action?"

Sensing he was getting off the hook more easily than he deserved, Sullivan said, "Yes, sir. I'll go over there right now."

"Thank you, Sergeant. There's one other thing I want to say to you. The only reason I'm not going after your badge is that you treated us with respect and courtesy. That's the way a good cop is supposed to act. Also, I hope you will remember the respect I'm showing you now in the event I need a good cop on my side in the future. Is that fair?"

"Yes, sir."

"Good. Now you had best go out and see to Officer Ike before he eats your tires or something."

Sergeant Sullivan grinned a little at that and said, "Very well, Mister Kinney. Have a good afternoon."

The minute he was out the door, I rushed to Eliza and she promptly collapsed in my arms. I carried her into the bedroom and laid her on the bed. She began sobbing uncontrollably, just as she had during much of the night before.

"Eliza, listen to me carefully. Everything is okay now. The police realize your father lied to them. Do you understand me?"

She sobbed, "I hate that man! I don't care if he is my father, I wish he was dead!"

"Darling, what we need to do right now is forget about everyone else and concentrate on you. Okay?"

Eliza was clearly feeling panicky. "Oh, Lester, I'm doing it again. I'm losing control. I can't help myself."

"Yes you can. With a little help you going to get your control back, right now. Slide over on the bed and make some room."

She did as I asked and I slid onto the bed next to her. Eliza rolled toward me and I put my arm around her.

"Do you feel safe now?"

"Yes . . . yes, I feel very safe."

"Good. Now focus on breathing at a slower, more normal rate."

Eliza's respiration changed almost immediately, slowing and becoming less erratic. "Good, darling, keep it up and start to feel other things like my arm around you and your head on my shoulder. How does that feel?"

Her tone of voice was less whiney and more natural. "It feels wonderful, Lester. It really does."

"It does to me, too."

Suddenly I felt her stiffen. "What's the matter, Eliza?"

"What if father comes to the library and makes a scene while I'm at work?"

"I thought of that possibility, too, and we are not going to let it happen. Do you have any vacation or sick leave time coming?"

I felt her nod. "I have earned two weeks of vacation time."

"Perfect. In the morning I think you should call whoever makes decisions at the library and tell them you need a little time, say a week, off to take care of personal business that came up suddenly. Do you think that would work?"

"Yes, my superior is very understanding. I think she would give me the time without asking any questions."

"Great. Now I have just one more question for you. Do you know how much I love you?"

"I don't know any way to measure it, but it must be an awful lot for you to put up with my . . . nonsense."

"What nonsense? Listen to yourself. You're fine now."

"Yes, I think so, but only because you helped me through the crisis."

"But isn't that what we agreed one of my jobs in our partnership would be? To help you keep things in balance when times get tough? Isn't that what we said this morning?"

"Yes it is. And, darling Lester, I love you with all my being for that."

"I know and it feels very good. Now close your eyes and let's get a little rest. After last night, I think we've earned a good nap."

TEN

Sunday - September 9, 1928

When I first woke up, the world around me didn't make any sense. My old wind-up alarm clock was trying to tell me the time was four in the morning, but there was too much light coming in the window for that to be right. Okay, the alarm clock has run down. No, I could hear it ticking. That meant it had to be four in the afternoon.

Next a memory popped into my mind explaining how Eliza and I came to be in bed at four in the afternoon, but that part was out of whack, too. My memory said when I stretched out next to her for a short nap, she was wearing her just-in-case outfit from the library, but now she wasn't. My arm was still around her waist and her head was still on my chest, but now she was wearing the threadbare pale blue shirt I gave her to use for a nightgown and we had a green army surplus blanket over us.

With a little more mental effort I came up with an explanation for how those things could be. It made sense that she did not want to wrinkle the skirt and blouse from the library because it was all she had to wear at the moment, so she must have gotten out of bed and changed clothes. I further concluded that was also when she found the blanket in the bottom drawer of the chest. That had to be what happened, even though I had no recollection of it.

Feeling Eliza's head move on my chest, I looked at her. Looking back at me through big brown sleepy eyes, she stretched like a cat awakening from a nap and said, "Are you awake, darling?"

"I think so."

Eliza was on her left side and I felt her rest her right leg on mine as she pressed herself closer to me. She purred, "Mmm, good. Sleeping with you is wonderful, but snuggling with you is even better."

I tightened my arm around her waist. "You know, strange as it may seem, I too have discovered that to be true."

Eliza slid up a little for a kiss, and the inside of her thigh brushed against the beginning of my perfectly natural male reaction to being in such close proximity to the most beautiful and sensual woman on Earth. Eliza giggled. "Oh, oh."

I rolled toward Eliza, pushing her onto her back and kissing her long and hard. Eliza arched her back, thrusting her body against me. I pressed my hand over her right breast and instantly felt the nipple stiffen. Eliza groaned softly.

When our lips parted, I said, "Oh, oh is right, kiddo."

Eliza's eyes glistened as she said, "I think it's more like oh . . . oh!"

I slowly and methodically unbuttoned the pale blue shirt while tracing a line of soft kisses down her throat. My lips had nearly reached her breasts when Eliza said softly, "Is now the time I finally and totally become your woman, darling?"

While I did not think it was the reaction she intended, her words began a tickertape of thoughts racing through my mind. My conscience was sending me an urgent message.

I kissed her forehead and rolled over onto my back again, gently pulling Eliza with me. She raised herself on her left elbow and said in an almost panicky voice, "Darling! What did I say? What did I do wrong?"

I shook my head gently. "You didn't do anything wrong, Eliza."

"Than what . . . ."

"You just made me think, that's all. Eliza, in my mind, you are already totally my woman. I don't need sex to feel that."

She sounded near tears. "I feel that, too. I said it wrong. Oh, Lester, what have I done?"

"Nothing bad, darling. We have a long way to go in our life together. Would it be okay with you if we saved some of the good things to celebrate the milestones we have yet reach?"

Eliza sounded more frustrated than panicky now. "What milestone do we have to reach before we can make love?"

"How about the day we exchange our wedding vows and become wife and husband? I guess I'm old fashioned enough to want that day to be the beginning of new things for us."

She tilted her head to one side and I thought I saw understanding in her eyes. "You mean if we've already done everything husbands and wives do together, getting married will be nothing more than a formality?"

"Something like that. Yes."

"And that is important enough for you to stop cold in the throes of passion?"

I nodded. Looking into her big brown eyes, I saw tears forming there yet again. "Oh, dear Lester, what in heaven's name have I done to deserve a man who loves me as you do?"

Trying to take some strain out of the situation, I said, "I don't know, but if you figure it out, I'll bet you'll think twice before doing it again."

Eliza lowed her head to mine and kissed me tenderly. "I know you said earlier that I had control of my mental balance, but I don't think that is entirely true. A few minutes ago when we were . . . you know, the thoughts that kept going through my mind were 'make him want you . . . make him love you' as if being as good for you in bed as I could possibly be would somehow make our love grow even stronger."

"Eliza . . . ."

"Lester, please let me say this while it is clear in my mind. Now, lying here next to you and thinking about your words, I realize my thinking was backward because I still fear I'll wake up and find that you were just a dream. It's the love we already have between us that makes everything else as good as it can possibly be.

"Darling, I want to be everything a woman can be in your eyes. Maybe that's selfish of me, but it is what I want. Do you understand?"

"Yes, Eliza, I understand. The thing is, you have nothing to fear because you are already everything a woman can be to me. That comes naturally because of who you are."

The tears were rolling down her cheeks now. "I come to you frightened and unsure, but leave feeling safe, loved, and very special."

Smiling, I said, "Special enough to make us some coffee?"

Eliza gave me a quick kiss. "Two cups of proper coffee coming up."

I noticed with a little twinge of disappointment that Eliza was fastening the buttons on her shirt as she walked out of the bedroom. Me and my Victorian morality, phooey! I got up, splashed some cold water on my face, and brushed my hair.

When I got to the kitchen, Eliza was putting my old coffee pot on a stove burner. "It's going to take ten or fifteen minutes, but it will be good, I promise."

"I don't doubt that. In the meantime, would you care to join me in the office? I could use some help setting things up to do some work in there."

Eliza actually seemed excited about helping. "Sure, darling.

Lead the way."

In the second bedroom, I said, "Let's begin by closing those curtains. I would just as soon not have the whole neighborhood looking over my shoulder."

Pulling the curtain drawstring, Eliza said, "Or anyone else. By the way, darling, I was very impressed with the way you handled those policemen this afternoon. They intimidated me awfully, but you ended up intimidating them. You have a lot of nerve, you know that?"

Laughing, I said, "It's easier to be nervy when you know you are right. At first I was a little worried, though, because I didn't really know how old you are. Thank God you're past your twenty-first birthday."

Putting her hand over her mouth in a surprised gesture, Eliza said, "Oh! I was wondering how you knew my age, but I figured you must because of what you said."

"I didn't then, but I do now. And just for the record, I celebrated my twenty-fourth birthday last June."

"Cradle robber."

While we were talking, I moved a cardboard box to my desk/table and removed the black carrying case that held my trusty Underwood portable typewriter. After removing the typewriter from its case, I put the case back in the cardboard box and set the typewriter in front of the kitchen chair I planned to use at my desk.

"Wow, I guess you really are a writer. You have a typewriting machine and everything."

"You, bet I do. It doesn't spell for beans, though. Would you please look in those boxes over there? One of them has some spare ink ribbons and a package of typing paper. I will need both."

Eliza rummaged for a moment, and then came up with the items I needed. Handing me a ribbon and setting the package of paper on the desk, she said, "You were serious, you really are going to do some work."

"Yes, I am going to write a news story based on our interview with Al Stone this morning. It may never be published, but for some reason it seems important to finish the job I set out to do."

"Would you mind if I stick around and read over your shoulder?"

"I'm counting on that. You can be my editor. I bet you're better at it than that editor over at the *Tribune*."

"I doubt that, but I would love to watch you work." Pointing to the stack of cardboard boxes where she found the typing paper,

Eliza asked, "Is that a radio in that box over there?"

I set about installing the new typewriter ribbon. "Yes, it was given to me as a birthday present two years ago. It's an Atwater-Kent and it works very well."

"Would it bother you to have some music playing softly in the background?"

"Eliza, I'm used to working in a newsroom full of loud-mouthed reporters yelling at each other. I doubt very much that I could function in a quiet place. So, if music would please you, plug the radio in and find us something tuneful. You can set it on top of the filing cabinet. It should get good reception there."

"Okay, I'll do that right after I check on the coffee. I will be right back."

Eliza first returned with another kitchen chair and set it at the table/desk opposite the one in which I was seated. She stood there a moment looking at me with an unspoken question on her face. When I nodded my approval of the chair's new location, she left again and returned with two mugs of steaming coffee.

Setting one of the mugs beside my typewriter, she said, "Here you are, darling. Taste that and tell me it isn't the best coffee you ever tasted."

I took a sip, and then another. "You have to be some kind of miracle worker to get coffee that good out my old beat-up coffee maker."

Standing behind my chair, she was already engrossed in reading what I had typed so far. "I told you the coffee would be good. Wow! That's quite a headline you've written there."

MONTECITO IN DANGER OF DEVASTATING CONTAMINATION

Summerland Oil Drags Feet on Capping Leaking Well

By Lester Kinney

According to a veteran Summerland Oil Field employee the crude oil contaminating the beach at Fernald Point is leaking from Summerland Well Number Sixteen. The well's casing is cracked and performing the necessary repairs will require shutting down the unit's pumping operation. Summerland management is reportedly reluctant to do so because Number Sixteen is one of the company's top producing wells . . . .

"I hope so. Wherever this story ends up, I would like it to ruffle some feathers."

"That should do it, but I'm not sure if ruffling feathers is a good thing or a bad thing."

"Trust me, it's a good thing. It made Lincoln Steffens and Upton Sinclair household names a decade ago."

While I turned to my stenographer's notebook to refresh my memory of Al Stone's comments, Eliza set up the radio. After a few moments strains of Paul Whiteman's orchestra playing George Gershwin's *Rhapsody in Blue* drifted across the room.

Eliza said, "Is that okay? Not too loud?"

"It's perfect. Where did you learn to tune a radio like that?"

She grinned. "It's just one of my special talents."

"Of which I'm discovering there are many."

Eliza seated herself in the chair opposite me. "If you really must know, father bought mother a Zenith console radio for her birthday one year, and since nobody seemed able to make it work right, I sat down and read the instruction manual from cover to cover. I am now an expert radio tuner. Your little radio works just like the big ones."

"I'm impressed."

"Thus proving what somebody I love dearly said about knowledge being power."

I couldn't help laughing. "It certainly does."

I spent the next twenty or thirty minutes finishing my story. After typing "X X X" at the bottom of the last page, I added it to the four previous double-spaced pages stacked next to the typewriter. Then I handed the stack to Eliza.

"Okay, your turn. Tell me what you think."

She went through the story slowly and carefully. When she handed the stack back to me, Eliza said, "Holy smoke! I guess this is what is meant by the 'power of the press.' I hope Estelle never reads that. She'll have a fit."

"After that rotten business she pulled on us last night, it would please me no end to cause her a fit or two."

"Lester you have to be careful! Estelle is a dangerous woman. She is perfectly capable of hurting those who cross her . . . I mean hurting them physically."

"Somehow I can't imagine Estelle Abernathy taking a poke at me."

"Not her, Lester. She has others to . . . hurt people. I once saw Estelle have Armando beat a man senseless because he spoke harshly to her."

"Who is Armando, that dandy butler of hers?"

Nodding, Eliza said, "Yes, his name is Armando Delgado, and do not underestimate him. He may look . . . effeminate, but he knows . . . knows how to hurt people, how to hurt them badly."

"Don't worry, darling. I won't do anything stupid. When I have a plan in mind, I will discuss it with you. Now, what do you say we go in and fix a couple of sandwiches for dinner before I type up two more copies of that story? I'm starving."

I had the idea our discussion concerning the power of Estelle Abernathy was far from over, but Eliza seemed willing to let it go for now. "I'll go you one better. I'll fix the sandwiches while you get started with the typing. Would you prefer tuna salad or bologna sandwiches?"

"Tuna salad, please."

"Good choice. My tuna salad sandwiches are the best in town."

"Oh, boy! I can hardly wait."

Rolling two pieces of paper onto the platen with a sheet of carbon paper between them, I got to work with my typing. I was just using paperclips to organize the three copies of my story when Eliza stuck her heard in the door and sang out, "Soup's on!"

On the kitchen table there were two plates, each holding a diagonally sliced tuna salad sandwich and a garnish of carrot sticks, tomato slices, and olives on a lettuce leaf. I was impressed and said so, "Gosh, you're gonna spoil me with this kind of cooking. My sandwiches are usually eaten off of a paper napkin, which is why as much sandwich ends up on my shirt as inside me."

"You don't 'cook' tuna salad, silly. You mix it in a bowl."

"Oh."

By the time dinner was done, we both belonged to the Clean Plate Club. It seemed like a very long time since we ate a cold poached egg and oatmeal at the Montecito Inn.

As I popped the last olive into my mouth, Eliza said, "Would you like something sweet for dessert? We have a can of peaches and one of pears."

"Peaches sound good."

Clearing our plates from the table, Eliza said, "Oh, I meant to ask you. There was a copy of today's *Post-Dispatch* on the table. Do you want it or shall I line the garbage pail with it?"

"I got that on my way out of the sundry store, but I haven't looked at it yet. In fact, I was just wondering what I did with it."

Eliza brought the newspaper over to me, asking, "Why on earth did you buy the *Post-Dispatch*?"

"I want to see what Tom Wigand wrote about his failed attempts to get a statement about the oil spill from Estelle Abernathy at the donation ceremony. He was so obnoxious about it the cops had to intervene."

Setting a small bowl of peaches and a spoon in front of me, Eliza said, "That sounds just like Mister Wigand. I have never met the man, but I know him by reputation. I think I can safely say he is not the most popular newspaper reporter in town."

I turned the paper over so the front page was up. "Well, let's see what he wrote."

Between bites of peach, I turned pages. Finally, arriving on the last page of the news section, I said, "Now that is mighty strange. There are absolutely no articles by Tom Wigand or about the oil spill or about Estelle Abernathy's donation ceremony in this newspaper."

"You're right, that is odd."

"Tell me something, Eliza. Has the *Post-Dispatch* ever gone up against Summerland or Estelle Abernathy in the past?"

"Yes. In fact, they have tangled so often it has become a standing feud."

"So this guy, Storche, who runs the *Post-Dispatch* isn't in the habit of backing down from Estelle or Summerland?"

"Oh, he wins some and loses some, but he has always been ready to take up a new crusade against them."

"I think I might pay Mister Storche a visit tomorrow."

"Why, darling?"

Holding up the Sunday *Post-Dispatch*, I said, "To see if he will tell me why he dropped the Summerland oil spill story. If he dropped it because Wigand couldn't come up with an article beyond what they printed Saturday morning, I might be able to sell our story to the *Post-Dispatch*."

Eliza smiled, "Well, that would certainly teach father a lesson, but I cannot help worrying what Estelle Abernathy would do if she reads what you wrote. That still scares me."

"I think we have to take this a step at a time. If I can get in to see Mister Storche, and if he seems amenable to the idea of buying our story, I'll offer it to him because we can certainly use the money. If he buys it, then we'll worry about dear sweet Estelle."

After cleaning up the kitchen, we sat close to each other on the living room sofa. While the radio in the office played romantic dance music, Eliza read a novel by Agatha Christie entitled *The Mystery of the Blue Train*, and I worked the *Post-Dispatch* crossword puzzle. The puzzle was much too easy.

Around ten we decided that despite our afternoon naps, it was bedtime. While Eliza got ready for bed, I turned the radio off and checked the doors and windows. When I walked into the bedroom she was just climbing into bed.

Feigning a shiver, she said, "Hurry, darling, this bed needs warming up. Besides, I'm anxious to see what you wear to sleep in when you actually sleep in a bed at night."

"Well, that presents a bit of a problem. I've been living alone so long, I don't even own a pair of pajamas."

Propping herself up on one elbow, she gave me a lascivious grin. "Then, pray tell, what do you sleep in, your birthday suit?"

"No! I normally sleep in boxer shorts, or shorts and a shirt if it's cold."

"Oh, poo! I was hoping for the birthday suit."

"Sorry to disappoint you."

Still grinning, Eliza said, "Well, if you're going to be that way about it, at least leave off the shirt."

"I thought you just said it was cold in the bed."

Giving me a wink that closely matched the nature of her grin, she said, "It won't be for long."

Shaking my head in mock disgust, I complained, "We have to do something about this streak of vixen in you. I'm almost afraid to get into that bed."

"Don't worry, darling, I don't bite . . . much."

I went into the bathroom to brush my teeth and change. I did not wear a shirt, but I did manage to ruin some of Eliza's fun by turning off the overhead light just as I left the bathroom.

"Hey! Why did you turn out the light? Don't tell me you're shy all of a sudden. Heavens, you've seen all there is to see of me from head to toe!"

Sliding into the bed, I said, "Eat more carrots so you can see better in the dark."

I felt her hands slide around my shoulders. "I don't need to see in the dark. Feeling is much more fun!"

After exchanging some relatively tame kisses and doing just a little petting, Eliza said, "I hope you know I was teasing you before. I remember what we talked about earlier, and I agree waiting is the right thing to do."

"You know, there is another good reason for waiting."

After a moment's hesitation, Eliza said, "I think I know what you're going to say, but tell me anyway."

"I sincerely hope we have kids one day, but I am fairly certain now would not be a good time to start a family."

"I thought that was what you were getting at. I have read about new methods of preventing pregnancy, but none of them are foolproof, so your point is well taken." Eliza snuggled a little closer and added, "There are times, however, when those important reasons for waiting do not really seem all that important,"

In a whisper, I said, "I know, believe me, I know."

ELEVEN

Monday - September 10, 1928

Eliza and I were sitting across from each other at the kitchen table. We each had a mug of her proper coffee and she was making a list on a fresh page in one of my stenographer's pads.

"Okay, here's what I have so far. One, call library. Two, try to see Mister Storche at *Post-Dispatch*. Three, County Bank withdrawal. Four, wardrobe shopping at Trenwith's. Five, grocery shopping—Piggly Wiggly. Can you think of anything we have forgotten to put on the list?"

"Actually, I can, but I'm hesitant to mention it."

Eliza cocked her head and gave me her question expression. "Oh? What did you think of?"

"When I was talking with Estelle Abernathy Saturday night, she said there was more she wanted to discuss and she invited me to come to her house tonight at eight."

Now her face was expressing something between anger and suspicion. "Is that so? You aren't planning to keep that rendezvous are you?"

"After we figured out what she was up to Saturday night, I was planning to stand her up, but now I'm not so sure."

"Lester!"

"I know you would rather I stayed away from Estelle, but after what she pulled on us, I no longer feel bad about using her to get what we want. Doing that, however, will require seeing her again."

Eliza's tone of voice was starting to sound panicky. "Lester, you're frightening me."

"I told you I wouldn't do anything until I had a plan and until you and I discussed that plan. I meant that. Okay?"

I could still see the anxiety in her eyes as she quietly said, "Okay."

Removing the percolator from the stove, I said, "More coffee?"

Shaking her head, Eliza said, "No, thank you. If I drink too much I get all jittery."

I poured myself half a cup and sat opposite her at the table again. Looking at her list, Eliza said, "We have a lot to do today. I wish I had my bicycle. It's in father's garage, and if we could sneak it out, I could use it to get some of these errands done."

"Not unless you bolt a second seat on that bicycle."

She looked confused. "What do you mean, darling?"

"I mean where you go, I go and vice versa. Now that I've landed the most wonderful girl in the world, I'm taking no chances of something happening to you."

Eliza's complexion got a little rosier for a few seconds. "You mean father, don't you?"

I nodded.

"Okay, darling, whither thou goest, I go."

"Ruth one-sixteen."

"Who?"

"That was a biblical quotation you just used. It comes from the book of Ruth, chapter one, verse sixteen."

Eliza laughed. "I must have missed Sunday School that day. Oh, look! It's eight already. If I'm going to take a few days off, I need to call the library and talk with Missus Whitley."

"All right, you call in while I do a chore of my own."

When I walked into the office a few minutes later, Eliza was speaking into the telephone. "Thank you so much, Missus Whitley. I am sorry for giving you such short notice, but I had no choice."

I found my metal-edged ruler and used it to neatly tear the headline from my original copy of the Summerland story. Then I put all the pages of the story, along with the headline piece into a business envelope and slipped it into my inside jacket pocket.

Next I ripped the Al Stone notes from my stenographer's pad and slipped them into another envelope with one of the two remaining carbon copies of the story and sealed the envelope. Finally, I placed the last copy of the story into a third envelope and sealed its flap.

While I was busy trying to keep track of which copy of the story was in which envelope, Eliza finished her conversation and disconnected her telephone call. She said, "I hated doing that, but Miss Whitley was very understanding. She was also very curious, but I got away with telling her I need the time off to take care of a very personal matter that would require me to be in and out of town during the next few days. What on earth are you doing with those envelopes?"

"Preparing for multiple eventualities."

"There you go talking in riddles again."

"Just follow me and you'll see what I'm up to."

With Eliza trotting along behind me like a curious puppy, I went into the kitchen and opened the corner cabinet we use as our pantry. From the pantry, I removed the round cardboard box of Quaker Oats we opened for our breakfast. I pulled the top off and pushed the envelope containing one copy of the oil spill story and the interview notes into the box until it was entirely covered with oats. Replacing the lid, I tapped the Quaker gentleman whose picture was on the label and said, "Mum's the word, pal."

"You're hiding copies of your story? Why?"

"I know it doesn't look like it, but the story in that envelope is worth a pretty penny, at least it is for a day or two. I want to make sure nobody gets a free copy of it so I'm hiding two of the three copies for safekeeping."

"Oh. Where are you going to hide the other one?"

"I'm not sure. Where would you hide it?"

Eliza frowned in concentration for a moment, and then grinned. "I know the perfect place! Follow me."

She led me into the bedroom and lifted the covers from her side of the bed. I shook my head. "Not under the mattress, that is the first place anyone will look."

"Not under the mattress, in it. When I was making the bed this morning I noticed there is a rip in the cover down at the foot end. It's hidden by the welting around the top of the mattress. See?"

Eliza was right, and when I tried slipping the envelope into the opening, it disappeared from sight completely. I said, "Brilliant idea!"

"Thank you, Mister Kinney. Now, let's get on to item number two on our list."

The offices and pressroom of the *Post-Dispatch* occupied a long narrow building on Ortega Street between State and Anacapa, right around the corner from the *Tribune*. I pulled into an empty parking place at the curb almost directly in front of the building.

"Eliza, I don't like leaving you here by yourself, but I doubt if having the daughter of the *Tribune's* Managing Editor with me will make getting into see Mister Storche any easier."

"Probably not, plus Mister Storche and I have met, so he knows what I look like. It's okay, darling, I'll wait right here for you."

"It's not okay, but it's what we have to do. I'm going to leave the car key with you. When I get out, please lock the doors. If you see any kind of trouble coming, start the car, and drive out of here."

"Yes, darling. I'll do exactly as you say."

Lastly, I opened the envelope of the oil spill story I had with me and removed the torn off headline. I put the headline back into my pocket, and handed the envelope to Eliza. "Please take good care of that for me, and how about a kiss for good luck?"

After receiving a smooch that was certainly chock full of luck, I walked briskly into the lobby of the *Santa Barbara Post-Dispatch*. I held out little hope of seeing Clarence Storche without an appointment, so I was quite surprised when I was ushered directly to his office.

The Managing Editor of the *Post-Dispatch* had quite different ideas about offices than his counterpart at the *Tribune*. Storche's domain occupied a corner of the newsroom and had but one window through which to survey his domain. The window was equipped with Venetian blinds and the slats were closed.

Preparing to walk into Storche's office, I put on a blank expression I hoped would not give anything away about the purpose of my visit. Actually, not giving away the reason for my visit was easy because I, myself, did not know for sure what that reason might be. I was playing this tune strictly by ear.

Storche, a balding rotund gentleman with a ruddy complexion, looked up from the papers on his desk and I said, "Good morning, Mister Storche, my name is Lester Kinney."

He leaned back in his desk chair and sized me up for several seconds. Finally, he said, "So you're Fred Hamm's new hotshot reporter, ay?"

I could either play my cards close to the vest or play them face up. I decided to play them face up and see if my hand was strong enough for a bluff when the time came.

"Not any longer."

Storche laughed. "It certainly didn't take you long to figure out Hamm is a tyrant to work for. If you don't mind me asking, what did he do that made you walk out?"

"He fired me. Mind if I sit down?"

I had his interest now. "Yeah, sure, have a seat. So Hamm gave you the sack, huh? What terrible sin did you commit to bring his wrath down upon you?"

Sticking with my cards up approach, I said, "I fell in love with his daughter."

The big man laughed so hard his multiple chins jiggled. "Kinney, you take the cake. That's rich!"

I simply sat back in my chair and watched the man. Finally

his laughter died away and he said, "So, why are you here? You lookin' for a job? I have to warn you, though, I don't have any beautiful daughters." His attempt at humor set off another spasm of laughter.

"No, Mister Storche, I'm not looking for a job. I'm here to ask some questions."

Somewhere in his head gears meshed and his expression shifted from joviality to suspicion. "Questions? What questions?"

"Let's try this one on for size. What's happened to Tom Wigand?"

A momentary change in Storche's face told me I had hit a nerve. "Wigand? What makes you think anything has happened to him?"

"Wigand covered Estelle Abernathy's donation ceremony Saturday morning. He also tried to pin her down for a statement about the Summerland oil spill, but there wasn't a single story by Wigand in yesterday's edition of the *Post-Dispatch*, not even an article on the ceremony. What's more, you completely dropped what might be the hottest story of the decade. So what's happened to Wigand, and while we're at it, why did you drop the oil spill story?"

"Damn, Kinney, you get right to it, don't you?"

"I don't see any purpose to pussyfooting around with you. Either you're going to answer my questions or I'll find the answers elsewhere."

"All right, I will save you some trouble. I have no idea what's happened to Tom Wigand. He has completely disappeared from the face of the Earth."

Storche had thrown me a tidbit when I threatened to go looking for Wigand. Was that to keep me from poking my nose where he didn't want it poked?

I asked, "And the Summerland oil spill story?"

Clarence Storche's eyes looked from my face to the top of his desk to some point out in space and back to my face, all in less than a heartbeat. I had asked the jackpot question, but I still didn't know what the jackpot was.

"There was no story yesterday because we didn't have any accurate new information on the spill."

"Now, that's strange because, from what I hear, a lack of accurate information never stopped you from coming up with a story before."

That raised Storche's ire. "Okay, Kinney, that's enough. Tell me why we are having this conversation or get out of here."

I still didn't know what he was hiding, but the welcome mat was wearing thin. If I was going to get anything tangible out of my visit to the *Post-Dispatch*, I had to make my move now. I removed the oil spill headline from my inside coat pocket and tossed it on his desk.

Picking up the slip of paper, he said, "What the hell this?" He read the headline, then held it up and asked, "Are you trying to tell me this is legit?"

I nodded. "It is one hundred percent legitimate. The article includes all the damning details and names names. I have the facts Wigand was guessing at."

"Yeah? So where is the rest of the . . . oh I get it. I have to pay to see your hole card. Is that it?"

"That's it."

"Damn, you are a nervy cuss! Okay, if I was interested—and I'm not saying I am—what would the article cost me?"

"A byline, no editing, and fifty dollars cash on the barrel head. In return, you get exclusive rights to this story on the Summerland oil spill."

"Fifty? Your story isn't worth half that."

"It will be when the national papers pick this thing up."

"What makes you so sure they will?"

"Because California is the largest oil producing state in the country, pumping up to forty percent of the country's oil, and southern California's oil fields are the largest source of oil in California. When the good citizens of Santa Barbara demand the closing of the Summerland oil fields because they're ruining some high-priced real estate, the rest of the US will want to know about it."

After staring at me for several more seconds, Storche said, "Tell you what, Kinney, I'll give you twenty-five for the story. That's my best offer."

Standing up to leave, I played my last card. "All right, Mister Storche, I'll take my offer to Jim Richardson at the *Los Angeles Examiner*. I'm pretty sure he will see the wisdom in buying it. Thank you for your time."

I walked out into the newsroom figuring I had overplayed my hand, but I hadn't gotten far when Storche bellowed, "Come back here, Kinney!"

Turning around, I looked back into his office, but took no steps in that direction. Storche made a come-here gesture with his arm and picked up the handset of a fancy intercom system on his desk. From the doorway I heard him tell someone to pull fifty from petty cash and bring it up to his office.

To me, Storche said, "Okay, the fifty is on its way. Where is the article?"

"It's in my car parked at the curb out front."

He stood. "Okay, as soon as the cash gets here, we'll go down and make the exchange, but bear in mind that I make no promise to publish your story."

What the heck was he up to? Why would Storche pay fifty for a story he might not publish?

Five minutes later we were walking across the sidewalk toward my Chevrolet. Eliza looked surprised to see me and Storche together, and I winked to put her at ease. I also made a cranking gesture, indicating she should open the passenger side window.

Through the open window I said, "Hello, darling, I believe you know Mister Storche."

Eliza put on a smile and said, "Hello, Mister Storche. It's nice to see you again."

Storche smiled back. "And you, my dear."

I said, "Eliza, please hand me the envelope."

"Here you are, darling."

"Thank you."

Turning to Storche I said, "Here's the story."

He held out five ten dollar bills and we made the exchange. Then I leaned against the Chevrolet's fender while he opened the envelope and read its contents.

Finishing the last page, Storche said, "Damn! And you're absolutely sure all of this is legit?" Looking at Eliza, he quickly added, "Apologies for my language, miss."

I answered his question with a slight exaggeration. "Every point in that story can be documented in a court of law if it ever came to that, although I doubt Summerland Oil wants to go anywhere near a court of law."

Nodding almost absentmindedly, Storche turned back toward the *Post-Dispatch* entrance and said, "All right. Good luck to you, Kinney." To Eliza he said, "Good to see you again, Miss Hamm."

When Storche was out of earshot, Eliza said, "Well, congratulations on selling your story."

"I'll tell you all about it, but first, let's find a less prominent location to park."

"Yes, that would be a good idea. Father drove by a little while ago. He didn't see me or recognize your car and kept going, but I don't think we can count on that happening twice."

I followed Ortega Street across State and parked in front of a vacant lot in a residential area a few blocks further south. I shut the engine off and told Eliza the main points of my conversation with Clarence Storche.

When I finished the story, she said, "That has to be one of the strangest deals in the history of journalism. Why did he buy a story for top dollar if he isn't sure he will publish it?"

"We don't know for certain he isn't going to print the story, but he would not have said that if there wasn't at least some question in his mind about using it. Just as puzzling to me is how Tom Wigand's disappearance and Storche dropping the Summerland spill story are connected. Obviously something is out of whack there, but I have no inkling what it could be."

Eliza shook her head. "Neither do I, but it might be a good idea if we found out."

"Agreed. For now, though, we best get on with our errands. What's next?"

"The County National Bank and Trust. It will be on our right in the fourth block up State from Ortega."

TWELVE

Monday - September 10, 1928

The County National Bank and Trust Company, to which Eliza entrusted her checking account had all of the traditional confidence-inspiring icons associated with a successful financial institution. These included a high-ceiling lobby with an abundance of dark wood paneling, a highly polished granite floor, and gleaming brass bars in front of the teller windows.

After spending a few minutes in line we eventually arrived at one of those teller cages. A neatly lettered card alongside the teller window informed us we were about to be served by one Edward Lange. Eliza presented a withdrawal slip in the amount of forty dollars to Mister Lange, who read the slip carefully through horn-rimmed glasses.

Apparently satisfied that the withdrawal slip was properly filled out, he carried it to a large, impressive looking clothbound account book on a desk behind the counter. He turned pages in the book until he found her account number and studied the information there for a long moment. Mister Lange then returned to his cage and I could tell by his expression we were about to encounter yet another problem to overcome. He handed the withdrawal slip back to Eliza and said, "I'm sorry, Miss Hamm, but it seems your account has been frozen."

Somewhat confused by Mister Lange's terminology, Eliza said, "Frozen? What does that mean?"

"It means you cannot make a withdrawal from the account at this time."

"Why is it frozen? There is plenty of money in the account."

"Yes, there are adequate funds in the account, but someone who is signatory to it has ordered that the account be frozen."

Now thoroughly puzzled, Eliza said, "That cannot be. The account is in my name. There are no co-signers."

Speaking quietly as if he did not want to be heard giving away bank secrets, Lange said, "It was your father, Miss Hamm. He came in this morning and ordered the account assets frozen."

Eliza's response, however, was anything but quiet. "What gives him the right to do that!?"

"He is your legal guardian, Miss Hamm. He has every right to make changes in the account."

"He is NOT my legal guardian. You take that freeze or whatever you call it off my account right this minute!"

Mister Lange was obviously growing weary of dealing with the dumb Dora at his cage window. "Miss Hamm, perhaps you should come back at another time and take this matter up with our branch manager, Mister Peters. Now, please step aside so I can help the next customer in line."

I was deliberately keeping my mouth shut, letting Eliza handle the matter. At that point, however, she looked up at me, and I could tell she was close to tears. She needed a little help.

"Mister Lange, my name is Lester Kinney. I am a close personal friend of Miss Hamm's. She wants this issue resolved right now, so please trot your Mister Peters out here to set matters right."

Lange gave me a glare. "Mister Kinney, as you might imagine, Mister Peters is very busy taking care of pressing banking matters. Miss Hamm will have to make an appointment with Mister Peters' secretary. Now, if you would kindly step aside so the next customer . . . ."

Calmly, but in a clear voice that was loud enough to echo off the bank's high ceiling, I said, "Mister Lange, would you agree that a violation of federal banking regulations is a pressing matter?"

He looked at me as if I had just sprouted horns and a tail. "Please lower your voice, Mister Kinney."

"I'm speaking loudly because you seem to be having difficulty hearing me, Mister Lange. I repeat, would you agree that a violation of federal banking regulations is a pressing matter?"

He made a palms-down gesture with both hands in effort to make me lower my voice. In a hushed tone just above a whisper, Lange said, "Yes, Mister Kinney, I would agree . . . ."

"Then get your Mister Peters out here to deal with this pressing banking matter and do it now!"

Apparently Mister Lange came to the realization he was in well over his head and decided cooperation was the better part of valor. "Yes, sir. I will be right back." He almost ran to a desk in the teller area and used its telephone.

Eliza looked as if she might fall apart at any moment, so I leaned over and quietly said, "Try to stay calm, kiddo. We'll get this straightened out. Don't let it upset you."

A moment later an office door on one wall of the lobby opened and a slender man in a gray suit that matched his hair walked in our direction. When he reached us, he spoke directly to Eliza. "Good morning, Miss Hamm. Please step into my office."

Eliza said nothing and we followed Peters into his office. When I walked in behind Eliza, he appeared ready to say something, but chose not to. That was a wise decision.

After seating us in chairs opposite his desk, Peters said to Eliza, "Now, Miss Hamm, how may I be of service?"

Eliza looked at me without saying a word. I said, "Mister Peters, I am Lester Kinney, a close personal friend of Miss Hamm's, and it appears you have a major problem on your hands."

Peters took umbrage at my blaming Eliza's problem on him. "If you have reference to the freeze we placed on Miss Hamm's account, we were simply acting at the behest of her legal guardian, Mister Frederick Hamm."

Looking him square in the eye, I said, "Tell me, Mister Peters, what makes you think Frederick Hamm is Eliza Hamm's legal guardian?"

My question threw Peters for a brief moment. I guessed he was experiencing the first inklings that he really did have a serious problem on his hands. "Why, he is her father. Until she reaches the age of consent that makes him her legal guardian."

I looked at Eliza. "Eliza, please show Mister Peters your driving license."

She removed the license from her purse and handed it to Mister Peters. He accepted the license, gave me a wary look, and read what was printed on the white card. His haughty expression and the attitude that went with it instantly evaporated.

"I see. Apparently Mister Hamm misrepresented the facts of the matter."

Speaking in a tone more than loud enough to be heard in the lobby beyond Mister Peters' office door, I said, "That is a very polite way of saying Mister Frederick Hamm is a damned liar. Now, kindly release the funds in her account and give Miss Hamm the forty dollars she wishes to withdraw so we can get on with filing a police report."

Mister Peters was a proud man. It took a lot of effort on his part to apologize for the mistake, but he did so, and then went out to a teller cage and exchanged Eliza's withdrawal slip for two twenty dollar bills, which he handed to her personally.

Outside in my Chevrolet parked at the curb, Eliza sat for a

moment pulling herself together before saying, "I never realized my father was such a vindictive man."

"I would say he is a very childish man. Surely he must know that lying to the police and then to the bank about your age would not stand up."

"The thing that worries me is what he will come up with next. If I didn't know better, I would question his sanity."

I gave that a moment's thought and said, "Do you know better?"

Eliza turned to me with a startled expression. "What do you mean?"

"I mean he may actually be suffering from some kind of mental breakdown. Your father strikes me as rather high strung. Maybe something pushed him over the edge into a state of temporary insanity."

"Oh, I hope not. How could we find that out?"

"I can only think of one way. You could swear out a police complaint and let them deal with him. You certainly have good cause to do that."

Eliza shook her head. "I can't do that."

"Why not?"

"I simply cannot have my own father arrested."

I felt like telling her she most certainly could have her father arrested, but decided saying so would not improve the situation. Instead, I said, "Regardless of that, I thought you handled the situation in the bank quite well."

Going by her expressions, Eliza thought I was making some kind of bad joke at first, but when it became apparent I was serious, she said, "Only because you were there. I was so upset at that teller, I would have run out of the bank crying if you had not stepped in and made things right."

"Eliza, give yourself some credit. You were dealing with him quite well until he stonewalled you with that hogwash about talking to the branch manager. I think it is much more accurate to say we handled the situation as a team."

She reached for my hand. "I know you're being kind, Lester, and I appreciate you trying to boost my confidence."

"I hope I succeeded."

Eliza smiled and lit up the day. "Actually, darling, I think you have . . . at least a little."

"Good. Now here's something I hope will boost your confidence a little more." I handed her two of the ten dollar bills Storche gave me. "Put this with the forty you withdrew for clothes shopping so you can splurge a little."

"Lester, we are on a budget, remember?"

"Yes, but this is part of what Storche paid for our story. It's found money, so it doesn't count."

Eliza leaned over and hugged me. "What am I to do with you?"

"I'm afraid I'm a hopeless case, you'll just have to put up with me. Now, tell me how to get to this department store where you will attempt to do the impossible by making yourself even more gorgeous than you already are."

"Lester, stop exaggerating. Trenwith's is on the right two blocks south of here"

"I am not exaggerating. On State?"

"Yes, on State Street. Are you going to come in and help me make good choices again?"

"I'm going into the store, but I can watch from afar if you would prefer."

She thought for a minute. "Darling, if you don't mind, I think I would prefer that. It's not that I don't enjoy shopping with you, it was fun yesterday, but this time I would like some of what I pick out to be surprises. Do you think I can be trusted to pick out outfits that will please you?"

"Eliza do you remember when I came by the library last Wednesday and invited you to be my guest at Estelle Abernathy's shindig?"

"Of course I do. I am not likely to forget one of the most exciting moments of my life!"

"Okay, but do you remember what you said after you accepted my invitation?"

She had to give that some thought. "Gosh, darling, I think I told you I was honored you chose me. Is that what you mean?"

"You also said you would make me proud I chose you to be my guest."

Eliza looked genuinely surprised. "I did? That was rather audacious of me."

"But you did make me proud. I could not have been prouder of the way you looked when we walked into the reception. That experience convinced me that whatever you choose to wear, you will look terrific in it."

I would swear she blushed again. I kind of liked that.

Trenwith's Department Store was in a two-story commercial structure called the Howard-Canfield Building, and the women's departments—there seemed to be several—took up most of the first floor on both sides of the main entrance. I wished Eliza happy shopping and took up a station just inside the entrance doors, trying my best not to look at the women's lingerie display not more than five feet from where I stood. As it turned out I had plenty of opportunity to stand in less embarrassing locations because Eliza's shopping expedition lasted more than an hour.

When Eliza returned to the main entrance she was followed by a young fellow in a bright blue uniform with a little round pillbox hat that made me think of a hotel bellboy. He was loaded down like a pack mule with packages in a variety of sizes and shapes.

I held the door open for both of them, and then hurried ahead to open the Chevrolet's trunk. When we were done stuffing it full of packages, there was not room left over for so much as a hanky. I opened the passenger door for Eliza and tipped the boy a dime, for which he seemed grateful.

Behind the steering wheel, I turned to Eliza. "You got all that for sixty bucks?"

"No, darling, I got all that for fifty-seven dollars and twenty-six cents. You have change coming. Your future wife knows how to shop for bargains."

Chuckling, I said, "I guess you do."

Sounding quite proud of herself, Eliza enumerated her purchases. "All told, I bought three skirts, two dresses, four blouses, two sweaters, a leather purse, a nice warm jacket, two pairs of shoes, two cloche hats, two pairs of gloves, six pairs of silk stockings, six pairs of undies, two silk slips, and assorted accessories, including a couple of belts and a beautiful tiny cloisonné typewriter pin."

"Typewriter pin? Why on earth did you buy a typewriter pin?"

Eliza leaned over and kissed me on the cheek. "I bought a typewriter pin because it makes me think of you."

"Oh."

"Yes, oh. We only have one item left on our list, grocery shopping. Shall we do that now or stop for lunch?"

"To be honest, I have felt rather conspicuous all morning. It would suit me fine if we bought our groceries and got out sight."

"I have felt the same way. Let's go to Piggly-Wiggly and then head for home."

"All right. Where is this Wiggly-Piggy?"

"Piggly-Wiggly, darling. It is about three blocks further south on State. It will be on our right and there is a good produce market right next door."

We made quick work of the grocery shopping because we only needed some staples, meat for dinners, and fresh fruit. It is fortunate we did not need more because getting it all home would have required a trailer. As it was, Eliza had to share her side of the seat with a sack of potatoes.

As before, I pulled down the central drive of the garden court and parked at the rear close to number ten. That made unloading easier and kept the Chevrolet somewhat out of sight. I was not exactly hiding the car, but I saw no reason to advertise our whereabouts.

Once we carried everything into the cottage, Eliza disappeared into the bedroom to unpack her new wardrobe. While she did that, I stowed the groceries away. When that chore was done, I set about fixing our lunch.

From the kitchen, I hollered, "Shall we finish off your tuna salad sandwich makings for lunch, or would you prefer something else?"

"A tuna salad sandwich sounds good to me, unless you don't want it two meals in a row."

"Doesn't bother me in the least."

I set about making two tuna salad sandwiches just as Eliza made them last night, right down to the garnish of carrot sticks, tomato slices, and olives. Then I upped the ante by opening a wax paper package of Laura Scudder potato chips, one of our few non-essential grocery purchases, and poured some into a bowl, which I set at the center of the table.

When Eliza arrived in the kitchen for lunch, she looked the table over and said, "Wow, you really know how to set a great table."

"I have a good teacher."

"Gee, we even have some of those crispy potato things." Eliza tried a potato chip. "I only had these things once before, but they were homemade. I think these are better because they aren't so greasy. Kind of salty, though."

"That's what the beer is for."

Eliza made a show of looking around the table. "What beer?"

"The beer we would have if those do-gooders in the Women's Christian Temperance Union hadn't hornswoggled the blue noses into believing America would be paradise if booze was outlawed."

Eliza laughed. "Oh, that beer."

"Mark my words, booze will be back. There are already movements afoot to repeal the Eighteenth Amendment because it has been a miserable failure. I'll wager prohibition doesn't last more than a few more years."

"Well, prohibition certainly hasn't been more than an inconvenience to people like Estelle Abernathy. Gin was flowing like water at her party."

"It was, indeed, and the elected officials who are supposed to be setting good examples for us impressionable citizens were bellied right up to Estelle's bar. It's almost laughable."

During my tirade a worried expression appeared on Eliza's face. "Lester?"

"Yes, darling?"

"Have you decided if you are going to keep your appointment with Estelle tonight?"

I shook my head. "With everything else going on this morning, I haven't given it much thought."

"Oh."

"I know you would rather I didn't go up there, but it could be an opportunity to learn something useful from her, and if the *Post-Dispatch* publishes our story tomorrow morning, this could be the last such opportunity I have."

The tone of her voice rose higher. "What more do you need to know about her, Lester? Estelle Abernathy is an evil, wicked woman!"

"What I want to know about her is where her weaknesses lay. I owe her something for what she pulled Saturday night and for what she has done to you."

"What she did to me, I allowed her to do. If you have to punish someone, punish me! Please don't go up there!"

I thought about what Eliza said, and made my decision. "I have no choice, Eliza. I have to see her."

She jumped up from the table and ran into the bedroom, slamming the door behind her. I didn't see her again until seven-thirty, when I was about to leave the house.

I knocked softly on the bedroom door, and then opened it. Eliza was laying across the bed. I sat on the edge of the mattress and took her hand in mine.

"Eliza?"

A small voice in the darkness said, "Yes, Lester."

"I'm going to see Estelle now. Please don't worry. I will be very cautious and I'll be back soon."

She said nothing for a long time. Finally, as I stood up to leave, Eliza said, "Lester, I love you with all my heart.

THIRTEEN

Monday - September 10, 1928

For some reason the night was darker than usual as I made my way along the Riviera's winding roads. The closer I got to the Abernathy mansion, the more I suspected I was on a fool's errand. Besides that, Eliza's reaction to my visiting Estelle tugged at my heart. I felt bad for hurting her, maybe unnecessarily.

Estelle's mansion was definitely darker than it was two nights earlier. The sole light outside the house was a porch lamp alongside the big oak door. The air outside was deathly still and the only sound I heard was the quiet ticking of my engine as the metal cooled.

I removed the key from its slot in the ignition switch and sat there for several seconds with the key in my hand. A voice in my head was telling me to poke the key back into its slot and get the hell out of there. I was very near to doing what the voice said when Estelle Abernathy's front door opened and I was committed.

I climbed down from the seat and walked toward the entrance, where Armando Delgado stood in the shadows holding the door open for me. As I approached, he smiled wolfishly. "Good evening, Señor Kinney. Señorita Abernathy awaits you in the library."

The heavy library door slammed closed with the finality of a jail cell when Armando shut it behind me. The grand dame was at her desk and knowing what I now knew about her, the smile with which Estelle Abernathy greeted me looked as authentic as a three-dollar bill.

"Good evening, Lester. How are you?"

Having already decided to tell her about Frederick Hamm firing me to see how she reacted, I set the stage for that announcement. "I have had better days, Estelle. How are you?"

"I am fine Lester. I am always fine, but you seem troubled. Has something happened?"

The tone in which she asked the question implied she already knew the answer. Seating myself in one of the leather chairs near the desk, I said, "Yes. To say it frankly, Frederick Hamm has dismissed me from the *Tribune* staff."

Estelle put on a look of surprise. "Oh? Why on earth did he do that?"

Now I had to be careful because I did not want Estelle knowing the truth of the matter. I said, "It had nothing to do with my skills as a reporter. Mister Hamm is upset over my relationship with his daughter."

She turned up the volume of her surprised expression. "Heavens! I am shocked. Frederick has a tendency to be impulsive, but this time I fear he has made a costly error in judgement."

I gave her a small smile. "Thank you for saying so, Estelle."

"If I may ask, what specifically did he object to concerning your relationship with Eliza?"

"I think Mister Hamm suspected we were sharing more intimacy than he felt was appropriate."

Estelle appeared to give that some thought, and then said, "And was he right?"

I deliberately hesitated. She was watching my face carefully and when I did not answer her question promptly, Estelle said, "Forgive me, Lester. I have no right to ask you such a question. Tell me this, though, what are your employment prospects?"

That question I answered promptly. "Not promising, especially without a letter of reference from Mister Hamm, and since there are only two newspapers in Santa Barbara, I fear I will have to go back to the Los Angeles area in order to find employment."

My answer caused Estelle to put on a sad face. "That seems a shame. I have the impression you enjoy being in our town."

"Oh, I do. Who wouldn't enjoy living in such a beautiful place?"

Estelle's sad face was quickly replaced with a happier expression. "And it seemed you fit in quite well here."

She let that sink in a few moments, and then said, "Lester, what would you say if I told you I may be able to have you reinstated in your position at the *Tribune*?"

I was genuinely surprised. "I'm not sure, Estelle. How could you do that?"

Estelle stared at me intently for quite a while before saying, "Lester, I'm going to acquaint you with a little known fact about the *Santa Barbara Tribune*. It happens that I own fifty-one percent of the newspaper."

Again, I was surprised. "I certainly did not know that."

"It was never my intention to be in the publishing business, but when Frederick decided he wanted to publish a paper to compete with the *Post-Dispatch*, I thought it was an excellent idea to have newspapers reflecting different points of view in our town. Unfortunately, Fredrick could not raise the capital to carry out such a venture. When he seemed ready to abandon the enterprise, I contacted him with an offer to finance his dream in exchange for controlling interest in the newspaper. Frederick accepted my offer. So, you see, a word from me puts you back on the *Tribune* staff."

What I had just learned not only surprised me, it made my meeting with Estelle well worthwhile. The news also put me on the spot. I knew I had to proceed cautiously because, under the current circumstances, I could see no benefit whatsoever in having her intervene with Frederick Hamm on my behalf.

With a frown, I said, "Estelle, I am honored that you would consider doing such a thing for me, but I cannot imagine any circumstances under which I would be willing to submit to Frederick Hamm's tyrannical methods."

"Now, Lester, don't you be guilty of the same foolish impulsiveness as Frederick. I can assure you his tyrannical methods will cease where you are concerned. You will be free to do your job as you see fit."

"In my experience, albeit somewhat limited, a good newspaper staff works as team. While certainly appealing, I fear your offer simply would not work out in the long run."

Estelle frowned. "Lester, I beg you to give my offer further consideration before you reject it. In fact, I insist that you do so. Now, it has been a long day and I feel in need of some rest. Thank you for coming to see me."

With that, Estelle stood up, and wishing me a good night, she left the room. I barely had time to stand up before Armando was at my side escorting me to the front door. Obviously the grand dame was displeased with me. Too darn bad.

On the way to the entrance we passed through the sitting room where Aurora Abernathy was seated on a couch reading. It was the first time I was close enough for a good look at her. The younger Miss Abernathy possessed a slim body and her features we're clearly Latin—coal black hair worn long, full lips in a bright shade of red lipstick, and dark brown eyes that stared intently at me until I reached the entryway. Her expression struck me as contemptuous.

Armando led me all the way to my car and surprised me further by saying, "Señor Kinney. Señorita Abernathy is very disappointed in your decision not to accept her offer."

Surprised that he even knew what Estelle and I discussed, I turned to look at him. Armando grabbed the front of my jacket with both hands and slammed me back against the Chevrolet. "I strongly urge you to reconsider her generous proposition, Señor."

Before I could react, he sucker punched me in the solar plexus hard enough to take my breath away, and followed that by slapping my face with enough force to snap my head to one side. I tasted blood at the corner of my mouth. It felt like a lot more than a trickle.

"If you do not reconsider, Señor Kinney, we will speak again, only perhaps not so pleasantly as now."

He was holding me upright against the Chevrolet with his left arm. When he let go and turned toward the house, I slowly slid down the side of my car and ended up hunched over and gasping for breath on the running board.

I heard the front door of Estelle Abernathy's mansion close, but it was several moments before I was able to regain my feet and climb onto the Chevrolet's seat. After fishing the ignition key out of my trouser pocket, I started the engine. As I drove slowly away, I glanced up and clearly saw Estelle watching me from an upstairs window. Her expression showed no sympathy for my pain.

Making my way down the hill, it occurred to me that I still had no idea what Estelle originally intended the subject of tonight's meeting to be. It could not have been my job at the *Tribune* because I was still employed when she arranged the meeting.

The lights were out in cottage number ten when I parked the car. As I opened the front door, Eliza came running out the darkness and hugged me with all her might.

When I winced at the pain her hug caused, Eliza stepped back and looked at my face. "Darling, you're bleeding. There is blood all over your face and shirt. What happened?"

Leaning lightly on her, I said, "I learned a valuable lesson tonight."

She frowned in the darkness. "What do you mean?"

"I mean the next time the woman I love warns me not to do something, I will listen and follow her advice to the letter. I have to sit down."

She helped me into the bedroom, where I sat on the edge of the bed. Eliza turned the overhead light on and gasped. "Lester, your face looks horrible. I'll get a washcloth."

While Eliza ran into the bathroom I began unbuttoning my shirt, but I did not get very far. My lower chest throbbed with pain from Armando's punch. All I wanted to do was sit perfectly still.

Eliza gently cleaned my face with the washcloth. "The cut on your mouth doesn't look too bad, but you have a large ugly bruise on the side of your face. Here, let's get your shirt off."

When I winced, she said, "Are you hurt somewhere else?"

"Yes, my chest. I feel like I might have a broken rib."

"Oh, darling!"

Together we managed to get my shirt off, and I stretched out on the bed. Eliza said, "I am going to feel your stomach and your ribs. This might hurt a little, but we must find out if you have any broken bones or other serious injuries."

I was proud of myself for only cringing a few times as she gently poked and prodded. Finally, Eliza said, "I don't feel anything out of place or broken, but you have another nasty bruise down there. There is a bottle of aspirin tablets in the medicine cabinet. I'll get a couple for you."

Eliza returned with the aspirin and a glass of water. I swallowed two tablets and Eliza said, "The aspirin should start working soon. Now, tell me what happened. I have to know."

Speaking slowly and deliberately I gave her a condensed description of my visit to Estelle Abernathy. When I finished, Eliza said, "I'm just glad you weren't hurt more seriously."

"I think my pride is hurt as badly as any other part of me. Despite your warnings, I let that Mexican fop catch me unawares."

"I believe Armando is Spanish, darling."

"I don't care what he is. I shouldn't have . . . ."

"Relax, darling. If you are up to it, we can talk more about what happened later, but first, I think we should put you to bed. I will join you unless my being there will make it difficult for you to sleep."

Taking a gentle deep breath, I said, "Not at all, but I need to get out of my pants and use the bathroom."

"Okay, I'll help you."

Eliza did indeed help. First, she helped me stand up, and then unbuttoned my trousers so I could step out of them. Finally she assisted me to the bathroom door.

"Can you handle it from here, darling?"

For the first time in hours, I genuinely felt like smiling, so I did. Of course Eliza noticed.

"What do you find so amusing?"

"Your choice of words, and yes, I think I can handle it from here."

Eliza looked up at me with a puzzled expression, and then my meaning sank in. She grinned. "For a guy who is extremely vulnerable at the moment, you are being awfully brave. Now, get in there, you goof."

After I finished in the bathroom Eliza used it while I hobbled back to the bed and stretched out again. I was stark naked because finding a pair of clean shorts seemed like much more work than it was worth Still, the aspirin tablets were beginning to have some effect and, as long as I didn't move, I felt almost human.

When Eliza joined me in bed, I noticed something strange. She was wearing my pale blue shirt.

"Eliza, what happened to your new nightgown?"

She looked puzzled. "What new nightgown?"

"Didn't you get a real nightgown when you went shopping today so you wouldn't have to wear my hand-me-down shirt to bed?"

"No, I did not get a new nightgown. I like wearing your shirt and I am going to continue wearing it to bed until it falls apart, but you have to put it on once in a while so it still smells like you a little."

Gently pulling her toward me, I said, "You are amazing." Then we kissed, gently at first, and then with more enthusiasm.

"Easy, darling. I love kissing you, but that cut on your lip is still pretty raw and we don't have another clean set of sheets until I do some washing tomorrow."

"I can help with that chore."

Smiling, Eliza said, "I don't think so. I hope I'm wrong, but I imagine you are going to be pretty sore for a few days. Now, tell me about the part of your visit to Estelle's you left out before."

Surprised, I said, "How do you know I left anything out?"

Propping her head up on the pillow next to mine, Eliza said, "I'm not sure how I know, I just know you have more to tell me."

"Well, you're right I do, but this is the really strange part."

"As long as I know you're okay, I can handle it."

"Do you remember me saying Estelle wanted me to go back to work at the *Tribune*? In fact she was so insistent, Armando beat me up for turning her down."

"Yes, I remember, but I don't know how she could make such an offer. Father runs the *Tribune*."

"According to Estelle, your father only owns forty-nine percent of the paper. She owns the rest."

Eliza sat up abruptly. "What?"

"She claims she gave your father the money to start the *Tribune* in exchange for controlling interest."

"I never heard that before! Do you think she was telling the truth?"

"I don't know that for sure, but I can't think of any reason for Estelle to lie about it. She said she invested in the *Tribune* because she felt there ought to be two papers in town to represent differing points of view."

Eliza slid over without saying anymore and rested her head gently on my chest. She was quiet for a long time before saying, "You know one reason why I like to rest my head on your chest?"

"Tell me."

"Because I can hear your heart beat. I can even feel it, which is very important right now. While you were gone tonight I was afraid I would never hear it again."

"Eliza, Armando wasn't trying to kill me. He was just showing me what happens to people who don't do what Estelle wants them to do."

"Lester, if Estelle told Armando to beat you up just for not accepting her offer to put you back on the *Tribune* staff, have you stopped to think what she is likely to have him do when she reads your oil spill article in the *Post-Dispatch*?"

"I doubt if she would send him to do me serious physical injury just for that."

"What about Tom Wigand?"

"What about him?"

"Lester, Tom Wigand bothered Estelle trying to get a story, and he suddenly disappeared into thin air. Do you think that was a coincidence?"

"I don't think she had anything to do with . . . ."

"Don't lie to me, Lester. You do think she had something to do with his disappearance."

"What?"

"Darling, I'm listening to your heart, remember? When I asked you about Tom Wigand your pulse rate increased noticeably."

"Oh."

"Yes, oh. When you came home tonight you said you learned a lesson. You said the next time I gave you advice you were going to follow it to the letter. Well, I'm about to give you another piece of advice."

"What advice?"

"If your oil spill appears in tomorrow's *Post-Dispatch*, we need to pack some bags and get out of Santa Barbara for a while; maybe forever."

"Do you really think that is necessary?"

"Lester, my father is trying to ruin my life and Estelle Abernathy has already had Armando beat you up, plus you just sold a news article that is guaranteed to send her through the roof. Don't those things make you think Santa Barbara might not be the best place in the world for us to be?"

"All right, Eliza, we'll get a copy of the *Post-Dispatch* first thing in the morning. If my story is in it, we will pack up and leave Santa Barbara."

She breathed what sounded like a long sigh of relief. "Thank you, darling."

"Do you have any idea where we ought to go?"

Eliza gave that a little thought. "Well . . . do you know how far it is to Las Vegas, Nevada?"

I was surprised. "Las Vegas? I don't know; about three-hundred-fifty miles or so—maybe a nine hour drive across the desert. What do they have in that little cow town that would make you want to go there?"

She gently cuddled closer. "It's what they don't have in Las Vegas that attracts me."

"Okay, what don't they have in Las Vegas?"

Carefully sliding her right leg over mine in a manner to which I was already quite accustomed, Eliza said, "A waiting period to get married. Tonight taught me a lesson also. Life is much too precious to waste any part of it. I would gladly start being your wife tonight if I could."

"All right, Las Vegas it is."

Eliza slid up alongside me and pressed her lips against the side of my mouth that still functioned more or less normally. We kissed as deeply as circumstances allowed and it wasn't long before she felt me pressing against the inside of her naked thigh as I had on previous occasions. Propping herself up on her elbows, Eliza gently rolled a little further over me and suddenly I was between her legs and we were inches from consummating a marriage that was yet to be.

"Eliza . . . ."

She giggled just a little. "Don't say it, darling. I'll move. I just wanted to be sure that part still works."

Even though it was painful, I lifted my hips slightly and pressed myself against her.

"Oh, God, darling!"

"Are you convinced everything still works?"

Between rapid breaths Eliza said, "Oh yes, very convinced . . . very, very convinced!"

Despite my discomfort, some part of my mind wanted desperately to know what Eliza would do next, so I stayed right where I was. She pressed herself down against me even more firmly for a brief moment, and then abruptly but gently rolled back on her side.

"Damn you, Lester Kinney! How is a girl supposed to abstain when you do things like that?"

"But you did."

Still breathing in rapid gasps, she said, "Proving what? That I have as much willpower as you?"

"No, kiddo, proving you love me an awful lot."

"Oh, God, yes. I love you more than I could ever tell you."

"You don't have to tell me, Eliza. You show me how much you love me in everything you say and do."

She carefully pressed her face against my chest and with a sob in her voice, said, "Oh, Lester."

I felt her tears on my chest. "I sure hope those are happy tears."

"They are the happiest tears a girl ever cried." After a pause, she said, "And I sure hope your heart is in good shape because from the way it sounds right now, your ticker is certainly getting a workout tonight."

FOURTEEN

Tuesday - September 11, 1928

As she is about so many things, Eliza was right about my condition Tuesday morning. It was all I could manage to stagger into the bathroom. A hot shower and two more aspirin helped matters some, but getting through the day was going to be a challenge.

While Eliza made us some of her proper coffee, I drove up to State Street and purchased a copy of the *Post-Dispatch* from a young man in a snappy tweed cap. Back at the kitchen table, I went through the entire newspaper page by page.

Eliza was watching me intently. "Is it there?"

"No. There is not a word about the oil spill written by me or anyone else."

She looked a little sad when she said, "Oh, darn. I guess I have to unpack my new white dress."

"Keep that dress handy. You will still be needing it very soon."

"I know, darling. Truthfully I am grateful your story is not there."

"So am I, but I am puzzled by it. Like you said the other day, why would Storche pay top dollar for a story he had no intention of publishing. It makes no sense."

Eliza stood up. "Changing the subject slightly, how do scrambled eggs with grated cheese and minced ham sound for breakfast?"

"Sounds good."

Beginning the preparation of our scrambled eggs, she said, "You know, Mister Storche's decision not to print your story does make some sense if you consider Tom Wigand's disappearance as part of the picture."

I looked across the kitchen at Eliza while I thought about what she said. "You think Wigand's disappearance was meant to scare Storche off the Summerland story?"

"It is a possibility, isn't it?"

"I suppose so, but that still leaves the question of why Storche paid fifty dollars for a story he knew he would not publish. Why not save the money and just send me packing?"

"Maybe he was just curious about what you had on Estelle."

That got me thinking in a new direction. "Or it could be Storche has something else in mind. Maybe he is planning on discrediting her with a major exposé in which my story is just one part."

Eliza turned to look at me with her spatula in hand. "You know, darling, you could be right. If the *Post-Dispatch* hit her hard enough with irrefutable facts, Estelle might be powerless to stop him. The damage would already be done."

I gave that idea some thought. It had merit.

When Eliza brought two plates of scrambled eggs to the table a few minutes later, I said, "The more I think about that, the more I think we are on the right track, and if we are, I might be able to help Storche out with another story that would go a long way toward exposing Estelle Abernathy's misdeeds and crimes."

"Just remember last night, darling. We have to be careful. Estelle is not going to forget you rejected her offer."

I smiled. "Like I said, don't put that white dress too far from reach."

Our conversation continued along the same lines as we devoured Eliza's delicious scrambled eggs. They were just the ticket. After my last bite, I stood up a little shakily and said, "More coffee, kiddo?"

"Oh, I'll get it, darling. Sit down before you fall down."

With a smile, I said, "I'm tough, I can take it. Besides, I cannot sit on my . . . laurels all day."

I had just finished pouring Eliza a half cup and a full cup for me when someone knocked on the front door. She got the panicky look on her face again and I said, "Drink your coffee. I'll get the door."

Upon opening the front door I was surprised to see Sergeant Danny Sullivan of the Santa Barbara Police Department standing on my porch again. His partner, Ike, was nowhere in sight.

Sensing my displeasure at finding him at my door again, Sullivan quickly explained, "Relax, Mister Kinney. This is just sort of a courtesy visit."

"Oh? In that case come on in. We were just finishing breakfast in the kitchen."

"Good Lord, Mister Kinney, what happened to your face?"

"For now, let's just say I ran into a door . . . several times."

Expressions of concern, and then suspicion crossed the Sergeant's face, but he let the matter pass.

Intending to warn Eliza as to who was about to enter our kitchen, I called out, "We have a visitor, kiddo. Sergeant Sullivan says he's here on a courtesy visit, so let's show him some courtesy."

Eliza had a somewhat reluctant smile on her face when Sullivan and I entered the kitchen. "Hello, Sergeant Sullivan. Would you care for some coffee?"

Sullivan smiled back. "No thank you. I stopped by because we had an interesting complaint filed yesterday, and I thought you might want to hear about it because the complaint indirectly involves you, Miss Hamm."

Eliza put her panicky expression back on and I asked, "What is the complaint?"

"The complainant is Mister Oswald Peters of the County National Bank & Trust Company and he charges Mister Frederick Hamm with bank fraud. Now, bank fraud is covered by federal statutes, but we're doing the initial investigation before the case is handed over to federal authorities."

I glanced at Eliza. She had a faraway look in her eyes.

To Sullivan I said, "I see. Thank you for letting us know. What can we expect?"

"Well, statements will be needed from Miss Hamm and from you, Mister Kinney, for the official investigation, but I was hoping you might unofficially tell me what happened from your point of view. I mean just between us so I have a little more insight into the matter before we make an arrest and the lawyers start trying to twist the facts around."

"I don't know, Sergeant. What do you think, Eliza?"

She looked up at Sullivan. "What happens if I refuse to make a statement? Would you still have to arrest my father?"

Sullivan glanced at me, apparently surprised by her question. "I'm afraid so, Miss Hamm. You see, Mister Peters provided us with bank documents proving without question that your father ordered a hold be placed on your bank account by virtue of a claim to be your legal guardian. All we really needed to make the case complete was evidence of your date of birth, which we have already obtained from the County Recorder's office."

Eliza simply said, "Oh."

I thought about asking why he had not thought of checking Eliza's birth records before showing up to arrest me for kidnapping an underage minor. I decided, however, there was nothing to be gained by criticizing Sullivan at this point.

In light of the events occurring during his previous visit two days earlier, Sergeant Sullivan was now quite obviously puzzled over Eliza's reaction to the news her father was about to arrested on federal charges. He said, "Unfortunately, there is more to the story."

I said, "Let me guess. There is also the unresolved issue of a fraudulent kidnapping charge in the files of the Santa Barbara Police Department."

"Your guess is correct, Mister Kinney. That report establishes a pattern of similar criminal activity. It is certain to become part of the investigation."

"Sergeant, I think we definitely need to have that off-the-record conversation you mentioned. I suggest we go into my office and get comfortable. Eliza, I know you aren't feeling very good about things right now, but I think it is important to enlighten Sergeant Sullivan on some points. Are you up to doing that?"

Eliza looked at me. Her big brown eyes were as troubled as I had ever seen them, but she said, "I'll try, darling."

Realizing the office would be one chair short for the three of us, I started to pick up one of the chairs still in the kitchen. The pain of lifting the chair surprised me and I involuntarily winced.

Sullivan quickly said, "Let me get that chair, Mister Kinney."

When we were all seated around my table/desk in the office, I took Eliza's hand in mine and said, "Sergeant Sullivan, I don't think it will come as any surprise to you if I say Miss Hamm has been through quite a lot during the past few days."

Sullivan said, "No, Mister Kinney, I can see that. I can also see you have been through a few rough moments yourself."

Trying to keep the conversation on the light side, I said, "True, but my physical discomfort is not directly related to the matter you have come to discuss with us, so we can set that aside for now. The crux of the matter from Miss Hamm's point of view is that, regardless of what her father has done, Mister Hamm is still her father."

Sullivan nodded. "I can understand that."

"And as you can imagine, Miss Hamm and I have discussed her father's behavior at length, trying to understand why he has done the things he has done. Eliza, would you care to tell Sergeant Sullivan what we have concluded?"

She looked at me, and then took a deep breath. "Sergeant Sullivan, by nature my father is not a bad man, of that I am certain. Knowing that leads Lester and me to think father has suffered some kind of mental breakdown that is affecting his behavior, causing him to do awful things."

As if saying all those words wore her out, Eliza sat back in her chair and looked at me. I gave her a "well done" nod and said, "Sergeant Sullivan, we understand that determining a suspect's sanity is not your job, but I hope you will take our assessment of the situation into consideration in your handling of the case. Also, knowing what we believe has happened might help you understand Eliza's reluctance to make a statement that is likely to contribute to the criminal case against him."

Sergeant Sullivan looked from me to Eliza. "It does help me understand Miss Hamm's predicament, and your assessment of the situation also might provide the answer to a question that has been bothering me."

I asked, "What question is that?"

"I have been curious as to Mister Hamm's motives for doing what he has done. Some kind of mental problem is a plausible explanation for why he did things a sane person would realize were not only illegal, but also could not solve any problem."

I agreed. "It certainly seems that way to me."

Eliza then asked, "When will you arrest father?"

Sullivan said, "Soon. I have an arrest warrant issued by Judge Williams in my automobile and I intend to serve it and make the arrest when I leave here. I wanted to speak with the two of you first, and I am glad I did."

I asked, "Will he be eligible for bail?"

"Yes, bail could be granted after arraignment, but because we are looking at federal crimes, the arraignment will not happen for at least forty-eight hours."

"I see."

"Now, I am afraid I must get on with my duties, unpleasant though they may be."

I said, "Sergeant Sullivan, before you leave, I have an unofficial problem with which I am hoping you might be able to unofficially help me."

"If I can, certainly."

"Am I correct in assuming that adoption records are kept on file in the County Clerk's office?"

"If the adoption occurred in this county, yes."

"Are those records public or private?"

"According to the State of California they are public records, but the Clerk's office is extremely protective of the information in those records. In order for anyone to obtain the information they contain the person must fill out a form that is reviewed by the

County Clerk, himself. If there is any question in his mind that the requested information might be used in a harmful way, the request usually is misplaced or permanently delayed."

"Does that procedure apply to police officers as well as the general public?"

"Generally not. What are you getting at Mister Kinney?"

"Sergeant Sullivan, I have in my possession knowledge of what appears be a heinous crime, actually, several heinous crimes, but I do not yet have the necessary evidence to support a formal charge. Three pieces of information from a particular adoption record would allow me to verify the accuracy of my information and turn the matter over to you for criminal investigation. The nature of the crimes and the people involved are such, however, that I dare not say anything about it, even to you, without first making sure of my facts."

Sullivan stared at me across the table for several seconds. "All right, Mister Kinney, I owe you and I am willing to trust the voracity of what you are saying. What facts do you need and what is the name of the adoptee?"

Looking the Sergeant straight in the eye, I said, "The facts I need are a date of birth, the date of the adoption, and the names of the birth parents. The adoptee's name is Aurora Abernathy."

Both Eliza and Sullivan looked shocked, but I knew they had different reasons for being surprised. Sullivan shook his head. "Mister Kinney, you are treading on very thin ice. I hope you know that."

"I do. That is why I need to do this carefully and discreetly."

"All right, Mister Kinney, I will stop by the County Clerk's office this afternoon and see what I can do, but I want your promise that any information I give you will remain between us."

"You have my promise, Sergeant."

With that, Sergeant Sullivan turned to leave, but he stopped before he was out of the room. "Would you like me to carry that chair back into the kitchen?"

I smiled my appreciation of his consideration. "No, thank you, Sergeant. I think Eliza and I can manage it."

After seeing Sergeant Sullivan to the door, Eliza and I successfully moved the chair back to its place at the kitchen table. That done, I began walking back to the office, but Eliza stopped me in the hallway.

"Lester, what on earth are you up to with that business about Aurora Abernathy's adoption papers?"

"Come on into the office so I can sit and I'll tell you."

We sat at the desk again and I said, "Simply stated, what I am up to is this: We already know Estelle is a lesbian. If we can prove Aurora Abernathy was under age at the time of her adoption, we can put Estelle away for years on a variety of charges. Homosexual behavior is a crime in the State of California, as is statutory rape, regardless of the participants' genders."

Eliza's face turned pale. "Lester, if you do what you are planning, I will no longer be able to show my face in Santa Barbara!"

"Eliza, how old were you when you worked for Estelle?"

"I had just turned eighteen."

"Then you were the victim of statutory rape. However, that you were ever involved with Estelle in any way need not become public knowledge. There are certain to be other young women she molested."

She nodded slowly. "Yes, there were. I even know who two of them are, but still . . . ."

"Eliza, we will do this one step at a time, and we will do nothing unless we both agree it is the right thing to do."

"Lester, this is scaring me, I mean REALLY scaring me. Can't we just go away and forget Estelle Abernathy?"

"That may still turn out to be the best course of action, but even leaving Santa Barbara would be safer if we could take Estelle out of the picture."

Eliza's expression told me she did not think that was possible, but she said, "I guess so."

"I have another question for you. How well do you know Mabel Stafford?"

"The *Tribune's* archivist? We are good friends. I know her not only through my father, but also through the library. We call on one another frequently for information. Why are you asking about Mabel?"

"After you helped me research Estelle's background at the library, my next stop was the *Tribune* morgue. When I mentioned Estelle Abernathy to Mabel, she reacted with what I felt was animosity. I would like to know why. Would you be willing to set up a meeting with Mabel so we can ask her?"

In the next moment or so I got the definite idea Eliza knew exactly why Mabel did not care for Estelle, but all she said was, "I guess so. I'll call Mabel."

I slid the telephone across to Eliza and she dialed the *Tribune* office. The long and the short of their conversation was Eliza told Mabel she was no longer living at home and missed seeing her friends. She invited Mabel over for dinner. Mabel accepted.

After Eliza disconnected the call, she said, "Lester, if we are right about father having a mental breakdown, it brings up another problem we haven't discussed."

"What problem is that?"

Her expression turned sad and she said, "Insanity can be hereditary. That might be why I have so much trouble maintaining my mental balance."

I shook my head. "Eliza, you are no longer having trouble maintaining your mental balance. You are doing fine."

"I do fine with you here to hold my hand and get me out of trouble, but on my own it is different story."

"Eliza, with all the catastrophes we've experienced lately, anyone would get a little unbalanced."

"Lester, we have to take this seriously. If I have a mental sickness, we can never have children. We should not even be talking about marriage."

"Darling, believe me, you are perfectly sane."

"Am I? Was it sane for me to have sexual relations with a woman, an old woman, I didn't even like? Was it sane to move in with a man I had known less than a week? Is it sane for me to try to seduce you every time we are in bed when you have made it clear you don't want me that way? Is it sane . . . ."

"Eliza! Stop it!"

It was the first and only time I ever raised my voice to Eliza and it got her attention. She sat there trembling and staring at me with her big brown eyes open wide.

"Now, please listen carefully to what I am saying. Last night you saw me come home all beat up because I was not smart enough to see the truth in what you told me, and you just learned your father is being carted off to jail for trying to control your life. Those are not normal daily occurrences. They are horrible experiences that would distress anyone. It is perfectly reasonable for you to feel confused and upset. That is extraordinarily normal behavior under extremely abnormal circumstances.

"I love you very much and I will do anything you ask, but first you must get your thoughts straightened out and make an intelligent decision as to how we should proceed with our relationship, and you will have to make that decision entirely on your own. I cannot make it for you. So please go into the bedroom and think things through. When you have decided what you really want to do, come back and tell me. Now, go."

"Lester . . . ."

"Go, Eliza."

She got up from her chair and stood there looking at me for another long moment before spinning around and running into the bedroom. I sat there listening to her sobbing in the bedroom and feeling very low about what I had just done to the woman I love. I am certainly not a doctor. I have never even read a book by Sigmund Freud, but I knew I had to get Eliza thinking clearly. I just hoped I'd done the right thing and not made matters worse.

I looked at my watch after Eliza had been in the bedroom for quite a while, and I was surprised to see it wasn't even eleven o'clock yet. Time was passing slowly. I thought it ought to be at least the middle of the afternoon.

A little later, Eliza came softly to the office door. I looked up and she said, "Lester, my thoughts are straightened out and I know what I want to do."

"All right, Eliza. Come sit down and tell me what you decided."

She had taken her shoes off at some point and her bare feet made no sound walking across the hardwood floor. Eliza sat down and folded her hands on the desk like a school girl.

We sat there looking at each other for what seemed a long time before Eliza said, "Lester, what I want is what we talked about last Sunday. I want us to share our lives together as equal partners with each of us carrying our own weight, but also helping each other through the hard times, just as I helped you last night, and you helped me this morning. Is that still acceptable to you?"

"It is. Can you tell me how you came to that decision?"

"Yes. I have told you I seemed to know we were meant for each other from the day we met. With each day since then I have learned things about you to make that feeling stronger. You are not perfect, I know that. I am certainly not perfect either, but I do believe we are perfect for each other."

"That sounds like a thoughtful decision, but tell me how we should deal with situations like this morning when life heaps more on you than you feel you can handle."

"If the load gets too heavy, I become panicky and I can't seem to think straight. I think what I need when that happens is a mental slap in the face just like the one you gave me a little while ago."

"I hope you know I got no enjoyment out of that."

Eliza smiled a little for the first time since coming back to the office. "I know you didn't, Lester. I could see the pain in your eyes. Seeing that pain is one of the things that helped me get my thoughts straight. It seemed to me that if you were willing to endure that pain for me, I could do the same for you."

"All right, I have one more question. Earlier you asked if it was sane for you to try to seduce me every time we were in bed, even when I have made it clear I don't want you in that way. Do you remember saying that?"

She nodded. "Yes, I remember saying that."

"Do you really believe I don't want you sexually?"

"No, I know for an absolute fact you do want me. That's not something you could hide even if you wanted to. I was lashing out at everything and everyone then. I know I hurt you when I said that, and I know you asked me not to say 'I am sorry,' but if there is anything I am really and truly sorry for it is hurting you with the thoughtless things I have said when I was so wrapped up in my own misery that I gave no consideration to your feelings."

I slid my hand across the table and she took it. "Eliza, this is one of the most rational conversations you and I have had about us. That pleases me because it tells me your sanity is very much intact. I hope it helps you know that as well."

"It does, darling. I love you for at least a hundred reasons, and one of those reasons is the belief you have in me."

Smiling, I said, "I also love you for at least a hundred reasons, not the least of which is you are the most beautiful woman I have ever met, both on the outside and on the inside.

FIFTEEN

Tuesday - September 11, 1928

After a lunch of bologna sandwiches and more of Laura Scudder's potato chips, I cleared the table, and Eliza stood staring into the pantry cabinet. She was shaking her head.

"What's the matter? Do we have mice?"

"Worse. We don't have anything suitable to serve for dinner tonight. At least, not suitable to serve a guest."

"I take it bologna sandwiches don't make the grade."

"Most decidedly not. Would you mind if I took the car to the market?"

"Yes."

Eliza was surprised by my answer. I said, "We have a deal, remember? Whither thou goest, so go I."

"I know, darling, but I hate to put you through an expedition to Piggly Wiggly in your condition."

I laughed. "My condition? You make it sound as if I'm pregnant or something."

"I certainly hope not! That's my job. Okay, I'll make a list. How does swiss steak sound?"

"A multinational menu!"

She gave me a look of exasperation. "You goof, swiss steak has nothing to do with Switzerland. The name comes from the way the meat is prepared for cooking. It gets pounded in flour with a hammer. That is called 'swissing. You do have a hammer, I hope."

"Sure. I'll even wipe some of the dirt off of it."

"You'll clean all of the dirt off of it, please."

Sitting at the table with a notepad and pencil, Eliza said, "Now, let's see . . . three pounds of top round steak should be plenty. Then we need a large can of puréed tomatoes, and box of spaghetti. I think we have everything else. Oh, a garlic clove."

"I'm sure glad you know how to do this cooking stuff. If it were up to me, Mabel would get a hot dog and like it."

"See? There's another advantage to having me around."

"Okay, I'm sold."

"You are a wise man. Now we had better get going. Swiss steak has to cook for a while."

An hour and two stops later, we were back in the kitchen unpacking the makings for Swiss Steak Ala Eliza with strawberries and cream for dessert. The second stop we made at Eliza's insistence was a home goods store where we purchased two more coffee mugs at a total cost of ten cents.

Next the boss sent me out to clean my hammer while she did a great deal of chopping and dicing of vegetables and what I took to be spices. This was followed by beating a couple of defenseless top round steaks into submission with the hammer on a breadboard. During this process flour flew everywhere. Finally, Eliza consigned the meat and other ingredients to our one and only skillet on a back burner of the stove.

Joining me at the kitchen table from which I'd been watching the proceedings, Eliza said, "Okay, we are done for now. All I have left to do is clean the strawberries and cook the spaghetti, which only takes a few minutes."

"Thank you for all the work I'm putting you through with this harebrained scheme."

"Mabel is worth the effort. She is a truly nice person. I am glad to have her as a friend."

"She seemed quite nice to me."

We sat there for a few minutes just looking at each other. Eliza had a smudge of flour on her nose, and it somehow made her look even cuter.

"Lester?"

"Yes, Eliza?"

"Is everything between us really as wonderful as it seems right now?"

"I wouldn't be surprised. Why do you ask?

She glanced down at the table for just a second, and then looked back at me. "I guess I'm still feeling a little insecure. I really tried your patience this morning and I just cannot believe anyone can be as forgiving as you are."

I smiled. "Well, Eliza, I will let you in on a little secret."

"What?"

"I'm not really forgiving. I just can't resist a beautiful woman with flour on her nose."

She looked puzzled. "Flour?" Then the light dawned and she wiped at the tip of her nose. "Oh, good grief! I was being serious."

"Well, stop being so serious. I am enjoying every minute I

spend with you, even going to the Wiggly Piggy. You ought to try it."

Eliza jumped up and threw her arms around my shoulders. "Okay, Mister Kinney, kiss me. That would be extra enjoyable."

"Okay, Miss Hamm. Just don't get any flour on me."

By five-thirty the inside of cottage number ten smelled like a first-rate Italian restaurant. Coming into the kitchen from the bedroom, where I put on a fresh shirt and my dark brown sport jacket, I noticed the table was set, complete with a candle and the third kitchen chair, which had been transported from the office.

Eliza was standing at the stove adjusting the flame under the skillet. Upon seeing me, she said, "My, don't we look handsome!"

"Thank you kindly, ma'am."

"Come over here, handsome man, and be useful while I go in and make myself presentable."

"Okay, what do I do?"

"Just watch the skillet. If the sauce begins to boil instead of simmering like it's doing now, turn the flame down just a little. Okay? I'll be back in a few minutes."

About five minutes later I heard a knock on the door. Then Eliza said from the hallway, I'll get it."

A moment later, Eliza came into the kitchen. She was wearing a dark maroon pleated skirt and a white blouse that looked great on her. She was also carrying an envelope.

I gave her a questioning look and she said, "It was Sergeant Sullivan. He handed this envelope to me and said it was the information you asked for."

Taking the envelope, I said, "I'll put this away for now. We can look at it later. Oh, and by the way, you look even more ravishingly beautiful than usual in that outfit."

Eliza put on her coy expression. "Am I pretty enough to keep your attention from wandering off to other women with flour on their noses?"

"Well," I paused as if thinking about her question. "That would take a lot of pretty, but I think you win by a nose."

"Go put your envelope away, Romeo."

Mabel was expected at six and at precisely that hour by my pocket watch, we heard another knock at the door. Turning up the flame under our largest pot filled water, Eliza said, "That must be Mabel. Would you mind if I get the door?"

"Not at all."

"Thank you. This arrangement of ours is going to take some explaining, and I think we might get off to a better start if I answer the door."

"Have at it, kiddo."

I could hear Eliza welcoming Mabel and Mabel thanking Eliza for inviting her. Then Eliza said, "Come on into our kitchen/dining room."

As they walked through the door, I smiled a welcoming smile and Eliza said, "Mabel, I think you already know Lester."

Mabel said, "Why, yes I do. He is the silver-tongued devil who came down to my basement and gave me so many compliments my feet didn't touch the ground again for two days."

Eliza said, "That's Lester, all right, but he never says anything he doesn't mean, so whatever Lester told you he meant."

I was surprised when Mabel came forward to shake my hand. Apparently there were more liberated women in Santa Barbara than I knew.

"Good evening, Mister Kinney."

"Good evening, Missus Stafford, but I would be honored if you would call me Lester."

Her smile got a little bigger. "All right, Lester, but in return, you must call me Mabel."

"It's a deal, Mabel."

She took an appraising look around the kitchen and said, "This is a lovely little cottage you have here, Lester. I have driven past these garden court apartments many times and often wondered what they are like inside."

I tried not to show surprise that she knew the apartment was mine, and not Eliza's, as I said, "This was one of the first places I looked at when I arrived in town. It struck me as an ideal place for a guy on a budget to live."

From the vicinity of the stove Eliza said, "Dinner will be ready in just a few minutes. Take a seat at the table and relax while I finish getting things ready."

Mabel said, "Thank you. It seems I have been on my feet all day. Things were in something of a turmoil at the paper today."

To get out of Eliza's way and give my aching muscles a break, I held a chair for Mabel and then sat opposite her. In response to her comment about turmoil at the *Tribune*, I said, "I can understand why matters were a bit more chaotic than usual at the *Tribune*."

Mabel gave me what authors like to call a "knowing look." "I figured you were aware of what went on today."

I nodded and she said, "Lester, years of working in the *Tribune's* morgue have endowed me with an almost overwhelming and occasionally obnoxious curiosity. Fortunately, Eliza and I share a very open friendship. In other words, we seldom keep secrets from one another. Am I right, Eliza?"

Stirring the spaghetti pot, Eliza said, "You are absolutely right, Mabel."

"So, Lester, if I seem nosey, I come by it naturally, particularly where a friend's welfare is concerned."

I grinned. "All right, Mabel ask me what you want to know and you will get straight honest answers."

To Eliza, Mabel said, "Eliza, where did you find this wonderful man? I want to go there and see if there are any more like him."

Eliza laughed. "Actually he found me, in the library of all places."

"Okay, Lester, I'll ask the obvious question. Why is my friend living in your apartment instead of at home with her father?"

I saw Eliza turn to say something, but she stopped when I held my hand up.

"Simply said, Mabel, Eliza came to live here with me when the situation with her father at home became untenable. I will leave any further explanations of that situation in Eliza's hands because I do not feel right about discussing her private family matters."

"All right, Lester, I accept that. Now please tell me your intentions concerning my friend."

I looked at Eliza. "Shall I answer that one, or would you rather do it?"

She grinned at me. "You're doing fine, darling."

Turning back to Mabel, I said, "In general, my intentions concerning Eliza are to make the most wonderful woman in the world also the happiest woman in the world. Furthermore, we plan to enter the state of holy matrimony as soon as it is possible for us to do so."

Mabel seemed pleased with what I was saying. "And what will make that happy event possible?'

"In a word, employment. As I am sure you are aware by now, Frederick Hamm sacked me over the weekend."

"Yes, Lester, I heard he discharged you. People at the *Tribune* are genuinely puzzled by that. We all thought Mister Hamm was quite fond of you."

Eliza arrived at the table with three servings of Swiss steak. "What would you all like to drink? I plan to make coffee later, but if you would like some now . . . ."

Mabel said, "Water is fine for us, Eliza. Sit down and enjoy this delicious dinner. It smells heavenly."

We all dug in and the swiss steak really was delicious. After a few minutes of serious eating, Mabel said, "Lester, I have already asked you more intimate questions than I have any right to, and you have been very courteous about satisfying my curiosity. The only question I have left . . . well, the only question I have enough nerve to ask, is why were you fired?"

I was deciding how to respond when Eliza said, "That was entirely my fault."

Mabel looked at Eliza with surprise. "Your fault?"

"Yes, it is kind of a complicated story. Lester took me as his guest to Estelle Abernathy's reception Saturday night and some old history came up, history you already know about."

Softly, Mabel said, "Oh, oh."

"I was already upset, and then I found out Father had warned Lester about taking me out because of that history. I didn't even think he knew about it, but he does. Anyway, that upset me so much I knew I couldn't go home and face him. Lester and I were already falling in love by then, and I took advantage of that by asking if I could stay here . . . strictly on a platonic basis. He agreed after warning me it might not be the smartest thing I could do.

"Lester also insisted I call home and tell Father where I was so he wouldn't be worried about me. When father found out I was here, he blew up, demanding Lester bring me right home. Lester was very daring and told Father the decision to come home was entirely up to me. Father threatened to fire Lester if he didn't bring me home immediately, and Lester said his job was unimportant compared to my welfare.

"Then Father showed up here and I made matters even worse by behaving like a . . . well, behaving in a very unladylike manner. From that Father was convinced we were being anything but platonic.

"The saddest part is that, aside from sleeping in the same bed because it is the only bed in the cottage, we have not done anything for which we need to be ashamed."

Eliza looked at me with a soft smile and took my hand. Mabel looked at me, too. "It would seem, Lester, that you are the hero of that sad tale."

"I'm afraid I don't feel much like a hero."

"Well you are most certainly a hero in Eliza's eyes and, I must say, in mine, as well."

I smiled. Thank you for those kind words, Mabel. Now, if you don't mind, I would like to ask you a frank question."

Chuckling, Mabel said, "All right, Lester, it's your turn, as long as you don't ask my age."

"A gentleman never asks a lady her age. No, what I want to ask about is something that happened when I saw you down in the *Tribune* morgue. At one point you said Estelle Abernathy's name with what sounded like extreme distaste. Would I be correct in assuming that was because you knew about the 'history' to which Eliza referred a few minutes ago?"

"Yes, that and a general dislike for people who think they are better than everyone else based on the size of their bank account, but mostly because of what that awful woman did to Eliza and other young girls. Now, Lester, I have one more question for you."

Eliza interrupted. "Hey, don't I get to ask any questions?"

With a laugh, I said, "No. You are a librarian. You already know everything."

Eliza stood up and swatted me with her napkin. "We have strawberries and cream and for dessert. Does that sound good to you, Mabel?"

"It sounds wonderful, Eliza."

"All right, strawberries and cream coming up, and I'll put the coffee on. It's not quite as good as yours, Mabel, but it is close."

Mabel said, "Eliza, you have so many other amazing virtues and talents, the fact that you make decent coffee is like frosting on a cake. Don't you agree, Lester?"

"Oh, very much so."

"All right, Lester, now my last question. From the look of your face and from the way you moved earlier, it is pretty obvious that someone has given you a thorough walloping. Am I right?"

I glanced at Eliza and she, in turn, glanced at Mabel. Their unspoken communication was quite effective.

Mabel quickly said, "Oh, oh. I seemed to have stepped into a sensitive area. I withdraw the question."

"No, Mabel, I promised you answers and I will keep my word. Yes, someone gave me, as you put it, a thorough walloping."

"Lester, you strike me as a man who would be difficult to wallop, so I am going to put a lot of random pieces of the puzzle together and guess the walloping you received was at the hands of a man trained in the art of hurting people, a man of the sort a wealthy woman might hire as a bodyguard. Unless you tell me otherwise, I will assume my conclusion is correct and we will leave the matter there."

"Thank you, Mabel. You are very adept at solving puzzles."

As we enjoyed the strawberries, our conversation turned to

small talk. After dessert, our friendly conversation continued while I drank my coffee left-handed. Eliza was holding my right hand tightly, but there was nothing in her expression to indicate any anxiety. She appeared quite happy and holding my hand was a part of that happiness. Mine, too.

The evening was winding down, and Mabel said she needed to be going home. There was, however, something she wanted to tell us before she left.

"Eliza and Lester, this has been a very pleasant evening. I always enjoy spending time with you, Eliza, and getting to know you, Lester, has been a pure joy,"

I said, "Thank you, Mabel. Getting to know you has been enjoyable for me, as well. I mean that sincerely."

"Lester, I have always thought of Eliza as the daughter I never had, and now, I hope you will not object if I think of you as the son I never had. Individually, you are both special people, but together, you are the living example of what I imagine the Good Lord intended when He gave us the capacity to love.

"Over the years I have known many people who were deeply in love, including my beloved late husband and myself, but never before have I encountered a love between and man and a woman that is so strong I literally felt it the moment I walked into the room. Children, cherish and nurture the gift God has given you."

Eliza and I promised we would do exactly what Mabel suggested. Then I saw her to her automobile out on the street. I held the car door open for her and Mabel climbed into to her two-year-old Ford four-door sedan, but before I closed the door, she said, "Lester, I am not telling you anything you don't already know when I say Eliza is sometimes a troubled young woman. Until she met you, life had not treated her fairly, yet despite that, she is still a loving, caring person. Earlier you said you intended to make Eliza the happiest woman in the world. Please see that you do that for her, for yourself, and for me. Goodnight, Lester."

When I went back into cottage number ten, I found Eliza at the kitchen sink washing the dishes. I hugged her, kissed her, and picked up a towel to dry the dishes as she washed them.

As we worked side by side, Eliza asked, "Now that you have come to know Mabel better, what do you think of her?"

"I think she is a good, kindly person and a wonderful friend to have."

"Then you can see why she is so important to me?"

"Yes, I can.'

"Mabel has been part mother to me, part confidant, and my

best friend in the world until I met you."

"Eliza, I think there is room in your heart for two best friends. I am pleased to share that space with Mabel."

"Oh, Lester, you do understand!"

"I think I do."

With the dishes done, we decided to turn in. Eliza went to get ready for bed while I did my nightly walk around the house to make sure the doors and windows were locked tight and that all the lights were off.

As I walked into the bedroom, Eliza came out of the bathroom in my faded blue shirt. She ran up to me and said, "I have been very inconsiderate of your discomfort this evening, Lester. How do you feel?"

Slipping out of my shirt, I said, "Certainly better than I felt last night."

Eliza gently ran her hand over my stomach. "I hope so, darling. Please hurry to bed. I especially need to feel you close tonight."

When I slid into bed and pulled the covers up, I felt her warm body slid against me. She raised up so I could put my arm around her in our now standard sleeping position. Then she gently rested her head against my chest and she whispered, "You do, you know."

"I do what, kiddo?"

"You make me the happiest woman on earth."

"I'm glad, but be sure you mention that to Mabel occasionally."

"Why should I mention that to Mabel?"

"Because she told me I need to keep that promise for you, for myself, and for her."

Eliza giggled. "Then I will give her regular reports on how you are doing in that department."

"I hope you do. I wouldn't want Mabel to be displeased with me."

"There is no chance of that, darling. You won her heart tonight."

We just enjoyed being close for a while, and then Eliza said, "Do you really believe God meant for us to be together like Mabel said?"

"I can't say for sure because I don't know why He would think I deserve a woman like you, but it surely feels like somebody up there has His eyes on us."

"That's how I feel, too."

"Eliza, do you think Mabel believes we have kept our love

platonic, even while sleeping in the same bed?"

"I'm sure she does. For one thing, she knows I never lie to her, and for another, there is no reason for me to say that unless it is true. Besides, Mabel would not think less of us if it were not true."

"Good. I don't care what most people think, but Mabel is different."

"You don't know how happy I am to hear you say that."

Eliza propped herself on her pillow and slid up to kiss me. I noted that she did not rest her leg on mine this time. I was surprised to find myself feeling a little disappointed. The kiss she gave me, however, was pure, tender and so full of love I could feel it down to my toes.

"Good night, darling Lester. I love you with all of my being. Please dream sweet dreams about us tonight."

"Goodnight, Eliza, my love. Sleep well and know that I love you more than words can say."

"I do know that, Lester. I honestly know it and feel it.

SIXTEEN

Wednesday - September 12, 1928

Wednesday morning I awoke in an empty bed and to the smell of fresh coffee. I was also in considerably less pain than I'd been in twenty-four hours earlier, so much so that a hot shower and two more aspirin tablets left me feeling fairly spry.

When I walked into the kitchen, Eliza greeted me with a kiss and a cup of her proper coffee.

"Good morning, sleepyhead."

Nodding, I said, "I know. I saw the bedside clock when I woke up. I can't believe I slept past eight."

"You needed rest, darling. That's why I didn't wake you when I got up. How are you feeling?"

"Apparently a good sleep helped. I'm not quite up to running the hundred yard dash, but I feel much better than yesterday morning."

"Good! I'm tired of giving you gentle hugs. I want to squeeze the daylights out of you!"

"Put that on the calendar for first thing tomorrow morning and I'll be ready."

Her smile lit up the room. "Don't think I won't, mister."

"How did you sleep last night, kiddo?"

"Very well. I had no bad dreams and woke up feeling really refreshed. I think that talk we had yesterday helped a lot."

"I suspect spending time with Mabel last night helped, too. You seemed very relaxed and content when we went to bed."

"That is exactly how I felt. You are very observant."

"When it comes to you, I feel as much or more than I see or hear."

Eliza looked puzzled. "I'm not sure I understand. How does that work?"

"I'm not sure how it works. It is as if we are on the same radio wavelength and I receive messages from the way you stand or the tone of your voice or the tilt of your head. It isn't a mystical power or anything weird like that. In fact, I bet you do the same thing all the time without realizing it."

She slowly nodded her understanding. "You know, I think I do. I never thought about it before, but it is like a sixth sense tuned to you."

"The other thing about that sense is, if I try too hard, it gets messed up. I imagine things that are not really there. It only seems to work on a subconscious level."

"Sometimes you completely amaze me, Lester. You think of ways to describe things I would never come up with in a million years."

"That works both ways, kiddo. You have ways of thinking and doing things I could never duplicate, but I enjoy learning what you teach me that way. Maybe that is why we fit together so well. Individually we are two separate people, but together we are a whole that is more than the sum of its parts."

"Whatever it is, I like it."

"Me, too. Shall we go into the office and see what Sergeant Sullivan brought us last night?"

With a stop at the coffee pot for refills, we headed into the office and I opened the envelope Sullivan left for me. The single sheet of paper inside it made very interesting reading.

```
Adoptee: ABERNATHY, AURORA
Birth Father: DELGADO, ARMANDO
Birth Mother: (unknown), MARIA
Birth Date: NOVEMBER 28, 1910
Date of Adoption: DECEMBER 1, 1925
```

Looking over my shoulder, Eliza said, "Armando is Aurora's father! I never would have guessed that in a hundred years."

"I guess it makes sense in some twisted way. Now let's do some arithmetic. If Aurora was born in 1910, she was adopted right after her fifteenth birthday."

"Correct, and she will still be a minor for another three years, at least technically."

"Well, there is half of what we need. Now we need to put this together with evidence of Estelle's sexual proclivities and hand the whole works over to Sergeant Sullivan."

Eliza seated herself across the desk from me and said, "That's a case of proving something everyone in town already knows, but don't we have to prove Estelle . . . did bad things to Aurora?"

I shook my head. "Unless Aurora comes forward herself, I don't know how that would be possible. I think showing that an underage female is living in the home of a lesbian with no supervision is enough for legal action to have Aurora taken out of Estelle's home."

"Yes, but couldn't the fact that Armando is her father and he lives there too be considered a form of supervision?"

"No jury is going to buy that. If Armando was any kind of a decent father, he wouldn't permit his daughter to be there in the first place. Plus, Armando is presumably paid by Estelle to do what she tells him to do, which hardly makes him an impartial observer."

"All right, but how do you prove Estelle is a lesbian? Even if you got one or two of the girls she . . . molested to come forward, it would be a case of their word against Estelle's."

"True. It will take something with a little more authority behind it. I'm not sure what form that would take yet." At that point a thought occurred to me. "Eliza, do you think the nuns at Saint Andria's are aware of Estelle's preference for young women?"

Eliza looked thoughtful. "That is a good question. I can't imagine they would condone the adoption of a young girl by a lesbian, even in exchange for a fifty-thousand dollar donation. On the other hand, it is also hard to imagine Saint Andria's overlooking something everyone else in town knows or suspects."

"Even if they were looking the other way, the threat of a public scandal would get their attention in a big hurry."

"Lester, what are you thinking?"

"I'm trying to think of a way to find out what the Sisters of Saint Andria know and don't know, and if they don't know about Estelle, how I can reveal the facts to them."

Eliza frowned. "Anything you say to them is bound to get back to Estelle. Is there a way to do it anonymously?"

"I don't think so. Information from anonymous sources is naturally suspect. I think the information would have to come from a known and credible source."

Eliza gave her head what looked like an involuntary shake. "Lester, after what happened Monday night, I already feel as if we are living on borrowed time. If word somehow gets back to Estelle that we have been snooping in the adoption records . . . I'm sure Sergeant Sullivan was careful and all, but if someone in the County Clerk's office saw him and told Estelle, Armando will come after you with orders to do more than beat you up. Telling anyone, like the Sisters at Saint Andria's, what you suspect would be suicide."

I sighed. "You are right. I wish I knew more about the

Catholic Church. There must be somebody high enough up who could handle this discreetly."

Eliza looked as if she was trying to decide whether or not to say something. Finally, she made up her mind. "There is one man I know who might be in such a position, Monsignor O'Boylan. I think he is a Bishop or something like that.

"I know him from the library because he loves mystery novels and he comes in looking for books by authors like Dorothy Sayers and especially G. K. Chesterton. He thinks I'm the cat's pajamas because I find authors for him he has not yet read. Last time he was in I suggested *The Mysterious Affair at Styles* by Agatha Christie. It's a mystery with a new main character, a Belgian detective."

"Do you think he would agree to meet with me privately?"

"He might agree to meet with the two of us because he knows me, but what would you say to him?"

"I would lay out the facts and the suppositions we have about Estelle, and see how he reacts."

Eliza frowned. "Would you want me to tell him about my . . . experiences with Estelle?"

"No. I would never ask you to do something that painful."

She looked at me for several moments, and then said, "Do you have a Santa Barbara telephone directory?"

I picked up the directory I was given when the telephone was installed. "Right here."

Eliza began leafing through the directory. "I remember the address on his library card is the Pastoral Center on La Colina Road. Here it is. The number is nine-six-six."

She wrote the number down, and then asked, "When do you want to do this?"

"The sooner the better."

Eliza nodded and dialed the telephone number. After speaking to two or three people, she said, "Hello Monsignor O'Boylan, this is Eliza Hamm from the Santa Barbara library. Do you remember me?"

After a pause, Eliza said, "I'm doing all right, but my fiancé and I have a serious dilemma involving the church on our hands and I would really appreciate it if we could meet with you privately to discuss the situation."

Apparently she said the right things because a few minutes later we had an appointment to meet with Monsignor O'Boylan at one o'clock. The location of our meeting was to be the rose garden adjacent to the old Mission Santa Barbara.

I said, "Good work, Eliza. Thank you."

"You're welcome, darling. I sure hope this works."

"Me, too."

"I guess you know I'm getting scared again." After a brief pause she said, "Terrified is a better word."

I studied her face for a long time, long enough to make her say, "What? What are you thinking, Lester?"

Standing up, I said, "Come on, kiddo. Let's go pack a couple of bags. I think it's time for us to get out of Santa Barbara for a few days."

Eliza's smile instantly lit up the room. "Really? Are you sure?"

"I'm positive. We can make a stop at my bank on our way to the Mission so we have some cash and we can leave right after we meet this Monsignor O'Boylan. At that point we will have done what we can do for now and all that remains is waiting to see what grows from the seeds we've sewn. We don't need to be here to do that."

In addition to two suitcases packed with clothes for a week or so, I carried my typewriter and a few stationery supplies out and stowed them in the Chevrolet's trunk. Depending on what the Bishop had to say, this might be a working vacation. Either way, we picked a beautiful day for it. The usual thin morning overcast was gone and the sun was shining brightly in a cloudless sky.

Eliza heated up the leftover swiss steak for our lunch. Then we made quick work of the lunch dishes and I walked around making sure everything in the house was turned off and secure.

Around twelve-fifteen I locked the door to cottage number ten and we drove up to State Street, where I turned south and traveled seven blocks to the Central Bank at State and De La Guerra Streets. Eliza waited in the car while I ran into the bank and made a withdrawal. Since I had almost none of the money Clarence Storche paid me for the oil spill story left, I withdrew fifty dollars.

My banking completed, we made our way north and west of the downtown area to the old mission and parked alongside the formal rose garden. It was about five minutes before one when we locked the Chevrolet and strolled past a fountain and into the garden.

Eliza said, "Monsignor O'Boylan is here already. That's him sitting on the bench over there."

The older gentleman sitting on the bench wore a black cassock with reddish-purple piping around the edges. It seemed Bishops ate well. Monsignor O'Boylan was well padded. His sparse hair was gray and his complexion fair.

He stood and made a small waving gesture toward Eliza. As she approached, he said, "Good afternoon, Miss Hamm. It is nice to see you again."

"Good afternoon, Monsignor O'Boylan. I would like you to meet my fiancé, Lester Kinney."

The Bishop turned to me and I could tell by his reaction he was startled by the large bruise and cut on my face. He did not offer to shake hands. For all I knew shaking the hand of a Bishop was a mortal sin in the Catholic Church.

"Good afternoon, sir. Thank you for taking time from what I am sure must be a very busy schedule to see us."

"It is my pleasure, Mister Kinney. Shall we stroll through the garden while you tell me about the dilemma you mentioned, Miss Hamm?"

"Monsignor, I want Lester tell you about the dilemma. He is much better at explaining things than I am."

"All right, Mister Kinney, what is your dilemma involving the Catholic Church?"

As we walked along dirt path through the garden, I began my explanation. "First, please forgive me for not knowing the proper form for addressing you. I was raised in the Methodist Church."

"That is quite all right, Mister Kinney. I understand completely. I sometimes wonder if we of the Catholic Church have more rules than are really necessary."

I said, "As to our dilemma, I would prefer to discuss it as a hypothetical situation for the moment. I think you'll understand why."

"All right, son. Go ahead."

"Let us say there is an agency of the Catholic Church providing for the care and adoption of orphaned children. Let us also say that a few years ago, three to be exact, that agency arranged for the adoption of a fifteen-year-old girl by an unmarried woman of substantial means.

"Now let us suppose that the home provided by the woman is an extremely immoral and dangerous environment for the young girl. Finally, let us add to the situation that the woman has made very generous and substantial donations to the Catholic agency that arranged the adoption.

"My hypothetical question is this: if the Catholic Church became aware of such a situation and determined that the circumstances were as I have described them, what would the church be likely to do?"

Monsignor O'Boylan was strolling between Eliza and I with his hands clasped behind his back. "Mister Kinney, let me ask one or two questions to clarify your hypothetical situation. First, why would a person who had evidence of such a situation not take the matter to civil authorities, like the police?"

"That would be the logical thing to do unless the immorality of the home environment were of such a nature that those who witnessed it firsthand were reluctant to come forward and expose themselves to public humiliation."

"I see. Can you be more specific as to the nature of the hypothetical immoral environment, Mister Kinney?"

"I can. Let us say the immorality concerns abnormal intimate behavior. Let us say the woman prefers to be intimate with young women as opposed to men."

The Bishop stopped and turned to face me. "My goodness, Mister Kinney! What you suggest is not just immoral, it is also illegal and a sin abhorred by the Church. Such a claim would require strong evidence, which I gather is not available in your hypothetical situation. Is that correct?"

"Let us say that the woman's immoral proclivities are widely recognized within the community."

"It sounds as if you are saying the only evidence in this hypothetical situation consists of rumors. That being the case, I could not in good conscience take any action in your hypothetical situation. It is not that I doubt you, Mister Kinney. I am confident you believe what you are telling me, but unless a credible witness with firsthand knowledge came forward, well . . . ."

Surprising both the Bishop and me, Eliza said, "Monsignor O'Boylan, would you consider me a credible witness?"

I quickly said, "Eliza, no. We will find another way."

O'Boylan turned to look appraisingly at Eliza as she said, "Lester, this has gone on much too long. Worse, you were badly hurt acting on my behalf. I must speak up."

The Bishop, turned and looked at the damage to my face, and then turned back to Eliza. "You . . . you have firsthand knowledge of this woman's abhorrent behavior?"

"I do. When I graduated from high school four years ago, I . . . ."

I stepped around Monsignor O'Boylan and stood in front of Eliza. "Eliza, please. This isn't necessary. I'm not going to allow that woman to cause you any further . . . ."

The Bishop held his hand up to stop me. "Mister Kinney, I give you my word as a clergyman of the Catholic Church that what

Eliza tells me will go no further without her specific permission. I will treat what this young woman says now as I would the Holy Sacrament of Reconciliation, or as it is known in lay terms, confession."

Defeated, I sighed, and Eliza said, "When I graduated from high school and before I found my job at the library, I responded to a 'help wanted' advertisement in the newspaper. The position was for a clerical assistant to Estelle Abernathy, and I was hired."

I could see the tears forming in Eliza's eyes as she struggled on with her tale. "Within a few days Miss Abernathy began making uninvited advances of a sexual nature. I know I should have left the job then and there, but I needed the work and . . . well, I'm not sure of all the reasons, but I went along with her. By the end of the week she was urging me to move in with her and become . . . become . . . her live-in sexual partner . . . ."

Eliza was sobbing so hard she could not finish her story. As tears ran down her face, I put my arm around her, saying, "That is when she left Estelle Abernathy's employ. Is that what you wanted to hear, O'Boylan? Does that make you happy?"

The Bishop stared at me. "No, Mister Kinney, what Eliza has so painfully told me does not make me happy in any way. It does, however, convince me that the facts of your hypothetical situation are accurate. Tell me, is the injury to your face what she was referring to when she said you were badly hurt acting on her behalf?"

I nodded. "That and other injuries that are not so visible. I was beaten by a man named Armando Delgado at Estelle Abernathy's direction. Delgado is employed as Estelle Abernathy's butler."

Monsignor O'Boylan stood there on the path looking thoughtful while I tried to ease Eliza's pain. Finally he said, "Mister Kinney, Eliza, let me assure you of two things. One, I intend to see that the young adopted woman is removed from Estelle Abernathy's home as soon as possible regardless of the cost to Saint Andria's Orphanage. Two, I will do so as discreetly as possible.

"I should think Miss Abernathy will be cooperative because she will want to avoid civil proceedings and the publicity they generate. Beyond what I intend to do, the Church will surely investigate Saint Andria's to learn what effort they made toward determining that Miss Abernathy was a suitable adoptive parent. There will no doubt be other ramifications from this that I cannot clearly foresee."

"Thank you, Monsignor O'Boylan. Hopefully this will turn out to be an unfortunate incident with a happy ending."

"I will pray for such a happy ending. I also want to thank you for coming forward, especially you, Eliza. I can see how painful this was for you. Perhaps having gotten the matter off your chest so to speak will lift the burden you have carried in your heart for the past few years. I can see that you are sincerely penitent for your sins."

I cringed. If calling what Eliza went through at the hands of Estelle Abernathy a sin is how the Catholic Church comforts victims, I wanted nothing further to do with it. I was tempted to say so, but decided that would be counterproductive. Instead, I said, "Monsignor, Eliza and I are leaving town for a while." Pointing to my face, I added, "I do not want to see her looking like this."

The Bishop said something that sounded like a short prayer and ended with, "May God bless you, my children."

Fifteen minutes later Eliza and I were driving south along the coast on US Route 101. She was sitting close to me, but had not said a single word since we left Santa Barbara. Thinking it might help matters for us to talk things over, I turned off the highway onto a small road that paralleled the beach just south of the Summerland Oil Field.

I parked in a spot alongside the road from which we could see the surf rolling in and switched off the Chevrolet's engine. "Eliza, what are you thinking?"

In a soft voice, she said, "I just feel very confused right now, darling. I know you didn't want me to tell Monsignor O'Boylan what I told him, but I was afraid this horrible thing would go on and on forever if I didn't."

"You made our case for us, but putting you through more pain was the last thing I wanted to do."

"I know that, darling. Besides, you didn't cause the pain. That was my decision."

"Eliza, you are an amazing woman. Do you mind if I ask you one more personal question?"

She frowned a little. "No, darling. I'll answer any question you ask."

"I know, but this question is really personal."

At that point Eliza realized I was playing with her. She put on an impatient look. "I said it was okay. Get on with it!"

I leaned close to her and softly asked, "Will you do me the honor of becoming my wife? I mean like tomorrow?"

Eliza grinned from ear-to-ear. "Well, I should think about it for a while, but since I packed my white dress, yeah, sure."

Then she threw her arms around me. "Oh, Lester, you always know just what to say to put a great big smile on my face!"

We were about to seal the deal with a kiss, when movement beyond the Chevrolet's rear window caught my eye. I turned and saw a dark red Cadillac Phaeton rolling along the road toward us. I knew that Cadillac, and what I knew about that Cadillac was it meant trouble. Without explanation, I turned and started the Chevrolet's engine.

"Get down on the floorboard, Eliza. We've got trouble coming our way."

She took one quick look at me and slid off the seat onto the floorboard. I had the Chevrolet rolling by then, but it was too late. I heard a loud crack and felt a hot, stinging pain in the right side of my neck. Suddenly my vision began to dim like the theater screen when a motion picture fades to black at the end of a scene. The last thought I had was to stomp on the brake pedal and stop the car before it rolled into a drainage ditch alongside the road.

SEVENTEEN

Thursday - September 13, 1928

I awoke to find myself in a hospital room that seemed quite nice. Besides the bed I was in, the room was furnished with a small bureau below a mirror on one of the pale blue walls, a snazzy wicker wastebasket, and a colorful rug with blue and gray stripes. There were two windows, one on each side of the bureau, and a classy overhead light fixture with two electric light bulbs and a pull chain to turn them on and off.

Most important, there was a comfortable chair next to my bed. The chair was particularly important because Eliza was seated in it. To my relief she did not appear to be injured, in fact, she was leaning forward looking at me with a lot of concern in her big brown eyes. Eliza was also holding my hand. I liked that.

"Lester? Are you awake, darling?"

When I answered her my throat hurt a little and my voice sounded rough. "I think so. Are you okay?"

"I'm fine, darling. More important, how do you feel?"

"My throat hurts some and my voice doesn't sound right. I'm also a little groggy, but other than that I feel okay."

"Your throat hurts because you were shot. The emergency doctor says you were lucky. The bullet went in and right out again without hitting anything critical in your neck."

"I'm afraid the doctor's definition of lucky and mine differ somewhat."

Eliza squeezed my hand. "You are alive, darling. I call that lucky. The grogginess is probably due to the fact that twelve hours ago you were in an operating room having the holes in your throat sewn up."

Looking around at my surroundings again, I asked, "Where are we, Cottage Hospital?"

"No. I decided to take you to Ventura. This is Big Sisters Hospital?"

"Big Sisters? That sounds like a club for high school girls."

She smiled. "I'm glad you haven't lost your sense of humor in

148

all of this. The staff here has treated us very nicely. I'm afraid I was pretty panicky when I got you here. The nurses took charge and knew just what to do."

I thought about that for a moment. "When YOU got me here? You drove us to Ventura?"

Eliza looked hurt. "Why does that surprise you? You said I was a good driver, remember?"

"I remember that, but I'm just a little confused about more recent events. What day is this?"

Glancing at her wristwatch, Eliza said, "It's a few minutes after nine Thursday morning. We got here late yesterday afternoon. They rolled you into the operating room at seven last night and it took the doctor about two hours to sew up your wounds."

"I see. I remember being shot, but nothing after that. Maybe you'd better remind me what happened."

"All right, darling, but first, I need to call the nurse. She said I should tell her when you woke up this morning. I will be right back."

Eliza was as good as her word, returning to my room with a kindly looking dark-haired woman dressed in a crisply starched white nurse's uniform. She wore wire-rimmed glasses and a smile."

"Good morning, Mister Kinney. I am Nurse Clara. How are we feeling?"

Her smile was contagious. I smiled back. "Under the circumstances, I guess I am feeling better than I have any right to."

Nurse Clara gave the bandages on my neck an inspection. "I am happy to hear that, Mister Kinney. It seems you are quite fortunate. The damage is minimal considering what might have happened."

With everyone telling me how lucky I was, I wondered if I shouldn't be heading for a horseracing track to wager on the ponies. Keeping that thought to myself, I said, "Eliza tells me you folks have been taking excellent care of me. Thank you."

"You are quite welcome, Mister Kinney. I might add that your friend Eliza is quite a trooper. She got you here all by herself and saw to it our emergency doctor knew exactly what had happened to you."

I glanced at Eliza. She just gave me a soft smile.

Nurse Clara said, "Our next step is getting some nourishment into you. Do you feel up to eating a little applesauce?"

"I think I could manage that."

"Wonderful. I'll ask the kitchen to send some up. Also, there is a deputy from the Ventura County Sheriff's Department out in the hall waiting to speak with you. We had to notify them after your surgery last night because your wounds were caused by a gunshot. That's the law. He's been here ever since, but I think he could wait just a little longer until you are less groggy and have something to eat."

"Thank you, Nurse Clara."

"You are welcome, Mister Kinney. I will be back with your applesauce in just a few minutes."

With Nurse Clara out of the room, Eliza returned to her chair by my bed." I said, "Maybe you should finish telling me what happened before I have to talk to that deputy."

"All right, darling. I'm afraid I did not see much at first because I was still down on the floorboard of the car. I stayed there for a few minutes waiting to see what was going to happen next. I can tell you I was scared out of my wits. I couldn't tell if you were alive or dead.

"Anyway, when I heard a car driving away, I thought it might be safe to take a look. I saw a big dark red car going back toward the highway. It was almost out of sight. When it disappeared, I got out and went around to your side of the car.

"There was blood everywhere and you were unconscious, but your heart was beating and you were breathing. The blood seemed to be mostly from the wound in the front of your neck. Thinking I needed to stop the bleeding, I grabbed the first thing I could find that would make a proper dressing, which happened to be a pair of . . . ah . . . panties out of my suitcase. I wrapped them around your neck, and then I used my belt to hold them firmly against the wounds."

"I bet the doctor got a kick out of your choice of bandage material."

Eliza giggled a little. "If he did, he was gentleman enough to keep it to himself. He did say I had done the right things, though.

"Anyway, when I had performed all of the first aid I could think of, I managed to push you over to the right side of the seat and tried starting your car. It started right up.

"That's when I made the decision to bring you to Ventura. I think this place is about the same distance from where we were as Cottage Hospital, but it had the advantage of being as far from Santa Barbara as I dared go before getting you to medical care.

"I didn't know where the hospitals in Ventura are, so when I got into town, I stopped at a service station and asked the attendant. He gave me good directions and here we are."

I smiled at her. "Nurse Clara is right. You are quite a trooper, kiddo. Your quick thinking probably saved my life."

Eliza smiled back at me. "Oh, I don't know about that, but after all the times you've come to my rescue, it was about time I did something right for you."

"Kiddo, everything you do for me is right, speaking of which I think a kiss would be appropriate treatment for my condition."

Eliza laughed. "And just what is your condition, mister?"

"I am hopelessly in love with the most wonderful woman in the world."

"All right, darling, but just one. We don't want to over-medicate you."

She leaned over the bed and pressed her lips to mine for a quick kiss. Of course, it was precisely at that moment that Nurse Clara arrived with my applesauce.

With a smile on her face, she said, "Now you kids behave. At least until Mister Kinney has some nourishment."

Eliza blushed and I laughed. "Applesauce!"

After the nurse left and while I dipped a spoon into the applesauce Eliza said, "I'm so embarrassed!"

"For heaven's sake, why? I'll wager Nurse Clara has smooched a fellow or two in her time. She understands being in love."

"I suppose."

The applesauce was cool on my throat and tasted good. Dipping my spoon in for more, I asked. "If I was in here all night, where did you sleep?"

"I told the duty nurse I had no place to stay and she said it would be all right for me to stay here last night. It was my turn to spend the night in a chair. If they will allow it, I'll sleep here again tonight. I don't want to leave you here alone."

"I would be happy to share the bed with you, kiddo, but I'm afraid it is a little small for two."

"True, and I doubt if Nurse Clara is that understanding."

A few minutes later Nurse Clara returned with a deputy sheriff in tow. She said, "Mister Kinney, this is Deputy Tanner of the Ventura County Sheriff's Department. Do you feel up to answering a few questions for him?"

Figuring cooperation would get the gendarmerie out of our hair faster, I smiled and said, "Good morning Deputy Tanner. Sorry to keep you waiting so long."

The deputy responded in kind. "That's all right, Mister

Kinney. I have been kept waiting in far worse places."

"What would you like to know, deputy?"

He studied his notebook for a moment, and then said, "Well, Miss Hamm was kind enough to give me your names and addresses, but she was reluctant to tell me exactly how your accident happened. She said she couldn't see very well from where she was and it would be better for me to get the information directly from you."

I glanced at Eliza who was standing against the wall behind Deputy Tanner. She gave me a small shrug.

"Okay, deputy. I guess the first thing you need to know is that the incident occurred outside of your jurisdiction, in Santa Barbara County."

"I see. Exactly where in Santa Barbara County were you shot?"

"As close as I can place the location, it happened just north of the Carpenteria bluffs."

Nodding, Tanner said, "You're right, that's Santa Barbara County. So what I will do is complete my report and send it on to the sheriff's department up there. Now, would you please give me the facts of the incident?"

"Sure. We were on our way south from Santa Barbara for a few days of vacation when we decided to pull off the highway and take a walk on the beach. I drove a ways down a little road to the beach until I found a spot where I could safely park. We were just about to get out of the car when I heard what sounded like a gunshot some distance away. The next thing I knew I woke up here. Fortunately, Miss Hamm knew how to stop the bleeding, and then she drove me to the hospital."

Smiling as if he was thinking of something funny, Tanner said, "Yes, I heard that first aid in the form of a temporary dressing had been applied. That was very quick thinking on Miss Hamm's part, using materials readily at hand and all."

I glanced at Eliza. She actually stuck her tongue out at Deputy Tanner. She did so out of his line of sight, but he almost caught her as he turned to ask, "Out of curiosity, Miss Hamm, what prompted you to bring Mister Kinney to Ventura, instead of taking him back to Santa Barbara?"

Looking innocent as a lamb, Eliza said, "I came here because I thought it was closer than going all the way back to Santa Barbara."

Tanner studied her for a moment, and then said, "Actually, you were just about at the midpoint between here and there, but I can certainly understand your confusion at a moment like that."

Turning back to me, Tanner said, "You stated that the sound of the gunshot sounded distant, but you were shot with a point-three-eight caliber round. That means the bullet was most likely fired by a handgun rather than a rifle. Since pistols have a much shorter range than most rifles, I wonder why the gunshot sounded distant."

I put on a thoughtful expression. "As a journalist, I do my best to be succinct in my choice of words. The idea I was trying to communicate is that the gunshot was not as loud as it might have been if the gun was only a few yards away, like at a shooting range. Also, there is a grove of trees alongside the road on which we were parked. If the gun was fired from that grove, the sound would have been more muted than if it were out in the open. Additionally, the car windows were up, so they no doubt blocked some of the sound."

It was Tanner's turn to look thoughtful. "All right, I see what you mean. One more question if you don't mind."

"Not at all."

"Mister Kinney, do you know of anyone who might have it in for you? I mean someone with a grudge or something who might want to hurt you?"

"Well, as a newspaper reporter, I write about events and people, so I suppose it is always possible I offended someone along the way, but usually those people are quite vocal in their complaints. I don't know of anyone who is so upset with me that they would shoot me."

Closing his notebook, Deputy Tanner said, "Okay, Mister Kinney. I think those are all the questions I need to ask for my report. I'm sure the Santa Barbara County Sheriff's Department will be in touch with you, although this incident looks to me as if it is an accident. Someone was probably out taking target practice and a shot got away from them. If that's the case, it is unlikely the person will ever be identified."

"That seems likely to me, too, Deputy Tanner."

"All right then, thank you for your cooperation and I wish you a fast recovery from your injuries."

When the deputy left, Eliza returned to the chair next to my bed. "Gee, Lester, if I had not been there, I would believe every word you told that deputy. Now, please tell me why you made up that story."

"The automobile I saw behind us when I yelled at you to get down on the floorboard was Estelle Abernathy's Cadillac. If we had told him what really happened, the ensuing investigation would have alerted Estelle to the fact that Armando is a lousy shot and that he didn't make sure he got me. In that case, she would quite likely send him back for a second try. By the way, you were wise to tell the deputy he would have to talk to me about what happened. Most of all, thank God you didn't tell him you were on the floorboard of the car when I was shot."

Eliza looked puzzled. "Why, darling?"

"You being on the floorboard implies that I saw the danger coming, and that does not fit with the story I told him."

"Oh."

"Right now, though, our highest priority is getting out of this hospital. We're sitting ducks in here."

"Lester, you just got shot less than twenty-four hours ago! You have two holes in your neck. You need time to recover."

"Yeah, I know, but I also have a wedding to attend."

'Darling, you have a perfectly legitimate excuse for . . . ."

Eliza was interrupted by a new arrival to the room. This time it was a young fellow in white with red hair and freckles. From the stethoscope around his neck I deduced he was a doctor, just the man I wanted to see.

Addressing Eliza, the man in white put on a charming smile and said, "Hello, Miss Hamm. It's good to see you again."

It was obvious from his demeanor the doctor thought Eliza was hotsy-totsy from head to toe. With a tone of voice clearly chosen not to encourage him, she politely said, "Good evening, Doctor."

Looking a lot less charming and much more businesslike, he turned to me and said, "Hello, Mister Kinney. I'm Doctor Dillon, the surgeon who patched up your neck. I'm glad to see you awake and alert. How are you feeling?"

I gave him a cheerful expression. "Quite well, Doctor Dillon. You must have done a good job."

He smiled an obligatory kind of smile. "I hope so. I suggest, however, that you enjoy the lack of pain while it lasts. I am sure you are still feeling the effects of the anesthetic we used during surgery. It will wear off during the day and you are likely to experience an increase in pain. I have prescribed a pain reliever for you. Just tell your nurse when you are in pain and she will administer Laudanum."

"I see. Can you give me an idea of how long I need to remain in your hospital?"

"That depends largely on how quickly your body mends. Our

greatest concern is infection, so we need to keep your dressing fresh and clean. If I had to hazard a guess, I would say you will need to be here at least three to four days. Then, assuming we see no signs of infection and there are no other complications, you should be able to recuperate at home until the stitches can be removed."

Three to four days was not the answer I wanted to hear. I tried a different tack to see if I could get an answer that better suited our needs.

"Doctor Dillon, our home is in Santa Barbara. How would it be if Miss Hamm drove me up to Cottage Hospital and I did my recuperation there?"

He appeared to give my request some thought. "Well, Cottage is an excellent hospital, but let us see how you are doing tomorrow. I'll stop by around mid-morning. We can talk about that idea more then."

"Thank you, Doctor Dillon."

He nodded at me and to Eliza, he said, "Goodbye, Miss Hamm."

When the good doctor was gone and Eliza returned to her chair by my bed, I said, "If you ever wanted to marry a doctor, I think you have an excellent opportunity with Doctor Dillon there."

Eliza shook her head with vehemence. "I have no desire to marry a doctor. I want to marry a writer, and I have one all picked out, thank you very much."

"I'm relieved to hear that, but I am wondering how much of that wolf's lack of enthusiasm for letting us out here has to do with keeping you around."

"Lester, he is a doctor. I cannot imagine a physician and surgeon doing something that devious."

"I'm not so sure. Just to be safe, try looking a little less enticing when he's around."

She giggled again. "All right. I'll put a pillowcase over my head the next time he comes in. Will that do?"

"A pillow case will not cover the parts he was looking at."

Eliza stood, and leaning over the bed, she gave me another soft kiss. "I promise you, darling, you have nothing to worry about when it comes to amorous doctors, or anyone else. You are stuck with me forever. Now, try and get some rest."

On that pleasant note I closed my eyes. In a matter of moments I was dead to the world.

EIGHTEEN

Friday - September 14, 1928

I experienced a moment of panic when I awoke Friday morning and realized Eliza was not in her chair. I awakened several times during the night, and she was there every time. Now she wasn't.

Trying to convince myself that everything was okay and she had just stepped out for a minute, I decided to distract myself by trying something daring, like sitting up. After a moment of dizziness, I found I could manage all right with half of me vertical.

That success emboldened me to find out what would happen if all of me was vertical. I pivoted and let my legs hang over the edge of the bed. I was about to try standing when Eliza walked in. Her fresh outfit, a cheerful yellow pleated skirt and a simple white blouse, told me where she had been.

Calmly, but with concern, Eliza asked, "What are you doing, darling?"

"I am finding out if I can stand up. If I am successful at that, I shall attempt new heights by walking to the bathroom."

"I suppose it would do no good for me to suggest you wait until a nurse or Doctor Dillon tells you it is all right to do those things."

"You suppose correctly."

"How are you feeling this morning?"

"Not bad. Doctor Dillon's dire predictions of intense pain seem to have been a little off the mark. My throat is painful, all right, especially when I strained to sit up, but it is nothing I can't handle."

She walked to my side and gave me a kiss on the cheek. "All right, if I cannot dissuade you from performing death-defying gymnastic feats, I can at least be handy if you need to lean on something."

As I slid off the edge of the bed to set my feet on the floor, I said, "You're the prettiest crutch I have ever seen."

Eliza did not reply. She was completely focused on my

progress. As it turned out, she need not have been so concerned. With just one more short moment of dizziness, I was standing alongside her. Since my equilibrium seemed to be fully functional, I took a step, and then another one.

"Where's the bathroom?"

Eliza was smiling. "You can walk!"

"Unless I missed something in physiology class, one's throat is not directly involved in the process of walking. Where did you say the bathroom is?"

"Nurse Clara said you share a bathroom with the next room. It is through that door, but knock before you open it to make certain the bathroom is not already occupied."

I strolled as nonchalantly as I could manage to the indicated door and knocked. When there was no response, I turned the handle and went in. After taking care of business and washing my hands, I looked into the mirror on the wall above the sink. It seemed to me I was a little more pale than usual, but other than that and the dressing wrapped around my neck, I looked a lot like me.

As I turned to go back into the bedroom I heard Eliza's voice. She was talking with another woman. When I opened the door, a new nurse was standing there glaring at me. Eliza stood behind her and seemed to be suppressing a grin.

The nurse said, "Mister Kinner, you are supposed to be in bed, not strolling around the hospital!"

"The name is Kinney, and what I am supposed to be doing or not doing depends on whose opinion you ask. Now, where are my clothes?"

"They are where they belong, in the closet at the nurse's station."

"All right, which way is the nurse's station."

"Mister Kinner, I am responsible for your care. Please return to your bed!"

"Nurse, what is your name?"

She looked surprised for a moment. "I am Nurse Marion, why?"

"Nurse Marion, I have very little confidence in the ability of someone to care for me who cannot remember my name for more than ten seconds. I am Mister Kinney and I want my belongings now. It would probably be simpler if you just brought them to me, but if you will not, I am sure your nurse's station is not that difficult to locate, especially if someone with your memory can find it."

She stormed out of the room, yelling, "All right, Mister Kinner!"

I looked at Eliza and she had her hand over her mouth in an attempt to keep from laughing. "Lester, you really should be kinder to the nurses."

"I will let Mister Kinner, lord help him, be kind to that one."

"Seriously, darling, I'm afraid the clothes you had on Wednesday are not at all presentable. Your jacket has blood soaked into the collar and lapels, your shirt is drenched in it, and your slacks are even badly stained. I doubt if even a dry cleaning establishment could restore them to usefulness. Would you like me to get some fresh clothes for you out of your suitcase in the car?"

"Thank you, kiddo. That would be very helpful."

No more than a few seconds after Eliza left the room a husky white-haired nurse came into the room carrying a cardboard carton that by the printing on its side had once contained Johnson & Johnson Band-Aid brand adhesive bandages. It now contained my bloodstained clothes and a large white envelope.

This nurse at least got my name right. "Mister Kinney, I'm Pearl Norwood, Supervisor of Nursing. I understand you wish to have the clothes you were wearing when you entered the hospital. Is that correct?"

"That is correct."

Setting the cardboard box on the corner of the bed, Nurse Norwood asked, "May I enquire as to what you intend to do with these clothes?"

"I intended to put them on, but Miss Hamm tells me they are not fit to be worn, so she kindly offered to bring me some fresh clothes from my suitcase in our automobile."

"And, may I ask, why you want to put clothes on?"

"I could give you a long list of reasons, not the least of which is that this hospital gown is uncomfortable and drafty. In addition, getting dressed is going to do wonders for my disposition."

She gave that a moment or two of thought, and then said, "Those seem like sensible reasons to me. By the way, your personal items—wallet, watch, money, and so on—are in the envelope on top of your clothes. Before you put on a clean shirt, however, I suggest we change your dressing."

"That sounds like a grand idea as long as Nurse Marion is not going to apply the fresh dressing. At the moment I would be at risk of strangulation if she performed that task."

Nurse Norwood actually chuckled at that. "I doubt she would

really strangle you with it, but the dressing might also cover your mouth by the time she was done. To avoid any such risk, I will personally change the dressing for you, Mister Kinney."

"Thank you, Nurse Norwood."

By the time Eliza returned with a fresh suit of clothes, Pearl Norwood had removed my old dressing and was inspecting my wounds. Eliza looked surprised.

"Lester, are you all right?"

Smiling, I said, "Yes, kiddo, I am very all right. Nurse Norwood here suggested we change my dressings before I put a fresh shirt on. Nurse Norwood, have you met Eliza Hamm?"

As she turned toward Eliza, the nurse smiled. "Not yet, but I've certainly heard of her, including the creative technique she used to stop your bleeding before she brought you in here. Hello, Miss Hamm."

Eliza's complexion was suddenly a bright rosy red again. "Nice to meet you, Nurse Norwood. Tell me, is there anyone in this blessed hospital who hasn't heard the details of my 'creative' approach to saving the life of my fiancé?"

Nurse Norwood smiled at Eliza. "You know, Miss Hamm, what you did really was the best thing you could have done. The dressing you applied was absorbent and soft enough to prevent additional damage to the wound. Under the same pressure you were experiencing at the time, I doubt I would have come up with as good a solution."

Turning back to me, she said, "Looking at your wounds, Mister Kinney, I see no signs of undo swelling, infection, or other complications. Do not take that to mean you are healed and ready to resume normal activities. It simply means that, so far, you are doing well. I also urge you to remember that you lost quite a lot of blood. That is certain to make you feel tired and quite weak at times. If you feel those symptoms, pay attention. Your body is trying to tell you something.

"Now, I'm about to re-dress the wounds. Miss Hamm, might I suggest that you come over here and observe how this is done, so that in the event you need to replace the dressing at some point, you will know how to do it without increasing the risk of infection?"

Eliza gave me a quick questioning look and said, "Thank you, Nurse Norwood. That would be very valuable to know."

For the next fifteen or so minutes, we received a step-by-step account of the correct method for replacing my dressings. When Nurse Norwood was finished, I noticed that she put the large roll of gauze, the adhesive tape, and the blunt surgical scissors she had used into the cardboard box containing my old clothes, rather than returning them to the tray on which they were brought into the room.

Looking me in the eye, Nurse Norwood then asked, "Now I will leave you to get dressed, but first, I will offer a piece of advice."

Nodding, I said, "Certainly, we would be glad to hear it."

"I have a strong suspicion that you intend to depart Big Sisters Hospital soon. Obviously I cannot stop you from doing so, however, I suggest you stick around a little while longer. Breakfast will be served in just a few minutes, and I understand Doctor Dillon is planning to look in on you shortly thereafter. Some nourishment and counsel from the doctor certainly will not hurt you."

I glanced at Eliza. She looked surprised. I said, "Thank you, Nurse Norwood.

"You are welcome, Mister Kinney. Also, I have placed a cane next to the door. I suggest you make use of it. You are going to tire easily for a while because of your blood loss. The cane will help your stability. Good luck to you, and to you, Miss Hamm."

When we were alone again, Eliza laid my fresh clothes out on the bed and we began the dressing process by removing my hospital gown and putting a clean shirt on. From there, we did drawers, socks, and trousers.

Eliza said, "I think your shoes from yesterday are okay. They should be in the box."

She rummaged through the box and came up with my shoes. She also found the gauze, tape, and scissors. "Holding the roll of gauze up, she asked, "How did these get in here?"

"My new friend, Nurse Norwood, put them in there. I think she intended we should take them with us when we leave."

"Really?"

"Really."

"Did you say something to her about leaving the hospital? Is that why she said we should stick around to have breakfast and see the doctor?"

"I said nothing about leaving. Nurse Norwood is a sharp cookie. She figured that out all on her own."

"You mean we are leaving this morning?"

"That seems the smart thing to do."

Eliza was about to ask something else when a woman in a pale blue apron came in carrying two trays. She put them on a roll-around metal table next to the bed and left without saying a word.

"I think breakfast has arrived, kiddo, and I am very hungry."

While I tied my shoes, Eliza rolled the table between her chair and the bed. Then she cranked the bed down to an altitude that made eating off the table possible.

As we ate our scrambled eggs, sausage patties, and toast, Eliza asked, "Where are we going when we leave here?"

"I'll tell you what I think when we get to the car . . . just in case these walls have ears."

She leaned closer to me, and speaking just above a whisper, said, "Do you really think we are still in danger?"

"I don't know, but I wasn't paying attention when we left Santa Barbara and that lapse in caution darn near got us killed. No more lapses."

A quiet knock on the door was followed by Doctor Dillon's arrival. He put on his charming smile and said, "Good morning, Miss Hamm."

When Eliza just nodded at him, he turned to me. "Mister Kinney, the nurses tell me you have it in mind to leave us this morning. Is that so?"

"It is, Doctor Dillon."

"I suppose you can guess my thoughts on that."

"Doctor Dillon, my decision to leave is based on concerns of which you are unaware. Trust that I have not made this decision lightly."

Dillon frowned at me, then turned and walked out of the room without another word. I had the distinct feeling he was taking our premature departure as a personal insult. Eliza had the same thought. "Darling, I think you hurt his feelings."

"That was not my intention. He is a very good doctor and I cannot blame him for being unhappy when people choose to ignore his advice. On the other hand, I have bigger things on my mind than the good doctor's feelings. Let's get out of here."

On the way to the car we dumped my ruined clothes and the cardboard box that contained them into a convenient trash can. Eliza had parked the Chevrolet in a lot near the hospital entrance, and Nurse Norwood was quite right. By the time we got there, even using the cane she thoughtfully provided, I was huffing and puffing like a broken down steam locomotive.

We put the items thoughtfully provided by Nurse Norwood for changing my dressings into my suitcase. Then, leaning against one of the Chevrolet's fenders, I said, "Eliza, would you mind driving?"

She frowned. "I don't mind at all. Are you feeling all right? You look a little flushed."

"Yes, I'm all right, just feeling somewhat fatigued after hiking down here. Nurse Underwood warned me that was liable to happen."

As I climbed into the Chevrolet through the passenger door, I examined the two most noticeable consequences of our encounter with Armando Delgado. One was a half-inch hole in the rear window glass and the second was a small dent in the dashboard above the speedometer, which I figured was caused by the spent round after it passed through my neck. What I found surprising was the lack of blood Eliza had described.

"What happened to all the blood you told me about?"

"When I came down earlier this morning to get my clean clothes, I took a minute with a damp rag and wiped up most of the blood I could see. I'm sure I didn't get it all, but it looks better than it did."

Surprised that she would think to clean up the car in the midst of everything else going on, I said, "Thank you, kiddo. You never cease to amaze me."

Eliza leaned over from the left end of the seat and gave me a kiss on the cheek. "I hope to continue amazing you for many years to come. Now, darling, where am I driving us?"

"Well, when we left Santa Barbara, I planned that we would be in Las Vegas by now. So much for the plans of mice and men."

Her big brown eyes brimming with love, Eliza smiled at me. "I rather thought that's what you had in mind."

"It finally occurred to me, however, that there is another place without a waiting period that is much closer."

"Oh? Where is that, darling?"

"Tijuana, Mexico. It's only a little over two hundred miles from here."

"Really?"

"Really. They perform a civil ceremony there that is considered legal in the United States. I fully expect we will want to get properly married in a church later on, but a Mexican marriage would accomplish our immediate purpose."

Eliza was grinning from ear to ear. "Darling, a proper church wedding would be wonderful, but that can wait. Right now I just want to be Missus Lester Kinney with all the benefits associated with that title."

"All right, keeping in mind that you have to be back in Santa Barbara for work on Monday, assuming it is safe for you to do so, we don't have much time for a honeymoon now, but at least we won't be living in sin any longer."

With a hurt expression, Eliza said, "Lester, do you really think we have been living in sin?"

"No, darling, I know better. However, others, some of whom are important to us, may see matters differently."

The smile returned to Eliza's face. "Okay, how do we get to Mexico from here?"

"We get on US Highway 101 and keep rolling south until we reach the border, but first, I think it would be wise for us to find out a few things."

"What things do we need to find out?"

"Mostly, what is happening at home."

"How do we learn that without going there?"

I smiled. "A clever fellow by the name of Alexander Graham Bell came up with a wonderful invention a while back. He called it the telephone. That's how."

"Oh. Whom do we call on Mister Bell's wonderful invention?"

"I suggest we call about the only friend we can count on, Mabel Stafford. How much change do you have?"

Eliza looked puzzled. "What do we need change for?"

"Mister Bell's telephone company thinks they should be paid for the privilege of using their service."

"Why don't we just call the *Tribune* and reverse the charges? I'm pretty sure they will accept a collect call from the daughter of the paper's managing editor."

I thought about her idea for a moment. "The only thing wrong with that is that the telephone company's records will point to exactly where we are."

"Does that matter? We are only going to be here a little while longer."

"I guess it really isn't a problem. Even if Estelle gets wind of a call placed by you, she still won't know whether I'm alive or dead. Okay, let's give it a try."

Eliza drove us to a Gilmore gas station right on the highway and we pulled in to use their public pay telephone. The required instrument was installed in a wooden booth with glass windows right alongside the station office. Eliza stepped in to place the call. While she did that I managed to slide over behind the steering wheel and pull up next to one of the station's gas pumps. An attractive blonde woman—all of Gilmore's station attendants were attractive women—filled our tank with Gilmore's Blu-Green gasoline while I kept my eyes on Eliza.

It was apparent that the *Tribune's* telephone operator did indeed accept a collect call from the managing editor's daughter because Eliza spent several minutes in conversation with someone, presumably Mabel. After I paid for the gasoline, I drove back over to the telephone booth and waited for Eliza to end her call. I could tell by her expression that whatever she was hearing was not good news.

When Eliza finally ended the call and slid back behind the Chevrolet's steering wheel, she said, "Everything in Santa Barbara has gone crazy!"

"Oh? Let's get on the road while you tell me what has happened."

A few minutes later we were rolling through the town of Oxnard on our way to Mexico. Eliza said, "I have so much to tell you, I hardly know where to begin."

"You looked upset when you were talking with Mabel. Start with what upset you."

"Monsignor O'Boylan."

My blood suddenly ran cold. "What about him?"

Eliza sounded as if she was trying to keep her composure by reciting the words just as Mabel had said them to her. "According to a story the *Tribune* ran Wednesday night, he was found unconscious on the grounds of the old mission. The article speculated he had been attacked by a thug sometime between one-thirty and two that afternoon. Monsignor O'Boylan is in a coma at Cottage Hospital. The doctors say he is unlikely to regain consciousness."

"Eliza, pull into that parking lot there. Let's talk about this."

She pulled into the lot I indicated, parked, and immediately burst into tears. "Oh, Lester, we killed that kind man who was only trying to help."

Sliding over to put my arm around her shoulder, I said, "Eliza, we did not kill the bishop. He was killed by someone who did not want him to repeat what we told him—someone with a lot to hide. My money is on Estelle Abernathy. Unfortunately, it sounds as if she was successful. I doubt he had time to tell anyone about Estelle's nasty little secrets."

Eliza's expression told me she was trying mightily to remain calm. "That wasn't all of the bad news. Two boys hiking in the Riviera hills found an automobile that had run off the road and down into a canyon. It was Tom Wigand's car. The article said he had been shot in the head."

"It seems Estelle is on a killing spree. Counting me, that

makes at least three people she has tried to kill in the past week. Any other bad news?"

Her voice was growing softer as if the effort of relaying all the terrible news had worn her out. "Not really. The only other thing Mabel told me was that Father was released on bail, but he hasn't come back in to work yet. Mabel thinks he might be spending time with his lawyer."

"That would be my guess, too."

Eliza looked up at me. "Lester what are we going to do? The world is falling apart at the seams."

"I don't think there is much we can do at the moment about matters in Santa Barbara, so I suggest we continue with our plan to do something about us."

Looking at my pocket watch, I did some arithmetic. It was ten-thirty. If my calculations were correct, five hours of driving would put us where we wanted to be. That would make our time of arrival between three-thirty and four o'clock.

"Eliza do you think you can handle five hours of driving?"

She looked up at me, and wiping the tears from her eyes, said, "Yes. If it means getting us to the state of holy matrimony, I could get out and push the car there."

It was good to hear enthusiasm in her voice again, but I cautioned, "I'm feeling kind of peeked, so I won't be much help. Are you sure you want to try it?"

"You lean back and try to sleep. We're going to Mexico!"

NINETEEN

Friday - September 14, 1928

I was trapped in an insane dream world in which a gigantic Estelle Abernathy commanded dozens of little Armando marionettes with big guns. She was pulling their strings to make them shoot at me. Thankfully the deceleration of the Chevrolet brought me back to the real world, where I saw that Eliza was pulling into a Richfield service station.

She said, "Lester, are you okay?"

Groggily, I said, "Yes, why?"

"You were moaning and talking in your sleep. Were you having bad dreams?"

"Yes. Where are we?"

"Someplace called Carlsbad. The gas gauge is getting low, so I thought we ought to stop and fill up. Is that okay?"

Trying to pull my thoughts together, I said, "It beats walking."

My watch said two-fifteen. We were making good time. At this rate we would make Tijuana a little before four.

"Do you use regular or high-test?"

"Regular works fine."

Eliza instructed the attendant to fill our tank with regular and I dug some cash out of my wallet. I handed a few dollars to Eliza for the gas and said, "I'm going to visit the restroom. I'll be right back."

"Oh. Be very careful, darling."

I was stiff and in much more pain than I felt earlier in the day, but with the aid of my cane I made it to the men's room and back without incident. As I returned to the Chevrolet, I carefully looked for any signs of trouble. I saw nothing that set off alarm bells.

Watching me slowly hoist myself back onto the car seat, Eliza said, "You are in pain, aren't you, darling?"

Settling onto the seat, I said, "A little."

"More than a little. I can tell by the way you're moving. This station sells some sundries inside. I'm going in to see if they carry aspirin tablets."

Eliza paid for our gas and pulled up in front of the station office. Minutes later she came back carrying an open bottle of Coca-Cola and tiny white tin of Spartan aspirin. Reading the dosage instructions on the back of the tin, she said, "It says you can take up to three of these every four hours. Let's try two for now."

I put two of the chalky white pills into my mouth and washed them down with swallows of Coca-Cola. Leaning back in the seat, I said, "I think we are only an hour-and-a-half or so from the border."

Eliza put her hand on my shoulder. "Are you sure you are up to this, darling? We could wait, you know."

"No, we can't. We need to go to a government office to get married and this is Friday. They are probably closed on weekends."

"All right, darling. I just hate to see you in pain."

It turned out that my estimate of our arrival time was close. We pulled up to the border crossing a few miles south of San Diego at five minutes before four o'clock. From the number of northbound cars lined up next to the covered platform on the other side of the international border, I concluded that leaving the United States was easier than getting back in. There were only two cars ahead of us on the southbound side.

When it was our turn, a cheerful-looking fellow in a green Mexican Army uniform stepped up to the car. "Good afternoon, Señorita. What is the purpose of your visit to Mexico today?"

In a cheerful voice, Eliza said, "We came to get married."

The soldier's face lit up. "Ahhh, Bueno! The place you must go is the Registro Civil in City Hall. You drive ahead on this street until you come to Calle Benito Juarez. There you turn right and go to Avenida Constitución. The City Hall is at that intersection on your left, but you must hurry. The Registro Civil closes at five o'clock."

"Gracias Señor."

Still grinning like a Latin incarnation of the Cheshire Cat in *Alice's Adventures in Wonderland*, the soldier said, "De nada, Señorita. Que tu matrimonio sea feliz."

As Eliza drove away from the border, she smiled said, "He wished us a happy wedding."

"I didn't know you spoke Spanish."

"I don't. Well, I don't speak much of it . . . just enough to get by in a pinch. There is Calle Benito Juarez. The soldier said to turn right."

This was not my first trip to Tijuana, so I knew what to expect, but it always depresses me a little to see such poverty so close to home. The entire town is a slum. Except for the downtown area few of the streets are paved and most of the commercial buildings look like sets from old-time cowboy movies.

Only the popular tourist attractions are at all swanky, like the horse track at Agua Caliente, the new Hotel Commercial, and the Mexicali Beer Hall, which claims to have the longest bar in the world. Tijuana's City Hall also turned out to be one of the few attractive buildings in town. There was another building across the street that had a respectable look about it. The big red sign over the door said "JOYERIO."

"Eliza, what does joy-air-eye-o mean in the local lingo?"

Eliza looked where I was looking. "The word is pronounced hoy-air-ee-o. It means jewelry store."

"Good. Let's stop there for just a minute."

It only took five minutes for us to select two gold bands that fit. The proprietor of the joyerio assured us that the "14 Karat" inscriptions inside the bands were accurate. The two rings—mine a plain gold band and Eliza's a slimmer style with a scallop pattern engraved around its circumference—cost a total of seven American dollars.

As we crossed the street to City Hall, I said, "I promise you will have a proper engagement ring and a wedding band as soon as we can afford them."

Eliza held my arm a little tighter. "Darling, I would be happy to marry you with a ring from a box of Cracker Jack. That we have real rings to exchange just makes this all a little more special. Thank you for getting them."

The civil marriage ceremony took only a few minutes longer than picking out our rings. First, we filled out a form; second, we showed the clerk our drivers' licenses for identification; and third, the clerk typed our information on another form with the words "Certificado de Matrimonio" across the top.

Finally, the clerk signed the form he typed and said, "Ahora eres hombre y mujer. Felicitaciones! Esta oficina está cerrada para el día."

Holding the certificado de matrimonio in my hand I gave Eliza a puzzled look as we walked out of the office. "He said, 'You are now man and wife. Congratulations.'"

"It took all those words just to say that?"

"Well, he also said the office is now closed for the day."

Leaving the office of the Registro Civil we found ourselves in a pleasant paved patio area with shade trees around its perimeter at the center of City Hall. I said, "I guess it is up to us to complete the ceremony. This looks like a nice place to do that."

I took Eliza's ring out of my pocket and she held out her left hand. Sliding the ring onto the appropriate finger, I said the only thing I could think of to say. "Eliza, with this ring I thee wed."

She held her hand up to admire the ring and I handed her the second ring. Eliza slipped it onto my finger, saying, "Lester, with this ring, I thee wed." After a brief pause, she added with a grin, "You may now kiss the bride." I did.

Minutes later we were back in the Chevrolet and I was feeling weak as a kitten. Eliza noticed and said, "You were leaning on that cane awfully hard. Are you still in pain?"

"Not so much now. I just feel very weak."

Eliza took my hand. "That could be partly because you haven't eaten anything since this morning. Let's get some food."

I nodded. "That's a good idea, but let's drive back to San Diego first. If we encounter any problems I would rather it be in a country where I speak the language." In the back of my mind I was thinking Armando Delgado would be right at home in Tijuana.

"Okay, darling husband of mine. We are on our way back to the good old United States of America."

It turned out I was right about it being easier to leave the US than get back into it. We waited nearly half an hour for our turn with the border guard. Once there, we were ordered to present our drivers' licenses to prove who we were. Then came the questions. Where did we go in Mexico? How long were we in Mexico? What did we do in Mexico? Did we make any purchases in Mexico? Were we bringing any fruit or vegetables back into the United States? Did we have any items of contraband in our automobile?

When the guard was through giving us the third degree, he brusquely motioned us across the border. It was not only easier to enter Mexico, it was also a much more pleasant experience.

Around six-thirty we pulled up to a little storefront restaurant where Rosecrans Street meets US Highway 101 in San Diego. They specialized in chicken pot pies, but I was in no mood to be picky. With Eliza on one side of me and the cane on the other, I made it through the door and into a chair at the first vacant table we came to.

Eliza sat next to me and I said, "Some wedding dinner, huh?"

"Darling, you are alive and we are together. That is all I care about."

Our waitress showed up with glasses of water and menus. As I picked up my menu, the new band of gold on my left hand caught my eye. "Missus Eliza Kinney."

She looked at me with a big smile, "Yes, Mister Lester Kinney?"

"Oh, nothing. I was just trying it on for size."

"I see. Does it fit?"

"Perfectly, just like it was made for you."

"I'm glad to hear that because I plan on wearing that name for the rest of my life."

I smiled at her, and taking the little tin of aspirin from her purse, Eliza held it out to me. "I know you said you weren't in too much pain, but taking two more of these will help keep it that way."

Obediently swallowing two more aspirin tablets, I looked at my menu. Not surprisingly, the principal item on the menu was chicken pot pie. An ala carte pie could be had for twenty-five cents, or for a nickel more, the pie would be served with gravy, mashed potatoes, vegetables, Cole slaw, or soup.

I decided on just the pie, but Eliza urged me to have it with vegetables. I am not a big fan of cooked vegetables, and the pie already had carrots and other healthy things in it, but I ordered my chicken pot pie with vegetables. As I did so, it occurred to me that Lester Kinney was already turning into a henpecked husband. He did not seem to mind.

Over dinner we discussed our next step. Eliza said, "I think we need to find a place to stay and put you to bed."

I nodded my agreement. "But there is one thing I think we ought to do first."

"What, darling?"

"Figure out how to get in touch with Sergeant Sullivan."

"You think he can help our situation?"

"I don't know, but we can help him solve at least three major crimes he has on his hands, and that ought to get his attention."

"Monsignor O'Boylan and Tom Wigand, but what's the third one?"

"Your brand new husband. Sullivan should be receiving the shooting report from Ventura in a few days, assuming the Santa Barbara sheriff's office shares such things with the city police."

"Of course. I'm a little distracted I guess, but we know how to get in touch with Sergeant Sullivan. We can call him at the police station."

"Except he probably has enough seniority to claim weekends

off, so we aren't likely to reach him there until Monday. Besides, if he has a telephone in his home, he will be able to speak more freely there than he could at the station. Does Mabel have a telephone at her home?"

"Yes. Do you want me to call her and see if she can find Sergeant Sullivan's home telephone number?"

"That's exactly what I'm thinking. And we should do it before we leave San Diego."

"Leave? Aren't we staying here tonight?"

Shaking my head, I said, "If we make telephone calls from here, it would be smart to stay somewhere else. If you are up to another hour or so of driving, I spotted what looked like a nice little motor hotel in Carlsbad as we went through there earlier. It was just before we crossed that bridge over the estuary at the south end of town."

"I can do the driving, darling, but you look like you are on your last legs. Are you sure?"

"I'm sure."

Finishing our wedding dinners, we drove a block south on Rosecrans and found a Texaco service station with a public telephone. Eliza pulled up to a pump and we got the tank filled with gasoline before parking next to the station's telephone booth.

"Lester, should I get change for the telephone, or should I make the call to Mabel collect? She will accept the call and we can repay her when we get back."

"Better make this one collect. We will have to get coins for the call to Sullivan, though."

Glancing at the small gold timepiece on her wrist, Eliza said, "Okay, darling. It's about seven-thirty, so Mabel should be home."

Eliza got out to make the telephone call and I leaned back in the seat, intending to close my eyes for only a moment. When I opened them again, Eliza was gently rubbing my forehead.

"Sorry, kiddo. I guess I dozed off for a minute."

"Yes, you did. You were out like a light. I'm becoming concerned about you."

Fighting the urge to close my eyes again, I said, "Did Mabel find a number for Sergeant Sullivan?"

Eliza shook her head. "No. If he has a telephone, his number is not in the directory. She said it seemed unlikely that a policeman would not have a telephone, so she's going to check another source. Mabel said to call her back tomorrow afternoon.

"Now lean back. I'm taking you to Carlsbad and putting you to bed. Oh, and Mabel says 'congratulations on tying the knot'.

171

She is very happy for us."

I think I said something like 'that was nice of her,' but I am pretty sure I was out before we were back on Route 101. The next time I opened my eyes, we were pulling into the parking lot of a place called the Ponto Beach Motel.

Noticing I was awake, Eliza asked, "Is this the motor hotel you meant?"

"Looks like it."

The place had a new look about it and was built in the hacienda style of architecture with Spanish tile roofs and an adobe facade. Behind a low wall, the Ponto Beach Motel consisted of several buildings, including a two-story section with a balcony. The driveway was a rectangle around a central lawn and provided access to parking places in front of the rooms around its perimeter.

The office was in the two-story building and Eliza pulled up in front of its entrance. I started to get out, but she said, "Darling, let me do this. I can handle it."

"I know you can. I just . . . ."

"Sit tight, Lester, I'll be right back."

A few minutes later we were carrying our suitcases into room number ten, which was away from the highway at the back of the motel. Once inside, I sat on the comfortable double bed while Eliza locked the door and set our suitcases on a pair of those folding wooden racks they put in hotel rooms for luggage. That done, she sat next to me on the bed.

"How are you feeling, my dear husband?"

"Like something the cat dragged in."

"I'm sorry, darling. Let's take your shirt off so I can see how your dressing is doing."

After helping me out of my shirt, Eliza stood and leaned over and closely examined the bandage around my neck. Allowing the examination earned me a sweet kiss on the cheek.

"The dressing looks all right. I don't see any fresh blood and gauze is still where it should be. Nurse Norwood did a good job of putting it on. Are you feeling much pain in your neck?"

I managed a grin. "This whole situation is a pain in the neck!"

"Oh? Are you having second thoughts about marrying me already?"

"Absolutely not."

With a smile that gave me a lift, she said, "I'm certainly glad to hear that! Now give me a straight answer to my question."

I thought about how to answer her honestly, and then said,

"The discomfort in my neck is more of a dull ache than a sharp pain, but along with the aftereffects of the beating Armando gave me Monday night and sleeping in the car so much, all of my muscles are feeling stiff and achy, but that is nothing a couple of aspirin won't fix."

Eliza nodded. "I'll get them for you in a minute. Are you still weak?"

"Not so much. You were right. Having some nourishment kind of cured that."

She grinned again. "See what eating your vegetables will do for you?"

"Yes, Nurse Eliza."

"Do you still feel tired?"

"A little, but all things considered, I am really feeling a whole lot better than I did this afternoon. That part of the day is just kind of a blur."

"You do remember us getting married, don't you?"

Feigning a look of surprise, I said, "Married? Are we married?"

"You bet we are, Mister Kinney! Amnesia tricks will not get you out of that." She held up her left hand to show me her ring. "And I have the proof right here."

I put my arm around her and leaned back on the bed, pulling Eliza with me. She let out a surprised squeal and I said, "Good! That means I get to have my way with you, Missus Kinney."

"Mister Kinney, I doubt if you can even get undressed on your own, let alone have your way with me."

"I was not planning on doing either of those things on my own."

Eliza rolled on top of me. "That's different! Let's get ready for bed."

Deliberately leaving my cane by the bed to prove I didn't need it, I staggered into the bathroom and cleaned up as best I could without a bath. Then Eliza and I swapped places and I stretched out on the bed.

Coming out of the bathroom, she switched off the room light. She was wearing my faded blue shirt, but when she got to the bed, she took the shirt off, and stood there for several moments in the pale light from the windows.

Her breasts were firm, her tummy was flat, her legs flowed gracefully from her slim hips, and her face was aglow with a light that could not come from any manmade source. I gulped involuntarily.

Smiling lovingly, she said, "What do you think, darling? Will I do?"

"Eliza, you literally take my breath away. You are the most beautiful woman in the whole world."

She giggled and slid into bed, pressing her body against mine. "I'm still not sure why you think that, but whatever the reason, this woman is all yours to have and to hold for now and always."

We kissed a long, deep kiss that grew more passionate with each second of its life. During the kiss Eliza did the same thing she had done so many times before, rolling to her left and sliding her right leg over mine. I felt the warm skin of her thigh pressing firmly between my legs hastening my already growing arousal.

Breathlessly, Eliza said, "Oh, Lester, I love you so much and I love you more with every passing minute."

Then she rolled on top of me, positioning herself so I was pressed firmly against her moist warmth. Not able to wait another moment, I raised my hips and gently entered her.

"Ohh, darling, yes!"

We kissed again, savoring that wonderful moment in which we became one. I whispered, "Eliza, this is so much more than I ever imagined it could be."

For the next several minutes we alternated between moving together in passion and laying perfectly still to enjoy all the sensations of our joining. Soon, though, the rhythm and pressure of Eliza's hips began to increase, pushing me deeper inside her.

Only moments later her entire body began to tremble against me and she gasped, "Oh, Lester!" That was more than I could stand. I joined her in a climax that seemed it would never end. Finally, she collapsed on top of me and I held her tightly while we both caught our breath.

Still panting, Eliza said, "Oh, darling, I must be hurting you. Let me roll back onto my side."

"Stay where you are a little longer, Eliza. I want to remember this feeling for as long as I live."

She kissed me gently on the lips and I could feel her heart beating next to mine. "Lester, I now know all the parts that combine to make our love perfect—the happiness, the sadness, the pain, the understanding, and now the passion. And the amazing part is we have experienced it all in just seven days."

I rolled with her as Eliza slid off of me and back onto the bed. "You said that beautifully, Eliza. I am going to remember those words."

In a lighter tone, she said, "See? All one has to do is be loved deeply and completely by a writer and beautiful words magically come into one's mind."

I chuckled. "Sure they do."

We lay there for a while just holding each other and feeling our heart rates return to normal. I was close to dozing off, when Eliza asked, "Was it all right, Lester?"

"Was what all right?"

"What we just did, you goof."

"It was the most amazing experience of my entire life. What makes you ask such a question?"

"Well, I'm no expert on this subject, but I have read books, and as I understand it, the man is usually on top. I just thought it might be easier on you tonight if . . . ."

"Eliza, throw all that silly insecurity away right now!"

"But . . . ."

"But nothing! If there really are rules about such things, they are absurd and downright ridiculous. You were wonderful and considerate and . . . wonderful!"

"You said that, darling."

I looked at her. She was grinning. "I said what?"

"You said I was wonderful twice."

"Oh. Well, sometimes you leave even me at a loss for words. You are the most terrific lover I could ever imagine. You're . . . wonderful!"

She giggled. "That is three 'wonderfuls'."

"Missus Kinney?"

"Yes, Mister Kinney?"

"Shut up and kiss me goodnight."

TWENTY

Saturday - September 15, 1928

Even though it took me a moment to clear my head and figure out where the devil I was, I awoke Saturday morning with very little pain and a sunny disposition. The world outside Room Ten at the Ponto Beach Motel was another matter entirely. A storm moved in during the early morning hours and rain was coming down in buckets. I could hear thunder and see flashes of lightening through the window curtains.

Eliza was still sleeping with her head resting on my shoulder when a particularly close bolt of lightning set off a boom that rattled the windows. She jumped and I put both arms around her.

"It's okay, kiddo. Mother nature is just putting on a show for us."

She looked up at me and smiled. That at least brought the sun out in room ten.

"Good morning, darling. Is it raining?"

"Buckets, complete with lightning and thunder. That's what woke you."

She cuddled closer. "I'm glad you're here. Thunder and lightning are scary."

"Don't worry, I won't let donner or blitzen get you."

Sleepily Eliza asked, "Santa's reindeer are here, too?"

"In spirit only. Donner is the German word for thunder, and blitzen refers to a flash of lightning."

"Oh. What time is it?"

"Darned if I know. I think it is pretty early, though."

"Oh." Then her mind shifted gears. "Oh! How are you feeling this morning, darling?"

I kissed her softly on the lips. "Like a happily married husband."

"I'm happy to hear that, darling, but I meant physically."

Sliding my hand gently over her breasts, I said, "That, too."

"Are you trying to seduce me, sir?"

"I would never think of doing such a dastardly thing!"

With disappointment in her voice, Eliza said, "Oh."

Then, sliding her hand down over my stomach and abdomen, she found evidence to the contrary. "Oh, oh! You fibbed!"

"Just a little fib."

Stroking me slowly, she said, "That is not a little fib, darling. It feels like a rather large fib to me."

I trailed kisses down her neck to her right nipple and Eliza moaned softly. "I knew it. You are trying to seduce me, and it's working . . . oooh . . . it's working very, very well."

Having thus gotten the day off to a rousing start, we bathed, dressed, and packed. It was seven-thirty when I ducked under the awning over the Ponto Beach Motel's office entrance and checked us out of room ten. From there, we drove around to the other end of the building and parked outside the Ponto Beach Café, a coffee shop attached to the motel.

We took a booth near the front of the dining room, and as soon as the waitress brought menus and water, I got out the Spartan aspirin tin. There were only two tablets left. I swallowed them with a sip of water.

Eliza, of course, noticed and asked, "Are you hurting from too much excitement this morning?"

"Just a little, but it's worth it. As you have pointed out, taking aspirin before the pain gets bad helps keep it from getting bad."

She grinned at me. "See? You are trainable!"

I smiled proudly and said, "Put the right carrot on the end of the stick and I can learn all kinds of tricks."

"And what, may I ask, is the right carrot?"

"Specifically, a five-foot-four, hundred-and-five pound brunette with a smile I cannot resist."

"Well, dear husband, I hate to tell you, but that is not me."

"Oh? I thought it was."

"It was me when I got my driving license, but since then I've put on almost ten pounds. Mabel insisted. She said I was so skinny I didn't have any . . . well, any of the parts that are supposed to stick out on a woman."

"I see. Mabel knew what she was talking about. Those parts are now about as perfect as they could be."

I don't know if our waitress overheard part of the conversation, but when she showed up with Eliza's oatmeal and my scrambled eggs, she had a funny smile on her face. Having already worked up an appetite, we both dug right into our breakfasts.

After a minute or two, Eliza put her spoon down and frowned.

"What if I get pregnant?"

My fork stopped midway to my mouth. "Huh? Where did that question come from?"

Eliza hesitated, and then said, "Well, I know you're going to give me a lecture on my insecurities, but you keep telling me how beautiful I am. I won't look the same when I'm pregnant."

I set my fork down. "Kiddo, there is only one thing that could make you more beautiful than you are now, and that is the blush of motherhood."

She looked down at her oatmeal. "You're just saying that to make me feel better."

"No, I mean it. If what I said happens to make you feel good, so much the better."

Eliza looked up at me with love showing in her big brown eyes. "You know, darling, I do believe you. I really think you would love me even with a big belly."

"You bet I would. Now, speaking of Mabel . . . ."

"Were we speaking of Mabel?"

"In a roundabout way. What else did she have to say when you talked to her last night, I mean besides that Sergeant Sullivan does not have a telephone at his home?"

"I guess the most important item is Mabel found Sergeant Sullivan's home address in the city directory, and she is going to his house this morning and explain some of our situation to him. If he has a telephone number that is not listed in the telephone directory, Mabel will get it. I think I mentioned to you yesterday that she wants us to call her after noon today."

"I vaguely remember something like that."

"On other subjects, she said there was no change in Monsignor O'Boylan's condition, and the only new news is some sort of labor trouble down at the Summerland Oil Fields. Mabel also said father was in to work yesterday, but he is still letting Louis Arquette run the paper."

Louis Arquette is the *Tribune's* senior reporter, and he seems quite capable of holding down the technical responsibilities of the editor's job. Whether or not he could oversee the paper's editorial policy in keeping with Frederick Hamm's wishes, was yet to be seen.

"It is swell of her to go see Sergeant Sullivan for us. Mabel is a darn good friend."

Agreeing with my assessment of Mabel, Eliza said, "Yes, she certainly is. Now what will we do in the meantime? I know we need to stop at a drugstore and get you a bottle of aspirin, but what then?"

"If we can reach Sergeant Sullivan, I hope to meet him somewhere. Since we don't dare go to Santa Barbara, we will have to arrange a meeting someplace else. That means we should find a safe place to stay north of Los Angeles."

Eliza nodded her understanding of my reasoning. "You mean someplace like Oxnard or Ventura?"

"Possibly Oxnard, but not Ventura. By now Estelle might know we were at the hospital in Ventura."

"All right. Do you want me to drive again, or are you up to it?"

"So far, I am up to driving. You can take it easy for a while."

"Okay, Lester, but if you get to feeling tired or you are in pain, I can drive."

Just as we paid our breakfast bill, the power failed and the lights went out. Before we went back out into the storm, I asked our waitress if she knew of a drugstore nearby that would be open on a Saturday. She did and gave me directions to find it. By nine-thirty we were northbound on Highway 101 again with a full tank of gasoline, a full bottle of Bayer aspirin, and two Baby Ruth candy bars for emergency rations.

It soon became apparent that the storm was heading in the same direction we were going. Up ahead the dark clouds stretched as far as we could see, which was not very far because the Chevrolet's windshield wipers were fighting a losing battle against one cloudburst after another. The thunder and lightning were still with us, but the thunder was hard to hear over the rain drumming on our roof. The flashes of lightning around us, however, were nearly nonstop.

Another effect of the storm was a general deterioration of traffic. There were few cars on the road, but they were driving cautiously and we were seldom able to travel more than thirty-five miles per hour. The driving was tedious and I was grateful we were in no hurry.

As we approached the outskirts of Santa Monica, Eliza noted, "It is almost twelve-thirty. We should find a place to call Mabel soon."

"Okay. Route 101 turns left through downtown on Colorado Avenue in a few minutes. We ought to find a public telephone there."

The Santa Monica shopping district was deserted, so when Eliza pointed out a public telephone in front of a theater, we were able to park right next to it. She hopped out of the car and ran into the telephone booth.

As sheets of water blew across Colorado Avenue, I watched Eliza through the rain spattered glass in the booth's folding door. She dropped a nickel into the slot and dialed "0" for an operator. While she was asking to be connected to Mabel's number in Santa Barbara, Eliza retrieved her nickel from the coin return. It took a while for the connection to go through, but given the intensity of the storm, I was somewhat surprised she was able to get through at all.

Eliza spoke with Mabel for a minute or so, and then turned to give me an "OK" gesture with her thumb and forefinger. The conversation only lasted a few more seconds before Eliza returned the telephone handset to its hook and ran back to the car.

"Good news?"

"Yes. Let me write it down before I forget."

Eliza took a small address book out of her purse and found a small gold mechanical pencil in one of the side pockets. On the blank inside of the address book's rear cover, she carefully printed, "Sullivan—911."

Putting the address book and pencil away, Eliza said, "Yes, darling, very good news. Mabel spoke with Sergeant Sullivan at his home this morning. She told him some of what has been happening, and he said we should call him as soon as possible."

"Did Mabel tell you specifically what she told Sergeant Sullivan about our situation?"

"Yes. She told him we were out of town and that you had been shot. She also told him what I told her about helping the sergeant solve a murder case and two assault cases. Mabel said that was when Sergeant Sullivan said he would be home all afternoon and that we should call him as soon as possible." As an afterthought, Eliza added, "Mabel also said it is raining cats and dogs there."

Reaching over to start the Chevrolet's engine, I said, "I'm not surprised to hear that, this is a huge storm."

"Where are you going? Aren't you going to call Sergeant Sullivan?"

"We can call him from Oxnard, or wherever we end up. That way we can have a meeting place in mind. We're only about ninety minutes from there now."

So after filling up the Chevrolet's gasoline tank at a Shell station that still had electrical power for their pumps, we got back on Route 101 and continued slogging our way north. Eliza peeled the wrapper from one of our Baby Ruth bars and we nibbled on it as we drove. We also took stock of our financial resources.

Eliza counted thirty-nine dollars left in my wallet of the fifty I withdrew from my bank on Wednesday and what little I had left from the sale of the Summerland story to the *Post-Dispatch*, which meant we had spent forty-some dollars on gasoline, food, lodging, and our wedding rings. Eliza had ten dollars left in her purse, which gave us a grand total of forty-nine dollars. I judged that amount to be adequate for a few more days.

Handing my wallet back to me, Eliza said, "You know what?"

"What?"

"When this is all over, we need to have some pictures of us taken. I want you to have a photograph of me in your wallet and I want one of you in my purse."

"That would be nice, but if you are worried I will forget what you look like, I don't think there is much chance of that."

Out of the corner of my eye I saw Eliza shake her head in mock disgust. "Whatever happened to the romantic man I married?"

"That fellow has your face and most of your other parts etched permanently into his brain."

"MOST of my other parts? Mister, you'd better have ALL of my parts etched into your mind."

"I'll work on that, I promise."

It was a little after two-thirty when we arrived at the outskirts of Oxnard, and I was glad to be there. It is hard to understand how doing nothing more than sitting behind the steering wheel of an automobile could be so tiring, but I was feeling weary when we pulled to the curb in front of a Piggly Wiggly grocery market in what served as downtown Oxnard. The store was open and they had a public telephone booth on the sidewalk near the entrance.

I said, "This is as good a place as any to call Sullivan. I'll go inside and get some change for the telephone."

"I can get the change for you, if you'd like, darling."

"Thanks, kiddo, but moving around a little would do me good. I'll be right back."

Even with the help of my cane I was walking a little lopsided as I returned to the telephone booth with five dollars' worth of quarters, dimes, and nickels in my pocket. That condition did not last long though, because the long distance operator cheerfully instructed me to deposit two dollars into the telephone before she completed the connection to Santa Barbara exchange nine-one-one.

I only heard two ring signals before Sergeant Sullivan said, "Hello?"

"Hello, Sergeant, this is Lester Kinney."

"Glad to hear from you, Mister Kinney. I was starting to think something else had happened to you."

"Sorry to keep you waiting. We had some driving to do in the storm and traffic was moving at a crawl."

"I can imagine. Most of the streets in town here are running rivers. Now, I understand you have some information for me."

"Actually, I have a lot of information for you. I think it would be best if we met someplace where we can talk face-to-face."

"Am I understanding correctly that you have been shot?"

"You understand correctly."

"Then wouldn't it be a good idea for you to return to your home where we can give you some protection?"

"Not to question the abilities of the Santa Barbara Police Department, but this thing has gotten so big and out of hand that I am not willing to trust our safety to anyone but myself."

Sullivan seemed to give that some thought. "I see. And you are certain of the facts that make you say that?"

"Positive. I can show you the bullet holes in my neck, and tell you exactly who I saw put them there. Is that certain enough for you?"

"All right, Mister Kinney, I will meet you. I'm working an extra shift from midnight to eight tomorrow morning because of the storm, but that's my only commitment."

I thought about timing and a location for a moment, and then said, "Do you think you would be up to making a forty-five minute drive when you get off tomorrow morning?"

"I can do that. Where do you want me to go?"

"Do you know the Hollywood by the Sea resort in Oxnard?"

"Yes, I've been there."

"I'll meet you just inside the entrance arch at nine tomorrow morning."

"I will see you then."

I hung up the telephone handset and just as I slid the telephone booth door open, a brilliant bolt of lightning lit up the black clouds directly over my head. The strike was so close that the flash and explosion of thunder were almost simultaneous. Through the water cascading down the Chevrolet's passenger window I saw Eliza flinch.

I walked around to the driver side door as quickly as I could and climbed in. Eliza slid over next to me and I put my arms around her.

"It's okay, kiddo."

"I don't mean to be a scaredy-cat. I just hate electrical

storms."

"Would you like to hear what Sergeant Sullivan had to say?"

Eliza nodded. "Yes, please tell me."

"Well the upshot of it all is he's coming down here to meet us tomorrow morning at nine o'clock. At first he suggested we go home so the police could protect us, but I told him this thing is so out of hand I was not willing to trust our safety to anyone but ourselves."

"I don't like it that he wanted us to come home. Are you sure we can trust Sergeant Sullivan?"

I looked Eliza in the eyes. "I'm not sure of anything, kiddo, but if we ever want to go back to Santa Barbara, we have to trust someone to help us. Based on our experience with Sullivan, I think he is on the level."

Her expression told me she wasn't as sure as I was, but she said, "Okay, darling." Then another lightning flash lit up the interior of the car and she added, "Do you think we ought to go into the store as long as we are here and get some provisions so we don't have to go out in all this again after we find a place to stay?"

"I think that is an excellent suggestion. What would you like me to get?"

"I'm going in with you. I don't like it out here."

As we walked the two main aisles of the market, Eliza held on to my arm with one hand and carried a wire shopping basket in the other. When we reached the checkout counter, our provisions included a loaf of sliced bread, two bright red Delicious apples, a small block of cheddar cheese, a quarter-pound of bologna, a tin of Peter Pan peanut butter, a wax paper bag of Laura Scudder potato chips, a small jar of Best Foods mayonnaise, and a package of Oreo cookies. We also bought a small paring knife and a package of Nibroc folded paper towels. Our bag of groceries—enough to hold us over for two or three meals—came to a grand total of three dollars and some change.

Back at the car, the storm was still raging. In a nervous tone of voice, Eliza asked, "Can we go where we will be staying now?"

"Sure. I have a motor court in mind that is close to where we are meeting Sullivan in the morning. It should do nicely."

I navigated across Oxnard to the coast and a section of beach known locally as the Silver Strand. The place I was looking for was right where I remembered it. I pulled into the driveway of a small motor court with the nautical name of Sea View Cottages.

Situated at the intersection of Roosevelt Boulevard and Melrose Drive, the Sea View looked clean and expensive, being as it was, across the street from the beach and adjacent to the Hollywood by the Sea resort area. This time of the year, though, the beach was deserted, especially with a storm rolling through. I hoped the proprietors might be eager enough for business that they would go easy on our pocketbook.

Inside the office, I found exactly that to be the case. The manager even offered me an umbrella to use while we carried our luggage into the cottage he rented to us for three dollars per night. A sign on the wall indicated cottages rented for six dollars during the summer and five dollars in the "off season."

The cottages of Sea View numbered eight and were arranged in a line along a driveway running perpendicular to the street. We were in number one, the cottage closest to Roosevelt Boulevard.

After we carried our bags and groceries into the cottage, I took a closer look at our lodgings. Actually the room was quite nice, a fact that was not lost on Eliza.

"It's just like a fancy yacht in here. Look at the wooden platform around the bed and the round windows like portholes."

The room was indeed furnished like the main salon aboard a ritzy motor yacht. Nicely finished wood cabinets, curtains with anchor designs, and a chandelier resembling a hurricane lantern hanging on a metal chain combined to give the room a decidedly nautical feeling. Fortunately, the bathroom was more functional than nautical.

Feeling a little fatigued, probably from not eating anything since breakfast, I sat on the bed. Eliza came over and sat next to me. Holding my hand, she said, "How are you feeling, darling?"

"Okay. I'm just tired. I could probably use something to eat, too."

"Would you like a sandwich with baloney, cheese, peanut butter, or all three?"

"How about just the first two?"

"Coming right up. After we eat, I think we should change your dressing. It's looking a little worn around the edges."

"All right, Nurse Eliza."

A few minutes later she summoned me to the room's small table where our sandwiches, some potato chips, and apple slices were laid out on paper towels. Not a fancy feast, but one that tasted darn good to me.

I complimented Eliza on her cooking and she laughed, "It would be difficult to mess up a bologna sandwich, darling. I will say, however, doing the dishes is a snap."

Once done with our repast, Eliza led me into the bathroom

and removed my shirt. She used the blunt-tipped scissors Nurse Norwood provided to carefully cut the dressing and remove it. Then she examined the bullet wounds.

"The wounds look good. I don't see any inflammation or extra redness. You are healing quite well, darling."

Smiling, I said, "I am sure that is due entirely to the excellent medical care I have received since leaving the hospital."

"I doubt that. It is much more likely married life agrees with you and accelerates the healing process. Now hold still while I use a wash cloth with some warm water to clean your neck around the wounds."

I held still, and when she was satisfied with the cleaning job she performed, Eliza rewrapped my neck in fresh gauze and applied new adhesive tape.

Glancing at my pocket watch, I said, "It's only seven, but I feel like I could sleep . . . ."

An explosion of thunder interrupted me and caused Eliza to take a step closer to my side. "Darn. Except for the rain on the roof, it's been quiet since we checked in. Now the thunder is back. I brought a book along, but I don't know if I can read with all that going on outside."

"Tell you what, kiddo. Let's get ready for bed and you can prop yourself up and read while I get some sleep. That way I'll be close by if the thunder and lightning scares you and you need to hold on."

Eliza grinned. "You want me to read while you sleep? I guess the honeymoon is over."

Putting my arms around her I said, "Kiddo, the honeymoon hasn't even started."

A few minutes later Eliza was reading and I was drifting off to sleep when a bolt of lightning lit up the room through the curtains and a rumble of thunder shook the rafters. The next thing I knew the light was off and Eliza was cuddled against me. I put my arm around her and that's how we spent the night.

TWENTY-ONE

Sunday - September 15, 1928

I awoke early again Sunday morning, which isn't surprising since I'd been in bed for more than twelve hours. I was reminded of Nurse Norwood's warning about feeling weak and tired on a daily basis. Hopefully it would not be much longer until our situation was such that I could take things a little easier.

I lay in bed for a few minutes listening for sounds of the storm, but there were none. For Eliza's sake, I hoped the thunder and lightning had moved on up the coast to annoy the people in San Francisco for a while.

Slipping out of bed carefully so as not to awaken Eliza, I went into the bathroom, where I took a bath, shaved, and did the best I could to make myself presentable. Back in the bedroom I found Eliza sitting on the edge of the bed in my pale blue shirt. Upon seeing me, she jumped up and ran into my arms. We hugged for a long time.

"Is something wrong, kiddo?"

She shook her head. "Not really, I guess I'm just a little homesick."

"Homesick for your father's home, our home, or Santa Barbara in general?"

"Our home and Santa Barbara. If the situation were different, I would be fine, but knowing we can't go back upsets me. I told Marguerite Whitley I would be back to work on Monday. That's tomorrow, but I don't think we should be in Santa Barbara yet, do you?"

"Right now I would not feel good about going back, but let's hold the final decision in abeyance until we have had our talk with Sergeant Sullivan."

Eliza nodded. "Okay. That makes the most sense."

"You know, there is one thing we didn't purchase with our provisions yesterday."

With a smile, Eliza said, "I bet you mean coffee."

"I do. Not only am I addicted to you, I'm also addicted to your coffee. It won't be the same, but I suggest you get dressed so we can go out and find some."

"That sounds like a good plan. I don't have my watch on. What time is it?"

"It was seven o'clock when I looked at my pocket watch a few minutes ago."

"All right, darling. Give me fifteen minutes."

"Okay, but I'm going to time you."

Eliza was as good as her word and twenty minutes later we were driving up Victoria Avenue, a main north-south artery through the Oxnard harbor area, in search of a café or some other establishment that sold hot coffee. We found what we were looking for across the street from a small US Coast Guard Station. The little café was called The Anchorage and the breakfasts they were making smelled so good, we decided to splurge on some breakfast to go with our coffee. The scrambled eggs and sausages I ordered tasted every bit as good as they smelled when the cook was preparing them. The good smells even tempted Eliza to the point of ordering eggs and toast.

Fortified with a good breakfast, we drove to Hollywood by the Sea. I wanted to look the place over before our meeting with Sergeant Sullivan to be sure we weren't walking into a trap. I know a little something about the place because covering its grand opening in twenty-six was one of my first assignments for the *Glendale News Press*.

Hollywood by the Sea is a swanky beach resort capitalizing on the fact that nearby sections of sand dunes were used as filming locations for a few popular motion pictures, including Valentino's *The Sheik* and Douglas Fairbank's *Bound in Morocco*. A shrewd developer got ahold of the property and bulldozed it flat so the beach could be subdivided into lots. Of course the bulldozers also eliminated most of the dunes people came out there to see in the first place. The developer, however, did build a few other attractions, like a small lake and a forty room hotel. He even named some of the streets he created after famous thoroughfares in Hollywood. It was all quite snazzy and the developer's efforts were resulting in a profitable venture.

The main entrance to Hollywood by the Sea features a concrete arch supported by two square pillars. The sign on the arch says "Welcome to Hollywood by the Sea" and "Park Your Car/Enjoy the Beach." A concrete roadway under the arch runs parallel to the coastline and offers access to the home lots and attractions. The place reeked of money.

Taking it all in, Eliza said, "This is not my idea of going to the beach."

"Mine either. I guess this just proves there really is a sucker born every minute."

I kept looking for signs of potential trouble, but I detected none. The only people in sight were a few hearty souls who were braving the morning chill for a swim in the surf. I parked next to a building called the Beach House, a sundries store with a walk-up window where snacks and drinks are sold. I bought two cardboard cups of coffee to help keep us warm, and then drove back to the entrance where we were to meet Sergeant Sullivan in about fifteen minutes.

Eliza slid over on the seat to share a little body heat and said, "I certainly hope Sergeant Sullivan is able to help us. Do you have any idea what to do if he cannot or will not?"

"I'm afraid I do not. I must say, though, I am quite tired of hiding from Estelle Abernathy and her thugs. Tell me something, kiddo. Would Mabel have told you if Clarence Storche ever printed my oil spill article in the *Post-Dispatch*?"

"I'm sure she would have said something. Mabel reads and clips the *Post-Dispatch* as part of her job, so if it was there, she would have seen it. Are you still thinking of sending Mister Storche an article on Estelle adopting Aurora?"

"It's on my mind, but judging by his lack of activity, I'm guessing Storche has dropped his crusade against Estelle, assuming we were right and that's what he was planning. If we have some time to kill, I might just write that story anyway, depending on how Sergeant Sullivan reacts to what we tell him."

Just then a two or three year old black Model T sedan drove under the Hollywood by the Sea entrance arch and pulled to a stop across the street from us. I said, "Speak of the devil. There's the sergeant. Sit tight for just a minute, kiddo, and I'll see how he wants to do this."

I got out and walked across the street to the Ford's driver-side door. Sullivan waved at me, and then opened the door."

"Hello, Mister Kinney."

"Hello, Sergeant. Thank you for coming."

I noticed him eyeing the dressing on my neck as he said, "You are welcome, Mister Kinney. I see you brought Miss Hamm with you."

"Yes, but she is now Missus Kinney."

"Is that right? Congratulations. It would seem the two of you have been busy."

"We have, and our experiences are part of the story, or stories, we have for you. Shall we meet in your car to get out of the chilly air?"

"That is a good idea, but I think I'll turn around and park behind your machine so we can keep an eye on the entrance."

While Sergeant Sullivan turned his sedan around, I helped Eliza down from our Chevrolet. When we climbed into the back of the sergeant's automobile, he said, "Good morning, Missus Kinney. I understand congratulations are in order."

Eliza smiled a genuine smile and said, "Thank you, Sergeant Sullivan. I believe you are the first person besides Lester to address me by my new name. I rather like the way it sounds."

Sullivan laughed. "Good! If you don't mind me saying so, I could tell when I first met the two of you that a stroll down the aisle was in the offing. You just are not the kind of people to . . . well, to live under the circumstances that existed at the time."

I think Eliza may have blushed a little on hearing Sullivan's opinion of us. I said, "Well, Sergeant, are you ready to hear a rather amazing story?"

Turning sideways on his Ford's front seat so he was facing us, the sergeant said, "Yes, quite ready."

"I guess the best place to start is with the information you provided us on Aurora Abernathy's adoption. There was only one surprise in that information. We had no idea that Estelle Abernathy's employee, Armando Delgado, is Aurora's real father.

"He is? You are right, that is a surprise, and a rather odd one at that."

"Once we had the facts of the matter, we began debating how best to put the information we had to good use. We know for certain Estelle is a lesbian. I would rather not tell you exactly how we know that to be a fact quite yet, so please take my word on it for the time being."

Sullivan did not look surprised. He simply nodded and I continued my narrative. "We knew your hands would be tied without evidence that living in Estelle Abernathy's home put her adopted daughter at risk, so we looked for another way of having her removed from the Abernathy house and we came up with an idea we thought would work.

"We contacted Monsignor O'Boylan, thinking he would take steps to solve the problem through the church if he knew the facts. He agreed to meet us at the old Mission rose garden. That meeting took place last Wednesday at one o'clock in the afternoon. We laid out the facts for the Bishop and he agreed it was an intolerable situation. He also indicated he would take some action to have Aurora Abernathy removed from Estelle's home, although he did not say specifically what form that action would take. Included in those facts we gave the Bishop was also firsthand proof that Estelle Abernathy is a lesbian."

I did not look at Eliza when I said that, but I felt her squeeze my hand. I noticed however, that Sergeant Sullivan took an involuntary glance in her direction.

"After that meeting with the Bishop, Eliza and I left town because we had reason to believe we could be in danger, depending on what Monsignor O'Boylan did with the information we gave him."

Sullivan finished the next part of the story for me. "And shortly after that Monsignor O'Boylan was attacked. By the way, he is still in a coma and his doctors are certain he will never regain consciousness."

Eliza said, "Oh, no."

I said, "I'm very sorry to hear that. He seemed like a good man to me."

Frowning, Sergeant Sullivan said, "By all accounts, he is. If, however, Estelle Abernathy had anything to do with the beating of Monsignor O'Boylan, she would have to know what you told him. How could she have known that?"

"Sergeant, we are dealing with a shrewd and powerful woman. She has what she described to me as a 'grapevine' of informants who keep her up to date on almost everything that happens in Santa Barbara. I'm guessing somebody in the County Clerk's office knew you looked at Aurora Abernathy's adoption papers and reported that to Miss Abernathy.

"It is also a safe bet that, after a meeting I had with her last Monday night, Estelle already had someone keeping an eye on Eliza and me. If they reported that you came by our house and dropped something off, she had a connection between you, the adoption papers, and us. Then when we met with the Bishop, she realized what we were up to."

Sullivan thought about my scenario for a moment, and then said, "Yes, it could have been that way, but what makes you think Estelle Abernathy had someone watching you?"

Pointing at the fading bruise on my face, I said, "As you noticed the last time we met, I received a very thorough beating prior to all of this. The man who attacked me was Estelle Abernathy's butler, Armando Delgado.

"As you may already know, Frederick Hamm fired me over a

personal matter. It turns out that Estelle Abernathy owns controlling interest in the *Tribune* and she offered to reinstate me in the position from which I had been fired. When I turned her down, she ordered Delgado to convince me I should accept her offer. Estelle does not tolerate rejection well."

By this time, Sergeant Sullivan was taking notes of our conversation. He looked up from his notebook with a shocked expression. "Estelle Abernathy had you beaten?"

"Yes, it happened in her driveway as I as was leaving the Abernathy mansion after meeting with her last Monday night. Delgado sucker-punched me and proceeded to inflict quite a bit more damage while telling me I should reconsider Estelle's offer or we would be having another, even more unpleasant conversation.

"Afterwards Estelle had to be wondering why I turned down her generous offer to put me back on the *Tribune* staff. She did not get where she is by ignoring details like that, so that is why I suspect she had someone watching us."

"Yes. I wish I had known about that beating, but I can see why you thought reporting the incident would make matters worse."

"In retrospect, it might not have made any difference because things got worse all on their own."

Sullivan glanced at the dressing around my neck. "Is that when you were shot?"

"Yes. We drove down Highway 101 after our meeting with Monsignor O'Boylan Wednesday afternoon and decided to stop along the beach and discuss things. We were sitting in my car when a movement through the back window caught my eye. I turned and what I saw was Estelle Abernathy's Cadillac Phaeton, the red one with the gold monograms on the doors, coming toward us. I could see Delgado behind the wheel.

"I yelled for Eliza to get down on the floorboard and started our car to get us out of there. That's when I heard the gunshot and felt a pain in my neck. You can see the bullet hole in the rear window of my car."

Sullivan looked up at the back window of my car and nodded. "Yes, I see it."

"I lost consciousness almost immediately. All I had time to do was slam on the brakes to keep us from going into a drainage ditch beside the road. Eliza will have to tell you the rest, because I was out like a light."

I looked at Eliza and she said, "I stayed on the floor of the car for what seemed like a long time before I heard a car drive away. I looked out the back window and saw Estelle's big red car leaving.

"When it was gone, I got out and went around to Lester's side of the car. I did my best to stop the bleeding from the wounds in his neck, and then pushed him across the seat so I could drive us to a hospital. At that point I didn't know if Lester was going to live or die. I decided on a hospital in Ventura because we were about halfway between there and Santa Barbara, and I didn't think going back was a good idea. I took him to Big Sisters Hospital and the doctors and nurses there took over."

I said, "A Ventura County Sheriff's deputy took a report of the shooting at the hospital, and because the crime actually occurred in Santa Barbara County, he said he would send the report to the Santa Barbara County Sheriff's office. When you see that report you will find that it differs considerably from the account we just gave you. I gave a false report because I didn't want an investigation alerting Estelle Abernathy to the fact that Delgado didn't kill me and leading her directly to our location at that time."

Looking at Eliza, Sullivan smiled and said, "You picked a good woman to marry, Mister Kinney. Sounds to me as if she saved your life."

Squeezing Eliza's hand, I said, "I'm certain she did."

From that point I related our "escape" from the hospital in Ventura, our trip to Mexico, and our drive north to Oxnard in the storm. I concluded that part of the story by saying, "That's it for our adventures. Now, the matter of Tom Wigand."

Sullivan looked surprised yet again. "You can tell me about that, too?"

"We have no specific evidence other than some personal observations made the day he disappeared."

The sergeant turned to a fresh page in his notebook, and I said, "That was on Saturday, September Eighth. The *Tribune* sent me to cover the ceremony at which Estelle Abernathy was to make her presentation of a fifty-thousand-dollar donation to Saint Andria's Orphanage at the County Courthouse.

"I was just about to leave for the ceremony when Frederick Hamm called to tell me about a major story in the morning's *Post-Dispatch*. It concerned the oil spill down at Fernald Point. Specifically, Mister Hamm expected Tom Wigand to be at the ceremony and that he would use the opportunity to badger Estelle Abernathy into making a statement about the oil spill. Any statement she made would be news because she owns a large part of the Summerland Oil Field Company. Mister Hamm was warning me to stay away from Wigand because, at the time, Miss

Abernathy had indicated a fondness for my writing, and Mister Hamm did not want her to get the idea I was in league with Wigand.

"At the conclusion of the ceremony Wigand did exactly what Mister Hamm predicted. He stopped Estelle Abernathy as she was leaving and twice demanded statements from her. After his second attempt Delgado and Miss Abernathy's driver advanced on Wigand and ran him off with the help of Santa Barbara police officers who were providing security for the event."

Sullivan said, "Yes, I believe I heard something about that. I didn't think much about it because the behavior was typical for Tom Wigand."

"Well, that night there was a reception at Estelle Abernathy's mansion and Wigand knew I was on the guest list. That must have really burned him up because he surely figured I would take advantage of the situation to get the oil spill statements from her that he could not get.

"Now, from here on I'm speculating, but I have faith in my speculations. Events like the reception that night are always a little chaotic, and I suspect Wigand drove up there with the intention of slipping into the party and cornering Estelle again for a statement, hopefully beating me to the punch.

"My guess is he showed up and Estelle's people headed him off, making sure he would never bother her again. I know that seems rather drastic, but human life, especially among the lower classes, means little to Miss Abernathy. I think killing Wigand might have also been a warning to Clarence Storche at the *Press-Tribune* to back off on his stories about the Summerland oil spills. He dropped the story and has published nothing negative about Estelle since."

Sullivan stopped writing. "Your speculation sounds quite plausible, but unless someone actually saw Wigand on the grounds or saw him with Estelle Abernathy's men, it's all circumstantial."

"I understand that, Sergeant, but knowing what probably happened may still turn out to be important. You might at some point be able to use the knowledge as leverage, or at the very least, it is a warning about the dangers involved in dealing with a powerful woman like Estelle Abernathy."

"Point taken, Mister Kinney. Do you have anything else you feel I need to know?"

"We may think of something along the way, but you have the main points of which we wanted you to be aware."

"All right, Mister Kinney. Thank you. Now, what can I do for you in exchange?"

Sergeant Sullivan surprised me with that. I thought what we wanted him to do was fairly obvious. "Go arrest Estelle and her gang so we can go home and pick up our lives where we left off."

The Sergeant laughed at that. "I wish it were that easy, Mister Kinney, but I understand your dilemma. I am going to investigate what you told me about the beating of Monsignor O'Boylan, and of course I will look into you getting shot, but making arrests that result in convictions requires rock solid evidence, especially when the defendant is a prominent citizen. Now I have your statements and those of Missus Kinney, but I need corroborating witnesses and physical evidence. Otherwise making the arrests is a waste of time."

I could tell Eliza was disappointed. I was, too. I was also formulating a plan to take matters into our own hands. I said, "Sergeant Sullivan, may I expect that you will also open an investigation into the circumstances of Aurora Abernathy as they pertain to Monsignor O'Boylan's beating?"

Sullivan eyed me suspiciously. "Yes, Mister Kinney, you may expect that, but only in so far as those circumstances pertain to the attack on the Bishop or at such time I have solid evidence that Estelle Abernathy is, as you say, a . . . person with abnormal sexual tendencies."

"Thank you, Sergeant."

I opened the back door on my side of Sullivan's sedan and was stepping down on the running board when he said, "Hold on, Kinney. I am getting the distinct impression you have something up your sleeve. If you are thinking of taking matters into your own hands, I strongly advise against doing so. As you, yourself, pointed out, Estelle Abernathy is a powerful woman. I doubt if you are any match for her on your own."

Helping Eliza down out of the sedan, I said, "Thank you for your opinion, Sergeant Sullivan, but I would not wager money on that if I were you."

"Wait! What if I need to reach you?"

"As a direct result of your inability to protect and serve the innocent citizens who pay your salary, we can no longer be reached. Good day, Sergeant Sullivan."

TWENTY-TWO

Sunday - September 16, 1928

We left Sergeant Sullivan's Model T in our rearview mirror, and as we drove under the Hollywood by the Sea arch Eliza said, "Sergeant Sullivan sure isn't being much help. He sounds more afraid of Estelle than we are."

"It does seem as if that is the case. Looks like we will have to get out of this mess on our own."

I sensed Eliza looking at me. "How are we going to do that, darling?"

"I think our original idea of embarrassing Estelle Abernathy in the press still has merit. If we can turn public opinion against her, her power will decline. With a little luck she could even end up behind bars."

"But Clarence Storche has lost interest in attacking Estelle in the *Post-Dispatch* and she has control of the *Tribune*, how are we going to accomplish that?"

"Perhaps we have been thinking too small. There are other newspapers in this part of the world that are big enough to have no fear of Estelle. When you think about it she is really only a big fish in a small pond."

"I see that, but why would a newspaper outside of Santa Barbara have any interest in articles about her?"

"Because stories about sex and scandals, especially among the rich and famous, sell newspapers. Writing stories in that genre is not what I consider good journalism, but they are good for circulation. When we get resituated I'll show you what I have in mind."

"Where are we going to get resituated?"

"Away from here. Sergeant Sullivan last saw us in this area, and while I don't really believe he is in Estelle's pocket, there is no sense in taking chances. What do you think?"

"I agree there is no sense in taking chances, but we can't hide from Estelle indefinitely. That reminds me, I must telephone Marguerite Whitley first thing in the morning to tell her I will not be coming back to the library for a while longer. I have another week of time off coming, but I really hate to put the staff in a bind at the last minute like this."

"On the other hand having you in the hospital or dead would put them in a worse bind."

"I know, darling. It's what we have to do. What else is on the list?"

"We need to get our hands on more cash. We are not out of money, but if we're going to stay on the road another week or so, we will need more. Unfortunately, that means going to a bank in Santa Barbara. I don't know how else we can do it."

Eliza was quiet for a minute, and then she said, "I do. I will call Mabel and ask her to meet us so we can give her a check to cash. Then she could bring the cash to us."

"That is asking a lot of her."

"Mabel knows I would gladly do the same thing for her."

"All right. Let's check out of the Sea View Cottages and get on the road."

By eleven o'clock we had loaded our bags into the Chevrolet, checked out of the Sea View Cottages, and were parked at a public telephone booth next to a Gilmore gasoline station near State Route One, or the Pacific Coast Highway as it is known locally. Eliza was in the booth speaking with Mabel, and I was standing just outside keeping an eye on the traffic going by. I was concerned that Sergeant Sullivan might follow us, but his Model T was nowhere to be seen and there were no signs of anyone else having the slightest interest in us.

Eliza put her hand over the telephone handset and asked, "How much cash do we need, darling?"

"Another fifty dollars will keep us going for a while."

She nodded and put the handset up to her ear again. "Lester thinks fifty dollars will get us by." After a pause, Eliza said, "That would be wonderful! Mabel, I don't know how to thank you."

Eliza covered the handset again. "Where would you like to meet her tomorrow afternoon?"

"Pick a place somewhere a little closer to Santa Barbara so Mabel doesn't have to drive as far."

Finishing her conversation, Eliza ended the telephone call and said, "Mabel is such a dear person. She is bringing us the fifty dollars tomorrow at four o'clock and we can give her the check then."

"That's awfully kind of her. When I write the check, I'll make out it for a little extra to cover some of the telephone charges we owe her."

"I'm sure she would appreciate that, but why don't I write this check on my account? I think it is my turn."

"You can get the next one, kiddo. Where are we supposed to meet her?"

"At the Summerland Market. It's right on Route 101. Mabel grew up in Santa Barbara just like I did, so she knows her way around."

"Good. Now let's get out of here."

Back in the Chevrolet, Eliza asked, "Where are we getting out of here to?"

"That is an excellent question. We are running out of nearby places to stay. About the only choices we have left are to travel back south toward Los Angeles or return to the Ventura area. Returning to Ventura is risky, but it will save us some driving back and forth. I think I know of an inn there that will not be too busy this time of year, and it is relatively secluded. It's just up the coast highway nine or ten miles. What do you think?"

"I don't know what to think, darling. Please make the decision for us."

The Pierpont Inn was exactly where I remembered it being, on a bluff overlooking California Route One and the Pacific Ocean. I pulled into their drive and we looked things over. The hotel was a two story craftsman style building within a grove of trees that sheltered the grounds from offshore winds.

"What do you think, kiddo? Will this do?"

"It looks expensive. I wonder what they charge for rooms."

Climbing down from the Chevrolet's seat, I said, "I'll find out."

The entrance to the Pierpont Inn was a tall door with inset glass panels. The lobby was finished with polished wood paneling and large windows. The furnishings were also wood with brown leather cushions. The setting seemed quite homey. I hoped such hominess did not come at too great a price.

A few moments later I exchanged five dollars for the key to room twelve. Twelve was a first floor room on the back side of the hotel. An honest to goodness bellboy carried our bags for us along with my typewriter and stationary supplies. I tipped him twenty-cents and we explored our new accommodations.

We were in a corner room with two large windows, both overlooking the panorama of beach through the trees behind the hotel. The room was furnished in a fashion similar to that of the lobby, with a table, two chairs, a commodious armoire, and a large bed with a massive wooden headboard. The bathroom featured a combination bathtub/shower enclosure with an abundance of fresh towels and soaps.

According to my pocket watch it was a few minutes past eleven when I wearily sat on the edge of the bed. Eliza sat next to me.

"You look tired, darling. How are you feeling?"

"The way I look. I just don't have any stamina since I was shot."

"The nurse said that would pass in time."

"I know. I'm just tired of feeling like a slug all the time."

Eliza smiled. "I surely would not have mistaken you for a slug when you told Sergeant Sullivan off this morning."

"That may not have been the smartest thing I ever did, but he made me mad, darn mad."

"I am pretty sure you did not burn any bridges we will need to cross again, and for what it's worth, he made me awfully mad, too. Now, how about a peanut butter sandwich? I think peanut butter has a lot of protein in it, so it should be good for you. We also have an apple left, and if you eat all that healthy stuff, I might give you an Oreo cookie or two for dessert."

"All right, kiddo, you sold me. Bring on lunch."

We ate our peanut butter sandwiches, apple slices, and Oreo cookies at the table and it all tasted good. I wished, however, we had something other than water to wash down our lunch.

"I noticed a soda pop cooler in the gift shop, and they also have complimentary coffee at the front desk. Right now a soda would taste pretty good. I think I'll walk to the lobby and get one. Would you like a soda or a cup of coffee?"

"I might. Why don't we walk down there together?"

I don't know whether Eliza just felt uneasy about being in the room alone or if she was afraid I might not make it all the way to the lobby and back on my own. Whichever it was, we returned from the sojourn with two icy cold bottles of Coca-Cola and a bottle of Orange Crush.

We shared the orange soda while I turned our table into an office by means of my typewriter and stationary supplies. Eliza propped herself up on the bed with a copy of *Beau Geste*, and I began writing the first of two feature articles I had in mind.

An hour later I sat back in my chair to read what I had written. When Eliza noticed I was no longer typing, she stood behind me with her hands on my shoulders. I looked up and saw she was wearing the little typewriter pin purchased with her new wardrobe at Trenwith's Department Store.

"I like your pin."

She smiled. "I thought it was appropriate since you are writing again. How is it coming?"

"All right. I'm just editing the first article."

"Do you mind if I read over your shoulder?"

"Not at all. I welcome your opinion."

SANTA BARBARA POLICE INVESTIGATE BIZARRE ADOPTION

Catholic Church Condones Homosexuality?

By Lester Kinney

The story, itself, summarized the potentially fatal attack of Monsignor O'Boylan and the ensuing police investigation. I placed emphasis on the suspected motive being information the Bishop had just received regarding the adoption of a female child from Saint Andria's Orphanage by a wealthy and powerful business woman in Santa Barbara who is widely suspected of being a lesbian. The story also mentioned a large monetary donation to the orphanage by the unnamed business woman.

I quoted Sergeant Sullivan of the Santa Barbara Police Department as saying, "You can expect us to open an investigation into the circumstances of the adoption as they pertain to the beating of Monsignor O'Boylan." I further quoted Sullivan as saying, "We will be looking for solid evidence that the woman in question is a person who engages in abnormal sexual behavior."

After reading the article, Eliza said, "You certainly do have a way with words. The implications are there without any false statements that I can see."

"Again, this is yellow journalism at its worst, but that's what I was trying for."

"You succeeded, darling, but if this article is published, there will be no question of who you are talking about among Santa Barbara readers. Estelle will really be out for blood."

"That is why we have to stay on our toes. I don't intend to give Armando a second chance at us."

Eliza leaned over and kissed my cheek. "I'm counting on that, darling."

With that Eliza went back to her book and I finished editing my first draft of the story. I typed the final version with a carbon copy and filed the original in my suitcase. I slipped the carbon copy into the stack of blank paper I brought from home. Finally, I tore the first draft into the tiniest scraps I could manage and flushed them down the toilet.

Returning to my makeshift office, I rolled a fresh piece of paper into the typewriter and sat thinking about an attention-grabbing headline. This is what I finally typed:

JOURNALISTS BEATEN AND SHOT

Santa Barbara Newspaper Owner Implicated

I left my byline off of this article because it was partly about me and I felt the content would carry more weight if readers believed it was an entirely objective report. The first part of the story accurately described the beating and subsequent shooting of former *Santa Barbara Tribune* reporter Lester Kinney at the hands of Armando Delgado, an employee of wealthy Santa Barbara businesswoman Estelle Abernathy. I added that, by her own admission, Miss Abernathy is a silent partner in the company that publishes the *Tribune*. I quoted myself as an "eye witness" positively identifying Delgado as the perpetrator of both the physical assault and the shooting.

The second part of the story included a decidedly lopsided version of the incident in which *Santa Barbara Post-Dispatch* reporter Tom Wigand was strong-armed by employees of Estelle Abernathy at a civic function and a report about the subsequent discovery of his dead body in the Riviera district of Santa Barbara not far from Miss Abernathy's mansion. The implication that the two incidents were related was clear.

The article concluded by saying that despite the statements of credible eye witnesses, an unnamed spokesman for the Santa Barbara Police Department insists further investigation into the matter is necessary before arrests can be made. The exact quote I used is, "We need corroborating witnesses and physical evidence. Otherwise making arrests is a waste of time."

To that I added "Lester Kinney, the victim in one of the two cases is quoted as saying, 'I have the distinct impression the Santa Barbara Police Department is reluctant to tangle with a powerful citizen such as the Abernathy woman. If so, that is a shameful attitude for an organization charged with protecting the public.'"

The second article took longer to write than the first because I named Estelle Abernathy as being involved and I had to be very careful in my choices of words. It was nearly two o'clock by the time I rolled the last page of the second story out of my typewriter.

Turning to Eliza, I said, "Care to read story number two?"

Tucking a bookmark into *Beau Geste*, she hopped off of the bed and trotted over to the table. I handed her the five double-spaced pages comprising the new article. Eliza sat in the other chair at the table and dove into the draft I just finished.

When Eliza set the final page on the table, she said, "Holy smoke, Lester. You certainly are not pulling any punches."

"I can't be subtle if we expect to get these stories published."

Eliza looked sad as she put the pages on the table in their proper order. "What are you thinking about, kiddo?"

"Oh, I was just wondering about father and how he is doing. Reading your article made me think of him and how Estelle caused me pain in one way and caused him pain in another way. We are both victims of Estelle Abernathy and her cruel behavior. I never realized that before."

"That sounds like an accurate description of the situation."

Eliza gave me a small smile. "Thank you, darling. Sometimes it takes me a while to look beyond the trees and see the forest."

Thinking that an outing might cheer her, I said, "How about some fresh air and a change of scenery? If you can wait just a little longer while I type a final draft of this article, I'll take you out for an ice cream cone. Okay?"

She put her arms around my shoulders and gave me a kiss on the cheek. "You are the only treat I need, but I would not turn down a chocolate ice cream cone."

"Okay, kiddo, I'll get to work."

By three o'clock I had an original and a carbon copy of the second article. After destroying the first draft, I stashed the carbon copy with the copy of the first story in my paper stack, and then I removed the original of the first article from my suitcase. I decided the originals might be safer locked in the Chevrolet's trunk while we were out. I slid the pages into a manila envelope and we carried them to the car on our way out for a Sunday drive.

Ventura's downtown business district is about a mile north of the Pierpont Inn and a tour of the area turned up an open-for-business ice cream shop near the intersection on Chestnut and Santa Clara Streets. The results of that discovery were one chocolate ice cream cone and one strawberry cone.

There is a block-square park across the street, so we took advantage of what turned out to be a warm sunny day by making ourselves at home on a bench. We were just finishing our cones when I said, "We should probably give some thought to our plans for tomorrow."

"Okay, darling. Besides calling the library first thing in the morning, what do you think we should do?"

"I have been thinking about visiting Summerland to take a look around. Mabel said something about the Summerland Oil Field Company having labor problems. I would like to see what's going on. There could be another story in it."

"If we do that in the afternoon, we can just wait around there until Mabel arrives about four."

"Okay, that's what we will do. We will have to keep a sharp eye out, though, to avoid anyone we know tomorrow at Summerland."

"Lester?"

"Yes, kiddo?"

"Do you think we will ever be able to go home again?"

"I hope so. That's the purpose behind all of this."

Eliza frowned. "I guess what I really want to know is if we should just give up on going back and find a new place to live. Those articles you're writing scare me. I'm worried about what Estelle will do when she sees them."

I nodded. "I understand, but moving away is not as easy as it sounds. First, allowing that woman to control our lives galls me no end. Second, we would have to change our identities, especially if I continue on as a newspaper reporter. All it would take is somebody noticing my byline in a paper somewhere and we would be back in the soup."

"Darling, have you ever thought about writing novels? You write so well, I bet you could write great stories, and novelists use pen names."

I smiled. "I think every journalist has a secret ambition to write a great novel, and I'm no exception. The problem is it takes time to write a book and get it published, often a lot of time. That means a writer must already have a source of income to live on while writing a novel."

"But we do have a source of income. I am a good librarian and there is demand for people with the skills I have. Plus, there are libraries everywhere. We could move just about anywhere."

"I appreciate your willingness to contribute, but what about raising that family we spoke about?"

With sincerity on her face, Eliza said, "We're still young, darling. We could postpone starting a family a few years."

The last thing I wanted to do at that moment was crush the self-confidence Eliza was exuding. On the other hand, I had no intention of making her be the breadwinner of the family.

"All right, let's give the idea some thought."

"Please do, darling. I have all the faith in the world in you. Nothing would please me more than helping patrons find your books in a library somewhere."

I leaned over and kissed her. "Thank you, kiddo. Knowing you believe in me means more than I can tell you."

TWENTY-THREE

Monday - September 17, 1928

After stopping by the Pierpont Inn's front desk to say we enjoyed their hospitality so much we wanted to stay another night, Eliza and I ventured into the hotel's dining room for coffee and breakfast. My bride had flapjacks and I enjoyed a tasty Cheddar cheese omelet with toast.

Eliza was nervous about calling the library to tell her supervisor she would be gone longer than expected, so a few minutes after eight, we found a Seaside service station with a payphone just off the coast highway not far from the hotel.

While I got our gasoline tank topped off, Eliza walked to the station's telephone booth and placed her call. She was still on the line when I parked the Chevrolet alongside the booth. There was a frown on her face when she finally hung the handset on its hook and climbed into the car.

"I'm glad that is over and done. Marguerite approved the extra time off, but she also said someone has called to speak with me nearly every day since I've been away. The staff tried to get the person to leave a name or a number, but the caller just keeps saying she will call back."

"The mystery caller could be anyone, but it could also be Estelle or someone in her employ trying to locate us. If you were harboring any doubts about not going back to work, that should eliminate them."

"I have no doubts about that, darling, but our situation gets scarier every day. I just want to run away and hide."

"I understand, kiddo, but we know the problems with doing that." Then a thought occurred to me. "Eliza, do you have any family nearby besides your father?"

Eliza looked hurt. "Yes, my father has a sister in Los Angeles. Why? You aren't trying to get rid of me, are you?"

"Not at all, I just thought you might be a little less fearful if . . . ."

"No! We are getting through this together. If we were apart, I would be worried sick about you all of the time. That would be much worse."

"Relax, kiddo. I was just trying to offer you a safer alternative. I definitely do not want to get rid of you."

"You better not." Then with a little smile, Eliza added, "After all, if I were not here, who would make you eat your vegetables?"

Smiling back at her, I said, "That's right, dear."

She leaned over and gave me a gentle kiss. "That's better. Where are we going now?"

"It's too early to go to Summerland, so I think we should do some library research."

Eliza gave me a real grin. "Now you're talking! That is my specialty. I even know where the Ventura County library is. Turn left and go up to Main Street."

A few minutes later we pulled to the curb in front of a three-story brick building. A large sign out front said, "E. P. Foster Library."

I looked at Eliza. "I hope they don't know you here."

"I don't think that is a problem. I have only been inside once. That was when I applied for a job several years ago. They needed someone with more experience, so I wasn't here long. I'm certain no one on the staff would remember me today."

"Good. What I want to find are copies of the local newspaper, the *Ventura County Star*, since Friday, the fourteenth."

"That should be easy, but it would have been even easier to simply visit the newspaper office."

I nodded. "Yes, it would, except there are at least two people on the *Star's* staff who know me. I went to school with them."

"Oh. Okay, we'll do it here. Let's go."

I brought my stenographer's pad in for notetaking and sat at a table while Eliza went in search of the periodical section. She returned with three newspapers, each bound by a long wooden rod to keep the pages together.

She said, "The *Star* is a morning paper that publishes six days a week so there is no Sunday edition. What are we looking for?"

"Anything about labor problems at the Summerland Oil Field Company. I want to be prepared when we go up there this afternoon."

I began with the Friday edition and Eliza picked up the Saturday paper. I found what I was looking for right on the front page under the headline, "Summerland Union Negotiations Fail."

The story summarized four days of negotiations between the

Summerland Oil Field Company and the International Association of Oil Field, Gas Well & Refinery Workers of America. During the negotiations workers argued for the unionization of Summerland. The negotiations broke off when they reached a stalemate Thursday night. The IAOFGWRWA promptly ordered workers who support a union shop to begin picketing Summerland Oil Field's facilities Saturday morning.

The article Eliza found in Saturday's edition of the *Star* carried statements from both the company and the union. A spokesman for Summerland said, "We have always treated our workers fairly and paid them well. They have no need for a union."

A union spokesman fired back, "Summerland's treatment of its employees is fair only if you consider eight hours pay for a ten to twelve hour day being well paid. We do not!"

The article also reported the presence of sign-bearing pickets along the coast from Fernald Point to Loon Point. So far the strike had been peaceful, but the Summerland Oil Field Company said it intends to bring in nonunion workers, called "scabs" by the union, to maintain the smooth and safe operation of the oil pumping operations. I wondered if those smooth and safe operations still included the leak in well sixteen.

This morning's *Ventura County Star* reported that picketers were back and in larger numbers than were reported Saturday. Santa Barbara County Sheriff's deputies were being brought in to help control the situation and to prevent traffic backups on the state highway running through Summerland.

I completed my notes from Monday's *Star* and Eliza returned the newspapers to wherever they were kept while I reviewed what I had just learned. Unless the *Star* was drastically exaggerating the situation, Summerland was in hot water with only two choices for getting out of it. They could sign a contract with the union, or they could try to outlast the union.

The latter option was unlikely to succeed because the IAOFG . . . etcetera was part of the American Federation of Labor, and even though its founder and leader, Samuel Gompers, died a few years back, the A F of L was still strong under its current president, William Green. They had the resources to maintain a long work stoppage if it came to that.

The ultimate question, whether the union knew it or not, was what were Estelle Abernathy's thoughts on the situation? Estelle was not the kind of person to take a labor strike in stride. If things got out of hand, I had no doubt it would be at her instigation.

After lunch at a small café on Thompson Boulevard we figured it was time to head north for Summerland and see what was going on there. The Summerland oil fields and Ventura are separated by about thirty miles of California Route One, but we had only traveled about twenty of those miles and were just approaching the little town of Summerland when we began seeing the effects of the strike. Traffic in the northbound lane of the highway suddenly slowed to a crawl. When we finally got through Summerland, we saw the reason for the traffic jam.

The derricks, piers, and railroad tracks of the oil field stretch along the beach below a bluff next to the highway. In order to be seen by motorists on California Route One, the pickets were marching on the bluff next to the highway, which put them within a few feet of the southbound traffic.

Black and white Santa Barbara County Sheriff cars were parked at intervals between groups of pickets to help drivers see the danger. There really was not much likelihood of an accident, though, because the strike had all but closed the highway.

The signs the striking workers carried looked just like the hodgepodge of placards carried in every other labor strike:

```
------------------------------------
         A. F. of L.
       OIL WORKERS
        ON STRIKE
------------------------------------
      OIL FIELD WORKERS
            want
      AN HONEST DAY'S PAY
            for
      AN HONEST DAY'S WORK
------------------------------------
      SUMMERLAND UNFAIR
            to
        OIL WORKERS!
------------------------------------
```

Gesturing toward the chaos on the other side of the highway, Eliza said, "Why don't the cops get those men off the edge of the road so traffic can move again?"

"My guess is the sheriff's deputies have orders to avoid any kind of confrontation with the strikers. Either that, or the deputies are sympathetic to the union cause."

"Making drivers angry surely cannot be helping the union cause."

"That is probably true, but I would be willing to bet that half of these drivers are here to see the show just like we are. I'm going to get us a better vantage point."

Turning off the highway to the east, I drove up a narrow road leading to the top of a small hill just north of Summerland. Several automobiles were already parked at the top of the hill, and after making certain there were no cars up there I recognized, I parked the Chevrolet and we got out to look down on the scene below.

The air had a nip to it and we could see dark clouds gathering in the south. The day was turning dismal. Between the clutter of oil derricks and piers below and the rapidly approaching storm clouds overhead, the sunny California beaches with which they illustrate travel brochures were nowhere to be seen.

Looking north, cars and trucks were lined up in the southbound lane of the highway as far as we could see. The line was moving, but only barely.

Eliza put words to the same thought I was thinking. "I cannot believe Estelle has let things get this far out her control. That isn't like her."

"It surprises me, too, but short of giving in to the union's demands, there is no quick solution to this situation. In the long run, however, I'm sure Estelle will take some sort of action. It's just a matter of time."

Only moments later we saw exactly what Estelle Abernathy intended do about the situation. A large stake-bed truck was nearing the front of the southbound line of traffic, and as it passed the last sheriff's car parked next to the highway, the truck swerved right onto the shoulder of the road and accelerated. In an instant at least eight or nine picketers were down, either pushed off the bluff or run over by the truck.

Eliza saw what the truck was doing before I did and gasped, "Oh, God!"

We could clearly hear the shouts of the strikers below as the truck sped off down the southbound lane of traffic. By the time the nearest deputy got to his car and took off in pursuit of the truck, it was out of his sight around a bend in the highway. What we saw from our high vantage point that the deputy could not see was the truck turning left, pushing its way across the northbound traffic, and disappearing into the little town of Summerland.

The shoulder where the truck had passed was littered with a half dozen bodies the truck ran over and the smashed remains of picket signs. Other strikers were running to help their comrades, but it seemed unlikely there was much they could do for those who were down.

Eliza turned away and pressed her face into my side as if not seeing it would somehow make the carnage disappear. I too was shocked, but I also clearly saw what needed to be done. "Come on, Eliza. Let's get out of here."

In the Chevrolet with the motor running, I said, "I want to see where that truck went. Any suggestions?"

Still in shock, it took Eliza a minute to come up with an answer. "Yes . . . I think so. Drive south on this road. It will wind down the hill and end up a block this side of the highway. If you turn left at the first big intersection, you should be on the street the truck took." After a second or two she added, "Lester, that was horrible, all those men . . . ."

"I know, kiddo. There's going to be hell to pay and it will be very interesting to see who does the paying."

As we approached the street on which Eliza said I should turn left, a large black car flashed through the intersection heading toward the highway on our right. Even though the automobile was moving fast, it was distinctive enough to recognize from a quick glance. The big black car was a custom Packard limousine, one I thought I had seen before. There just aren't many six-thousand-dollar custom limousines around, even in Santa Barbara. The only other details I could make out in the brief glimpse we had of the car were the two men in the front seat. The man in the passenger seat was Armando Delgado.

"Eliza, did you see the big black car that just went through the intersection?"

"Yes. Is there something special about it?"

"I think so. It is a custom-made Packard limo and I am certain I have seen it before."

"Do I need to ask where you have seen it before?"

"I think you can figure that out when I tell you that particular car cost at least six grand."

A hint of panic crept into her voice. "Did the people in it see us?"

"I don't think so. There were two men in the front seat and they were looking straight ahead at the highway. The fellow in the passenger seat was our friend Delgado. I am tempted to follow them, but I want to know for sure I'm right about what it is going on here."

Still sounding nervous, Eliza said, "How will you know you are right?"

Making my left turn, I said, "By driving up this road. If we find a black stake-bed truck up here somewhere we will know."

"Wouldn't it be better to let the police find it?"

"We can do it quicker than they can because we saw which way it went from our vantage point on top of that hill. The sheriff's deputies only know it went south on the highway. Don't worry. If I am right about this, the bad guys are long gone."

It turned out that Evans Avenue, the street we were on, extended less than a mile east of the highway. It was an uphill residential street with about a dozen houses on it and there was only one cross street. Evans ended at a hillside gully filled with oak trees and scrub brush. I stopped near the end of the pavement and turned around.

Leaving the engine running and making sure the brake lever was pulled, I said, "I'm going to take a look in that gully. Slide over here, and if you see anyone coming up the street toward us, honk the horn and I will come running. This should only take a minute."

Eliza started to protest, but before she got the words out, I was walking as quickly as I could toward the trees. The ground was still damp from the most recent rain we had and there were clear tire impressions in it. The tire impression were fresh and made by a large vehicle.

I didn't need to go more than a few feet beyond the first trees in the gully to see what left the tire tracks. Up ahead was a recent model black Ford stake-bed truck with its cab doors hanging open. I had seen what I came to see.

Sliding back onto the Chevrolet's seat, I saw the relief on Eliza's face. Starting back down the hill, I said, "The truck is back there in the trees, all right. My guess is Delgado and the other man drove the truck and the Packard up here and left the car while they used the truck to kill a lot of picketers. Then they drove the truck back into the trees and left in the Packard that passed us on our way up here."

"So Estelle broke up the strike by killing her own employees, and unless someone can trace the truck to her, she will get away with it."

"That's about the size of it, but I'm going to see if we can throw a monkey wrench into her plan by making an anonymous telephone call to the nearest sheriff's station and telling them where to look for the truck."

We were within a block of the highway when Eliza pointed to our right. "There's the post office. I bet they have a public telephone."

The post office was a tiny building with four parking spaces in front of it. Beyond the parking spaces I could see a public telephone booth. On our left there was a small drug store facing the highway. The store's parking lot was on our end of the building. I pulled in and parked with the Chevrolet facing Evans Avenue.

"Eliza, I'm going to walk across the street to use the telephone. That way the people in the post office will be less likely to notice our car and remember it if the sheriff's deputies ask. I would like you to slide over behind the wheel, and if you see any trouble approaching, drive back up Evans and wait for me there. Okay?"

"Okay, darling. Please hurry."

"Sliding off the Chevrolet's seat, I said, "I will, kiddo."

My hike up into the gully at the other end of Evans Avenue had already taken a lot of the starch out of me, but with the help of my cane, I got to the telephone booth in reasonably speedy fashion. Once in the booth, I dropped a nickel in the coin slot and dialed zero for an operator.

When the operator came on the line, I said, "This is an emergency call to the Santa Barbara County sheriff's office closest to Summerland."

One thing that can be said about the telephone company's operators is they know how to handle emergencies. Less than a minute later another woman's voice said, "Santa Barbara County Sheriff's office, Carpinteria Station."

I said, "I have important information for you, but I can only say it once. Please copy what I tell you carefully and give it to your watch commander immediately."

She said, "Who is calling please?"

"That's not part of the information you get. Now, write this down: The truck that just ran over strikers on the Coast Highway was left up at the top of Evans Avenue in Summerland. It is hidden behind the trees in the gully at the end of the street. Also, tell your deputies to ask the neighbors on Evans if anyone noticed a custom-made black Packard limousine parked near where the truck was left. That's the car the killers used after they hid the truck in the gully. If you can find a witness to the Packard being there, you will find it belongs to Estelle Abernathy in Santa Barbara. Got it?"

"You said a Packard limousine, sir?"

"That's right. It was last seen about half an hour ago traveling northbound on the Coast Highway. That's it."

I hung up the telephone and walked as briskly as I was able back to where Eliza was waiting in the Chevrolet. I climbed in on the passenger side and said, "It's your turn to drive. I'm running low on energy."

Putting the transmission into first gear, she said, "Where do you want to go?"

"Back up to that hill we were on when the truck hit the strikers. We can see what's going on from there and do some thinking."

I leaned back and during the less than ten minute trip to the hilltop, I was out like a light. When Eliza parked, she leaned over and kissed me on the cheek. "We're here, darling."

Dragging myself back to consciousness, I said, "There I go again, falling asleep at the switch."

Holding the collar of my shirt out of the way, Eliza looked closely at the dressing on my neck. "Not to change the subject, darling, but when we get back to the hotel we need to change your bandages. These got all sweaty and they are discolored. They are probably okay on the inside, but let's not take any changes."

I nodded and turned to look down at the highway. Southbound traffic was now at a dead stop, but cars in the northbound lane were being hurried along by deputies attempting to clear the highway. There was not a picket in sight, but a man on a gurney was being loaded on an ambulance at the southbound shoulder.

The ambulance drove away at a leisurely pace, leading me to think its passenger was not severely injured or was passed the need for urgency. At the same time we heard a siren coming from the south. Eliza said, "There's another deputy."

The sheriff's car pulled across the highway and stopped next to two deputies standing around alongside the highway with apparently little to do. The new arrival said something to them and the deputies jumped into his patrol car. They roared off back down the highway, but they didn't go far. The patrol car made a left turn across the highway at Evans Avenue and disappeared from view.

"I bet we can guess where they are going."

"It took them long enough! You called the sheriff's office almost thirty minutes ago."

"I'm guessing the first deputy drove up there to see if my call was on the level. When he found out it was, he came back for some help to get the truck out of there and canvass the neighborhood."

I stifled a yawn and Eliza said, "Darling, why don't you take a nap. I can keep an eye on things, and if anything changes, I will wake you."

"What time is it?"

Looking at her wristwatch, she said, "It is three o'clock. We have an hour before Mabel gets here."

"All right, you talked me into it."

The next thing I knew I got another wake-up kiss on the cheek and Eliza said, "It's about ten to four. We should get down to the market where Mabel is meeting us."

"Okay. You drive and I will wake up."

As Eliza pointed our Chevrolet back down the hill toward Summerland, I noted that traffic on the highway was moving normally again. There was no sign of the carnage we witnessed two hours earlier.

The Summerland Market was directly across US Route 101 from the drugstore where Eliza waited for me to call the sheriff's office. As is the case with many small towns, the highway follows Summerland's main street through town. I spotted Mabel's black Ford sedan as we pulled into the market's parking area.

Eliza and Mabel hugged each other, after which Eliza proudly wiggled the ring finger of her left hand under Mabel's nose. "See? I an old married woman now!"

"Congratulations, child!"

By this time I arrived at the party and Mabel said, "Lester, you have married a wonderful woman. You take very good care of her, you hear?"

I smiled. "Well, I don't seem to be doing a great job so far, but things will get better."

Mabel smiled back at me. "I have no doubt of that, Lester. From what I gather, you two are up against a powerful enemy, but I have faith you will prevail."

"Thank you, Mabel, and thank you for driving all the way down here to help us out this afternoon."

She handed me two twenties and a ten from her purse, and I

gave her the check I had written for fifty-five dollars, explaining that the extra five dollars should go toward the damages we had done to her telephone bill. Mabel said that wasn't necessary, but I could tell she appreciated the gesture.

Finally, Eliza and Mabel hugged goodbye and we went our separate ways, Mabel north toward Santa Barbara and Eliza and I south to Ventura. Eliza volunteered to do the driving and I did not argue with her.

TWENTY-FOUR

Monday - September 17, 1928

By six o'clock we were back at the Pierpont Inn and I was leaning hard on Nurse Norwood's cane. I was not in pain, just very fatigued.

I flopped into my chair at the table. Eliza gestured toward the typewriter. "Are you planning to write tonight?"

"If I can stay awake I am. Things are moving fast. If we are going to turn the events of the past few days to our advantage, we need to have our articles published quickly, but we cannot sell what has not yet been written."

"All right, darling. What can I do to help?"

"I think a bath might bring me back to life. Could you change my dressings after that?"

"Of course I could, but first, how are you doing for clean clothes? I'm running low."

"Me, too. I wonder if the hotel has an overnight laundry service."

"I'll call the desk and ask. Go take your bath."

The warm bath water felt good and it gave me a few restful moments to think about the next article I needed to write. By the time I was dried off and dressed, I had the story written in my mind.

When I came out of the bathroom, Eliza said, "The hotel does have an overnight laundry service and they have already picked up our clothes."

"When will they be done?"

"Before seven o'clock tomorrow morning. Now, let's go back into the bathroom where the light is better so I can change your dressing."

While the old dressing was off, Eliza inspected my wounds. "I think your stitches are ready to come out."

"Do you think they will last until Wednesday? That will be a week since they were put in."

"I think so. Otherwise everything looks okay. How is the

pain?"

"Mostly gone. I have not taken any aspirin today."

"That is wonderful! Now, how about something to eat before you put your journalistic skills to work?"

"I guess I could use a bite, but I hate to waste the time."

Eliza walked over to the dresser. "There is a room service menu here. How would it be if we splurged a little and had something sent to the room? That would take less time than going to the restaurant and get you some nutrition."

Rolling a fresh sheet of paper into my typewriter, I said, "Okay, what have they got?"

She studied the menu for a moment. "How does broiled fillet of salmon in parsley butter with succotash sound?"

"It sounds good up to the succotash part."

"Well, darling, it's either that or cauliflower in cream. One way or the other, you are going to get vegetables."

"Can I have mashed potatoes? Potatoes are vegetables."

"Succotash or cauliflower in cream. Pick one."

"You are worse than a mother!"

"Pick one, darling."

"Oh, succotash."

"See, that wasn't so hard."

"Saying it isn't so hard. Eating the stuff is another matter."

While Eliza placed our dinner order via the room telephone, I typed the headline I dreamed up in the bathtub.

SUMMERLAND OIL STRIKERS STRUCK DOWN IN COLD BLOOD

By Lester Kinney

I described the slaughter next to the highway exactly as it played out, estimating the number of victims at eight. Next I reported how the Santa Barbara sheriff's office received an anonymous tip about the location of the Ford murder truck and the black Packard limousine thought to have been used by the killers to flee the area.

It was necessarily a relatively short article because the only details I had to work with were those we personally witnessed. It did contain, however, facts pertaining to Estelle Abernathy's involvement, which no other reporter was likely to have so quickly. I was reasonably certain, therefore, the story would serve the purpose for which I had written it, that being getting through the door of a major Los Angeles daily.

I was editing the article when our dinners arrived. At least that was the assumption I made when someone knocked on the door.

The next thing I heard was Eliza's scream and the door slamming wide open. I swung in that direction and found myself staring down the barrel of a large revolver in the right hand of Armando Delgado. Estelle Abernathy's driver was there, too. He had his arm around Eliza's neck and a pistol pressed against her temple.

Delgado walked slowly toward me. His revolver never wavered. "Do not move, Señor Kinney. If you do, I will surely shoot you dead here and now."

I glanced at Eliza. She and Estelle's driver stood to the left of the door. There was utter panic in her eyes. I slowly raised my hands.

Stopping about ten feet from me, Delgado said, "That is very good, Señor Kinney. You are a hard man to kill, but you have just run out of luck. Now stand up slowly."

I stood, looking for a way out of this new predicament. I saw none at first. It appeared as if Delgado was right about me running out of luck. Then I noticed my cane on the bed where I tossed it when we got back to the room. Would Delgado let me pick it up?

"Now walk to the door, Señor Kinney." With a nasty grin, he added, "You should say goodbye to the señorita. I assure you this will be the last time she sees you alive."

Exaggerating the difficulty I had walking so as to demonstrate my need for the cane, I followed a slightly staggered path to the door that brought me next to the bed. Delgado stayed ten feet ahead of me with his back to the door. Just as I got close to the bed, providence arrived in the form of the room service waiter. Looking through the still open door, he saw the two men with guns and shouted, "Hey!"

Surprised, both men spun toward the door and I grabbed the cane, swinging it in a horizontal arc toward the side of Delgado's head. He must have seen my movement in his peripheral vision. He took a quick step away and raised the revolver intending to shoot me.

His quick reflexes made me miss my intended target. Instead, the cane whacked his gun hand. Delgado yelped and the revolver went spinning across the room. Trying to press my momentary advantage, I stepped toward him, thrusting the cane toward his face like a rapier. The tip of the stick caught him squarely in the left eye. Delgado screamed and stumbled backward.

While all this was happening, Estelle's driver had his hands full trying to cover me and the room service waiter while keeping his hold on Eliza. She broke free of his grip and the waiter shoved the cart carrying our dinners into the driver's legs from behind. He lost his footing long enough for me to put the cane to good use again. I swung at his head hard enough to hit a baseball clear out of the park. He went down hard.

Delgado was on his feet again with blood streaming down his face. He shoved the room service waiter aside and ran out of the room. Even injured as he was, I knew there was no possibility of my catching him, so I did not try. Instead, I took stock of the chaos in room twelve of the Pierpont Inn.

Estelle Abernathy's driver was still unconscious on the floor amidst the remains of our dinners. The room service waiter was using our telephone to call the front desk, presumably to summon the police. Eliza was leaning against the wall next to the door sobbing hysterically. She seemed the most urgently in need of my attention.

I put my arm around her and helped her to the edge of the bed, saying, "Everything is okay now, kiddo. Just catch your breath for a minute."

She looked at me and her expression clearly said, "This is it. I've had all I can handle."

The room service waiter set the telephone receiver down in its cradle. "The front desk is calling the sheriff. Should we get an ambulance for this guy?"

I said, "Hell, no. If he needs medical attention, let the cops worry about it, and thanks for your help. You just saved our lives."

With a grin, the young man said, "You're welcome, Mister Kinney. That's the most excitement we've ever seen around here! By the way, my name is Raymond, but you can just call me Ray. That's what my friends call me."

Shaking his hand, I said, "I am very pleased to be among your friends, Ray. I'm Les."

"Say, should we round up the guns on the floor?"

"I don't think so. As long as this fellow can't reach them if he wakes up, let's leave everything as it is. That will help the cops see what happened in here."

Ray took a look at Estelle's driver and said, "I don't think he'll wake up very soon. You're pretty good with that cane. You conked him a good one."

I looked at the driver and noticed his head was laying in succotash. I couldn't help chuckling. "I think I finally found a good use for succotash."

I glanced at Eliza on the edge of the bed. Even in her current state, she saw the humor in what I said. Sitting next to her, I said, "You going to be okay, kiddo?"

She leaned against me. "I don't think so, Lester. I can't take any more of this."

A familiar voice from the doorway said, "Don't tell him that, Miss Hamm. I am making a terrific career out of investigating attempts on Mister Kinney's life."

I looked up to see Deputy Walter Tanner, the Ventura County Deputy Sheriff who interviewed me at Big Sisters Hospital. "Good evening, Deputy. I'm happy to see you again."

"I can imagine you are. What on earth happened in here?"

Pointing to Raymond, I said, "Thanks to this young man's timely arrival, you only get to investigate another attempted homicide instead of a murder. Ray, shake hands with Deputy Tanner."

As the two men shook hands, I added, "Deputy, you might want to cuff that fellow on the floor there, and then see if he needs medical attention."

Tanner leaned over and felt the man's wrist for a pulse. "His heartbeat is strong, but we'll call for a doctor just in case."

Ray said, "I can tell the front desk to call for an ambulance if you'd like me to."

Snapping a pair of shiny handcuffs onto the driver's wrists, the deputy nodded. "Yeah, that would be good." Then, after looking around the room, Tanner said, "Also, tell them to call the sheriff's office again and say Deputy Tanner requests two extra men to assist.

Looking up at me, Tanner said, "Just for the record, who the heck am I handcuffing, anyway?"

"I don't know his name, but he's Estelle Abernathy's driver. He also figures significantly in several other crimes, including the killing of all those pickets out at the Summerland Oil Field."

Looking in the man's wallet, Tanner said, "Says here his name is Peter Mikhailov. Sounds Russian." Standing, the deputy said, "Now, Mister Kinney, if you don't mind, please tell me what the heck happened here."

"Well, first of all, I need to correct you on one detail." I looked at Eliza. "It is no longer Miss Hamm. Eliza is now Missus

Kinney."

Tanner shook his head. "You're just full of surprises, aren't you? Now, what went on here, or haven't you had time to dream up another good story like the last one you told me?"

"Deputy Tanner, I resent that."

"Resent it all you like, Mister Kinney, but it doesn't change the facts. I drove up to where you claim you were shot for a looksee. What you told me happened doesn't jibe with what I found."

"That might be, deputy, but that location is out of your jurisdiction, so what I told you isn't your problem, is it?"

"No, Mister Kinney, but now we are well within my jurisdiction, so how about just giving me the true story this time? It will save us both a lot of trouble."

I spent the next fifteen minutes giving him the true story from the time we witnessed the truck killing Summerland pickets to Tanner's arrival in our room at the Pierpont Inn. I left out our meeting with Mabel, but I went into great detail about Armando Delgado and Peter Mikhailov crashing into our room and my use of the cane to subdue them. I also made sure Tanner understood that both Delgado and Mikhailov were in the employ of Estelle Abernathy.

The Deputy's first comment was, "I heard about the anonymous phone call to Santa Barbara's Carpinteria substation. I should have figured you were involved somehow."

Turning to Eliza, Tanner asked, "Is that how you remember what happened, Missus Kinney?"

Nodding, she answered him with a quiet, "Yes."

"Anything you want to add to what your husband told us?"

She just shook her head. Deputy Tanner then turned to Ray. "Son, is that how you recall the events from the time you got here?"

"Yes, sir. Mister Kinney told it exactly like it happened. He didn't miss a thing."

I was thinking how annoying it must be for Tanner not to have any nits to pick with my story when our room suddenly became very crowded as a doctor, two ambulance attendants, and two additional deputies simultaneously arrived at the party. The doctor immediately turned his attention to Mikhailov while Deputy Tanner gave his men their marching orders, which included making a sketch of the room noting the location of both guns and various other items, and using a public telephone in the lobby to call in a "be-on-the-lookout" bulletin for Armando Delgado.

The deputy charged with that task had some questions for me. "Can you describe this Delgado character?"

"Yes, mid-thirties, slight build, maybe five-ten or so, swarthy with one of those thin little pencil moustaches. He is Spanish and looks it."

"Any idea what kind of car he would be driving?"

"When seen earlier in the day, Delgado and this fellow here were in a black Packard custom limousine, but he has other cars available, including a dark red Cadillac Dual Cowl Phaeton, and I think there is also a Stutz Black Hawk Speedster, the boattail model, painted black. It could be one of those or something else entirely."

The deputy was writing feverishly in his notebook. "Any idea which way he would have gone from here?"

"He lives in Santa Barbara at . . . ." I looked at Eliza.

"1919 Las Tunas Road."

"That's his address, but he was pretty badly injured, so he might have gone somewhere else for medical attention."

"What part of him was injured?"

"He took a cane tip to the left eye. The wound was bleeding heavily when he ran out of here."

"Okay, I will have them check all of the hospitals between here and Santa Barbara."

The doctor finished his examination of Mikhailov and instructed the ambulance attendants to put his patient on the gurney and wheel him out to the ambulance. Tanner quickly ordered one of his men to accompany them and not to let the man out of his sight, even for a second. He had a big time killer on his hands now and he wasn't taking any chances, which suited me just fine.

Finally, Tanner slipped his notebook back into his uniform jacket pocket. "All right, Kinney. As usual you've left me another fine mess to clean up. There will be pure hell to pay when the Santa Barbara guys discover we can identify the Summerland killers and we even have one of them in custody. That's to say nothing of having an eye witness to the whole thing. They'll be arguing who gets the first shot at them from now 'til Christmas. In the meantime, I have to keep tabs on you. What are your plans from here?"

I looked at Eliza. She wanted to hear the answer to that question, too. I said, "Well, I think we'll be in Los Angeles for most of the day tomorrow. I have some business to take care of there. Tomorrow night we should be back here, assuming the

Pierpont Inn doesn't throw us out for redecorating their room with blood and succotash. Wednesday I need to go back to the hospital and have the doctor take the stitches out of my throat wound. After that, I don't know."

Tanner looked thoughtful. "I suppose you know the two of you are still in danger. You've eliminated two of this Abernathy woman's thugs, but she is bound to have more."

I nodded, "Deputy, I'm damned tired of hiding from her. Besides, we're just about out of hiding places. What do you suggest?"

He looked around. "First, I suggest we get you into another room. Then I'm going to post an around-the-clock guard."

"I appreciate that, Tanner."

"Don't kid yourself. I'm not doing any of this for your benefit, Kinney. I need your testimony to straighten out all the messes you've created around here. Otherwise, I'd let Estelle Abernathy have you on a silver platter just to get you out of my hair."

I was thinking how reassuring it was to have Deputy Tanner so concerned with our welfare when my typewriter caught my eye and I realized I was missing an opportunity to add some detail to my Summerland story. "You're concern overwhelms me, Deputy Tanner. Would you mind answering a question for me?"

He put on a suspicious expression. "What do you want to know, Kinney?"

"I was thinking about what happened to those Summerland pickets this afternoon. How many were killed and injured?"

"The last word I got said eight were killed and four were injured, but the injured are all expected to pull through. Why?"

"Just curious. It looked pretty bad from our vantage point."

"Okay, I've got a question for you. Why the cloak and dagger routine with the anonymous telephone call to the Santa Barbara Sheriff's substation?"

"We were trying to avoid exactly what happened here tonight by keeping our whereabouts a secret. I thought we were doing pretty well. I still have no idea how these two guys found us. It has to be more than a lucky guess."

Tanner shook his head. "Kinney, I don't know what you did to upset Estelle Abernathy, but it must have been a humdinger."

"Oh, it is, Deputy, and I'm just getting started."

While we were talking, Ray called the desk and explained our need for a new room. He also ordered a bell boy to help move our bags. To me he said, "Someone will be here in a minute to move you into a new room. Now, would you like me to reorder your dinners?"

I looked at Eliza still sitting on the edge of the bed. She shook her head. I said, "Ray, do you think they could just make us a couple of sandwiches and a pot of coffee?"

Smiling, he said, "I know they could, Mister Kinney. I'll place the order right now."

Noticing Tanner looking at something in his notebook, I asked, "Deputy Tanner, would you care for a sandwich or something?"

He must have been deep in concentration because it took him a minute to shift gears and answer my question. "No, I don't think so, but thanks for asking."

It took about an hour to get moved into our new room and to get everyone else moved out of our new room. We were now in twenty-two which was on the second floor directly above our old room. If I had not struggled up a flight of stairs to get there, I would have sworn I was in the same room.

Eliza was rehanging some items in the armoire. I interrupted and led her to the bed. We sat down and I said, "Okay, kiddo, let's talk. What are you thinking about all of this?"

The tone of her reply took me aback. "What do I think? What do you think I think? Lester, I have taken all I can take. I'm so upset I can't see straight!"

"I understand you are upset. What can we do to make things better?"

"Nothing! That's the problem. No matter what we do or where we go Estelle will always be there. I hate that woman. I hate her!"

I leaned over to put my arm around Eliza and she pushed me away. "No, Lester! Words and hugs will not make this one bit better."

"Then . . . ."

Eliza jumped up and ran toward the bathroom. She practically shouted, "Just leave me alone!" The bathroom door slammed behind her.

My stomach felt like I had swallowed hot coals. I knew Eliza was disappointed because her knight in shining armor was failing miserably at his mission to slay the evil dragon. I also knew she was wrong about one thing. Words could make things better. They could slay the dragon.

I walked to the table where my typewriter sat beside the sandwiches and coffee Ray brought us. I poured a cup of coffee from the porcelain decanter and sat at the typewriter. With pencil in hand, I made a few changes to my first draft, including inserting the number of killed and injured as a quote from Ventura County Deputy Sheriff Walter Tanner. I also rewrote the section about the black Packard limousine, identifying Estelle Abernathy employee, Peter Mikhailov, as the driver, even though I had not gotten a clear look at him. That part was a fabrication, but only a small one. Who else would be driving Estelle Abernathy's automobile but Estelle Abernathy's driver?

Rolling a fresh piece of paper into the typewriter, I began typing the second draft of my story. I was still on the first page when Eliza came out of the bathroom. She was wearing her nightshirt and she carefully avoided looking in my direction.

As she climbed into bed, I said, "I'm typing the final draft of our Summerland story, but I won't be long."

She tucked herself in on her right side, facing the opposite wall. "Take your time."

I thought I heard her crying a few times during the hour it took me to finish the final draft of the story. I wanted to go to her, but Eliza had made it clear she wanted to be left alone. I left her alone.

The sound of her breathing when I went to bed made me think Eliza was finally asleep. I wanted to put my arm around her as I usually did, but decided that did not come under the heading of leaving her alone.

TWENTY-FIVE

Tuesday - September 18, 1928

I lay there worrying about Eliza for a long time. When I finally dozed off, it seemed I only slept for a few minutes when I was jolted awake by a scream.

Eliza was in the throes of a nightmare, a bad one. Her body shook violently as her fists beat the mattress furiously. In a voice so shrill and laden with panic I hardly recognized it as Eliza's, she shouted, "Lester!"

That was all I could take. Sitting up, I gently shook her arm. Her skin was damp with sweat. "Eliza! Eliza! Wake up."

It took a second try before her eyes opened wide. Panicked anguish distorted her features until she recognized me and grabbed my arm. "Oh, Lester! I'm sorry . . . I'm so sorry!"

"Easy, kiddo. You were having a bad nightmare. It's over now. You're safe."

As I pulled her closer she began to cry. I just held her and said nothing.

After what felt like a very long time her sobs gradually subsided. I thought she might be falling asleep again, but she said, "Lester, can you forgive me for being so thoughtless?"

"You weren't thoughtless, you were scared out of your wits when those guys showed up. There is nothing to forgive."

"Yes there is. All I could think about was how bad things were for me when you are the one who has been hurt physically and nearly killed twice. That's the part that scared me so. I couldn't imagine how I would go on if you were . . . if you weren't here anymore."

"I understand, Eliza. I feel the same about you. We had a close call, and when I saw that Russian holding his gun to your head all I could think was, if he hurt you, I would kill him."

Eliza's wet brown eyes looked up at me. "But that's just it! When we were both in danger you were thinking of me. It was me you were worried about, not yourself."

I had to smile. "That's not true, kiddo. I was plenty worried about myself, too. If Ray had not shown up when he did, I don't know that things would have turned out so well."

Eliza just pressed her head to my chest and held on tight, and then something occurred to me. Reliving the evening's events reminded me that Deputy Tanner said he was posting a twenty-four hour guard outside our room, and yet, despite Eliza's nightmare screams, there had been no knock on the door to make sure everything was all right.

"Sit tight for just a moment, Eliza. I need to check on something."

I got up, put on my pants, and walked to the door. I opened it slowly and looked into the hall. It was quite clear why there was no response to Eliza's screams. The deputy Tanner left to ensure our wellbeing was snoring softly in a chair next to the door. I resisted the temptation to slam the door and wake him. Instead, I closed the door quietly and walked back to the bed shaking my head.

Eliza was sitting on the edge of the bed when I got there. "What is it, darling?"

"You screamed quite loudly during your nightmare and I got to wondering why the guard Tanner put on our room didn't come running."

With a concerned expression, she asked, "Isn't he out there?"

"Oh, he's out there, all right. He's also sleeping like a baby."

Eliza frowned. "Oh, swell. So much for around the clock protection."

With a grin, I whispered, "Shush! You'll wake him up!"

As I sat next to her on the bed, Eliza hugged me and bestowed a kiss upon my cheek. "Thank you for still being my knight in shining armor, even if I don't deserve you."

"In truth, you deserve better than me, but I'm what you got, for better or worse." Then, pulling my watch out of the watch pocket in my slacks, I said, "It's about two a.m. Do you want to try for a few hours more sleep?"

"If you'll hold me so the nightmares stay away."

We both slept on and off, but by seven Eliza and I were both up and dressed. While I waited for her to put the finishing touches on her face and hair, I contemplated our situation. It did not seem to me that the lack of diligence on the part of the deputy outside our hotel room made much difference in the overall scheme of things.

Armando Delgado had already demonstrated his cleverness at locating us despite the care I exercised in selecting hiding places.

That after two attempts he had still not managed to carry out the assignment Estelle Abernathy gave him owed more to dumb luck than a lack of skill and dedication. While I didn't know if, after last night, Delgado was in any condition to further pursue that assignment, it made little sense to hang around the same place he last saw us.

Then there was Eliza's safety to consider. I was sure she was not exaggerating when Eliza said she had taken all she could take. Eliza was stronger than she thought she was, but going through another experience like last night could push her over the edge, assuming she survived the encounter physically. No, I needed to come up with a better way of dealing with our circumstances.

Eliza had just come out of the bathroom when there was a knock on the door. Her features froze in an expression of panic. I was not far from feeling the same way myself, and then we heard, "This is Deputy Barber."

I opened the door and found the deputy in a slightly rumpled uniform that looked as if he had slept in it, which he had. He handed me a brown paper package that contained our clean clothes from the laundry and said, "Mister Kinney, Deputy Tanner said I should go off duty when you folks left for the day. I heard you moving around in here and was wondering if you were leaving soon."

An idea occurred to me that might put us in a slightly better situation. I said, "Yes, Deputy, we are on our way out the door. I see no reason for you to hang around any longer."

"Thank you, sir. What time do you expect to return tonight?"

"Oh, I'm certain we'll be gone until early evening, maybe seven o'clock or so."

"All right, Mister Kinney. I'll plan to be back between five and six so I'll be here when you return."

"That will be fine, Deputy. You go get some sleep."

He was wearing a slightly guilty expression when he nodded his thanks. As the deputy walked down the hall toward the stairway, I closed the door and looked at Eliza.

"All right, Lester, why did you lie to him?"

I tried to look puzzled. "Lie to him? What makes you think I lied to him?"

"This is me, remember? I can always tell when you're fibbing."

Grinning, I said, "Yes, I guess you can. I lied to him because I think hanging around the same place where Armando Delgado last saw us is a monumentally stupid thing to do. We need to move on and I see no reason to let the less than vigilant Ventura County sheriff's department in on our change of plans."

"Well that makes sense and I'm sure that deputy will sleep much more comfortably in his own bed than out in our hallway."

"Yes, I'm sure he will. Now let's pack up our belongings and get out of here."

By eight o'clock we had checked out of the Pierpont Inn and the bellboy we called to move our bags down to the car finished loading the Chevrolet's trunk. While I made certain the original copies of the three stories I had written were secure in their large manila envelope, Eliza procured two cardboard cups of coffee from the lobby.

I made a slow circuit of the Inn's parking area to see if anyone was watching us. Nobody was paying the slightest attention to us, so I got our Chevrolet headed south on the coast road. The first Auto Club directional sign we saw said Los Angeles lay seventy-nine miles beyond our front bumper.

As our route turned east and became Ventura Boulevard through the San Fernando Valley, Eliza asked a very good question. "Do you know where we're going?"

"Yes. We are going to start at the top and work down from there."

"What is the top?"

"In this instance it's the *Los Angeles Examiner*."

Eliza sounded pessimistic. "The Hearst paper? Do you think you can get in to talk with someone?"

"I think I might. I know the Metro editor. In fact, he was one of my journalism professors at Occidental College."

"Wow, that's a break!"

"Especially since he thought I had great promise as a journalist. He may, however, change his mind about that when he hears I was fired after less than a week at a backwater newspaper like the *Tribune*.

"Darling, you know very well that had nothing to do with your ability as a journalist. You were fired because you fell in love with the wrong woman."

"Actually, I fell in love with the right woman. I went to work for the wrong editor, but Professor Carlson may not consider that an acceptable justification for ending up on the street with your father's boot print on the seat of my pants."

Shaking her fist at the windshield, Eliza said, "He will if I explain it to him."

"Well, let's hope it doesn't come to you having to beat him up.

Besides, I don't want a job, I just want to sell him three stories."

William Randolph Hearst publishes his *Los Angeles Examiner*—which he claims is one of twenty-eight publications in eighteen major cities with a total circulation of twenty-million copies—from an impressive building in what locals refer to as "downtown" Los Angeles. More specifically, the Examiner Building is located at 1111 South Broadway.

Once over the Cahuenga Pass and into Hollywood, Route 101 turns east on Sunset. We followed Sunset all the way downtown to Broadway. The Examiner Building takes up more than half of the block between Eleventh and Twelfth Streets. It is a long narrow two-story building of Spanish architecture with a large third floor cupola. Architecturally, the most notable features of the Examiner Building are the fifteen arches spanning the Broadway side of the structure. The center arch contains three sets of double doors, which are the main public entrance to Hearst's Los Angeles Empire.

The closest parking place I found was across Broadway and Eleventh Street. Not knowing how long I was likely to be, we decided Eliza would come in and wait for me in the *Examiner's* lobby rather than in the car. We found a comfortable seat for her in the elaborate two-story guilt and marble lobby, and after consulting the directory, I rode the elevator to the second floor.

The central section of the *Examiner's* second floor was a large open area jammed full of desks and abuzz with activity. This typically hectic newsroom was surrounded by offices, one of which was room two-two-four, in which the building directory had assured me I would find Robert Carlson. Lettering on the frosted glass window in room two-two-four's door said, "Metro Editor." I gave the door a hopeful knock.

A hearty, deep bass voice responded brusquely to my knock. "Enter."

Professor Carlson is a big man who does everything with energy and vigor. At that moment he was energetically reading what turned out to be the morning's edition of the *Examiner*. He looked up, recognized me, and jumped up from his desk, saying, "Lester! This is a pleasant surprise. How are you, son?"

We shook hands and I said, "I'm well, Professor Carlson."

"Go lightly with that 'professor' stuff, Lester. Around here I'm mostly known as either Bob or just Carlson."

"Yes, sir."

He waved me into one of the straight-back chairs facing his desk and said, "Have a seat, Lester, and tell me what brings you to the big city. The last I heard you were on your way up to Santa Barbara to work for Fred Hamm at the *Tribune*. How does it feel to be a genuine working Journalist?"

"It felt pretty good for about a week."

His eyes widened. "Don't tell me you got yourself sacked!"

"I'm afraid so, sir."

With a thoughtful expression, Carlson said, "That's unexpected. I don't know him well, but I would have thought Hamm would appreciate your writing ability."

"I'm afraid my dismissal had nothing to do with my journalistic skills. It was a personal matter between Mister Hamm and me."

Despite his words, he looked puzzled. "Oh. I see. Well, that's a different matter entirely. So, tell me, Lester, how can I help? I'm afraid we don't have any staff openings at the moment, but . . . ."

"I'm not job hunting, Mister Carlson, but I do have a couple of things you may find interesting."

"Oh? Show me what you have, Lester."

The first story I handed him was the article about Aurora Abernathy's adoption and the attack on Monsignor O'Boylan. Carson put on a pair of wire-rim spectacles and looked at the top of the first page. His eyebrows shot up the instant he read the head. I had his attention. Now I hoped he would think the story was worthy of publishing.

I watched Carlson's expressions as he read the story, and by the time he finished I was fairly certain I was about to sell an article. He stacked the pages on his desk, and then spent a moment neatening the stack. He seemed to be thinking about what he just read.

Finally Carlson removed his spectacles and looked at me. "Lester, I'm not even going to ask you if you verified your facts because I know you would not bring me an article, especially one that calls the Catholic Church into question, without thorough research."

"No, sir, I would not. Every word of that story is verifiable."

"All right, now tell me why you brought this to me."

We were down to the brass tacks. "I brought it to you because it is one of three stories I would like to sell the *Examiner*."

Mister Carlson nodded as if I had confirmed his suspicions. Then, holding up the story he had just read, he asked, "Are the other two stories you brought on the same subject?"

"No, sir. They are indirectly related, but they concern different matters."

Leaning back in his chair, Carlson appeared to think for a moment, and then said, "And are they as volatile as this one?"

"One of them certainly is. It concerns the murders of the Summerland Oil Field pickets yesterday."

"I see. Okay, Lester, I think we can do business, but at least the one I just read is going to take approval from a higher authority. Tell you what, let me read the other two stories, and then we'll take them down to Jim Richardson. If he gives us a thumbs up, you've sold at least one, and maybe three stories."

"Fair enough, sir."

Half an hour later we were sitting in front of the City Editor's desk. James Richardson is a narrow-faced man with glasses and thinning hair. He chain-smokes cigarettes, lighting new ones from the still glowing butts of the old ones.

I knew we were in Richardson's office because, despite his title, he pretty much ran the newspaper from top to bottom. If the *Examiner* was going to take on the Catholic Church, Estelle Abernathy, and a wealthy oil company, it would only do so with Richardson's approval.

Since we arrived in his office, Richardson had read my stories on Monsignor O'Boylan and the Summerland Oil Field murders. He was just finishing my third story, the one that covered my attempted murder and the disappearance of Tom Wigand.

Richardson tossed the pages of the third story on his desk and pointed to the stack. "This one is about you, right? I mean you're Lester Kinney, right?"

"Yes, sir."

"Well, that explains the bandage on your neck." After a pause, Richardson shook his head. "Kinney, I don't quite know what to make of you. You either have the best nose for news on the West Coast or you are the best fiction writer since Sinclair Lewis. Either way, I'd bet money if W. R. were here, he'd be offering you my job."

I wasn't quite sure what to make of that when Bob Carlson, sitting next to me, laughed. That, I figured, probably made Richardson's comment a positive thing.

Richardson rummaged through the stacks of paper on his desk and came up with the Monsignor O'Boylan story. Holding it up, he said, "Okay, here's what we're going to do. This goes on this afternoon's front page, just below the fold. I'll take care of that."

Next the City Editor picked up my Summerland story. "Bob, I think the Summerland story is worthy of front page Metro. What do you think?"

"I agree, Jim."

Richardson tossed the stacked pages to Carlson and said, "That's your baby."

Finally he picked up the article about my getting shot. "Let's hold on to the third article until we see the reaction to the first two. There is a common thread to these articles—that Abernathy woman—and we might want to use this article to tie it all together and summarize the situation as it stands tomorrow afternoon." He looked in my direction. "Kinney, you gonna be in town for a couple of days?"

"I can be."

"Good. Tell Bob where he can reach you . . . no, better yet, Bob, put him up at the Biltmore on us. That way he'll be where we can get to him if we need him." Richardson turned to me. "I want you here no later than nine tomorrow morning. We should be . . . ."

Bob Carlson interrupted my marching orders. "Sorry to interrupt, Jim, but we don't own the rights to Mister Kinney's stories yet. I wanted you to read them before I committed to buying them."

Richardson's hands went up in a what-is-the-problem gesture. "Well, buy them, for crying out loud. We have work to do."

"All right, Jim. What would you like to offer Mister Kinney for his stories?"

The City Editor's expression turned hard. "I won't let you hold us up, Kinney, no matter how good your stories may be. You get one-fifty total for the first two stories we're using and we'll figure out what a rewrite of the third one is worth when we know what we're going to do with it. That's my top offer. Take it or leave it."

I looked at Carlson. He smiled at me. To Richardson I said, "You drive a hard bargain, but you've got a deal."

"Good." Richardson picked up the telephone handset on his desk, listened a minute, and then said, "Carol, get two checks for seventy-five bucks cut for Lester Kinney right away. Yeah, that's k-EYE-n-n-e-y. Have 'em charge the checks to our stringer budget. Also, fill out two article release forms for Kinney to sign. He'll help you fill in the blanks on the forms.

"After that, call the Biltmore and get Mister Kinney a room . . . no, make it a suite, he's gonna need space to work. I don't know how long we'll need him so leave the checkout date open."

Richardson tossed the telephone handset back in its cradle and stood up. Offering me his hand, he said, "Pleasure doin' business with you, Kinney. See you tomorrow."

Fifteen minutes later, just before eleven o'clock, I stepped out of the elevator and into the *Examiner's* lobby. Eliza was sitting near the entrance doors, but she trotted across the wide open space to meet me halfway. "I'm sure glad to see you. I was starting to get a little worried."

"I'm sorry, kiddo. It's been one heck of a morning."

"Does that mean good or bad, darling?"

I slipped the *Examiner's* checks out of my inside jacket pocket and put them in her hand. "I would call it very good."

Eliza looked at the amounts of the checks. "Holy smoke! They bought your stories?"

"Yes, except that's just for two of them, the Monsignor O'Boylan story and the Summerland Oil story. It looks like they want the third one, too, but we will deal with that one tomorrow."

She said, "Wonderful!" with such enthusiasm, her voice echoed all around the two-story room. Eliza gave the high ceiling an embarrassed look and softly said, "Oops." After that, she gave me a hug and said, "You did it again, Mister Knight in Shining Armor."

"I got lucky, kiddo, but luck or hard work, it all pays the same."

"Where are we going now?"

"The *Examiner* has booked us a suite at the Biltmore at their expense."

Eliza looked impressed. "Suite at the Biltmore? These people must think you are the second coming of Johann Gutenberg or somebody. Let's go. All this sitting around waiting has made me hungry."

"Okay, but we need to be a little tricky about this."

"We do?"

"Yes. I kept an eye on the review mirror in the car all the way down here from Ventura and saw no sign of anyone following us, but before we go to the hotel, I want to be doubly certain of that."

"How?"

"Instead of going straight to the Biltmore, we are going to use a random roundabout route and make an unexpected stop along the way. Do you feel up to driving in the downtown Los Angeles traffic?"

"I think so." Glancing out the glass entrance doors toward Broadway, she added, "It doesn't look that busy out there at the moment."

It took about five minutes to hike back to the Chevrolet. After opening the door for Eliza and helping her into the driver's seat, I walked around to the passenger door. By the time I was in and closed the door, Eliza had the engine running and was waiting for instructions.

"Let's start out by driving straight ahead on Broadway."

Eliza took a look over her shoulder to be sure the way was clear, and then pulled out headed more or less north on Broadway. After Olympic, we were crossing numbered streets in descending order. When we got to Grauman's Million Dollar Theater I figured we had gone far enough and asked Eliza to turn right. That put us on Third Street.

On Third we passed Spring and Main before coming to Los Angeles Street, where we made another right. A block later, at Fourth, we turned right again. Crossing Main, we completed a circle and I asked Eliza to pull over and park. We were in front of the Barclay Hotel and directly across Fourth Street from the Los Angeles Farmers and Merchants Bank where the *Examiner* did its banking.

Using my cane to speed up the process, I made quick work of cashing one of the *Examiner's* seventy-five dollar checks. The second one was safely folded away in my wallet. We really didn't need the extra cash right away, but having it in my pocket gave me a more secure feeling.

Before returning to the car, I spent a few minutes staring out the bank's windows for any sign that someone was following us. Seeing nothing to indicate a problem, I returned to the Chevrolet and directed Eliza five blocks up to Olive. We turned left just beyond Pershing Square, and then right into an alleyway that led to the underground guest parking area for the Los Angeles Biltmore Hotel.

TWENTY-SIX

Tuesday - September 18, 1928

Along with many other curious folks, I visited the Los Angeles Biltmore Hotel soon after it opened about five years ago. My impression of the place now is the same as it was then. The Biltmore is a monument to ostentatiousness with all the warmth and charm of a Victorian mausoleum. It is as if the Biltmore's public rooms were designed as picture frames for the self-admiration of its guests. In short, the hotel is an enormous gilded cage looking for a bird.

That having been said, and while the Biltmore is not generally included in lists of the world's seven wonders, it is still the sort of spectacle everyone should see at least once in their lives, and as we walked through the lobby trailing a bellman with our luggage, Eliza was experiencing her first views of that which defies description. There is quite literally so much detail that even the most conscientious observer is at a loss to absorb it all.

Leaning close so as not to be overheard, Eliza said, "Lester, are we in the right place? This looks more like a gaudy bordello than a hotel."

I almost laughed out loud. "Eliza, please show a little respect. Some fool spent a fortune building and decorating this barn. Besides, how would you know what a bordello looks like?"

"I read books, darling."

"I see."

From twenty feet away I could already see the desk clerk looking down his nose at us. Everything from our clothes to our luggage told him we were not of a class that could afford accommodations at the Los Angeles Biltmore, and yet here we were.

When we arrived at the highly polished registration desk, he snooted, "And how may we be of service to you?"

His tone of voice was such that, in less than ten words, the clerk succeeded in making us feel only slightly less welcome than the plague. Showing more respect than the clerk deserved, I said what I needed to say in just two words: "Reservation. Kinney."

The word "reservation" took a little wind out of his sails, but not much. He spent a moment shuffling through a short stack of reservation slips, and then stopped short. The clerk's eyebrows raised a bit in surprise, but his tone of voice was no less snooty.

"Yes, Mister Kinney, here is your reservation. We have you in the Ambassador Suite."

Feeling I had been patient with the clerk's insolence long enough, I looked him in the eye and said, "You HAVE us in the Ambassador Suite?"

Without missing a beat, he said, "I apologize, sir. What I meant to say is that we have prepared the Ambassador Suite for your use during your visit to the Biltmore. Now, if you will please sign the registration book, we will have your bags taken up."

The pages in his registration book had four columns of information—two for guests to fill in, and two for the clerk to complete. In the NAME column I wrote, "Mr. & Mrs. L. Kinney." Beneath RESIDENCE I added, "Santa Barbara, Calif."

The clerk printed "1135" under ROOM NUMBER and a six digit number in the FOLIO column. After that he handed me an oval sterling silver key fob with a stylized B on one side and the number of the Ambassador Suite on the other. Our key dangled from a silver ring at the top of the fob.

As I accepted the key, the clerk oozed, "Enjoy your stay at the Los Angeles Biltmore Hotel, Mister Kinney."

I gave him a curt nod and followed Eliza and the bellman toward a bank of elevators. On the eleventh floor, the bellman led us down a thickly carpeted hallway to a pair of elaborate doors next to a large bronze plaque announcing: "Ambassador Suite."

The Ambassador Suite, we soon discovered, consisted of three rooms. What appeared to be the living room was dominated by a white marble fireplace accompanied by an assortment of armchairs, a sofa, end tables, and a writing desk, all in a modern style and made of blond woods.

The light woods continued into a homey bedroom equipped with the same sort of furnishings one might be likely to have in their bedroom at home. These included a large double bed, nightstands, a chest of drawers, a rocking chair, and a stylish dressing table below a large oval mirror. The walls were covered in a pale blue wallpaper with a subdued pattern of tiny flowers.

The bathroom was a study in white. Everything from the paint and tile on the walls to the toilet, pedestal sink, and bathtub were white. With a large wall mirror reflecting more white, the effect was rather dazzling.

After surveying our new temporary domain, Eliza stood at one of the living room windows for several moments. Looking over her shoulder, I saw an expansive view of downtown LA south of the hotel. I put my hands on her shoulders and Eliza turned her head to look up at me.

I smiled. "Welcome to the Honeymoon Suite."

She beamed up at me. "You read my mind again, but it seems like much longer than five days ago that we were in Tijuana being married by a government clerk."

"We may have gotten off to an inauspicious start, but that just means the best is yet to come."

She frowned a small frown. "Oh, I wasn't complaining! I'm happier than I've ever been before. I even got tingles when I watched you register us as Mister and Missus L. Kinney."

"Good. I like it when you get tingles."

"Joke if you must, but I'm serious. This is all pretty exciting to me."

I kissed Eliza on the cheek. "Me, too. Now, how would it be if we got some exciting lunch?"

"That would be just peachy, but I need to make a telephone call first."

"Who are you going to call?"

"Doctor Otto Becker."

Having no idea what she was up to, I asked the next logical question. "And who, pray tell, is Doctor Otto Becker?"

"According to this card by the telephone, Doctor Otto Becker is the Biltmore Hotel house doctor, and before you ask, I'm calling him to see if he will remove your stitches. They have to come out, and if Doctor Becker will do it, we can save a trip to a local hospital."

While Eliza made her telephone call, I visited our bathroom to comb my hair and freshen up. When I'd done what I could in that department, I went back to the living room, where Eliza was just returning the telephone handset to its cradle. "Doctor Becker would be delighted to be of service by removing your stitches."

"Delighted?"

Eliza shrugged. "He has a European way of speaking. I suspect that is for the benefit of his ritzier patients."

"I see. Do we go to Doctor Becker or does he come to us?"

"He said it would be his pleasure to perform the procedure in our suite at two o'clock this afternoon. He did not say what his fee would be for the 'house call.'"

Trying to maintain a serious demeanor, I asked, "More important, do you tip a hotel house doctor?"

That got a laugh out of Eliza. "No, darling, I don't think tipping is appropriate for professional people."

"Oh good. Let's get lunch."

The Biltmore's less formal dining establishment, simply known as the "Coffee Shop," was a study in maroon, and could be entered from the street through a stylish stainless steel revolving door to the left of the hotel's main entrance or through double glass doors from the hotel lobby. We entered via the lobby.

Coffee shop diners were seated in upholstered booths, at free-standing tables, and on stools along a serpentine counter against one wall. Since the lunch rush was on, the hostess asked if we would mind sitting at a regular table, or would we prefer to wait for a booth. We said a regular table would be fine, and a minute later we were studying the Biltmore Coffee Shop menu.

A single six-page menu covered their offerings for breakfast, lunch and dinner. Such economy seemed out of place at the Biltmore. For some reason, an "All Day Special" sounded particularly good to me. It consisted of Canadian ham slices, two eggs, buttered toast, and fried potatoes. Eliza decided on a lettuce and tomato sandwich with mayonnaise. We both ordered iced tea as our beverage.

While waiting for our lunches to arrive, Eliza smiled across the table and said, "Well, darling, are you feeling proud of yourself? You should be, you know."

"I should?"

"Yes, you should. You just sold two stories to one of biggest newspaper chains in the country. That is no small accomplishment."

"Then remind me to thank Estelle Abernathy for being a coldblooded killer. Without her I doubt if would have accomplished the feat of which I should be so proud."

Eliza's smile faded. "What's the matter, darling?"

"I guess it comes down to feeling less than thrilled about the stories the *Examiner* bought. They are not journalism by any definition. They are sensational, scandalous articles raising indecent behavior to a far higher level than it deserves."

Eliza nodded. "I thought that might be what's bothering you. Look at it this way, though, it is something you felt needed to be done in order to save our lives, and the *Examiner's* willingness to buy the stories proves you are even capable of writing trash well."

I couldn't help laughing at her view of the matter. I reached across the table and took Eliza's hand. "Once again your unique way of looking at things has given my sagging morale a boost. Thanks, kiddo."

"You are quite welcome, Mister Journalist."

After finishing our tastily prepared lunches, I signed the bill. It came to a dollar and a quarter, including tip. From there we ascended to the eleventh floor, arriving at the Ambassador Suite about ten minutes before two.

At precisely two o'clock a pleasant door chime rang. It seemed you did not knock on the door to Ambassador Suite. That would be far too plebeian. Instead, visitors announced their arrival by pushing a small brass button to sound the chime. Doctor Otto Becker had arrived at our door.

Middle-aged and perfectly groomed, he looked more like a prosperous businessman than a doctor, but he went straight to work proving appearances can be misleading. After fastidiously washing his hands, Doctor Becker removed the dressing from my neck and closely examined my wounds.

Completing his examination, Doctor Becker said, "It looks as if everything is healing as it should, but I am rather curious why you called me to remove the sutures instead of returning to the doctor who did the original surgery."

Not feeling the need to give Doctor Becker our life histories, I said, "It's a matter of poor timing. The surgeon is up in Ventura and we are stuck down here for several days. Since it seemed the stitches needed to come out promptly, we called you."

Becker nodded. "You were quite right about the sutures needing to be removed, so let us get to work, shall we?"

He opened his bag and I glanced at Eliza. She grinned and gave me her "I told you so" look while Doctor Becker removed an implement I thought might be some sort of surgical scissors and a pair of tweezers from his bag.

I felt him snip the first of twenty-some stitches and he said, "All right, Mister Kinney, I will be as gentle as possible, but this is likely to sting some."

By the time he removed the final stitch I had come to the conclusion that suture removal was invented by Ferdinand and Isabella as a particularly diabolical form of torture for the Spanish Inquisition. Doctor Becker said, "There you go, all done. I recommend keeping a dressing in place for a few more days to avoid infection in the suture holes. After that, you're all done."

"Thank you, Doctor Becker. How much do we owe you for your services?"

He looked thoughtful. "Oh, I should think twenty dollars will cover it."

As I handed him a twenty dollar bill, Becker said, "Tell me, Mister Kinney, what caused those wounds in the first place?"

Figuring Doctor Becker recognized a bullet wound when he saw one or he would not have asked the question, I said, "A point-three-eight caliber bullet, Doctor."

"Am I safe in assuming the doctor who performed the surgery followed proper procedures for reporting the treatment of a bullet wound to the authorities?"

"Yes, the surgeon reported the gunshot wound to the authorities. The surgery was performed at Big Sisters Hospital in Ventura. You are welcome to check with them if you need to."

"Oh, no, Mister Kinney. I felt obligated to ask, but I would never doubt the word of a Biltmore guest. Have a pleasant afternoon."

With that, Doctor Becker removed himself from our suite, and Eliza came over to give me a hug and a kiss on the cheek. "You were very brave, darling. Pulling those sutures out must have been painful."

So as not to disillusion Eliza in the matter of my bravery, I said, "Oh, it stung a little, but not too terribly."

Giving me a look that told me she knew I was understating the case, she said, "So what shall we do now, darling?"

"Put on your typewriter pin, kiddo. I am fairly certain I know what Richardson, the *Examiner's* City Editor, will expect in the way of rewrites for my third story, so I might as well start revising it now."

"All right, darling. Do you think it would be safe for me to call Mabel? I think it is a good idea for us to keep up to date on what's happening at home."

I gave the safety aspect of her question a moment's thought. "I think it would be okay. Call from the room phone here and we'll let the *Examiner* pay the long distance charges. That way the call won't show up on the *Tribune's* telephone record, just in case anyone is paying attention to such things."

The room brightened with Eliza's smile. "Thank you, darling. There is an extension telephone instrument in the bedroom. I'll use it so I don't disturb your work."

I set up my typewriter on the living room writing desk as Eliza placed her long distance call to Santa Barbara, and I was off to a good start on my rewrite of the "Journalists Beaten and Shot" story by the time Eliza returned to the living room. I noted that she was, indeed, wearing her little typewriter pin. She was also wearing a somewhat glum expression.

"Bad news?"

Perching on the arm of a chair a few feet from the desk, Eliza said, "Not really bad, just discouraging. Mabel said father is not at the paper again today."

"Maybe he's still working on his defense with his attorney."

"I suppose that could be. I only hope he is getting along all right."

Despite our earlier conclusion that Frederick Hamm's behavior was a symptom of a mind sickness, I still had trouble working up much sympathy for his plight. On the other hand, he was not my father. Trying to give Eliza a boost, I said, "He surely has a lot on his mind right now. Under similar circumstances I would find it difficult to settle back into a daily routine of work."

"Lester, what do you think the court will do to father?"

"Assuming his attorney uses an insanity defense, along with the fact that your father's crimes are of a technical nature and did not actually hurt anyone significantly, the court might simply require a treatment program of some kind. The State of California has statutes governing the commitment of those suffering from mental sickness, so those might come into play."

Eliza's eyes were full of sadness. "That is what I fear most. I've read about the things that go on in mental asylums. Some of it is dreadful—straightjacket restraints and injections of poisonous drugs . . . they even use patients for testing experimental vaccines. Father does not deserve to be treated like that."

She was right. Frederick Hamm had done nothing to deserve the sort of treatment she described, although I had no idea how to go about preventing it. For the first time it was occurring to me that a legal defense of insanity could backfire and do more damage than a jail sentence.

Eliza came over to stand beside the desk. "The worst of it is that my behavior set him off. If I had not behaved so badly the night of Estelle's party . . . if I had not flown off the handle and acted like . . . like I did, none of this would have happened. This is all my fault."

I stood and put my hands of her shoulders. "Listen to me, Eliza. This is not your fault. Yes, some of your decisions that night triggered his behavior, but if they had not, something else would have set him off sooner or later."

She leaned her head against my chest, but said nothing. I gave voice to a thought that occurred to me. "Tell me, Eliza, do you know your father's lawyer?"

Looking up at me, she said, "I've never met him, but I know his name is Tailor, Elias Tailor, I think."

"Do you think he would talk with you if you telephoned him?"

Eliza seemed to think about my question for a moment. "Maybe. I don't know. Why?"

"If you could talk with him, he might give you some idea of what to expect and you might be able to give him some insight into the situation he does not have."

Nodding, Eliza said, "I guess it wouldn't hurt anything to try. Should I use the telephone here to call him?"

"I would, but the choice to call him is up to you."

Eliza hugged me tighter. "I would like to try. Thank you, darling."

Once again, she disappeared into the bedroom and I went back to my writing, at least I tried to go back to it. Concentration on the sheet of paper rolled around the platen in my typewriter eluded me as my attention drifted off to the next room and Eliza's telephone conversation. I could not hear many of the words she spoke, but the tone of her voice told me that suggesting she call her father's defense lawyer was not one of my better ideas. When she returned to the living room Eliza's expression confirmed that impression.

Eliza said, "Well, that was a thoroughly unpleasant experience."

"What happened?"

"Mister Tailor would not speak with me except to say I should be ashamed of myself for the anguish I have caused my father and that I was the one who ought to be on trial."

Eliza's eyes were moist and I suspected the only thing holding back the tears was her anger. "He is an awful man!"

Nodding agreement with her assessment of Elias Tailor, I said, "Regardless of his opinions, it is not his place to speak to you in that manner."

"No, it is not!"

Replaying Eliza's brief account of her conversation, something else occurred to me. "That he said those things, however, might tell us something about the defense he is planning."

That seemed to puzzle her. "What do you mean?"

"Well, I might be reading too much into what little was said, but I have to wonder if this fellow Tailor has in mind trying to justify a desperate father's actions by condemning his daughter's immoral conduct and outrageous behavior. We may be way off the mark with our assumption he is planning a temporary insanity plea."

Eliza's immediate reaction to my comments was infuriation. "Immoral conduct? Outrageous behavior? That is . . . that's . . . ."

I finished the sentence for her. "That is a very effective way to win the sympathy of a jury consisting of parents. It would cause men and women with children to put themselves in your father's shoes when he was confronted with what they might well see as the immoral disobedience of a daughter who was out of control."

That unleashed the tears. They started rolling down her cheeks as she asked, "Oh, Lester, do you think I was immorally disobedient?"

Picturing Eliza's near naked confrontation with her father in the living room of my cottage, I felt it prudent to stretch the truth somewhat. "There were extenuating circumstances, but to someone with a biased view of the facts, it could appear that you were."

"Oh, God! If what I did comes out in court, I will never be able to show my face in Santa Barbara again. I will lose my job!"

The anguish on Eliza's face was overwhelming. I stood and took her in my arms. "Slow down, kiddo. We need to learn more before we make assumptions about what is going to happen."

She looked up at me. "How can we learn more?"

"We could try going through the backdoor."

"What do you mean?"

"I think we should place another call to Mabel and ask her if she knows of any connection between Elias Tailor and Estelle Abernathy. Also ask her to find out who is prosecuting the case and if he has any connection to Estelle."

Eliza looked surprised. "You think Estelle is behind what the lawyer said?"

"I don't know, but it seems like a good idea to find out the extent to which she could be involved on both sides of the case."

Nodding, Eliza walked out to place a second call to Mable. Meanwhile, I tried to sort the situation out in my mind. Matters were complicated to begin with, and when this afternoon's *Examiner* hit the streets, there would be even more complication.

My first priorities were Eliza's safety and wellbeing, but insuring those things was becoming increasingly challenging. Besides Estelle Abernathy trying her darnedest to bring my life to an untimely end, I now had to deal with some shyster besmirching Eliza's reputation in order to save her father from a prison sentence.

While I personally did not give one whit what happened to Frederick Hamm, Eliza did, so that meant I had to take his welfare into consideration as well, even if that consideration came into conflict with my first priorities. Circumstances were also complicated by the knowledge that Eliza brought much of our situation on herself, but I knew that when I asked her to marry me.

On the positive side of the equation I now had a formidable ally in the form of W. R. Hearst and his *Los Angeles Examiner*. If my articles exposing Estelle Abernathy's dirty deeds did not end her private reign of terror, nothing could. Also, with a good deal of help along the way, I managed to eliminate two of Estelle's tools of destruction. As Deputy Tanner pointed out, that did not mean there were not more thugs at her disposal, but I thought taking Delgado and Mikhailov out of the equation improved the odds somewhat.

It turned out that reducing our situation to the lowest common denominators contributed nothing to a solution. Then, just to complicate things further, Eliza returned with more unsettling news from Mabel.

"You were right, darling, at least as far as Elias Tailor is concerned. Mabel clearly remembers him representing the Summerland Oil Field Company in the past. That connects him to Estelle. Mabel said she hasn't heard who is prosecuting the case against father, but she promised to find out for us."

"That is not particularly good news about Tailor."

Eliza said, "Isn't that a conflict of interest or something?"

"I don't see how it would be. Estelle is not legally a party to the case against your father and neither is Summerland, so there are no grounds for conflict, at least not one on the surface of things."

Eliza just nodded. I had a feeling she was feeling pretty worn out emotionally. Glancing at my watch, and then giving her a hug, I said, "It's almost four. The *Examiner* will be hitting the streets very soon. They truck the newspapers for out of town subscribers, so Santa Barbara won't see a copy for at least another hour or two. Why don't you relax and read or take a nap until five? Then we can get a copy of the paper from the newsstand in the lobby and see what they did with our stories."

Eliza simply nodded again. "But please don't go downstairs without me, okay?"

"Promise."

TWENTY-SEVEN

Tuesday - September 18, 1928

I still had trouble concentrating, but managed to bang out a decent rewrite of the "Journalists Beaten and Shot" story, updating it to include events happening since I wrote the original. That effort took up most of an hour, so it was time to wake Eliza.

Having checked on her a time or two, I knew she was sleeping, but not soundly. I could not blame her for being distraught, but every time I figured she was down for the count, Eliza seemed to bounce back.

After taking a moment in our dazzling white bathroom to freshen up, Eliza was ready to accompany me on an expedition down to the lobby newsstand. As expected, they had a stack of hot-off-the-presses *Examiners* prominently displayed on their counter. I purchased a copy and we ascended back up to the Biltmore's stratosphere to see how my stories were treated.

Robert Carlson and Jim Richardson had done the stories justice. A one-column photo of Monsignor Cullen O'Boylan appeared with my story about him being attacked on the grounds of the Santa Barbara Mission. Carlson obviously did some additional research. It was the first time I had seen the Bishop's given name. I didn't even know bishops, popes, and the like had first names.

A larger two-column photo of the Summerland Oil Field was prominently displayed below the headline, "Summerland Oil Strikers Struck Down in Cold Blood," on the first page of the Metro section. The photo was captioned, "Scene of labor massacre." The story appeared word for word as I wrote it.

Eliza pointed to the short lines of bold twelve-point text just below the headlines that said "By Lester Kinney." "There you go, Mister Journalist, your bylines in a major west coast newspaper. We need to put these in your clippings scrapbook."

"I don't have a clippings scrapbook."

She grinned at me. "You will have as soon as I get my hands on a book to paste them in. Everything else aside, these articles mark a major milestone in your career."

"If you say so. I think I'll turn over such important responsibilities to the president of my fan club."

"That would most certainly be me. What's next on our agenda this evening?"

I shrugged. "Darned if I know. I finished my rewrite of the third story, and I'm not due back at the *Examiner* until nine o'clock tomorrow morning. I guess we have some free time on our hands."

As if on cue, the Ambassador Suite's telephone rang. Eliza gave me a questioning look and I picked up the handset. "Hello."

"Hello, Lester, Bob Carlson here. How's the Biltmore treating you?"

"A trifle ostentatiously, but we're quite comfortable. I even got some writing done this afternoon."

"Good. Say, what are you doing for dinner?"

"No plans so far, what do you have in mind?"

"I was thinking it would be nice if the *Examiner* bought us dinner in the Biltmore's Gold Room. About seven o'clock?"

"Sounds good, Bob. Okay if I bring a guest?"

"Sure. The more the merrier. W. R. can afford it."

"All right, see you at seven."

I returned the handset to its cradle and Eliza said, "We have a dinner date?"

"We do, Missus Kinney. In the Biltmore's Gold Room, no less."

A tenor of excitement crept into her voice. "And with whom are we rendezvousing?"

"Bob Carlson, the *Examiner's* Metro Editor and part time journalism prof at Occidental College."

Eliza gave me a small frown. "Oh, a business dinner. Are you sure I won't be in the way?"

"Eliza, there is no place I will ever go where you would be in the way. In fact, I'm looking forward to showing you off. Bob will be impressed with my good taste in women."

She flashed her coy look. "Oh, my. In that case I shall wear something dazzling. What time?"

"Seven, but you don't worry about wearing something dazzling. You would dazzle in a potato sack."

"That's kind of you to say, but I suspect the Gold Room's maître d might consider a potato sack too gauche for such a swank milieu. Besides, I enjoy dressing up for you."

I laughed. "Okay, kiddo, get yourself dressed to the nines. I will even try to find a tie."

At seven o'clock we passed through a pair of elaborate eight-foot gold-painted ornamental iron gates and entered the Gold Room, where a fellow in a tux was tinkling his way through *Fascinating Rhythm* on a grand piano. As a similarly clad maître d approached, I saw that Bob had already arrived. I gestured toward Bob's table and the maître d escorted us in that direction.

Following Eliza, I was yet again taken by her beauty. She was wearing her "wedding dress" and the effect of the simple white frock in contrast to her dark hair was stunning. I could tell Bob agreed with that assessment because he jumped to his feet as we approached. That was not something he would have done if I had arrived solo.

To me he said, "Good evening, Lester. You didn't tell me we were dining with a beautiful motion picture starlet tonight."

Eliza smiled a small smile in subtle acknowledgment of Bob's compliment as the maître d seated her. Seating myself, I said, "Eliza, meet Professor Robert Carlson. Bob, this is my wife, Eliza."

"Good evening, Missus Kinney. Thank you for brightening up our dreary little dinner party."

The piano player launched into *My Heart Stood Still* and Eliza said, "Good evening, Professor Carlson and thank you for including me in your invitation."

"Please call me Bob, and if I'd known who Lester's 'guest' was going to be, I would have suggested he send you in his stead."

She smiled again, but said, "Then I fear you would be dining alone tonight. Now that I have managed to catch a handsome, talented writer, I am taking no chances."

Bob looked at me. "I assume she's referring to you, Lester, although how you landed such a stunning and obviously intelligent woman I will never understand. You hardly struck me as a budding Valentino during your college days. Back then you were strictly business."

Winking at Eliza, I said, "I had to be strictly business. My journalism professor insisted on it."

Bob chuckled. "It seems my insistence on hard work paid off. You, my boy, have officially made it to the big time. Jim Richardson is quite impressed, and he does not impress easily."

"Thank you, Bob, but I never would have gotten past the *Examiner's* front door if it had not been for you."

"Yes you would. It might have taken a little longer, but you would have gotten there."

At that point we were politely interrupted by a waiter who

asked if we would care for a libation. His question reminded me that in addition to being an elegant restaurant, the Biltmore's Gold Room was also widely known to be a speakeasy. It is said they even have a "secret door" providing imbibing patrons a hasty exit route out to Olive Street in the event of a raid.

Knowing Eliza's feelings on the subject of Demon Booze, however, I said, "The lady and I will have Coca-Cola. Bob?"

Bob clearly did not share Eliza's distaste for alcohol. "I'll have Rye rocks."

The waiter acknowledged our orders and left large leather-bound menus on the table for our perusal. He promised to return shortly with our drinks.

Ignoring his menu, Carlson turned to Eliza and said, "So, Missus Kinney, how does it feel to be the wife of a top notch journalist?"

"It is quite exciting, but I grew up with a journalist, so I knew what to expect."

"Oh? Was someone in your family a newspaper man?"

Eliza realized her mistake. Now it seemed she would have to open the whole can of worms about her father. She shot a side glance at me.

I made an effort to get her off the hook. "Eliza's dad was a journalist. Now, tell me, Bob, have you had any reaction to either of the articles yet?"

Bob seemed to accept my explanation and responded to my question without asking any of his own. "Only from the legal department. Jim ran your stories by them and the response was that you did a good job of putting the onus on your sources. In other words, the *Examiner* simply reported the facts as provided by credible sources. So, unless we misquoted somebody, if anyone gets sued, it won't be the paper. Lawyers go in for that kind of reporting, especially on a paper like ours."

Nodding, I said, "Good. We have to keep the lawyers happy."

"You bet we do. Now, let me ask you a question. I know darn well I did not teach you to write in the style of the stories you sold us. Where did you learn to write for the yellow press, as we are so disrespectfully known?"

"Truthfully, I never tried it before." Grinning, I added, "It would seem writing trash comes naturally to me."

"Trash? Remember, Lester, that trash earned you a C-note-and-a-half today. A little respect please."

That is when our waiter returned with our drinks. Bob promptly raised his glass in the manner of a toast. "To Missus

Eliza Kinney, the loveliest woman in this or any other room!"

I clinked my glass against Bob's and took a swig of Coca-Cola. Eliza looked properly appreciative, and then we turned our attention to our menus. The selections were numerous and covered just about every imaginable type of cuisine.

After a few moments, I looked at Eliza. She turned her open menu toward me and pointed to her choices so when the waiter returned for our dinner orders, I was able to say, "The lady will have Sole Meuniere with Green Beans Almandine as an accompaniment."

I chose a sautéed shrimp and ham over rice dish also with Green Beans Almandine as a nod to Eliza's firm belief that I should consume vegetables by the bushel basket. I received a pleased smile of approval for doing so.

Bob's dinner choice was a rare T-bone steak and a baked potato drowned in melting butter. I am certain the Gold Room's chefs would have taken the way we devoured our dinners to the last morsel as the highest form of compliment.

Over cups of coffee that was only a small step below Eliza's on the epicure's scale of deliciousness, we chatted about a variety of subjects, most of them pertaining to my school days at Occidental or the state of modern journalism. Eliza entered into the conversation and was not hesitant about expressing her opinions. I observed that, once Bob got used to the idea of a woman having intelligently stated views, he enjoyed the exchange immensely.

Bob and I were both mildly surprised, however, when Eliza asked a question neither of us anticipated. "Bob, you obviously know Lester well, and now that you have seen samples of his versatility, how would you rate his chances of securing a reporting position with a large metropolitan newspaper?"

He considered his answer for a moment, and then said, "I think his chances are mighty good, but it would take some time to find the job that fit just right." Bob turned to face me and asked, "Is that what you want, Lester, to be a reporter on a major daily?"

"Yes and no. I'm not sure what I want at the moment. As you might have gathered from the stories I wrote, things have been kind of crazy for us during the past few weeks. I am without a source of income, but I don't think we're in a position to make a move right now. As I said, I'm just not sure what I want at the moment."

I looked at Eliza and said, "What are you thinking about all this, kiddo?"

She stared back at me for a moment, and then said, "This isn't the place to air our problems, but it is a distinct possibility that all of this craziness could cost me my job at the library. If that happens, our financial future will be dismal. We have to do something, and I was just trying to think ahead. On the other hand, as you said, we are not in a position to make permanent decisions right now. Do you see what I'm getting at, Mister Carlson?"

Bob nodded. "I do see the problems you are facing, but let me ask you something, Missus Kinney, do you know what a stringer is?"

"I think so. Isn't a stringer like a correspondent, a freelance journalist who contributes articles to a news organization on a semi-regular basis?"

"Yes, that's it in a nutshell. I asked that question because, at the moment, that is exactly what Lester is to the *Examiner*. We are paying him on a per-article basis for his coverage of at least two on-going stories, and it looks to me as if either or both of those stories could continue for some time to come, especially the Summerland story.

"I'm pretty sure Jim Richardson would be inclined to continue using Lester as a stringer if we approached him on that subject. As you discovered today, the *Examiner* pays its stringers quite well when the story warrants it. What do you say, Lester? Are you interested in continuing in that role for us?"

I nodded enthusiastically. "Very much so."

"Now, I don't know how long Jim will go along with a suite at the Biltmore, but it seems to me you could work out of your home in Santa Barbara or rent a small place here in LA. I'll speak to him about it first thing in the morning if you'd like."

"Yes, I think that would be just the ticket. What do you think, Eliza?"

She smiled a smile that told me she was pleased we had negotiated a favorable, if temporary, outcome to one of our problems. "I think Bob just provided the solution to our dilemma." Looking over at Carlson, she said, "Thank you, Bob."

"You are most welcome, Eliza." With a wink, he added, "It's a pleasure doing business with you."

After I signed the check charging our dinner, sixteen dollars including tip, to room 1135, we parted company with Bob Carlson and ascended to the rarified atmosphere of the Ambassador Suite. There, with an expression of concern clouding her pretty face, Eliza asked, "Was that all right, darling, I mean what I said to Mister Carlson?"

"Certainly. At least we have a temporary solution to one of our employment problems."

"I wish I could have spoken to you before asking him, but the idea only occurred to me during dinner and I thought we should take advantage of the situation while we had Mister Carlson's attention. You aren't obligated to the *Examiner* if you don't want to be a stringer for them."

Removing my tie, I said, "Don't worry, kiddo. I think you did a good thing for us. Thank you. Now, unless Jim Richardson doesn't go along with the idea for some reason, we need to make some choices."

Turning her back to me, Eliza said, "Would you please unzip me, darling?"

I fulfilled her request and gave her a hug just because it felt good. As Eliza walked into the bedroom, she said, "What choices do we need to make?"

"I guess the first decision must be where we want to go from here. For you to go back to work, we must return to Santa Barbara by the end of the week. That assumes, of course, you want to go back to work."

Moving to the bedroom doorway so she could see me, Eliza said, "Going back to work at the library might be difficult if I no longer have a job there. Remember the conclusions we drew after talking with father's attorney this afternoon?"

I joined her in the bedroom. "Yes, I remember. We should also bear in mind that those conclusions were largely guesswork. They could be completely incorrect."

Eliza paused in the midst of hanging her white dress in the closet. "Can we take the risk that they are correct? Wouldn't it be better to prepare for the worst?"

I hung my jacket next to her dress. "That could mean burning some bridges behind us. Are you sure you are ready to do that?"

"Darling, when you woke me from my nap this afternoon, I had what might be called an epiphany."

"Oh?"

"Yes. What I realized is our world is transforming into a completely different place than it was the day we met. Things are changing very quickly and we have no control over most of what is happening so if we are going to survive the changes, we have to change with them."

I added my trousers to the closet and thought about what Eliza was telling me. She had clearly put a lot of thought into her revelation and, so far, I could not fault her logic. Seeing her standing there in the slip she wore under the white dress, however, made concentration on our conversation a little more difficult, but I managed to ask, "What sort of changes do you think we need to make, Eliza?"

I must have sounded worried, because she prefaced her answer by saying, "Don't worry, darling, I'm not proposing anything outlandish. In fact, we have already made the first and most important change."

"Oh? What change was that?"

She gestured toward the small gold band on the ring finger of her left hand. "We got married. You do remember that, don't you?"

Smiling at the humor she added to our serious conversation, I said, "Yes, I do recall something to that effect."

Eliza returned my smile, something that always raised my spirits. "And do you also recall why we got married?"

"Seems to me it had to do with loving each other."

Choosing that moment to pull her slip off over her head, she said, "Yes, but there was more. We also got married because we decided we need each other, and one of the reasons we need each other involves keeping up with the changes occurring in our world. Right?"

I found myself responding more to her standing there in her panties than to her words. "Ah . . . right."

Eliza grinned. "Keep your mind on our conversation for just a few more minutes, darling. The other changes we have to make in our lives concern what we do and where we do it. Those are the sorts of choices we must make. Does what I'm saying make sense?"

"You are making a lot of sense, Eliza. We must figure out the best way to survive the changes and adapt our plans accordingly."

She stepped out of her panties. "You've got it! See, my revelation, though a little late in arriving, makes good sense. So, I suggest we begin discussing those changes and deciding what course they will take."

"Ah . . . would putting that discussion off until morning be too much procrastination?"

Stepping into my arms, Eliza said, "No, darling, it would not. Besides, you clearly have your mind on other things at the moment."

"And you don't?"

"There you go trying to put the blame on me just because I'm standing here naked and wanting you so much it hurts."

We kissed and I said, "It hurts? Really?"

Eliza cocked her head to one side as if thinking about my question. "It's more of an all-consuming need than an actual pain, darling."

"I see. In that case perhaps we should find a way of filling that need before it consumes you entirely."

"Yes, darling, we should."

We did.

TWENTY-EIGHT

Wednesday - September 19, 1928

Mornings are busy times for afternoon newspapers and when I arrived a few minutes before nine Wednesday morning, the *Examiner's* newsroom shared many similarities with a three-ring circus. Amazingly, it is in such environments of barely controlled chaos that daily editions of the world's greatest newspapers are born.

Dodging copy boys, assignment editors, and reporters with pencils behind their ears, all scurrying to wherever they needed to be, I made my way to the door marked Metro Editor. Bob Carlson's office was like the eye of a hurricane, calm and peaceful.

Bob looked up from a page of copy he was marking with a red pencil and said, "Morning, Lester. Have a seat. I'll just be a few minutes."

I sat across from his desk and swallowed some coffee out of a cardboard cup I poured on my way through the newsroom. Eliza would not have approved of the mud in my cup.

We decided she should again accompany me to the *Examiner* this morning. I had seen no specific signs of danger leaving the Biltmore, but given the fact that everyone who mattered had now seen my articles, this seemed like an inappropriate time to let our guard slip.

I had swallowed about half of my coffee when Bob finally pressed a button on his desk intercom and said, "Copy." After that he leaned back in his swivel chair and turned his attention in my direction.

"Mister Kinney, if you intended to stir things up with your articles, you have succeeded and then some. I expected responses, but this reaction is bigger than anything I anticipated."

"It is? What's going on?"

"Well, let's see. First, the Catholic Church is in an uproar. We received a copy of a letter they apparently sent to everyone with a mailbox in southern California. In it, the Archbishop of the Los Angeles Archdiocese demands all manner of investigations into the beating of that bishop up north. Also, even though it is a Catholic charity, he wants that orphanage investigated for allowing a young girl to be placed in what he termed an 'immoral environment.'"

"I guess we did stir thing up a bit."

"Yeah, and neither of those events even occurred in the archbishop's bailiwick. Obviously the church believes the best defense is a loud and vocal offense, and if you know anything about the Catholic Church, you know that even an archbishop does not have the authority to send such a damning public letter without approval from a higher authority. Clearly, a lot of midnight holy oil was burned last night."

I smiled. "Apparently."

"And that's just the beginning. An hour ago we received a long distance telephone call from the mayor of Santa Barbara, what's his name?"

"Finley."

"Yeah, Finley. He wanted to assure us that he is ordering his police department to double their efforts in finding the thug who beat up the bishop."

I laughed. "All he has to do is call the Ventura County Sheriff. They have the guy in custody."

Bob also saw the humor in the situation. "So it says in your article. Being from the sticks and all, perhaps the mayor does not read well."

By this time I was making copious notes in my stenographer's book. "Anything else?"

"A few minutes ago Jim told me he had a call from the managing director of the Summerland Oil Field Company, a guy by the name of Brinkley. He denies any knowledge of who is responsible for the dreadful slaughter of the company's valuable and loyal employees. He claims he has offered the company's full cooperation in locating the killer or killers."

"Of course he has. What else?"

"Our switchboard has been lit up like a Christmas tree since last night, so I'm sure there is a good deal more, but those are the main things I know about so far, except I have a stack of telephone messages for you here."

Bob handed me the messages and I shuffled through them quickly. Not too surprisingly, Sergeant Danny Sullivan wanted to talk to me. So did Deputy Walter Tanner of the Ventura County Sheriff's Department. There were a few calls from people I did not know, and one I found particularly interesting. Estelle Abernathy wanted me to call her. I bet she did.

I moved Estelle's message to the bottom of the stack and said, "I will return these calls in a while. In the meantime, here's my rewrite of the third story you saw yesterday.

He took the copy and gave it a quick read-through. "Good job of keeping the ball rolling. Jim will be happy to have this. It connects your shooting with the assault on that bishop and further implicates the Abernathy woman. It also has a lot of drama in it. Readers like stories about people getting shot and that sort of thing, especially newspaper men."

"Good. I wouldn't want your readers getting bored."

Ignoring my comment, Bob said, "Jim also wants you to get hopping on anything new you can put together on the progress of the investigation into the beating of that Bishop, O'Boylan. He wants that by one this afternoon, if you can manage it."

"I'll have to do it long distance, but I think I can come up with something worth reading."

"Good. I talked to Jim this morning about you staying on as a stringer, and he's all for it. He also said you can keep the Biltmore suite through Friday."

"Thanks, Bob. I really appreciate you acting in our behalf."

"Don't thank me, thank your wife. Give her half a chance and she'll put a Pulitzer in your pocket."

Smiling, I said, "That's my gal. Now, do you have anything else for me, or can I go get started on the new article for Jim?"

"Only that we owe you another seventy-five for your third story. You want that now or should we wait and see what else you have for us?"

"Hold it. I'm okay for now."

"Then go to work. The minute you have the bishop update on paper, call it in. I'll have a stenographer take it over the phone. Remember, we need it by one at the latest."

"You'll have it."

I hurried down to the *Examiner's* lobby where Eliza was waiting for me. Of course, she wanted to know what the reaction to our stories had been. I said I would give her a full report on the way back to the Biltmore because we had to get moving. I had only two-and-a-half hours to research and write another article.

So as we negotiated another roundabout route to the hotel, I filled Eliza in on the responses Bob told me about. When I finished, her reaction was much the same as mine.

"Wow. Talk about the power of the press! Your stories have probably upped the *Examiner's* readership a percent or two. They ought to like that."

"I think they do. Jim Richardson even said we can stay at the Biltmore through Friday."

With exaggerated enthusiasm, Eliza said, "Oh, boy!"

We pulled into the Biltmore's underground parking area and elevatored up to the eleventh floor. In our suite, I asked Eliza for some help with the story I needed to write.

"Anything, darling. What do you need me to do?"

"I think the first step is to call Mabel and find out if she can add anything to what we know about reactions to the stories. Maybe she also has the name of the attorney who is prosecuting your father's case."

"Okay. I'll get busy."

I gave her a kiss on the cheek. "Thanks, kiddo. I'll get busy, too."

After staring at the blank sheet of paper in my typewriter for a minute or two, I started the story:


```
         SUSPECT ARRESTED IN BEATING OF SANTA BARBARA
                             BISHOP

         Meanwhile Bishop O'Boylan Near Death in Santa
                       Barbara Hospital.

                      By Lester Kinney


        A man identified as Peter Mikhailov, is now
     suspected by authorities of being the assailant
     who attacked Santa Barbara's Bishop O'Boylan one
     week ago.  Mikhailov was arrested Monday night
     during an assault incident at Ventura's Pierpont
     Inn.
        A second assailant at the Pierpont Inn,
     Armando Delgado, was injured during the incident,
     but managed to flee the scene.  Delgado has also
     been identified as the man who shot newspaper
     reporter Lester Kinney last Wednesday.  Both
     Mikhailov and Delgado are known to be employees
     of prominent Santa Barbara businesswoman, Estelle
     Abernathy.
```

I was mentally composing my next paragraph when Eliza returned to the living room. "Stop the presses."

Looking up, I asked, "What's up?"

"Mabel says Cottage Hospital announced early this morning that Bishop O'Boylan passed away last night. There were multiple causes of death all from injuries sustained when he was beaten a week ago."

"I'm sorry to hear O'Boylan didn't make it, but his death puts Estelle one step closer to the gallows. What else did Mabel have to say?"

Looking at notes she made, Eliza said, "This is good news. Mabel said the *Tribune* carried a story last night about a nun coming forward to say she saw a stranger leaving the old mission grounds in a hurry around two o'clock on the day Monsignor O'Boylan was beaten. She described the person she saw as a big man with black hair and a large, bushy moustache."

"That fits Peter Mikhailov to a T, right down to the mustache."

"It sure does."

"Anything else?"

Nodding slowly, Eliza said, "She found out that father's case is being prosecuted by an Assistant US District Attorney named William Edwards. His office is here in the Los Angeles Federal Building. She gave me the telephone number."

The name William Edwards struck a familiar chord in my mind. Pulling the stack of *Examiner* telephone messages from my jacket pocket, I thumbed through them. Sure enough, there was one from William Edwards.

"I thought that name sounded familiar. He called the *Examiner* and left a message for me to call him."

Eliza frowned. "Oh, oh. I wonder what he wants."

"Since we never gave Sergeant Sullivan the statements he said they would need from us, I suspect that might have something to do with his call."

"I bet you're right. Are you going to call him?"

"Let's think about that for a little while. We can discuss it again after I finish this story."

Eliza nodded. "Okay. What else can I do to help?"

"How about calling Deputy Tanner to let him know we are okay and why we left the Pierpont?"

"You want me to tell him his deputy fell asleep while he was supposed to be protecting us?"

"Absolutely. That gives us a reasonable excuse for disappearing and puts him on the spot. That's a good thing, because it will make Tanner feel guilty."

"Okay, if you say so."

"I do. Be a little indignant with him. Feeling guilty might make him more eager to share information. I want to know what's going on with Mikhailov, and if Tanner is in a cooperative mood, he should have the latest news on that subject."

Eliza grinned at me. "Now you're talking like a real reporter."

I grinned back at her. "Hop to it, kiddo."

As Eliza left for the bedroom telephone again, I ripped the page out of my typewriter and rolled in a fresh sheet of paper. The new headline I typed was:

SANTA BARBARA BISHOP DIES OF BEATING INJURIES

Suspect Arrested in Beating Death of Bishop
O'Boylan

By Lester Kinney

Eliza was gone about five minutes. She returned with a few new facts to plug into my story.

"You were absolutely right, darling. Deputy Tanner was extremely apologetic when I told him we caught his deputy sleeping in the hotel hallway. He was also most cooperative.

"It turns out he just received an order from the Ventura County District Attorney to make arrangements for transferring Peter Mikhailov to the custody of Santa Barbara County. Deputy Tanner said the Ventura DA and the Santa Barbara DA, a man named John Gilbert, like the movie star, were still discussing who would prosecute Mikhailov first, but when the hospital announced Monsignor O'Boylan's death, Santa Barbara won the argument. I guess a murder charge trumps an assault charge in these matters."

"That and the Santa Barbara DA now has an eye witness to Mikhailov being at the scene of the crime. All he needs is a motive, and I gave him that in yesterday's story on O'Boylan's beating. What else did Tanner have to say?"

"You will get a laugh out of this. He said a high-priced attorney from Santa Barbara showed up to get Mikhailov released on bail, but with multiple felony charges pending across two jurisdictions, the Ventura County judge who heard the bail request was not having any part of that idea. Would you care to guess who the high-priced attorney from Santa Barbara was?"

I thought about it for only a moment before the light dawned. "You have to be kidding!"

"That's right, none other than Elias Tailor, father's defense attorney."

I shook my head in amazement. "If this whole mess wasn't so tragic, it would be funny. Estelle Abernathy is one nervy dame!"

"That is putting it mildly. How is your story coming?"

"Give me twenty minutes and we can call it in. In the meantime, how about ordering us some lunch from room service. Shoveling all this manure around is making me hungry."

"Sure, I can do that. What would you like?"

"You pick it, so long as there is some real food along with the vegetables."

Smiling, Eliza said, "I will do my best to meet that requirement."

While Eliza went to consult the room service menu, I filled out my story with the information from the *Tribune* article about the nun who placed a man matching Peter Mikhailov's description at the scene of O'Boylan's beating and Deputy Tanner's news about Mikhailov's impending transfer to Santa Barbara for prosecution in the case. I also mentioned that Mikhailov was denied bail. I concluded the story with quotes from the Archbishop of the Los Angeles Archdiocese and Santa Barbara mayor Theodore Finlay.

Reviewing the copy, I decided it was good. The article was more of a straight, factual news story than my sensational articles the *Examiner* had already printed. This time the news was strong enough to stand alone without me having to paint it with a yellow brush. Jim Richardson might not appreciate that aspect of it, but I did.

At precisely twelve-ten I placed a call to Bob Carlson. He got a stenographer on the line and I read the story to both of them.

When I was done, Bob said, "Nice, Lester. Do we have the scoop on that fellow's arrest for the murder of O'Boylan?"

"I think so. The decision to move him to Santa Barbara for prosecution was made about an hour ago. It's unlikely any other paper will make the connection between Peter Mikhailov in Ventura County and Bishop O'Boylan until Mikhailov is in the hands of the Santa Barbara DA."

"Terrific! Jim already told me if you had anything really newsworthy in your story he wanted to move O'Boylan to the front page. I'd say this story is loaded to the gunnels with newsworthiness."

"Thanks, Bob."

"Say, do you think you could come up with something on the Summerland Oil thing for tomorrow's edition? Of course, that would be in addition to anything new on the O'Boylan story."

"I will see what I can do. The O'Boylan story is moving fast now, so there ought to be something, at the very least a statement from the Santa Barbara DA on arresting a strong suspect in the case. That will make the DA and the Sheriff's Department look good. Anything new there?"

"Well, the switchboard has finally calmed down a little, but it was busy all morning. The only thing for you specifically is another telephone message. A guy by the name of John Gilbert, like the movie star, called. He wants you to return his call as soon as you can at a Santa Barbara number. It's two-one-eight. Santa Barbara only has three digit telephone numbers?"

"Most of them. They just started using four digit numbers. It is turning into a major metropolis."

"Sure it is. I don't see any reason for you to waste time coming in here tomorrow, unless you want your checks. We owe you one-fifty for two stories now."

"Just keep track of it. I will put the time to good use getting you some new copy. One o'clock deadline again?"

"Or earlier if you can. That would take some pressure off of us here."

"I'll do my best. Talk with you tomorrow, Bob."

While I was talking to Carlson, lunch arrived. Eliza instructed the waiter set it up on a folding table near one of the living room windows so we would have a view with our lunch.

I joined Eliza at the table and saw that my plate had one of those stainless steel domed covers over it to keep the food warm. She removed the cover with a flourish and said, "There. Does that fit your definition of 'real food'?"

My plate held about the biggest hamburger I have ever seen. Along with it was a pile of French fried potatoes and garnish for the burger consisting of lettuce, tomatoes, a slice of Bermuda onion, and dill pickle slices.

I smiled my approval. "I'll say so. The only veggies I see are tomatoes, lettuce, onions, and pickles."

Sitting opposite me, Eliza said, "Technically tomatoes are a fruit and the pickles don't count, but you'd better eat up every bite of lettuce."

Her lunch consisted of a large tossed green salad with some bay shrimp and oil and vinegar dressing served in cruets on the side. Eliza noticed me looking at her salad.

"Now this is a real helping of vegetables, darling. You would be much healthier if you ate things like this."

"If eating all that green stuff keeps you looking sexy, I'm all for it, but I don't think it would do the same for me."

Putting on her coy expression, Eliza said, "You think I look sexy? You never said that before."

"That is an omission on my part. You are . . . how shall I put this? You are sexier than Clara Bow, Marion Davies, and Greta Garbo combined."

"Oh? You left out Gloria Swanson and Norma Shearer. I must eat more vegetables!"

"No, I left them out intentionally. I don't want all this sexiness to go to your head."

Adding a little more coyness to her expression, Eliza said, "As long as any sexiness I may have goes to your head, I'll be perfectly happy."

"Control yourself, kiddo. I have more work to do after lunch, and if you keep this up, I will not be able to concentrate."

"You are the one who brought up the subject of sexiness. I was just eating my healthy rabbit food."

"You are absolutely right. I stand corrected and I will keep my mouth shut about such things in the future."

"See that you don't, darling. Tell me, what work do you have planned for after lunch?"

"I intend to write an amended statement about how I was shot to replace the one we gave Deputy Tanner at the hospital. This one will include our meeting with Monsignor O'Boylan at the old mission and name Armando Delgado as the man I saw shoot at us. I will also explain my reasons for not telling the truth in my first statement. When it's done I will send copies to the Ventura County Sheriff's office and the Santa Barbara DA's office."

Eliza looked puzzled. "Why change your story now?"

"There are several reasons. First, I need to set the record straight. Second, having the facts of the matter in hand will give the DA a motive for O'Boylan's beating. Third, an accurate statement will also give him grounds to investigate Armando Delgado on charges of attempted murder. Fourth, the DA is sure to notice the discrepancies between my original statement and the facts laid out in the article the *Examiner* will print in today's paper about me getting shot. I think it would be wise to set the record straight before that happens."

"I wondered about that."

"In fact, somebody in the DA's office may already smell a rat. Bob gave me a telephone message this morning from the DA himself."

"Oh, oh."

"That's one of the things that prompted me to get on this now."

"How will you get it to the DA?"

"I think I will send copies to the Ventura County Sheriff's office and to the Santa Barbara District Attorney in the mail, and then return the DA's telephone call. If necessary, I can read the statement to him over the telephone."

"How can I help with all that?"

"I can think of two things. First, see if you can find the addresses we need. Second, go down to the gift shop and see if we can buy some envelopes that don't say Biltmore Hotel all over them. No, scratch out that second one. We'll both go down to the gift shop for envelopes."

She smiled. "Still doing the 'Ruth' thing, I see."

"You bet. Until we are certain the dangers are past, we go wherever we need to go together whenever possible."

Eliza stood up and walked around to my side of the table. There, she gave me a kiss on the cheek. "I would not be too upset if we continued that policy even after the dangers are past."

I went to work typing my amended statement. It began with us meeting Monsignor O'Boylan in the mission rose garden at one in the afternoon on Wednesday, September Twelve and concluded with Eliza delivering me to Big Sisters Hospital in Ventura that evening. I included an apology for giving an incorrect statement at the time because we feared the danger to our lives would escalate if authorities approached Estelle Abernathy and Armando Delgado and they learned I was still alive.

I rolled the statement and two carbon copies out of my typewriter and asked Eliza to read it in case I left something out. After reading the document, she said, "That's exactly how it happened."

"Good. Were you able to find an addresses for mailing these?"

"Yes. I called the Ventura Sheriff's office to get their address, and I made another call to Mabel a few minutes ago. She gave me the Santa Barbara County DA's address."

"Good idea. Any further news from home?"

"Nothing since what she told me this morning. I did ask her if she had seen father today. She said he didn't come in to the paper again. That's really starting to worry me."

"Let's get these amended statements into the mail so I can make my call to the DA, and then we can talk about your dad and the attorney situation, okay?"

Picking up her handbag, Eliza said, "Let's go."

We purchased some two-cent postal stamps at the gift shop, but they had no plain envelopes. The front desk had some, though, so Eliza addressed two of them, stuck on some stamps, and we slipped the revised statements into the lobby mail drop.

Back in the Ambassador Suite, I sat at the table and dialed the Santa Barbara County District Attorney's office. I identified myself to the woman who answered the DA's telephone and said I was returning Mister Gilbert's call.

After a few moment's wait, a male voice said, "Mister Kinney, thank you for returning my telephone call."

"You are welcome, Mister Gilbert. What can I do for you?"

After a moment's hesitation, Gilbert said, "Well, Mister Kinney, I have in front of me the statement regarding the shooting accident in which you were wounded on the twelfth day of this month; the one you gave to a Deputy . . . ah . . . Tanner of the Ventura County Sheriff's department. Do recall that statement?"

"Yes, I do."

"Well, I've been going over what you said and I have a few questions about it. Would you mind answering them for me?"

"Not at all, Mister Gilbert."

"Thank you, Mister Kinney. The first question I have concerns your mental state when you gave the statement to the deputy. I'm wondering if you might have still been under the effects of medication given to you during the surgery when you made the statement."

I couldn't help chuckling. "Mister Gilbert, that is the most diplomatic way of calling someone a damned liar I have ever heard."

He stuttered. "I didn't mean to imply . . . ."

"Sure you did, and you are absolutely right, there is very little truth in that statement. That is why I posted an amended statement to you earlier today. I am also prepared to read the new statement to you over the telephone now if you would find that helpful."

Gilbert chuckled. "All right, Mister Kinney, thank you. I would very much like to hear your amended statement."

I read the statement to him, including my explanation for why I lied in the original statement. When I was done, Gilbert said, "To be truthful, I like your amended statement much better than the original, although it might have sped some things up if you had given us the straight dope in the first place. I understand your reasons for doing what you did, though, and I see no way in which justice would be served by prosecuting you for giving a false statement to a law enforcement officer."

"Thank you, Mister Gilbert. I understand you are transporting Peter Mikhailov to Santa Barbara for prosecution. Does the content of my amended statement help you in that case?"

"Well, if this fellow Mikhailov works for Estelle Abernathy, she certainly had good reason for not allowing O'Boylan to repeat what you told him that afternoon. I think that gives us a motive to work on."

"That's what I was hoping you would say. What about Armando Delgado? He is wanted by Ventura County on assault charges. Are you going after him for shooting me?"

"It is my duty to do so, but until we get the case against Mikhailov nailed down a little better, I think I will let Ventura do the legwork on Delgado. I will tell Santa Barbara PD to cooperate in that effort. Is there a place I can reach you directly in case we need to talk with you again?"

I gave his question a moment of thought and decided caution still needed to be our watchword. "For the time being the *Los Angeles Examiner* is the best contact."

"I see. All right, Mister Kinney. We will do it that way for now. I understand you have a home in Santa Barbara. Will you be returning there any time soon?"

"At this point I am not sure. I would like very much to go home, but until we know Delgado is out of the picture and Estelle Abernathy has not recruited new henchmen to send after me, I must remain flexible."

"Understood. I wish you good luck and look forward to meeting you in person one day. Good day, Mister Kinney."

TWENTY-NINE

Wednesday - September 19, 1928

By the time I concluded my telephone call to John Gilbert, the time was nearly three-thirty. As I replaced the receiver back in its cradle, Eliza said, "That sounded as if it went well."

"I think I like Mister Gilbert. For an attorney, he seems like an all right sort of fellow. Gilbert said that, under the circumstances, the reason I gave for not being truthful in the police statement was understandable."

"That's a relief. Is he going to have Armando Delgado arrested?"

"Ventura County is already looking for Delgado. Gilbert is letting them do the legwork while he prosecutes Mikhailov. Once Delgado is in custody, Gilbert will work out prosecuting him with the Ventura DA."

Frowning, Eliza said, "I hope that's soon; I mean that Armando is in custody. He gives me the willies."

"He has not endeared himself to me either. Now, what are you thinking about helping your dad?"

Eliza shook her head slowly. "I don't know that we can help him at all. I might even make things worse for him by being there."

"We may not have any choice about being at his trial if we are subpoenaed, but supposing I return the federal prosecutor's call and find out what he wants? That might give us a better idea of what's going on and how to handle it."

"All right, darling, but I'm not holding my breath for any good news."

"Just the same, I think it would be a good idea for you to listen to our conversation on the telephone extension in the bedroom. That way you will know exactly what's going on."

Eliza nodded and walked into the bedroom and I dialed the number for the Assistant Federal District Attorney on the *Examiner's* telephone message slip. That number, it turned out, connected directly to Edwards' office.

A woman answered my call. "Assistant District Attorney Edwards' office."

"Good afternoon. My name is Lester Kinney. I am returning William Edwards' call."

It took a minute or more for Edwards to pick up the telephone. While waiting I told Eliza to pick up the bedroom extension.

Then a voice in my ear said, "Edwards. Thank you for returning my call, Mister Kinney."

The assistant district attorney had a strong bass voice with an authoritative tone about it. He had the sort of voice I thought would command a jury's attention.

"You are welcome, Mister Edwards. What can I do for you?"

"We need to meet, Mister Kinney. I also need to speak with Miss Eliza Hamm. Would you know where I can find her?"

"I would, but her name is no longer Hamm. She is now Missus Lester Kinney."

After a short pause, Edwards said, "I see. Then, we can kill two birds with one stone. I want to see you and your wife here in my office at the Federal Building tomorrow morning at ten."

He was not requesting our presence, he was ordering it. Mister Edwards was taking a lot for granted. He needed some instruction in diplomacy and I was moved to give him that lesson.

"Tomorrow is not a convenient day for killing birds, Mister Edwards. In fact, I am fairly certain there is no convenient time for us to meet with you until I know exactly what it is you want to discuss."

That seemed to throw him for a loop. Technically, he was prosecuting a man for crimes in which Eliza and I were among the victims. He had every reason to expect our cooperation, and yet I was not cooperating. In typical lawyer fashion, he responded with a threat.

"Mister Kinney, must I remind you I have the authority to subpoena your testimony as hostile witnesses?"

With a lot more bravery than I actually felt, I said, "Then trot out your subpoenas, Mister Edwards, although it seems to me you could gain our cooperation more easily by employing a modicum of diplomacy."

I glanced into the bedroom and saw Eliza raise her eyebrows in surprise. Edwards was silent for several seconds. I hoped he was reevaluating the situation. He was. "All right, Mister Kinney. The subject I want to discuss with you and Missus Kinney concerns the case I am prosecuting against her father. For one thing, I need statements from the two of you regarding Mister Hamm's actions."

"That is not an unreasonable request, Mister Edwards, but we would prefer to preface our statements with an off-the-record conversation. Is that acceptable to you?"

I had, in effect, turned the tables on Edwards. Now getting what he wanted depended on him making a concession, albeit a small one. He apparently decided discretion was the better part of valor.

In a much friendlier tone of voice Edwards said, "I think that could be arranged. When can I expect to meet with the two of you?"

Feeling a little braver now, I said, "As you may know, I am a journalist writing for the *Los Angeles Examiner*. At the moment I am up against a couple of tight deadlines. Would you consider meeting us at our hotel in, say, an hour?"

He seemed to think that over, and then said, "That would be all right, but I need a stenographer to take your statements, so . . . ."

"I have a typewriter here. It would be a simple matter to type our statements and sign them in the presence of the hotel's notary public. Then we could hand them to you directly."

Fearing I might have pushed him too far, I held my breath while Edwards considered my suggestion. He asked, "At which hotel are you staying?"

"The Biltmore. We are in the Ambassador Suite, room eleven-thirty-five."

In a tone tinted with resignation, he said, "Very well. I will see you and Missus Kinney in one hour."

The next sound I heard was a click. Our telephone conversation was over.

Eliza walked back into the living room with a barely concealed grin on her lips. "My goodness, darling, I think you pushed Mister Edwards about as far as he can be pushed."

"He got what he wants and I saved us a trip to the Federal Building. That is important because I believe we will fare far better with Edwards in a friendlier environment."

She cocked head to the side. "You sound as if you expect to gain something from our meeting with him."

I smiled. "I'm playing this strictly by ear, kiddo. Now that we have a new idea about Elias Tailor's defense strategy, my greatest hope is to keep your father's case entirely out of court. That probably is not possible, but we might be able to work out a compromise of some sort."

Looking sad, Eliza said, "I don't know which is worse; the possibility that Father could end up in jail or the likelihood that I will never be able to show my face in Santa Barbara again."

"I am not convinced the latter outcome is as likely as we first thought. In fact, I am nearly certain your father's defense attorney will not be arguing your 'abnormal behavior' caused your father's trolley to jump its track."

"What he said to me over the telephone made it sound as if that is exactly what he is planning. If he does that . . . ."

"But he doesn't dare do that. Remember in whose pocket he sits."

Clearly puzzled, she said, "I don't understand."

"We now know Tailor is ultimately working for Estelle Abernathy. She will not allow him to use that defense because it opens the door for cross-examination that would bring up your experiences with her and things like your father's warning to me that implied you prefer women to men."

Eliza was doubtful. "But wouldn't the prosecutor have to know her secret in order to prevent that defense?"

"He would, and we now have an opportunity to be certain Mister Edwards not only knows what sort of defense Elias Tailor might use, but that he also knows Estelle's dirty little secret. Heck, if he reads the *Examiner*, he already knows part of it, and so does your father's attorney. As you pointed out yesterday, circumstances we face are changing rapidly. This particular situation has already changed considerably since you spoke with Tailor on the telephone."

The assistant federal district attorney rang our door chime at four-twenty, ten minutes before his anticipated arrival time. I opened the door to a tall slender dark haired fellow in a charcoal gray pinstripe suit. He carried a dark brown briefcase and a gray fedora in his left hand.

"Good afternoon, Mister Kinney, I am William Edwards."

"Good afternoon, Mister Edwards, please come in."

Inside, Edwards gave the Ambassador Suite an appraising look. I could not tell from his noncommittal expression if he was impressed.

Eliza stood and I said, "Mister Edwards, this is my wife, Eliza."

Edwards actually bowed slightly. "I'm pleased to meet you, Missus Kinney."

In a tone oozing propriety, Eliza said, "And I you, Mister

Edwards."

Gesturing toward the living room couch and chairs, I said, "Please take a seat, Mister Edwards."

He chose one of the armchairs. Eliza and I sat on the couch. Crossing one leg over the other in an attempt to look relaxed and at ease, I said, "Now, Mister Edwards, let's get down to cases. Do you have an idea as to the defense strategy Elias Tailor plans to use?"

I intended my opening question to surprise him and his expression told me I succeeded. After a moment's hesitation, he said, "Ah . . . not specifically. The defense is not required to notify us of their intentions. I have seen some indications of what they plan to do from their witness list and documents they have requested be entered in evidence. Why do you ask?"

"Because I suspect the circumstances surrounding your case may be far more complex than you currently understand them to be."

"Oh? How so, Mister Kinney?"

I had an approach in mind and I took another step toward my ultimate goal. "How much do you know about your adversary, Mister Tailor? For example, are you aware of his connection to Miss Estelle Abernathy of Santa Barbara?"

His expression told me Edwards was not sure where I was going with my question. He said, "I know he represents the Summerland Oil Field Company in which Miss Abernathy has considerable interest. Is that what you mean?"

I nodded. "That is certainly part of it. Are you also aware that Miss Abernathy holds the controlling interest in *Santa Barbara Tribune*, Frederick Hamm's newspaper?"

Edwards shook his head. "No, Mister Kinney, I did not know that. I do not see, however, how that enters into this."

"Tailor's loyalties are important because they tell us Estelle Abernathy is indirectly controlling Mister Tailor's defense strategy."

"I suppose that could be the case, but I still do not see how . . . ."

"Bear with me just a little longer, Mister Edwards, and you will begin to see the larger picture. Let us suppose for a moment that Mister Tailor's defense strategy is to claim Mister Hamm was driven to behave as he did by 'abnormal behavior' on the part of his daughter—that as her father, he was so concerned with her welfare he took extreme and illegal measures to control what he saw as destructive conduct on her part. Would not that approach gain Mister Hamm a good deal of sympathy from a jury that included parents who could imagine themselves taking similar extreme measures to protect their children?"

"Yes, I agree that could become a significant factor in the outcome of the trial. As a matter of fact, we have seen some indications Mister Tailor is planning a defense strategy along the lines you suggest. There is little, however, we can do about that."

I smiled what I hoped he would see as a knowing and slightly smug smile. "Then let us do just a little more supposing. For example, let us suppose for a minute you possessed knowledge that would prevent Mister Tailor from employing that strategy. Would not that give you a powerful advantage in prosecuting the case?"

His expression, which thus far had remained bland, turned to one suggesting curiosity. "What sort of knowledge do you think would prevent such a defense?"

In preparation for our conversation with Edwards, I had placed Tuesday's edition of the *Examiner* on the coffee table in front of the couch. It was open to the front page on which my article about Aurora Abernathy's adoption appeared. I stood and handed Edwards the paper.

"Bearing in mind that Estelle Abernathy is ultimately in control of the defense strategy employed by Mister Tailor, please take a moment to read this article in yesterday's *Los Angeles Examiner*."

He accepted the paper and began to read the article, but I sensed he was losing patience with me. A minute or two later, he said, "Aside from the fact that you appear to have written this article I still do not see how it pertains to Mister Hamm's case."

Gently squeezing Eliza's hand, I said, "I think that will become clear with the help of just two more suppositions. First, suppose that in addition to Aurora Abernathy, Eliza is also a victim of Estelle Abernathy's 'immoral environment,' and that her experiences at Miss Abernathy's hand were behind the so called 'abnormal behavior' Frederick Hamm witnessed—the behavior that drove him to commit illegal acts. Finally, suppose Frederick Hamm not only knew Estelle Abernathy was a lesbian, but also that his daughter had for a short time been involved with her. Would not the defense strategy you expect from Mister Tailor allow you to introduce those facts—facts Estelle Abernathy has for many years gone to great lengths to conceal—into evidence?"

He glanced at Eliza. "It might, but Missus Kinney is obviously not a . . . forgive my language . . . lesbian. For one thing, she recently married."

I smiled another knowing smile. We were on the homestretch. "You are quite right, Mister Edwards, Eliza is not a lesbian. Nonetheless, she was employed by Estelle Abernathy for a short time, and in order to keep her position, Eliza submitted to Miss Abernathy's deviant sexual demands. She left the job as soon as possible, but the experience troubles her even now, four or five years after the fact. If Mister Tailor knew you possessed such knowledge, and especially in light of the *Examiner* article you just read, might he abandon the defense strategy you are expecting? In fact, would not Estelle Abernathy demand that he change his strategy?"

William Edwards' expression became thoughtful. He sat there for quite a while, apparently considering the information I gave him.

Eventually, Edwards said, "Yes, from what you have told me, I imagine we can expect a change in the defense strategy from what we anticipate. What I do not understand, however, is your motive for telling me all of this. Exactly where do you and Missus Kinney stand in this matter, Mister Kinney?"

With an overabundance of sincerity, I said, "Why, Mister Edwards, we simply want to see justice prevail."

"Forgive my suspicious nature, Mister Kinney, but that sounds a lot like balderdash to me."

Smiling slightly, I said, "Whether or not my answer is balderdash depends largely on one's definition of the word 'justice'."

"Then, pray tell, what is your definition of justice?"

Taking a deep breath, I said, "Mister Edwards, this is a situation in which intensely emotional reactions to painful circumstances resulted in a deep rift between a father and his daughter. Eliza said and did things she now deeply regrets because she believes her father would have been less likely to behave irrationally if she had acted differently."

Edwards nodded what I took to be his general agreement with my analysis of the matter. Encouraged, I continued. "Yes, certainly laws were broken, but the principal victim of those transgressions is Eliza. Since there are no other seriously injured parties, perhaps justice would best be served by a sentence of court-ordered emotional counseling at a facility in which Mister Hamm would not be subjected to the extreme measures employed by insane asylums."

I felt Eliza's grip on my hand tighten as we awaited Edwards' response to my suggestion. We did not have to wait long. "Mister Kinney, it sounds as if you are suggesting the people offer Mister Hamm leniency in exchange for a plea of not guilty by reason of short-term insanity. Am I understanding you correctly?"

"Yes, that in a nutshell is what I am suggesting."

Edwards looked at Eliza. "What do you think of that idea, Missus Kinney?"

In a clear and unemotional tone, Eliza said, "I agree entirely with what Lester has proposed."

"I thought you might, especially since the offering and accepting of such a plea would eliminate the need for entering your . . . intimate . . . experiences with Miss Abernathy as evidence in a public trial."

I said, "Mister Edwards, we will not insult your intelligence by denying that fact, but it is secondary to Eliza's concern for her father."

The Assistant Federal District Attorney seemed to think the matter over for several moments before saying, "All right, Mister Kinney, I concur that court-ordered mental therapy would be a just outcome in this matter, however, several parties, including the judge and the defense must agree to such an offer. I will prepare a proposal based on our discussion and present it to my boss, the Federal District Attorney, for approval. If he agrees to the plan, I will then present the proposal to the judge and to the defense for their acceptance. The entire process will take a few days."

Eliza said, "Thank you, Mister Edwards."

"You are welcome, Missus Kinney, but I must caution you that there is a chance Mister Tailor will reject the offer because of the stigma attached to an insanity plea. With that in mind, it might be helpful if you spoke with your father and Mister Tailor after we make the offer and urge them to accept it."

Quietly, Eliza said, "I don't know if I can do that."

"Why not?"

I sensed Eliza looking in my direction, so I said, "She may not be able to do as you ask because she attempted to contact Mister Tailor by telephone yesterday and he refused to speak with her other than to make outlandish accusations to the effect that the entire matter is Eliza's fault."

Edwards nodded. "That does not surprise me. Mister Tailor has no more idea of where the two of you stand on this matter than I did at first, and he obviously is not curious enough to find out. Well, so be it. We will do our best to bring about a fair outcome to all this despite his attitude."

I offered Edwards another smile. "Thank you, Mister Edwards. That is all we ask. Now, what about those statements you need from us?"

He looked at his wristwatch. "It is growing late. I suggest we forego the formal statements for now. Please type your statements as you suggested and have them ready. As long as you keep me informed as to your whereabouts, we can finalize them later."

"All right, we will type them tomorrow."

Standing, the Assistant Federal District Attorney said, "Then I will bid you a good evening, Mister and Missus Kinney. This has been a most interesting conversation to say the least."

Eliza saw Edwards to the door and closed it after him, and then she trotted across the room and wrapped her arms around my neck. After an impressive kiss on the lips, she said, "You did it again, darling."

"I hope so, but let us not count our chickens quite yet. We still have some obstacles to overcome."

"I know, darling, but now I can at least feel hopeful that we might be able to help father."

"Yes, I believe you can do that now. William Edwards has turned out to be a decent fellow after all. I guess we just had to earn his respect."

Smiling, Eliza said, "You certainly did that. Listening to the way you put things, I found myself wondering if you might have missed your calling. You sounded just like a very convincing lawyer."

"In that case, please excuse me while I go and wash out my mouth with soap."

THIRTY

Thursday - September 20, 1928

Thursday morning found Eliza and me in the Biltmore Coffee Shop, having breakfast and editing the two *Examiner* stories I finished in the wee small hours of the morning. I could have waited until that morning to write them and still met Bob Carlson's deadline, but an odd restlessness kept sleep away.

As a result of having been written when I was tired, though, the articles were not my best work. I jotted many rewrite notes in the margins, and Eliza was finding more than a few typographical errors.

I cursed my carelessness and Eliza said, "Yesterday was an exceptionally long day, and I could tell you were exhausted. It is no wonder these stories aren't up to your usual standards, darling."

Taking a swallow of coffee, I shook my head disparagingly. "That is for certain."

"What was bothering you last night? You seemed . . . distracted."

"I don't know. I just felt anxious, as if the walls were closing in on me."

Eliza reached across the table and placed her hand on mine. "Maybe you are suffering from a case of cabin fever. After you finish rewriting these stories, how would it be if we went out and saw the sights or something? It could be you just need a change of scene."

I nodded. "That might help. Let's do it."

Back in the Ambassador Suite, I went straight to work on the rewrites. I tackled the Monsignor O'Boylan story first. It consisted mostly of a summarization, but mentioned that John Gilbert, the Santa Barbara County District Attorney, was in possession of new evidence giving Estelle Abernathy a strong motive for having Peter Mikhailov beat O'Boylan to death. The new evidence I referred to was my amended statement about the shooting incident six days earlier, but I left that part out.

While I rewrote the O'Boylan story, Eliza called Deputy Tanner in Ventura to see if there was anything new on the killing of the Summerland strikers. He told her that Mikhailov was now in Santa Barbara awaiting prosecution on a murder charge. I added that detail to the end of the O'Boylan story.

The only information Tanner had on the Summerland situation was that Armando Delgado seemed to have disappeared from the face of the earth and was now the subject of a state-wide manhunt. I added that as a quote to my Summerland story, which was also largely a summarization of the incident and subsequent investigation. I also included what Bob Carlson told me about the telephone call the *Examiner* received from a Summerland Oil Field spokesman promising the company's complete cooperation in finding the men who killed and injured their valuable employees. The article was weak, but I thought it might be enough to keep the story on the *Examiner's* front page.

At a few minutes before ten o'clock I called Bob Carlson and his stenographer took down my articles over the telephone. When we were done, Bob said, "Not bad, Lester, but not great, either. You did a good job of tying the stories to each other and to your shooting story, but I was hoping for something bigger."

"I know you were, Bob. I was, too, but we're kind of in a lull between storms right now. Do you have anything new at your end?"

"Nothing to speak of. We did receive a call from the union that represents the oil field workers, but it wasn't terribly newsworthy. They were just condemning the dastardly attack on their strikers, or words to that effect. I'll plug it into your Summerland story. The union official's colorful language will liven up the copy a little. What are you planning now?"

Glancing at Eliza who was sitting on the sofa taking in my end of the conversation, I said, "I can't say for sure, Bob. Eliza and I need to do some regrouping and figure out where we go from here."

"I understand. Listen, Lester, with the two stories you just gave me, I figure we owe you three-hundred bucks. Unless you would rather I didn't, I'm going to have checks cut and send them over to you at the Biltmore by messenger. Depending on what you and Eliza plan to do, that cash might come in handy."

"Thanks, Bob. I appreciate that."

"Give your next stories some thought and talk to me this afternoon. We can hash it all out and come up with a plan then. Okay?"

Knowing that unless something big happened by tomorrow morning my byline would not appear in Friday's *Examiner*, I said, "Fine, Bob. I will talk with you then."

As I replaced the telephone handset in its cradle, Eliza smiled and said, "Shall we regroup here or on our sightseeing tour?"

"Let's go out and about. I think you were right. I do need a change of scenery."

"How would beach scenery be?"

"It would be just fine, and I think I even know how to find an ocean from here."

"Oh, goody! Let's go."

Leaving the Biltmore, we drove a few blocks south and turned west onto Wilshire Boulevard. The people of Los Angeles have been complaining for years about not having a direct route from downtown to the coast, but so far Wilshire Boulevard is as close as they have come to that dream. Wilshire goes as far as the community of Westlake and ends.

From Westlake one can follow a zigzag route around MacArthur Park and pick up Wilshire again a couple of miles to the west. This section of Wilshire Boulevard is becoming a fashionable shopping district promoted as the "Miracle Mile." Several large modern department stores are going up along this four or five block stretch of the road. From there Wilshire makes a slightly bent beeline over hill and dale to Ocean Avenue in Santa Monica. Ocean runs along a bluff overlooking the beach and the Pacific Coast Highway. A daring descent down a short unpaved road a few blocks north brought us to the beach and the coast road.

All told the twenty mile trip took us nearly an hour, but it was well worth the time. The day was turning out to be a beauty. The sun had burned away the morning overcast and we were welcomed by lines of waves breaking on sparkling sand. My spirits were already on the rise.

A few miles north on Pacific Coast Highway we came across a substantial building attached to a mock lighthouse with signs announcing The Lighthouse Bathhouse and Restaurant. This establishment was perched on a small point of land which was paved for automobile parking. I pulled our Chevrolet into a parking spot overlooking the water and turned off the engine.

Eliza, who was sitting close to me on the seat with her head resting on my shoulder, said, "Gosh it feels good to see our ocean again."

"It really does. Seeing it again reminds me of sitting with you watching the waves after the movie on our first date."

"You know, Lester, if you consider going to Estelle's party business, that night was our first and only real date."

"True, but it seems to have done the trick, Missus Kinney."

"It certainly did, Mister Kinney. Now, tell me, did Bob Carlson have any other news for you?"

"Nothing of importance. Oh, he did say he was sending our checks over to the Biltmore by messenger. He figures the *Examiner* owes us another three hundred."

"Wow, those checks add up fast. That makes four-hundred-and-fifty dollars you have earned from them."

"Yes, this has been a profitable week, but I'm afraid that will be all we earn for a while. I've run out of news to report."

"Still, that puts us way ahead of where we were a few weeks ago, and what's more, we haven't had to spend any of what you've earned,"

"Unfortunately, that will change on Saturday."

Eliza made an exaggerated sigh. "I know. We have to go back to being regular folks. That will be hard after being treated as celebrities."

"I suppose we ought to figure out where we will go after the Biltmore throws us out."

"And I have to do something about either going back to work or resigning from my job. They expect me back on Monday."

"Okay, maybe that is where we should start our planning because it effects a lot of our other decisions. What do you think you want to do about your job?"

Eliza sat up on the seat, and after a moment's hesitation, said, "Well, even though it is seeming less likely that I'll be humiliated in front of the whole doggone town in court, there are still some unknown factors."

"Yes there are. Which of those factors concern you the most?"

Without hesitation Eliza said, "Estelle and Armando Delgado. I can only imagine Estelle's opinion of us right now. She is a vindictive woman. I don't think she will take what we've done to her sitting down."

"No, I don't suppose she will. I think, however, we may have seen the last of Delgado. With cops looking for him all over the state, we are the least of his worries."

Frowning, Eliza said, "I sure hope that is true."

"What else concerns you about going back to the library?"

"Honestly?"

"Of course, honestly."

"Darling, this will sound selfish, but I really don't feel like going back to the library. I have enjoyed working there, but with all that has happened, I feel like one chapter of my life has ended and it is time to turn a page and begin a new chapter. Does that make any sense?"

I nodded. "That makes a great deal of sense and it is a very strong argument for calling it quits with the library. As you pointed out not long ago, you have skills that are in demand. If you choose to do so, you can find a library job anywhere."

Eliza kissed me on the cheek. "Thank you, darling, but how will we get along without either of us earning a paycheck?"

"For one thing, we now have a fairly good-sized nest egg to keep us going while we figure things out, and there will eventually be more articles to write for the *Examiner*. So, I suggest you show up at the library on Monday and hand them your resignation."

With a concerned expression clouding her pretty face, Eliza said, "Do you think it is safe to go back so soon?"

"It is certainly safer now than it was, and we can make it a quick trip. I would also like to check on things at the cottage and I need to deposit the *Examiner's* checks. Maybe we could also pay a call on Mabel."

With excitement, Eliza said, "Could we? That would be swell!"

"I think we could safely do that. I suggest we find somewhere up the coast to stay Saturday and Sunday night, and then we can drive into Santa Barbara on Monday and take care of our business."

Smiling, she said, "It's a deal."

While we sat there in the Chevrolet enjoying our surroundings, I noticed Eliza looking at her wedding ring. She was holding her hand up and turning the ring on her finger. I said, "Tell me, Missus Kinney, do you still think you made a wise decision by marrying an unemployed journalist?"

Looking up into my eyes, Eliza said, "I think . . . no, I know . . . that is the best decision I will ever make."

"I intend to do everything in my power to make sure you never change your mind about that."

The kiss we shared then was tender and brimming with love. When it ended Eliza said, "There is nothing you could ever do to change my mind about that."

Then I took hold of her left hand and raised her arm so I could see her wristwatch. It showed the time as twelve-thirty. I said, "My stomach is telling me it is lunch time, and your watch confirms that fact. What do you think of seeing what the Lighthouse Bathhouse and Restaurant has on their menu?"

"Mister Kinney, I think that is an excellent suggestion. And while we are on the subject of time, I think we should splurge and buy you a wristwatch. Pocket watches are inconvenient and old fashioned."

"I'm not sure I want to make it so easy to know the time."

A few minutes later we walked hand-in-hand into the Lighthouse's dining room. We were seated at a table next to a window looking out over the ocean. Eliza and I both chose something called a "Shrimp Louie." The Louies turned out to be green salads piled high with tiny bay shrimp and other goodies like black olives and slices of hardboiled egg. The salads were served with a Russian style dressing.

Finishing lunch, we took a short walk out around the point of land on which the Lighthouse Bathhouse and Restaurant is located. The sea air was invigorating and we hated to leave, but it was time to point our Chevrolet back toward downtown Los Angeles.

By two-thirty we had parked in the Biltmore's basement parking area, I had picked up our *Examiner* checks at the front desk, and we were making our way toward the lobby elevators. That was when I sensed somebody close behind us. Before I could turn to see who was there, a female voice said a single word. "Eliza?"

We both turned at the same time, and I was surprised to see Mabel Stafford hurrying along to catch up with us. Mabel's expression told me something was very wrong.

Clearly surprised by the sudden appearance of her friend, Eliza said, "Mabel! What on earth are you doing here?"

"I must talk with you, Eliza."

"What's happened?"

Glancing at me, she said, "We should talk somewhere private, child."

I said, "The elevators are right over here."

We rode up to the eleventh floor in silence, but Eliza and Mabel held hands the whole way up. I opened the doors to the Ambassador Suite and we hurried in.

Eliza said, "Now, Mabel, please tell us what has happened."

Taking Eliza's hands in hers, Mabel said, "There is no easy way to put this, child, so I will just say it out. It is your father, Eliza. He has died."

It was as if Mabel had slapped her. Wide-eyed, Eliza jerked

backwards and shook her head, "No! No!"

Mabel looked at me with tears in her eyes. I put my arms around Eliza and held her close. She leaned on me heavily, sobbing uncontrollably. Fearing she would collapse to the floor if let go of her, I walked Eliza over to the sofa.

"Easy, darling. Let's sit down for a bit." Looking up at Mabel, I said, "Please, take a seat."

Mabel sat in an armchair across from the sofa and placed her purse on the floor. "I'm sorry, Lester. I did not know any easier way to tell you the news."

"There is no need for you to apologize. I appreciate you coming all the way down here instead of just calling on the telephone."

"Oh, I could not have delivered sad news like this over the telephone. Besides that, I have a good deal more to tell you about all of this."

"I see." Turning to Eliza, I said, "Darling, can I get you a glass of water or something?"

Between sobs that shook her entire body, she said, "No. I . . . I will pull . . . myself together. Just give me . . . give me a minute."

"Take your time."

Finally, she took a deep ragged breath and said, "I'm sorry, Mabel. This is just so . . . so unexpected. What happened?"

Mabel hesitated a moment, and then said, "I'm afraid he committed suicide."

"What? That could not be. He would not . . . ."

"I don't have all the details, child, but it seems that is exactly what happened. Sergeant Sullivan of the police department remembered me from when I contacted him for you. He called me this morning at work and asked if I knew where you were. I told him I did and asked why he wanted to know. He said he needed to notify you of your father's death."

I felt Eliza shiver at those words. I took her hand and Mabel continued her sad tale.

"He was quite relieved when I said I would talk to you. I asked him for the details, and he said Mister Hamm was found in Estelle Abernathy's study this morning by a maid. Estelle was there and she was also dead. The sergeant said the police think your father killed her and then shot himself."

Eliza looked as if she was in a daze, but I knew she was concentrating on absorbing what Mabel was saying. There was a lot to absorb. Mabel had more to tell us.

She reached down and removed a slip of paper from her

purse. "Sergeant Sullivan said they found a note to you in your father's pocket. He read the note to me and I wrote down the words. It said, 'Dearest Eliza, I fear you will feel some responsibility for what I am about to do, but do not. None of this is your fault. I have had time to think and to understand the situation more fully. You have been hurt badly and I intend to punish those responsible for your pain, myself and Estelle. I know you truly love Lester. He is a good man. Marry him and live a wonderful life together.' The note was signed, 'Your Loving Father.'"

Eliza began to cry again. "Oh, God."

I admit to feeling a little weepy myself in that moment. I was wondering if I had seriously underestimated Frederick Hamm.

Looking at Mabel, I said, "Thank you. I know this has been a terribly difficult thing for you to do. Your thoughtfulness is appreciated."

I felt Eliza nod and Mabel said, "The two of you are my closest friends. I hate the pain my news has caused you, but I hope it was easier hearing the news from me than from a policeman."

In a quiet voice Eliza said, "It was, Mabel. It really was. I do not know how to thank you."

"There is no need to thank me, child. This is the sort of thing good friends do for each other." After a short pause, Mabel added, "The last thing Sergeant Sullivan told me is that he wants you to come home as soon as possible so you can give him a statement to clarify some of what has happened. He included you in that request, Lester."

I nodded my understanding, but my mind was racing ahead. There was something I could do—had to do—to set the record straight, and I had to do it right away before the news of Frederick Hamm's death became common knowledge and people drew erroneous conclusions from the news.

"Eliza, there is something I must do. I do not want your father's actions to be misinterpreted. May I have your permission to write this story for the *Examiner* as a way of explaining your father's motivation for what he has done?"

She looked at me thoughtfully through wet eyes and nodded. "Yes, darling, please do that. Please tell people what a courageous man my father was, and how he died for the sake of destroying evil."

"That is exactly what I intend to do, but I must do it quickly or the impact will be lost. Will you be all right for an hour or so?"

Now Eliza's expression was pure determination. "Yes, Lester,

I will be fine. You do what we must do for Father."

Mabel said, "I can stay for a while longer if I can be of help."

Eliza looked at Mabel. "Yes, dear friend, it would mean a great deal to me if you could stay for a while."

Nodding with a determination of her own, Mabel said, "Then, that is what I will do. Lester, go to work."

I thanked Mabel, gave Eliza a kiss on the cheek, and sat down at my typewriter. Eliza went into the bedroom to freshen up. When she returned I caught a glimpse of the little cloisonné typewriter pinned to her blouse. It was her way of being a part of what I was attempting to do for her father.

Before committing words to paper, I placed a long-distance telephone call to Sergeant Danny Sullivan at the Santa Barbara Police Department. To write a meaningful story I needed more information than I had.

When Sullivan came on the line, I said, "Sergeant, this is Lester Kinney. Eliza and I have heard the news about her father's death. Do you have a moment to answer a few questions?"

Sullivan hesitated. "Well, I would much prefer to speak with you in person."

"That will not be possible until tomorrow morning. In the meantime, I need some information."

He hesitated again. "You wouldn't be planning to write another newspaper story, would you? The department has not yet made any of the details public. I cannot give them to you . . . ."

"Sullivan, there was a time when I thought you were a good cop, but when I gave you the opportunity to prevent exactly the sort of thing that has happened, you did nothing. This time you will cooperate or I will have the people of Santa Barbara demanding your resignation."

"Are you threatening me, Mister Kinney?"

"You are damned right I am, and it is a threat that will become a promise in about ten seconds."

Sullivan was quiet for about five of those seconds before saying, "All right, Mister Kinney. What is it you want to know?"

"Give me the details from the police report beginning with the telephone call from whoever notified you that the bodies had been found."

THIRTY-ONE

Thursday - September 20, 1928

At forty-four minutes past four o'clock I called Bob Carlson with my story:

SANTA BARBARA MAN AVENGES EVIL IN MURDER-SUICIDE

By Lester Kinney

In a nutshell, the lengthy article described in detail how *Santa Barbara Tribune* owner, Frederick Hamm, ended a rampage of murder and immorality—including the recent deadly attack on Summerland Oil Field pickets—through the only means available to him. He took the life of the woman he knew to be responsible for those depraved and evil acts, Estelle Abernathy. Then, to spare his family further indignities caused by his actions, Hamm took his own life.

When I finished reading the story, Carlson was quiet for several seconds, and then he said, "Lester, I'm going to ask you a question, but you don't have to answer it unless you want to. Was Frederick Hamm Eliza's father?"

"Yes, Bob."

"I had a feeling that was the case. Please tell Eliza I am deeply sorry for her loss."

"I will. Thank you."

"Now, I will tell you that is the best damned expose I have seen in a long time. It's got all the right stuff, drama, pathos, an evil villain, and a real life hero. I have to talk to Jim, but I think you can count on your story appearing above the fold on tomorrow's front page exactly as you wrote it. Well done, Lester."

"Thank you again, Bob."

"Now, what are your plans? I presume you will be heading north tonight or tomorrow?"

"Yes, we'll be leaving for Santa Barbara tonight. Eliza has a lot ahead of her when we get there. I'll do my best to help her through it all, but it will be a tough time."

"No doubt. Do not underestimate your gal, though. She is strong and smart. I predict Eliza will get through it and come out on top. On another subject, I am assuming you received the checks I sent over to the Biltmore?"

"Yes, I did. Thank you."

"Would you like to stop by here on your way out of town to pick up your check for the story you just gave us?"

"If it is possible to do that, it might be the safest way to handle it because I don't know exactly where we will be for the next few days."

"Consider it done, Lester. I'll leave your check with the receptionist. She's in the lobby until seven."

"Got it. We'll be there before seven."

"Lester, please stay in touch with me as much as you are able. I sure there will be follow-ups on all of the situations we have been covering."

"Yes, I'll check in with you tomorrow and let you know how things stand."

"Good. Have a safe trip north."

"Thank you for all your help and support, Bob."

Eliza and Mabel were sitting on the sofa, and when I hung up the call, Eliza asked, "What did Bob say?"

"Somehow he figured out you were Frederick Hamm's daughter and he sends his condolences. He also said they would print the story exactly as written on the front page of tomorrow's edition."

She got up and walked over to where I was sitting at the desk. "Thank you, darling. Your story made me feel somewhat better about things—like what Father did has been explained so his actions can be better understood by those who knew and respected him."

Mabel added, "And that includes many people, especially the *Tribune* staff."

Nodding, I said, "I wish I'd gotten to know him under better circumstances."

Eliza gave me a small smile. "I wish that too." After a pause, she said, "Well, I guess there is nothing left to do now but pack our bags and drive north."

"We need to make a quick stop at the *Examiner* on the way to pick up a check. Is that okay with you?"

"Of course, darling."

When we were ready to walk out of the Biltmore's Ambassador Suite, Mabel made the generous offer to put us up for the night. Eliza looked at me, read my mind, and said, "Thank you, Mabel. That is very kind of you, but we are both anxious to get back to our cottage."

At that point a bellboy arrived to take our bags down and we all headed for the elevator. We bid farewell to Mabel in the lobby with Eliza promising to call her first thing in the morning. By five-thirty we were turning out of the Biltmore's parking garage to head for the Examiner Building. After picking up our check, we had a three hour drive ahead of us.

Understandably, Eliza was not in a talkative mood. She sat quietly next to me for most of the trip. I suspected the reality of the sad news Mabel brought us was beginning to sink in for her. It certainly was for me.

Less than three weeks had gone by since I sat in Frederick Hamm's office receiving my first assignment for the *Santa Barbara Tribune*. That fateful meeting was the first in a series of events that were to forever change the lives of everyone involved. Later that same day, while engaged in my new assignment, I met the most beautiful woman I had ever seen and fell in love with her almost at first sight. Now that woman was sitting next to me and she was my wife. Those three weeks seemed more like that many years.

Other memories of the events transpiring since that day wandered through my mind. Two red welts on my neck reminded me of Armando Delgado and the nearly fatal bullet he fired through the rear window of my Chevrolet. I saw the hole in the glass created by that bullet each time I glanced in my rearview mirror.

Just below the rear window, in the space behind the Chevrolet's seat, was the cane I was given by an understanding nurse at Big Sisters Hospital in Ventura. I seldom used the cane now because I was no longer feeling as much of the weakness caused by blood loss.

I knew there was another reason I stopped using the cane. Walking with it brought back nightmare images of Armando Delgado showing up in our room at the Pierpont Inn to finish the job he botched when the bullet he fired out on the beach failed to kill me. With the help of a brave young room service waiter I had used the cane to disarm Delgado and disable Estelle's driver.

Luck was on our side throughout that and all of the other

crises Eliza and I had faced during the past three weeks—more luck than I had any right to expect. That left me with the lingering apprehension that, should we encounter another crisis, we had no luck left to help us survive it.

Then another image appeared in my mind and it made me smile. I was looking at Eliza in the shimmering beaded gown she wore the night we attended Estelle Abernathy's reception. If I had not already been head over heels in love with her, the vision of her in that gown would have clinched the deal. That gown was like a shimmering looking glass that reflected all of Eliza's wonderful qualities, even those in her mind and heart.

Those thoughts reminded me that the dress shirt I wore to Estelle's reception still had eye makeup stains acquired later that same night. That led to the image of Eliza standing in the middle of the cottage living room wearing nothing but my faded blue shirt in front of an enraged Frederick Hamm. That completed the circle of my thoughts by reminding me that Eliza's father was dead.

Apparently my mind was not content to end on that thought, though, because one more image popped into my head. It was the picture of Eliza standing next to our bed at the Ponto Beach Motel in Carlsbad removing that same faded blue shirt on our wedding night. That brought another smile to my lips.

Somehow Eliza sensed that I was smiling. "What are you thinking that makes you smile like that, darling?"

A little embarrassed at being caught enjoying such thoughts at a sad time in our lives, I said, "Oh, my mind has been showing me mental pictures of the past few weeks. Some of them make me smile."

"Oh? Which one were you just smiling at just now?"

"It's nothing. How are you doing, Eliza?"

"I'm okay, Lester. Now please answer my question. Heaven knows I could use a happy thought right about now."

Caught with no way out, I fessed up. "I was remembering our wedding night."

"Come on, Lester, the whole truth. What about our wedding night made you smile?"

"If you must know, my memory of you taking off my old shirt just before you got into bed."

Glancing at Eliza to see how she took my answer to her question, I was relieved to see a smile cross her lips, too. "I guess love had me feeling a little naughty that night. I'm glad I made a lasting impression, though."

"You certainly did that."

"You know, it's wonderful to realize we are already making memories that help sustain us through dark times."

Another thought occurred to me and it seemed important to put it in words. "There's something else this dark time is proving."

"What, darling?"

"Not too long ago we were having frequent conversations about what we called your 'mental balance' and how you wished you could handle emotional situations without falling apart. Judging by the way you are handling your father's passing, I think the days of worrying about your mental balance are in the past."

Eliza was silent for quite some time. Finally, she said, "I think you are right, at least I hope you are. The news about Father is a terrible shock and I am awfully sad about losing one of my heroes. I will miss him, but at the same time I feel a sort of calmness. I think it goes back to what I said this afternoon at the beach about returning to my job at the library. I feel as if Father's passing turns a page and we are beginning a fresh new chapter."

I could not help smiling again. Eliza noticed and said, "What? Are you thinking about me being naked again?"

"No, kiddo. I am thinking about how you amaze me in so many ways. What you just said describes a kind of epiphany and shows how far your thinking has come in just a short time."

"If that is true, I owe the improvement to you. You told me what I needed to know, and then you put your foot down that afternoon in the cottage when you made me stop whining and sent me to the bedroom to think things through. That was the turning point for me, and without your guidance it never would have happened."

"Yes, Eliza, it would have happened sooner or later. All I did was force the issue. That, as I told you, was a very scary time for me. I had faith in you, but I was also afraid I might have pushed you too soon."

"Darling, if you had not pushed me then, I would not have had the courage to do what needed to be done when we met with Monsignor O'Boylan and when Armando shot you and . . . ."

I was smiling again. Eliza said, "What's so funny now?"

"I was just remembering your first aid technique before you took me to the hospital."

Eliza almost laughed. "Hey, you goof, my panties saved your life!"

"I know they did, and I wish we still had them. I would frame those panties and hang them on the living room wall."

Eliza shook her head disparagingly. "You know, I believe you would actually do that."

"I certainly would."

At that point, Eliza kissed me on the cheek and rested her head on my shoulder. We didn't speak for a while. In fact, we were well north of Ventura when Eliza put words to what was on her mind.

"Darling, have you given any thought to what we should do tomorrow?"

"Some. What do you think we need to do first?"

"I have to make arrangements for Father's service. I wonder where his . . . his body is."

"Sergeant Sullivan mentioned he was at the county morgue."

"Then I guess I should contact a mortuary. Mister McDermott is a mortician and he was one of Father's friends. I think I will ask him to take care of Father."

"Okay, that's number one on the list for tomorrow. What else is on your list?"

"I need to go to the library and give them my resignation. I want to get that over with as soon as I can. It is something I want to do, but I'm not looking forward to actually doing it." After a moment's pause, Eliza asked, "Darling, are you sure it is all right for me to resign?"

"I'm sure. When I get to the bank, which I would like to do tomorrow, we will have more than five hundred dollars in that account, plus I still have more than a hundred in cash. That will get us by for a while, even if I don't sell any further stories to the *Examiner*."

Eliza nodded. "Okay, a trip to the bank is item number three on our list."

"And we will have to make a trip to the Wiggly Piggy for some groceries."

"Item number four, and it is still Piggly Wiggly, darling."

Another question was on my mind. "Eliza, you don't need to make this decision right now, but have you thought about what you want to do with your father's house? Do you think we should move there from the cottage?"

Eliza did not hesitate in saying, "No. I would rather stay at the cottage or find another place that is ours."

"Then what will you do with the house?"

"For one thing, we need to empty it out. That will be a big job. After that, I want to sell the house. Father paid off the mortgage a few years ago and it should be worth something."

"I'm sure it is. My guess would be six to seven thousand."

Eliza sounded surprised. "You think that much? Gosh, that would buy us a pretty nice house somewhere."

"Yes, it would, but whatever money the house might bring if you sell it is yours. You might want to put that money in the bank or invest it for the future."

"Darling, as you have so often reminded me, we are in this together. If I'm not contributing to our income for a while, it is only fair that I help us pay for a place to live. Besides, Father always said real estate was the safest investment there is."

"All right, we'll work that out when the time comes. Anything else we need to do tomorrow?"

"Yes, laundry. We have to unpack and wash some clothes to wear."

"That's probably a good idea."

It was about nine o'clock when we finally arrived at the cottage. With some trepidation, I unlocked the front door. Aside from a hint of mustiness in the air, everything looked just as it had the afternoon we left for our meeting with Monsignor O'Boylan. I asked Eliza to wait in the living room while I made sure there were no surprises waiting for us. There were not.

After an eventful day punctuated by a long drive, we were not up to unpacking. Instead, we moved our essential toiletry items back into the bathroom cabinets and got ready for bed.

By the time I finished in the bathroom, Eliza was already between the sheets. I slid my arm around her waist and we assumed our usual sleeping positions. As I kissed her goodnight, I felt wetness on her cheeks.

"Are you all right, Eliza?"

"Yes, darling. I'm just a little weepy tonight."

"I certainly understand that."

With her head on my chest, Eliza said, "It's more than Father. Some of my tears are for the happiness I feel being back in our home. Staying at the Biltmore was fun, but I would trade the Ambassador Suite for our little cottage in an instant."

"Me, too, kiddo. Me, too."

THIRTY-TWO

Friday - September 21, 1928

Friday morning we were early birds, partly due to the fact that neither of us slept well Thursday night, and partly due to the long list of items on the day's agenda. As a result of our early start we had crossed several items off that list before eleven o'clock.

A load of laundry hung on the clothesline behind the cottage, my bank account was fatter by more than five hundred dollars, and Eliza had made the painful arrangements necessary with Mister McDermott of McDermott & Associates for her father's funeral and interment.

When all was said and done, the service was scheduled for two o'clock on the afternoon of Monday, September Twenty-Fourth. It would be a simple memorial conducted where Frederick Hamm attended services for most of his life, at the All-Saints-by-the-Sea Episcopal Church. After the service he would be interred next to Eliza's mother at the Santa Barbara Cemetery on the coast in Montecito. Eliza decided against graveside services.

Our Chevrolet was parked at the curb outside McDermott's mortuary and we sat there for several minutes while Eliza collected herself. Finally, she quietly said, "I hope I made the right choices for Father."

"Seems to me you did fine, besides, funeral services are for the living, not the departed. I'm sure your dad's friends and associates will find what you have arranged a suitable memorial."

"I never realized there were so many details. I am certainly grateful Mister McDermott knows what needs to be done. He was very kind."

"Yes he was. Now, where would you like to go next?"

Eliza sighed. "Would it be all right if we went to the library so I can give them my letter of resignation?"

"Certainly. The only other urgent item on the list is meeting Sergeant Sullivan. I promised we would see him this morning."

"Could we see him after the library? I really want to get my resignation over with."

Starting the engine, I asked, "Sure. Are you having any second thoughts about resigning?"

From the corner of my eye I saw her shake her head. "No. I am sure it is the right thing to do . . . unless you think I shouldn't . . ."

"Not at all. You need to do what you think is right."

The drive from McDermott's at the corner of State and Haley Streets to the library was only about eight blocks, so less than ten minutes later I pulled the Chevrolet to the curb on Anapamu Street.

"Would you like me to come in with you, or is this something you prefer to do by yourself?"

"I think it would be better if I went in alone. I'll try not to be too long."

"Take as long as you need. I'll be right here when you're done."

Parked at the curb, I noticed Auntie Alicia's Tea Room in the Odd Fellows building across the street. I smiled at the memory of how nervous I was waiting for Eliza to get off work the afternoon we met there. I wondered if she had been nervous, too. If so, she showed no sign of it.

When Eliza returned she slid across the seat close to me and I gave her a hug. "Thank you, darling. It wasn't nearly as bad as I expected. Everyone was very nice to me. They were all sad about Father, and I showed them my wedding ring and they all congratulated me, and . . . I . . . I like all of those people very much. I will miss them."

"I don't doubt they will miss you, too. There is no reason you cannot stop by and visit them once in a while."

As I started the Chevrolet's engine, she said, "I know, and I plan to do that when things settle down. Are we going to see Sergeant Sullivan now?"

"Yes. As long as were getting unpleasant jobs out of the way, we might as well tackle Sullivan."

I pulled away from the curb and turned right on Anacapa. Eight blocks later I turned right again, this time into the City Hall parking lot across the street from the *Tribune* offices.

As I shut the engine off, Eliza asked, "Is there anything we need to talk about before we see him? I mean, to get our stories straight or anything?"

I shook my head. "I don't think so. Let's just stick to the truth. Sullivan already knows most of our secrets."

As I helped Eliza down from the seat, I noticed her take a

wistful look toward the *Tribune's* building across the street. I said, "After we finish with Sullivan, maybe we ought to drop in on Mabel . . . perhaps take her out to lunch or something?"

"That is a nice idea. I spoke with her on the telephone before we left the cottage this morning, but I'm sure she is wondering how we are getting on with all we had to do."

The Santa Barbara Police Department does not provide sergeants with an actual office, so Sullivan led us to a small room with a table and chairs. It was the sort of room where a few people could have a private discussion.

Sullivan started things off. "Missus Kinney, please accept my condolences on the loss of your father. I am sure this must be difficult for you, especially given the circumstances."

I detected a note of smarminess in his tone of voice. I was not sure what was behind it, but I'm certain Eliza noticed it, too. Her polite "thank you" had little sincerity to it. The Sergeant then turned to me. "Mister Kinney, I haven't seen the article you've written on Mister Hamm's death yet. I hope you made good use of the information I gave you yesterday."

The tone of that comment told me Sullivan was still smarting from the manner in which I treated him during our telephone conversation. "I did, Sergeant. The article will be on the front page of today's *Examiner*. Now, what do you need from Eliza and me?"

Opening a notebook, Sullivan said, "Just a couple of questions to help us get a handle on the . . . ah . . . crime. Missus Kinney, did you have any indications that your father might be planning to kill Estelle Abernathy of himself?"

In a tone of voice that told me she was annoyed by the question, or maybe annoyed at being questioned by the police at all, Eliza said, "Sergeant Sullivan, I have not seen or spoken with my father since you arrested him. So, no, I had no idea Father would do anything like this."

Sullivan made a short note in his book. "You both once told me you felt Mister Hamm might have been mentally ill and that was the reason for his strange behavior. Do you have anything to add to that statement?"

Now I was as annoyed as Eliza sounded. "Sullivan, those comments were made off the record. They have no place in your report or whatever you're planning to do with the results of this interrogation."

"This is hardly an interrogation, Mister Kinney. Besides, in a murder investigation, nothing is off the record."

"That may be true, but this was not a murder case when those comments were made. Sergeant Sullivan, we are through with this meeting." Standing, I said, "Eliza, I think it is time for us to leave."

Eliza stood and Sullivan quickly said, "Hold on, there! You can't just walk out of a police interview."

"We came here voluntarily and we can leave any time we choose. If you can convince a judge to issue a subpoena so you can drag us back in here, go right ahead. In the meanwhile, we are leaving." Just before I left the room, I gave the sergeant one parting shot. "Sullivan, I don't know who you are working for, but I have a strong suspicion it is not the people of Santa Barbara."

I closed the door on the glare Sullivan was giving me and Eliza took my arm. Walking across the city hall parking area, Eliza said, "That is the most irritating man I have ever encountered!"

"I have the distinct feeling he is up to something. I just cannot figure out what it can be."

As I opened the Chevrolet's passenger door for her, Eliza tilted her head to one side and said, "You know, it might just be he is mad at us for bullying him during our last few encounters. I have a feeling Sergeant Sullivan is sensitive about his authority."

She had a point. "You might be right. His nose is certainly out of joint about something."

We drove out of the city hall parking lot and I pulled to the curb in front of the *Tribune* across the street. There was the usual buzz in the air when we walked into the newsroom, but the huge space went silent almost instantly. Then, beginning with photographer George O'Conner, who was standing over in the corner by my old desk, everyone in the room began applauding.

Eliza's expression told me she was completely baffled by the welcome. I'm sure my expression was no less perplexed. After shaking my hand vigorously, acting editor, Louis Arquette, raised his hands and called for quiet.

When more than two dozen voices died away, Louis said, "Eliza . . . Lester, welcome home! We have been following your adventures in the *Examiner*, and I speak for everyone here when I say we are overjoyed to see both of you."

Turning to face Eliza, Arquette said, "Missus Kinney, you have our condolences. We all miss your father. He was our leader and we could have asked for no finer man to fill that role."

I looked at Eliza. I was not surprised to see her eyes filling with tears. At the same time, the crowd was waiting for her to say something. She looked around the room, and said softly, "Thank you, everyone. This is so unexpected and . . . ." Eliza looked up at me and said, "Lester?"

I nodded and took over the speaking chores. "Folks, I know you will forgive Eliza. The death of her father and everything else that has happened in the past few weeks is still quite overwhelming. I have an idea what is in her heart right now, though, and that is gratitude to all of you for your kind welcome and your support for her father during his trials and tribulations."

Eliza held my right arm tightly and I felt her nod her head. Continuing, I said, "I hope it goes without saying that I feel the same way. We're very glad to be home."

The applause began again, and I spotted Mabel Stafford working her way through the crowd to Eliza's side. Mabel embraced Eliza, and Louis Arquette said in a voice that was intended for my ears only, "Lester, I have no idea what is going to happen to the *Tribune* now, but I plan to keep publishing until somebody says we have to stop. Does that meet with your approval?"

Arquette's question brought me up short with the realization that he expected Eliza or perhaps me to become his new boss. It was unlikely he knew about Estelle Abernathy's partial ownership of the paper. With one question he threw open the door to an entirely new line of thought in my mind. Shortsighted as it might be, I had honestly not given a moment's thought to what would now become of the *Tribune*.

Trying to appear as if his question had not stirred up a hornets' nest in my head, I smiled at Arquette. "That is exactly what I would do in your shoes. We still do not know the details, but I'm sure Eliza will be in touch with you as soon as things are sorted out."

"Thank you, Lester."

Thirty minutes later Mabel, Eliza and I were seated in a booth at the café on State Street at Cota. Still looking somewhat bewildered, Eliza said, "Well, I certainly did not expect the reception we received at the *Tribune*."

Mabel smiled. "The people at the *Tribune* loved your father, Eliza. He was a good leader, and despite what some saw as his quirks, no one on the staff would have traded him for the world."

The questions raised by Louis Arquette's comments were still buzzing around my mind like a hive of angry bees. "Eliza, Louis Arquette raised a very good question. He was telling me of his plans to continue publishing the *Tribune* until he was told to stop when I realized he expected us, or at least you, to be making such decisions. That, of course, begs the question who actually owns the paper now that your dad and Estelle are no longer in the picture."

Eliza shook her head. "I have no idea, but I suppose that is something else with which we must deal."

Mabel appeared puzzled. "I don't understand. What does Estelle Abernathy have to do with the ownership of the *Tribune*?"

I gave Eliza a questioning glance and she replied with a nod, meaning it was all right to tell Mabel what we knew about the ownership of the newspaper. I said, "Mabel, with all that has gone on the past couple of weeks, there are a few things we have discovered that we have not had an opportunity to tell you. One has to do with the ownership of the *Tribune*."

Mabel's expression changed to suspicion. "What about the ownership of the *Tribune*?"

"According to what Estelle said the night Armando walloped me, Frederick Hamm wanted to start a newspaper in competition with the *Post-Dispatch*, but he could not raise the necessary capital. Estelle told me she financed Frederick Hamm's venture because she felt the town would benefit from a newspaper with a second point of view. She put up the money in exchange for fifty-one-percent interest in the *Tribune*."

After taking a moment to absorb the significance of what I told her, Mabel shook her head. "If that woman doesn't beat all! Suddenly events that have puzzled me for years make complete sense. Estelle had your father over several barrels, and there was absolutely nothing he could do about it." Almost as an afterthought, she added, "You are right, though, the ownership of the *Tribune* is certainly in question. I would presume fifty-one percent of it belongs to Estelle's heirs, whomever they might be, and the rest to Eliza."

A thought that made me question Mabel's assumption occurred to me. "Perhaps not. The possibility of Estelle Abernathy and Frederick Hamm dying at virtually the same time could not have seemed likely when their agreement was drawn up, so perhaps their contract offered a different sort of settlement in the event of one partner's death. The question is, who has the actual written agreement so we can find out?"

Eliza said, "Father has . . . had . . . an attorney who handled business matters for him. Would he be likely to have the agreement?"

I said, "That is one possibility, or it might be that your father secured his copy of the agreement in some safe place. I doubt he would have kept something like that at the *Tribune*, but maybe at home? Or in a safety deposit box at his bank?"

"I do not recall father ever mentioning a bank safe box, but he did have a floor safe installed in one of our bedrooms several years ago. The agreement might be in there. I have the combination, so we could check."

Mabel was listening to our conversation, and finally said, "You kids have your work cut out for you. If I know your father, Eliza, finding that agreement will not be easy. Is there some way I can help?"

Taking charge of the situation as though she thought it was expected of her, Eliza said, "I think we should go directly to the house from here. Mabel, would you please come with us and help in the search?"

Nodding, Mabel said, "I would be happy to do that, Eliza. If Lester will take me back to the *Tribune* after lunch, I will sign out for the afternoon and meet you there."

I thought the craftsman bungalow at the corner of Arrellaga and Laguna Streets had a lonely, empty look about it when we drove up. That appearance must have been a trick of my mind, though, because only two days had passed since Frederick Hamm's death. Or maybe the house's loneliness began weeks earlier when Eliza moved out. That made more sense. Eliza had qualities about her that would make a house feel full and lived-in, as a home should.

The Hamm house had a mail slot in the front door, so when Eliza unlocked the door, I knelt and reached around the edge of the door to pick up the accumulated mail from the floor. Stacking the envelopes neatly, I handed them to Eliza and in we went.

The living room was neat and tidy, as were all the other rooms. The only sign of human habitation were two dishes, some silverware, and a coffee cup in a dish draining rack on the kitchen counter. Standing at the sink, Eliza gently touched the coffee cup and let her fingers linger on it for several seconds.

I gave Eliza a small hug and kissed her cheek. Our feelings did not require words. A soft knock on the front door and a "yoo-hoo" in Mabel's voice interrupted the moment. I said I would get the door and headed off toward the living room.

Opening the front door, I said, "Hello, Mabel. Please come in."

"Thank you, Lester." After looking around the room and apparently noticing that Eliza was elsewhere, Mabel asked in a low voice, "How is she doing, Lester? Really?"

Smiling at her concern, I said, "She's really doing quite well,

Mabel. As you would expect, there are moments when something makes her feel the loss more acutely, but I think that is to be expected."

Mabel nodded thoughtfully. "Lester, I want you to know I have observed some very positive changes in Eliza during the past weeks. I suspect you might have something to do with that."

"Thank you, but the credit is entirely Eliza's. She is perfectly capable of figuring things out on her own. Eliza simply needed some confidence in her own judgement."

Eliza chose that moment to enter the living room. I don't know how much of what we were saying she heard, but it didn't matter. She already knew my feelings on the subject. Besides, her interest at that moment was in an envelope, apparently part of the mail pile we collected from the living room floor.

"Lester?"

"Yes, kiddo?"

"Do you remember I said father had an attorney he used for business matters?"

"I do. Why?"

"There is a letter here from that attorney and it is addressed to me at this address. At least, it is addressed to Eliza Hamm."

"Good. Do you suppose we ought to open it?"

Eliza shot me a look as she unsealed the envelope flap. "Nobody likes a smart aleck, mister."

She looked at the page for a moment, and then said, "It is addressed to Miss Eliza Hamm, Three-Three-Four East Arrellaga Street. Santa Barbara, California.

"Dear Miss Hamm . . . First, please accept my sincere condolences on the loss of your father. Frederick was one of my dearest friends and I shall miss him.

"I am sure it will come as no surprise to you that there are several matters concerning your father's estate we must discuss, including the disposition of the *Santa Barbara Tribune*. I would be most appreciative if you could contact me by telephone or letter at your earliest convenience so that we might arrange a meeting.

"Sincerely, Edward Ingraham, Esquire."

Eliza lowered the letter and looked at me. "I guess that answers one of our questions."

I nodded. "At least we know Mister Ingraham feels the need to address the issue of the *Tribune's* ownership with regard to your father's estate. Whether or not he knows about Estelle's involvement remains to be seen. What would you like to do?"

"I think we should see Mister Ingraham as soon as possible."

Eliza glanced at her wristwatch and added, "It's just two-thirty. We might even get to see him today."

"That sounds like a good plan to me, kiddo. Why don't you give Mister Ingraham's office a telephone call and find out if he can see you this afternoon?"

Eliza spent about ten minutes speaking over the telephone, and then replaced the handset in its cradle. "Mister Ingraham will be back in his office at three o'clock. We have an appointment for three-fifteen."

Mabel had been observing the goings-on without comment. Finally she said, "Then I must be getting along. I trust you will call me later and let me in on whatever Mister Ingraham tells you. This is almost as exciting as a good mystery novel."

"I will call you, Mabel, you may count on that."

THIRTY-THREE

Friday - September 21, 1928

The offices of Edwin Ingraham, Attorney at Law, were located around the corner from the Santa Barbara Superior Court and across Figueroa Street from the County Courthouse and Clerk-Recorder. I have heard the neighborhood referred to as "Lawyer Row" because it seems every attorney in town is entrenched there. If one happened to be allergic to practitioners before the bar, this was a swell place to develop a rash.

Eliza and I walked into Mister Ingraham's outer office a few minutes early for our appointment, but we were shown directly into his inner sanctum. Ingraham, it turned out, was a rotund fellow of at least six feet in height. If he had been wearing a powdered wig, his hair would not have been whiter. His complexion was somewhere in the middle ground between the pink of health and apoplexy.

Standing behind a huge mahogany desk that could have served as a ping-pong table, Edwin Ingraham seemed confused about my presence in the room. After Eliza explained our relationship in terms so simple even an attorney could comprehend them, he appeared to understand. From that point on, however, Ingraham began addressing all of his conversation to me, referring to Eliza in the third person almost as if she were not in the room.

After a few moments of that, I said, "Mister Ingraham, kindly speak directly to Eliza. She is your client's heir. I am simply here in a supportive role."

With an expression on his face I thought might be meant to convey enlightenment or perhaps even an epiphany, Edwin Ingraham said, "I see. Very well, Missus Kinney, I asked to see you because I am the executor of your father's estate. As such, my role is to see that the wishes he expressed in his last will and testament are carried out precisely.

"My tasks in that role are simplified by the fact that you are Frederick's sole heir. Ah . . . that means no other heirs are stipulated in his will. In simple terms, he left his entire estate to you, and we know of no other family members or interested parties who are likely to have grounds for contesting the will. Ah, that means no one we know of appears to have a legal claim on your father's estate.

"That being the case, I will have his property and banking accounts transferred into your name. That will be accomplished during the next week. I assume the name I should use is Missus Lester Kinney. Is that correct?"

Despite the maudlin nature of our business in Mister Ingraham's office, Eliza glanced at me with a twinkle in her eye and said, "Thank you, Mister Ingraham. I would prefer, however, having the property and accounts become the joint property of Missus Eliza Hamm Kinney and Mister Lester Kinney. Would you please arrange matters accordingly?"

Ingraham looked at me questioningly. I looked back at him without expression. Turning to Eliza, he said, "Of course, Missus Kinney."

Smiling, Eliza said, "Thank you, Mister Ingraham."

Clearing his throat—perhaps an indication that Mister Ingraham was not entirely comfortable dealing with a modern woman—he said, "Now, there is one additional matter to which we must direct our attention."

Still looking cheerful, Eliza said, "I see. What would that matter be, Mister Ingraham?"

"It concerns the ownership of the *Santa Barbara Tribune* newspaper. It seems Frederick had a partner in that venture, a Miss Estelle Abernathy."

Now we were getting down to the gist of matters. It was apparent that Frederick Hamm's confidential agreement with Estelle Abernathy was not entirely confidential because Ingraham produced a copy of it from a folder on his desk. Paraphrasing the paragraphs of the agreement rather than actually reading all of the legal verbiage, the lawyer described the general agreement almost exactly as Estelle Abernathy had explained it to me two weeks ago when I last saw her.

After covering the general terms of the contract, Ingraham got down to its special conditions. The first of these addressed the repayment of Estelle Abernathy's investment in the *Tribune*. The agreement required the company to repay the investment—in reality, a loan—in ten annual payments.

The payments were to commence at the end of the paper's second year of operation and continue for a period of ten years. In lieu of interest on the money she loaned the *Tribune*, Estelle was to retain her fifty-one percent ownership in the company after the original investment was repaid.

Setting the agreement on his desk, Ingraham leaned back in his dark red leather desk chair and said, "Missus Kinney, I want you to know that I strongly advised Frederick against entering into this agreement with Miss Abernathy. I felt the terms were extremely one-sided in favor of Miss Abernathy. Frederick, however, was passionate in his desire to establish the *Tribune*, and I could not convince him to renegotiate the agreement."

I glanced at Eliza. She simply nodded in response to Ingraham's comments about the agreement and the attorney continued his explanation of the document.

"To bring matters up to date, one year ago Frederick, actually the *Tribune*, paid the final installment on Miss Abernathy's loan, and the last time I saw him, Frederick asked what I thought about the idea of buying Miss Abernathy's interest of the company. I told him it was an excellent idea, but that it was unlikely his partner would be willing to settle for a reasonable amount, or that she would even consider selling at any price.

"You see, Missus Kinney, by this time it was clear to me that Miss Abernathy did not enter into the *Tribune* agreement for any purpose of financial gain. Rather, it gave her control over half of the news read by the citizens of this town, and even though Frederick denied it, I was certain she occasionally applied pressure to have him write stories that paralleled her views on matters in which she had a vested interest."

Glancing in Eliza's direction again, I got the distinct impression she was growing angrier by the moment. It seemed a shame to waste her anger on a dead woman, if that's what she was doing. I was not sure.

Ingraham continued, "That is more or less where things stood as of last Wednesday night when Estelle Abernathy and Frederick Hamm died. With their passing, we must refer to the section of the agreement specifying what was to happen to the *Tribune* if either partner died.

"This part of the agreement has a stipulation attached. The stipulation is that Estelle Abernathy's loan to the company must be repaid within thirty days of either partner's death. In the event she is the first partner to die, the loan must be repaid to her estate. The loan has been repaid, however, so this stipulation no longer applies."

I had a feeling I knew what was coming. If I was right,

matters were about to get quite sticky.

As if he read my mind, Ingraham looked at me and said, "Now, we come to the part of all this that becomes complicated. The intent of the deceased partner clause is very straightforward. It simply says that, in the event of a partner's death, the *Santa Barbara Tribune* and all of its assets become the sole property of the surviving partner. Period.

"Now, if events on that night unfolded the way the police believe they did, approximately fifteen minutes passed between the time Estelle Abernathy was shot and the time Frederick committed . . . ah . . . suicide." Ingraham turned to Eliza. "I know this must be unpleasant for you, my dear, but the matter must be addressed."

Eliza nodded slowly. "I understand, Mister Ingraham."

"The difficulty," Ingraham continued, "Is that establishing the precise time of a death is not an exact science and because Miss Abernathy and Frederick Hamm both died within such a short period of time, it is remotely possible she was still alive when Frederick turned the gun on himself. In other words, there is no irrefutable evidence to support a claim that Miss Abernathy predeceased Frederick Hamm.

"If we cannot prove that in a court of law, the ownership of the *Tribune* must be settled in arbitration between Estelle Abernathy's heirs and ourselves. In that case, it is quite likely the outcome would be an ownership split between the two parties in the same ratio stipulated in the original contract. I should add, however, that we have heard nothing from Miss Abernathy's attorney regarding her heirs and estate."

I asked, "Mister Ingraham, exactly what does the county coroner say about the times of death?"

Ingraham picked up two manila envelopes from the top of his desk. "I have his autopsy reports and the death certificates right here. I was at the coroner's office picking up our copies when you called earlier this afternoon."

He opened the one labeled ABERNATHY, slid out four or five typewritten forms, and studied the top sheet for a moment. Finally, he said, "According to the testimony of a neighbor, Frederick was seen arriving at the Abernathy residence around ten-thirty Wednesday night."

Ingraham scanned further down the report, and then said, "The coroner places the time of Estelle Abernathy's death at approximately three a.m. This time of death estimate is based on the testimony of another neighbor who was awakened by at least two loud popping sounds she recognized as gunshots followed almost immediately by Estelle Abernathy's office clock chiming the three o'clock hour. These sounds were clearly heard by the neighbor because it was a warm night and both the Abernathy office window and the neighbor's bedroom window were open."

Ingraham returned the Abernathy forms to their envelope and removed the contents of the envelope labeled HAMM. Again he reviewed the top page of the death certificate. Finally, Ingraham said, "Here it is. Sometime after hearing the first gunshots and the clock's chiming, the same neighbor heard another gunshot—this time a single shot. She got out of bed thinking to call the police about all the shooting and noticed that, according to the clock in her living room the time was three-fifteen a.m.

"After the third shot, however, there were no further noises and the neighbor decided to go back to bed rather than calling the police as she had first intended. Later, when she was interviewed by the police, they noted that the clock in her living room appeared to be accurate, as was Estelle Abernathy's office clock when investigators inspected it Thursday morning.

"As I indicated earlier, Mister Kinney, according to the witness's testimony, Estelle Abernathy was shot at three a.m. and Frederick Hamm shot himself at three-fifteen a.m., placing the shots about fifteen minutes apart."

Eliza sniffed into her handkerchief and stood up. Softly she said, "Please excuse me for a minute," and left the office.

Ingraham looked a little puzzled at her abrupt departure. I explained it to him. "The events of the past few days have been very difficult for Eliza. She needs some time to recover from the shock."

Nodding in a sagacious manner, Ingraham said, "I understand."

"Mister Ingraham, you have been most helpful in explaining matters to us. I think now, however, I will take Eliza out for some fresh air and a change of scenery. Do you need anything else from us in order to take care of the matters you discussed?"

"Yes, Mister Kinney, I need your signatures on limited powers of attorney that will allow me to shift Frederick's accounts into your names as per Missus Kinney's wishes. I will have my secretary type the forms right away. That will take about half an hour. Could you remain until that is done?"

"I think so. How would it be if Missus Kinney and I took a short walk while the forms are typed? It is four o'clock. We can return at four-thirty."

"That should work out about right. We will see you in thirty minutes, Mister Kinney."

Walking out of Ingraham's office I could not shake the feeling there was something wrong with the coroner's report. There were so many other thoughts flying around in my mind, though, I could not put my finger on exactly what was bothering me.

I found Eliza sitting in our Chevrolet at the curb outside Ingraham's office. I slid onto the driver's end of the seat and said, "How are you holding up, kiddo?"

In a quiet voice, Eliza said, "Not as well as I hoped I would. Mister Ingraham is so cold about everything. It is as if he is talking about characters in a book or a motion picture rather than real living, breathing people."

"I noticed that. I wonder if it might be his way of coping with matters of life and death. Remember, he was a friend of your father."

"I know and I realize I am not being fair to him, but I needed to get away from all those cold facts for a while. We can go back now."

"We don't need to go back quite yet. Ingraham's secretary is typing power of attorney forms for us to sign so he can take care of changing your father's accounts and property in our names, and by the way, it is kind of you to include my name in those changes, but regardless of what it says on paper, all of your father's estate is yours. I want no part of it. I have already said that, and I meant it."

Eliza smiled softly. "I know you did, darling. Just humor me, okay?"

"If you insist. What are your thoughts on the *Tribune* situation? It looks as if you are about to become at least part owner of the paper."

She shook her head. "I need some time to think about all that. Right now I can't imagine sharing ownership in father's newspaper with Aurora Abernathy, and she is the only heir Estelle might have."

"You know, we still might be able to get that adoption overturned due to the immoral aspects of it. That's probably a very long shot if she contests the will, though."

"I'm sorry, darling, but I just can't think straight right now. Could we talk about this later?"

"Sure we can. I need to call Bob Carlson, anyway. He's another person I promised to talk with today, and I'm rapidly running out of today."

Eliza and I walked half a block up Anacapa Street to a public telephone booth. There, I placed a collect call to Carlson at the *Examiner*.

After telling the operator he would accept the charges, Bob Said, "Hello, Lester. I had about given up on hearing from you today."

"I'm sorry to be so late, Bob. We've had a busy day—funeral arrangements, getting Frederick Hamm's affairs straightened out, police reports—things like that."

"I can imagine. Anything in all of that worth a story or two?"

"Actually, yes, at least one story. I have more details from the police report on the murder/homicide. Some of it is pretty dramatic . . . and strange."

That got Bob's interest. "What is strange about it?"

"The way in which the coroner established the times of death. It's rather unorthodox. I won't waste time with the details now, but I think it is unusual enough to warrant a story in the first section."

"All right, Lester, can you call it in to me this evening, say, by eight? Remember, we become a morning paper on weekends."

"I can and will . . . will you be there that late?"

"Lately it seems like I'm here twenty-four hours a day. I'll be here."

While Bob was answering my question, I heard the courthouse clock chime. I started counting the chimes purely from habit, but they only sounded once. As with clocks in many churches and public buildings, a single chime signaled the half hour. It was four-thirty.

Suddenly I knew what was bothering me about the coroner's time of death. I yelped an involuntary "Damn!"

Of course Bob Carlson heard me. "What? What's the matter, Lester?"

"Save a spot on the front page, Bob. I just caught the Santa Barbara coroner and the local cops in a big, big mistake. I have to go. Talk with you at eight."

I hung the handset in its cradle and burst out of the telephone booth. "Come on, Eliza. We need to finish things with Ingraham and then see Sullivan again."

She trotted along beside me as I quickly walked back to Ingraham's office. "Back to see Sergeant Sullivan? For heaven's sake, why?"

Grinning, I said, "To ensure your sole ownership of the *Tribune*, kiddo!"

It only took a few minutes to read through the powers of attorney Ingraham's secretary had prepared and to sign them. Ingraham was saying something about specifically what he was going to do with the forms, but I interrupted him.

"I am sorry, Mister Ingraham, but we don't have time for that right now. Just get ready to have sole ownership of the *Tribune* transferred into Eliza's name."

He started to question what I said, but we were already through his office door. Then we were in the Chevrolet driving southeast along the three-and-a-half blocks that separated us from the city hall. I swung into the parking area and started to get out of the car.

Eliza was looking at me as if I had lost my marbles. "Come on, kiddo."

"Lester, what has gotten into you?"

"The sure and certain knowledge that the coroner and the Santa Barbara police have made a major mistake in determining the times of death in the coroner's reports. Come on, this is going to be fun!"

Eliza shook her head dubiously. Still, she hopped down from the car and followed me into police department offices in the city hall, where I asked to see Sergeant Danny Sullivan.

THIRTY-FOUR

Friday - September 21, 1928

Santa Barbara Police Sergeant Danny Sullivan was clearly not happy about seeing Eliza and me back in his domain. "Kinney, you can't just walk out on an interview and then pop back in for a friendly chat whenever you get the notion."

Barely suppressing a grin, I said "Sullivan, I don't enjoy your company enough to drop in for friendly chats. I'm here to save you from becoming a laughing stock."

Sullivan was clearly not convinced I had his best interests at heart. "Oh? Just what makes you think I am in danger of becoming a laughing stock?"

Winking at Eliza, I said, "Your investigation of the Hamm/Abernathy case is way out of whack and so are the coroner's times of death."

Glaring, Sullivan said, "I don't know what you're trying to pull, but that is nonsense. Now get out of here."

I grinned in the face of his glare. "All right, Sergeant Sullivan, if you prefer to read about your blunder in tomorrow's *Examiner*, that's fine with me."

The confidence I exuded was getting to him. "All right, smart guy, go ahead, tell me what's wrong with our investigation."

"You need to go back and take another look at the clock in Estelle Abernathy's office, the one the neighbor heard chiming."

An expression of relief passed over Sullivan's face. Now he was certain I was trying to pull a fast one and he called me on it. "There is absolutely nothing wrong with that clock. It is an expensive precision instrument."

"Oh, you are absolutely right about that part. In fact, it is the ship's clock from Duncan Abernathy's first ship. You may have noticed it is even engraved with the name of that ship, *The Highland Unicorn, 1873*."

"I may have. What is so darned important about that?"

"What is so darned important is that a ship's clock chimes the time entirely differently than other clocks."

For the first time I saw a small expression of concern cross Sullivan's face. "What in blazes are you talking about? Time is time."

"Yes, time is time, but on a ship the time is kept according to a system of bells to help crewmen know when their watches begin and end. A sailor's watch is four hours long and the twenty-four hour day is divided into six four hour watch periods. The first watch, for example begins at midnight. Thirty minutes later, at twelve-thirty a.m. a ship's clock chimes once to mark the first half hour of the first watch. One o'clock a.m. is marked by two chimes, one-thirty with three chimes, and so on. Are you with me so far?"

He was with me, all right, but I could see he wished he wasn't. "Are you sure about that?"

"Positive. Your witness who saw Frederick Hamm arrive at the Abernathy mansion says he got there at ten-thirty, so the next time the *Highland Unicorn's* clock would have chimed three times was one-thirty a.m., but the neighbor who was awakened by the gunshots thought the three chimes meant it was three a.m.

"Then when she was awakened again and saw by her own clock it was three-fifteen a.m., she thought only fifteen minutes or so had passed since she heard the first two shots. Actually the elapsed time must have been an hour and forty-five minutes. Got it?"

Sullivan nodded half-heartedly. "Yeah, I have it. If what you have told me is correct, the coroner's time of death estimates are off by about ninety minutes, but what the heck was Frederick Hamm doing all that time?"

I glanced at Eliza, concerned that my conversation with Sullivan might be upsetting to her. It surprised me to see that she was listening intently and apparently taking it all in stride.

"I doubt if we will ever know how Mister Hamm passed that time, but he was not a person who would have taken the killing of another human being lightly. I can imagine he was very upset by what he had done. Perhaps he was trying to compose his thoughts before taking his next and final step in life."

Sergeant Sullivan appeared to be lost in thought. "I suppose."

"What is important right now is, unless you want the coroner to learn about his blunder in tomorrow's *LA Examiner*, you had best get on the telephone and show him the error of his ways so he can revise his time of death estimates."

The Sergeant said, "I don't much care whether the coroner gets egg on his face or not, but in the interests of justice, I have to set the record straight."

While his words sounded noble, I knew it was egg on his face and the face of the Santa Barbara Police Department that concerned him. I offered an incentive to ensure Sullivan's cooperation in making things right.

"Tell you what, Sergeant, if the coroner revises his time of death estimates on new death certificates by the end of business today, I will write my article so it appears the error was discovered and brought to the coroner's attention by Sergeant Sullivan of the Santa Barbara Police, but I will need to see the revised death certificates first."

The expression on Sullivan's face told me I had him. He looked at his wristwatch and said, "You aren't giving me much time, Kinney. It's almost five."

"Sorry, Sergeant, but I have a deadline to meet tonight. That's the best I can do."

Sounding resigned, Sullivan said, "Okay, Kinney, I'll do what I can. Where will you be in an hour or two?"

"We'll be at our cottage on Micheltorena. My telephone exchange is 1121."

Nodding, Sullivan said, "You'll be hearing from me."

I noted that my legs were a trifle wobbly by the time we returned to the Chevrolet. I knew I was right about the clock chimes going in. The challenge was to convince Sullivan I was right. Apparently I had succeeded, but he could have just as easily thrown me out on my ear. The issue would have eventually been sorted out in court, but that could have resulted in delays that affected the operation of the *Tribune*, so I gambled on my approach to Sullivan and I'd gotten lucky.

After helping Eliza into the car, I slid behind the steering wheel and Eliza hugged me with all of her strength. "You did it, Lester. That's at least the third time you have challenged Sergeant Sullivan and beat him. You were amazing!"

That comment made me laugh. "Amazing might be overstating the case, but if everything works, you are about to become the sole owner and proprietor of the *Santa Barbara Tribune*."

"No, not the sole owner. I'm going to become the joint owner of the *Tribune*, along with my clever and brilliant husband."

By six o'clock we had restocked our pantry from the Wiggly Piggy market and I was sitting at my desk readying my typewriter to create an article for the *Examiner*.

Eliza was talking with Mabel on the telephone. At one point I heard her say, "It's not a sure thing yet, but it looks promising."

With a laugh she added, "No, you won't have to call me 'boss'."

Around six-thirty there was a knock at our door. As I hoped, it was Sergeant Sullivan. He held two large envelopes in his hand. I invited him in, but he shook his head and handed me the envelopes. "Convincing the coroner took longer than I expected because he insisted on going up to Estelle Abernathy's residence to see the clock for himself. I guess he wanted to be thorough."

"About time he started paying attention to details. That's what coroners are paid to do."

Sullivan cleared his throat. "Ah, are we okay for time? I mean for your newspaper story?"

"Yes, Sergeant. Assuming these revised documents say what they are supposed to say, you have kept your end of the bargain and I'll keep mine."

He simply said, "Thank you, Mister Kinney," and left.

With Eliza looking over my shoulder at the desk, I opened the envelope labeled ABERNATHY and ran my finger down the entries on Estelle Abernathy's death certificate. The typing in the "Date/Time of Death" blank read, "20 Sept., 1928 / Approx. 1:30A."

I found the same blank on Frederick Hamm's death certificate. There, the "Date/Time of Death" was recorded as, "20 Sept., 1928 / Approx. 3:15A."

With a note of surprise in her voice, Eliza said, "He did it!"

"The coroner didn't have much choice. We had him over the proverbial barrel. If he was going to use the clock chimes to determine the times of death, he had no choice but to revise his estimates. I suppose we can chalk this one up to the power of the press, speaking of which, I had best get going on Bob's story for tomorrow's edition."

The article I read to Bob Carlson's stenographer via the long distance wires to Los Angeles was under the headline:


```
     SANTA BARBARA CORONER MAKES NINETY MINUTE
           ERROR IN MURDER/SUICIDE


              By Lester Kinney
```


The headline did not have much real news value, but it was sensational enough to grab the attention of readers and it gave me an opportunity to keep my promise to Sergeant Sullivan. After crediting Sullivan with bringing the times of death errors to the coroner's attention, most of the story was a summary of the facts in the case and more on Frederick Hamm's motivation for his actions. The article concluded with information about the service for Hamm on Monday.

With Eliza's help I had also dashed out an obituary for her father. After reading the story and the obit for the stenographer, I said to Carlson, "You don't owe me for the obituary. That one is on the house."

Bob said, "I like the coroner story, Lester. It's a good wrap-up with a strong head. You have anything else coming up?"

"Maybe. Tomorrow I'll try to get in touch with somebody in the county DA's office up here and see how they're coming with the murder of Monsignor O'Boylan. I don't see much purpose in checking with the federal prosecutor on Frederick Hamm's case. I'm sure they'll be dropping it, but I can check if you want me to."

"No, we can keep an eye on that down here. I think we'll just let the story die a natural death unless something unexpected happens. Anything else?"

"On Monday I can check with the Santa Barbara County DA and see what, if anything, is happening with the Summerland picket killings. Of course, I'll be at Frederick Hamm's funeral Monday afternoon. I don't expect anything newsworthy there, but I'll keep my eyes open. I guess that's about it."

"All right, Lester. Let me know if you get anything out of the DA up there. If you do, we can run it Monday."

After hanging up the telephone handset, I looked over at Eliza. She had moved the second chair in from the kitchen and was sitting opposite me with something like a wistful expression.

"What's on your mind, kiddo?"

"Oh, I don't know. My thoughts keep hopping from one thing to another. I think my mind is overloaded."

"I'm not surprised. A lot has happened and we still have a lot to do."

Eliza nodded. "Yes. One thing that concerns me is what we should do with the *Tribune*, assuming we end up with it."

"That is certainly something to think about. You can let Louis Arquette handle things for now, but you'll ultimately have to decide what you want to do with the paper."

Eliza frowned. "Lester, please stop saying 'you can do this or that.' I'm counting on you for help with this and you make me nervous when you say that."

"Of course you can count on me. It's just that I never

imagined running an entire newspaper. I'm still trying to get used to that idea." After a moment I said, "Do you have any thoughts on what you would like to see happen to the *Tribune*?"

"I'm afraid I'm not very objective on that subject. The paper is like a member of the family. I grew up with it. Do you think we could run it? Or do you even want to?"

I felt myself nodding. "Yes, I think we could run it, and we could do it well." Smiling, I added, "At least I would not have to argue with the editor about rewrites."

Eliza smiled with me. "That's a certainly a point."

"I'm afraid, however, the question is more involved than just whether or not we could run the paper. For example, taking over the *Tribune* would require us to remain in Santa Barbara. I'm not necessarily opposed to that, but it is a decision we should make consciously rather than just letting it happen to us. On the other hand, the *Tribune* could solve our employment problems. I don't know how profitable it is, but your father seems to have managed on what the paper brings in."

"We can find out more about that tomorrow. I should go by the house again and gather up father's financial papers so I can pay his bills next week when Mister Ingraham gets our names on the bank accounts. Can we do that?"

"Sure we can." That brought another train of thought to mind. "Something else we need to do right away is get these new coroner's reports to Ingraham. We'll have to check tomorrow morning and see if he is in his office. Since it is a Saturday, that's doubtful, though."

Eliza reached across the desk and picked up the Santa Barbara telephone directory. As she opened it, she asked, "What is his first name again?"

"Edwin."

"That's right." She ran a finger down a page and said, "Well, here's an E. Ingraham on Rincon Vista Road. That's in the Riviera down the hill a ways from Estelle's house. It the sort of area where a well-to-do lawyer might live. The exchange is eight-five-one. Do you think we should try to call him?"

"Tonight? What time is it? About eight?"

Glancing at her wristwatch, Eliza said, "A few minutes after."

"It's not too awfully late. If that is his number, calling him now might save us some trouble tomorrow. Besides, he should be relieved to hear about the revised death certificates. Do you want me to talk with him?"

"Yes, please, darling."

I heard the phone ring twice before a male voice I did not recognize answered, "Edwin Ingraham residence."

I nodded in Eliza's direction to let her know she had found the correct telephone number. "Good evening. This is Lester Kinney calling. May I please speak with Mister Ingraham?"

"One moment, sir. I will see if he is in."

I smiled at that. Assuming he was a servant of some sort, the fellow would not be worth much if he did not know whether or not his employer was home. His response, of course, was intended to cover the likelihood that Ingraham had no interest whatsoever in speaking with Lester Kinney at eight o'clock on a Friday night. Apparently, however, that was not the case.

A few moments later, I heard Ingraham say, "Good evening, Mister Kinney. How may I help you?"

"I apologize for interrupting your evening, but I have some news I thought you might want to hear before Monday."

I heard curiosity in his voice. "What news might that be, Mister Kinney?"

"I have in my hands revised death certificates for Estelle Abernathy and Frederick Hamm on which the times of death are now approximately ninety minutes apart."

Ingraham's response was full of astonishment. "How on earth did you manage that?"

"I discovered an error in the coroner's method of determining the times of death, so I let the police in on the mistake. They contacted the coroner and he concurred that my version of the events that night was correct. The details will appear in tomorrow's *Los Angele Examiner*."

"You alluded to something along those lines when you left the office this afternoon, but I certainly did not expect this turn of events, and so quickly."

"I think the power of press might have had something to do with the prompt revision of the death certificates."

He apparently had to think about that for a moment before he realized what I was getting at. "Mister Kinney, as an officer of the court, I cannot condone blackmail, but in this instance it may be justified. Regardless, congratulations are in order. You and Missus Kinney are almost certainly the new owners of the *Santa Barbara Tribune*."

We concluded our conversation by agreeing that I would deliver the revised death certificates to his office around nine Saturday morning. He seemed to think having the paperwork in his hands as soon as possible was a good idea. That was just dandy with me.

I ended the call and leaned back in my chair. Eliza heard my end of the conversation, but she was curious as to Ingraham's response.

"We just made Mister Ingraham one very happy attorney."

Eliza smiled. "He thinks there won't be any trouble with our gaining ownership of the paper?"

"In his words, we are almost certainly the new owners of the *Santa Barbara Tribune*."

Now Eliza was actually grinning. "Wonderful! I guess that means we will have to make some of those decisions we were talking about, doesn't it?"

"It does, but we have a little time for that. In the meantime we can celebrate what appears to be a small victory."

Eliza walked around the desk and dropped lightly into my lap. Putting on the expression of coyness I always find irresistible, she asked, "And how would you suggest we honor the occasion?"

I shook my head in feigned annoyance. "You sure ask a lot of questions, kiddo. Just use your imagination."

Without another word, her lips found mine and Eliza put her imagination to work on what seemed to me like an excellent cause. Later, she stretched luxuriously next to me in our bed.

"Was that imaginative enough for you, Mister Kinney?"

In a tone of indifference I certainly did not feel, I said, "I suppose so."

That earned me a playful poke in the ribs. "You SUPPOSE so? Listen, mister, if I had been any more imaginative, you'd be passed out cold!"

Cringing from her poke, I said, "That would never do. The night is still young."

Leaning across my chest, Eliza kissed me. "Am I to take it you expect more imaginative creativity from me tonight?"

"Well, if you have more, it would be a shame to let it go to waste."

Eliza slid her right leg over mine. "With the proper motivation I might be able to come up with an idea or two."

"What would you consider the proper motivation?"

Pressing her thigh against me, she said, "Never mind, darling. I just found all the motivation I need."

THIRTY-FIVE

Saturday - September 22, 1928

Eliza was in bright spirits Saturday morning. I could hear her singing to herself in the kitchen and when I came in she handed me a steaming cup of proper coffee and sweetened it with a kiss.

Even in my groggy state her smile was contagious. "You are certainly Little Miss Sunshine this morning."

"That is because I woke up counting my blessings instead of thinking about all of the bad things that have happened. I really have a lot of them, you know."

"A lot of what?"

"Blessings, you goof, and you know what?"

"What?"

"The blessing I am most thankful for was right there beside me."

While hearing Eliza say things like that never failed to raise my spirits, it always embarrassed me a little. Nothing in my life prepared me for such adoration and I simply did not feel worthy of it. I was just me and Eliza is one of God's most glorious creations.

When I did not reply right away Eliza looked frowned. "What is it darling? Did I say something wrong?"

I took Eliza in my arms and held her tightly. "No, but when you say things like that you remind me that I am the one who is truly blessed. I just cannot get used to the idea that such a unique and beautiful woman chose me."

In a soft voice, she said, "That's funny."

"What's funny?"

"That you should use those words."

Puzzled, I said, "I don't understand."

"Sometimes when you aren't looking, I watch you and almost the same words come to me. Why did such a courageous and intelligent man choose me? In moments like those I feel I am not worthy of you. I want to be . . . I try to be, but I cannot convince myself I am. That is why you are such a wonderful blessing to me."

"Maybe it is because we share those feelings that we love each other so much."

Eliza's lips formed a small smile. "I keep remembering what Mabel said that night she was here. She said she had never known two people to be so in love that she could feel it when she walked into the room."

Nodding, I said, "I remember. She also told us to cherish and nurture the gift God has given us."

"Oh, I do, darling. I do with all my heart."

"Me, too, Eliza. Me, too."

"Oh gosh, Lester. Do you have a handkerchief? I'm all weepy."

I reached into my back pocket and produced the requested item. "Here you are. Please return it when you're done. I need it too."

After that we sat at the kitchen table drinking our coffee and smiling goofy smiles at each other. I think we would have spent the rest of the day right there if Eliza had not reminded me of our responsibilities.

"It's almost eight-thirty, darling. What time did you tell Mister Ingraham we would drop off those papers from the coroner?"

I sighed. "Nine."

"Then I suppose we ought to get on with our day."

"All right, kiddo. After we see Ingraham are we going to your father's house?"

She nodded, "Yes, if you don't mind. May I borrow a couple of empty boxes from when you moved in here? I need something to keep father's papers together."

"Sure. I'll bring a couple from the office."

Eliza leaned over and kissed me on the cheek. "I really want to give you a better kiss than that, but I fear we will never get our errands done if I do."

I grinned. "You're right. I suppose we can manage to behave ourselves for a few hours."

It was a few minutes after nine by the time I pulled our Chevrolet to the curb in front of Ingraham's office. He must have been watching for us because I saw him open the door and walk across the sidewalk in our direction.

I climbed down from the running board and walked around to open Eliza's door, but Ingraham beat me to it. He was already helping Eliza down when I got there.

He was looking at Eliza curiously when he said, "Good

morning, Mister and Missus Kinney. Thank you for coming by."

I looked at her, too. Aside from her eyes being a little puffy and a silly grin on her face, she appeared perfectly normal to me.

"Good morning, Mister Ingraham. Here are the coroner's revised death certificates."

Apparently Ingraham was extremely anxious to see if what I told him the previous night over the telephone was true. He opened the envelopes right there on the sidewalk and examined the forms.

When he slipped the papers back into their envelopes, Ingraham said, "You weren't kidding about the times of death, were you?"

"That is not something about which I am likely to joke."

"I guess not. I will begin the paperwork this morning, and by Wednesday or Thursday we should have everything filed. At that point this will all be settled and you two will have complete control over the assets in Frederick's estate, including the *Tribune*. I'll keep you informed on my progress."

Eliza said, "Thank you, Mister Ingraham. I am anxious to pay father's accounts up to date."

"I understand, but I don't think any of his creditors are concerned. Despite his . . . difficulties, we all knew your father to be an honorable man and I see that is a family trait."

"Thank you, Mister Ingraham. I'll do my best to continue earning that respect. Will we see you at the service on Monday?"

"Most assuredly. I have it on my calendar. I will see you then."

By nine-thirty we were in the house on Arrellaga Street and Eliza was diligently going through her father's desk and filing cabinets, sorting out the items she wanted to take home. At one point she stopped and said, "I wonder where father's automobile is. He must have driven it to Estelle's house. Do you think it is still there?"

"I doubt it. Chances are the police took it somewhere. I'll find out from Sergeant Sullivan."

"Thank you. It is a very nice car—a Buick—and it is practically new. Father only bought it a few months ago."

Smiling, I said, "Beats driving around in a beat up old Chevrolet."

"Darling, your Chevrolet will always have a special place in my heart."

"For heaven's sake, why?"

She shot me an exaggerated glare. "Some romantic you are.

We were in that beat up old Chevrolet when we shared our first kiss."

As if a switch was turned, I suddenly began remembering moments Eliza and I shared in the Chevrolet. "You're right. I think my next best Chevrolet memory is assisting you onto the seat in the gown you wore to Estelle's party. You were amazingly beautiful!"

"Thank you, darling. I still have the gown, you know. All you have to do is find us another swanky soirée and I can be amazingly beautiful for you all over again."

I laughed. "You are always amazingly beautiful. What you wear is just frosting on the cake."

"That's very kind of you to say, Lester, but it won't get you off the hook. I want another opportunity to see the same look in your eyes I saw that night."

"You just want to give Chaplin another chance to pat you on the fanny."

"Lester!"

"Well, at least we got a free breakfast out of that deal."

Eliza abruptly returned to her files, muttering, "My honor for a free breakfast, indeed."

I responded as expected. I patted her fanny.

In addition to Frederick Hamm's papers, the three cardboard boxes I carried out to the car also held a pair of lacquered wooden jewelry boxes, and a selection of silk garments Eliza described as "unmentionables." She also carried some clothes from her closet out and laid them on the front seat.

I was about to inquire where Eliza planned to sit when she asked, "Lester, would it be all right if I rode my bicycle back to our cottage so I can have it there? I miss riding it."

While I wasn't pleased with the idea, I said, "Okay. I guess it would be all right, but please be watchful. I still cannot shake the feeling I need to be looking over my shoulder to make sure Armando isn't back there pointing a gun at me."

"I will be very watchful, darling. I also want to make a stop in town, so I'll be a little longer."

"Where are you going to stop?"

Eliza's coy look was seeing a lot of use today. "That's personal and none of your business, mister."

"All right, kiddo, but get used to the idea that I intend to make everything you do my business."

"Nosey."

It was eleven-thirty by my pocket watch when I helped her

wheel the shiny blue bike out of the garage and slide the door shut. Eliza was wearing a white skirt that fit quite nicely, and as she rode away, I decided I could not in all fairness be too upset with Charles Chaplin for wanting to pat that fanny.

After carrying Eliza's boxes into the office and her personal items into the bedroom, I went into the kitchen and warmed a cup of coffee. That was around noon. When Eliza had not returned by one, I was seriously considering going out to look for her. Then I heard the cheerful ding-a-ling of a bicycle bell and felt a great deal of relief.

She came in through the back door and I was about to give her the dickens for being gone so long, but she spoke first. "I parked the bicycle on the service porch. Is that all right? I don't want it to get rusty."

"The service porch is fine. Now, where in blazes have you been? I was getting worried."

Eliza looked at her little gold wristwatch. "Oh! I am later than I thought I would be. I didn't mean to worry you, darling. I should have stopped and telephoned. I'm sorry."

Her expression was that of a little girl who expected a scolding. That, of course, took the wind out of my sails and there was nothing left for me to do but give her a hug and tell her everything was all right.

"Don't worry about it, kiddo. Just try to stay in closer touch until things settle down more. I've gotten so used to knowing where you are every minute, I'm like a mother hen."

"To tell the truth, darling, I rather like having you know where I am every minute. I like it very much. I'm afraid I just got caught up in my errand."

Giving her a kiss on the forehead, I said, "Now, do I get to know what you were up to, or is it still a big secret?"

Eliza grinned widely. "I was going to wait until later, but I can't. I'm too excited. Here!"

She held out her hand. In it was a rectangular box nearly a foot long and about two inches wide. The box was covered in white tissue paper and tied up with thin red silk ribbon made into a bow.

"What's this?"

"This, my darling dearest, is what people call a gift."

"I guessed that much. Who is the gift for?"

"There is a little card under the ribbon on the bottom. It might answer your question."

I turned the package over and, sure enough, there was a small white card tucked under the red ribbon. I removed the card and read the printing on it. In Eliza's hand it said, "For the man I love with all my heart." The card was simply signed, "Eliza."

"Well, unless you have someone hidden away in the closet, it appears this gift is for me."

Grinning and nearly jumping up and down in her excitement, Eliza said, "Yes, Lester, the gift is for you. Now stop fooling around and open it."

I could not help teasing her a little. "Now, wait a minute. It isn't my birthday and Christmas is still a few months away. What special occasion has prompted this gift?"

"There doesn't always have to be a special occasion for a person to give someone they love a gift. Open it!"

"Now just hold on . . . ."

"Lester!"

"Okay, okay. I'll open it."

I carefully removed the ribbon and gently tore the little round white seals from the tissue paper. "My mother always said if I remove the wrapping paper carefully it can be . . . ."

Large gold letters on a dark green leather-grained box spelled out, "GRUEN." Gruen, I knew, was a manufacturer of very high quality and prestigious time pieces. I had often admired them in jewelry store windows. I lifted the top of the box and stared in amazement at the most beautiful wristwatch I have ever seen.

The case was a rectangle of gold. The watch's face was white with large square numerals in gold surrounded by thin outlines in black. The hands were a matching shade of gold. The strap was leather and smelled of quality.

As I stood there awestruck by the beautiful object in my hands, Eliza said, "Well? What do you think?"

"I think it is the most wonderful wristwatch I have ever seen, but why?"

"Why? Because I love you darling." She stepped closer to look at the watch with me, adding, "Mister Hess, says it is the newest style and it is waterproof. The hands even glow so you can see the time in the dark!"

"Eliza, Gruen watches are terribly expensive. I've looked at them. Some Gruens are as much as a hundred dollars and more! This is much too extravagant."

"Lester, you said the money from father's estate was mine to do with what I please, and giving you this wristwatch pleases me very much."

"Yes, but . . . ."

With a smile she added, "Besides, Mister Hess is an old friend of my father's. He was kind enough to discount the price a goodly amount. He even set it to the correct time. Aren't you going to put it on?"

I shook my head in amazement. "I don't know what to say."

"You could say 'thank you.' You might even throw in an 'I love you.'"

"Of course, thank you, and I love you more than I can say, but . . . ."

"You're welcome. Here, let me help you with the strap."

A moment later the Gruen was on my left wrist. It looked and felt swell.

I took Eliza in my arms. "Kiddo, this is the most wonderful gift I have ever received. It means more to me than I can say, and not because it is expensive. It means so much to me because you thought of it and picked it out for me."

She looked up at me. "Good. And now you won't have to carry that clunky old pocket watch around. You are in the height of style."

"I'm always in the height of style when I go out with you on my arm. That's plenty for me."

Grinning, Eliza said, "In case I forgot to mention it, darling Lester, I love you with all my heart."

We kissed a long warm kiss. When our lips parted, I held up my left wrist. "The official time of that kiss was one-twenty-seven p. m. I love you, too."

"You sound just like the man on the radio. Well, except for the 'I love you part.' The man on the radio doesn't say that."

I laughed. "That is as it should be. I'm the only one who gets to love you."

"And you are more than enough for me. Now, how about some lunch? I am starving."

"That sounds good. I will even take you out for lunch. I know just the place, and we can do a little newspaper business afterward."

By two o'clock we were sitting at a table in the Montecito Inn's dining room. Eliza ordered a green salad and I chose an egg salad sandwich.

Looking around the room, I said, "I don't see the louse anywhere. He must have returned to Hollywood."

Eliza brightened our corner of the dining room with a smile. "Don't remind me. I was terribly embarrassed that day. I had no idea Charles Chaplin owned this hotel."

"I thought the whole thing was hilarious, although I'm not sure Chaplin saw the humor in it."

"I'm sure he did not. I think he might have been as embarrassed as I was."

"Somehow I don't think he embarrasses that easily."

Changing the subject, Eliza said, "You said you wanted to do some newspaper business after lunch?"

"Yes. I would like to drive down to Summerland and see what's happening there. After that I will try calling John Gilbert at the Santa Barbara DA's office to find out if he might be there on a Saturday and if he has any news on the search for Armando Delgado. I promised Bob Carlson I would try to call in another article for Monday."

Eliza smiled. "Still working for the competition, I see."

"I'm afraid so. For the moment, the competition is paying our bills. That gives the *Examiner* priority."

My new Gruen wristwatch told me it was almost three o'clock when we passed Summerland on the southbound side of US101 and I immediately saw that the trip had been worthwhile. There were no pickets in view. They had been replaced by large wooden signs tacked to sticks and planted in the ground along the shoulder of the highway. The signs bore the same messages as the strikers' placards had—slogans proclaiming the Summerland Oil Field Company unfair to organized oil field workers and demanding fair wages for a fair day's work.

Eliza said, "They are still at it, but in a much safer way."

"Yes, and I'm somewhat surprised to see the signs have not been removed by the Summerland Oil management."

"Maybe the sheriff told them to leave the signs alone."

I nodded. "That's a possibility. Another is that Estelle's death has the company managers wondering how they are going to get out of the hot water they're in. My bet is they are much more eager to bargain with the union now."

On the way home I pulled off the highway at Fernald Point to see if Well Number Sixteen was still spewing crude oil. It was. The only difference from our last visit was that Al Stone was no longer there cleaning the beach with his tractor. It occurred to me to wonder if he was one of the strikers killed by Delgado and Peter Mikhailov. I hoped not. Al was a nice guy.

Back home, I called John Gilbert at the Santa Barbara County DA's office. He was there, but preparing to leave for the day. Gilbert took a moment to tell me he had no news on the search for Armando Delgado. The consensus of opinion was that Delgado was laying low in Mexico. The Mexican authorities had been asked to help with the search and they were providing some cooperation, but it was clear from his tone of voice that Gilbert expected little to come of their assistance.

Otherwise, the prosecution of Peter Mikhailov for the murder of Monsignor O'Boylan was proceeding. A grand jury was scheduled to hear the case on Tuesday. That was the sum total of his news.

I had not expected to learn that Delgado was in custody, but somehow actually hearing the DA tell me the man was still at large put a damper on what had otherwise been a very pleasant day. The mental image of that evil little man pointing a large revolver at my head in our room at the Pierpont Inn thrust itself into my mind. That I had bested Delgado that night and caused him what I imagined was considerable pain did nothing to elevate my mood.

Eliza, of course, sensed my mood, and guessing the cause of my depression, had the wisdom not to try kidding me out of it. She simply stayed close, giving me the comfort of her presence. Despite her efforts I spent a fitful night fraught with nightmares.

THIRTY-SIX

Monday - September 24, 1928

Monday was a perfect day for a funeral. With a sky darkened by storm clouds and a fine mist in the air, the world put on a melancholy face for Frederick Hamm's final public appearance.

Eliza's face mirrored that melancholy. She seemed drained of her usual vitality and moved about the cottage lethargically. I had little more enthusiasm for the day than Eliza as I went about the tasks I had set out for the morning.

After coffee to clear away some of the cobwebs, I reviewed the *Examiner* article I had written Sunday. It carried the headline:

```
SEARCH FOR SUMMERLAND KILLER EXTENDED TO MEXICO

              By Lester Kinney
```

The story began with quotes from Santa Barbara County DA John Gilbert about seeking Armando Delgado in Mexico, including a comment about not expecting much from the cooperation provided by the Mexican government. From there I discussed the replacement of pickets with signs along US 101. I concluded the article with two paragraphs about the crude oil still washing up on the beach at Fernald Point from leaking well number sixteen.

I figured there was enough drama in the words I'd typed to warrant a front page spot in the Metro Section. Bob Carlson agreed with that assessment when I called the story in a few minutes after eight Monday morning. After finishing our business, Bob surprised me with a perfectly logical question I would have anticipated if my mind had not been preoccupied with Eliza and the ordeal facing her in a few hours.

"Lester, I'm curious. Do you have any idea what will happen to the *Tribune* now that Fred Hamm is gone?"

"Well, yes. In a few days it becomes the property of Mister

and Missus Lester Kinney."

"Really? Going into competition with us, are you?"

That thought was so preposterous I almost laughed. "You can tell Mister Hearst he needn't be overly concerned about that turn of events."

"I'm serious, Lester. Are you planning to run the *Tribune*?"

"It is looking that way."

"You don't sound very excited about the prospect."

"To be honest, the idea is a little overwhelming."

"You know, Lester, you could turn that paper into a money-maker. With Eliza's good sense and your journalistic skills, I'm sure you could make a go of it."

"It looks as if we are going to find out if you are right. Say, Bob, would you be interested in a new job? We would make you editor-in-chief of the whole shebang. Of course you would have to take a small cut in salary, but it is a wonderful career opportunity."

Carlson laughed heartily. "Lester, I would surely take you up on that truly generous offer if it weren't for the fact that the *Examiner* would probably collapse if I left."

"I was afraid you would say something like that."

"I might be able to give you some help, though, assuming you want my help. I'm willing to sit down with you and Eliza and work out a plan for managing the *Tribune* and turning it into a profitable publication. Talk it over with that pretty wife of yours and let me know, okay?"

"Thanks, Bob. Your help would be most welcome. I'll talk to Eliza and you'll be hearing from me."

"Good. Take care of yourself, Lester."

"I will, Bob. You do the same."

After hanging up the telephone it occurred to me that Bob's final words were somewhat unusual for him. I couldn't remember him ever ending a conversation on such a personal note.

Eliza interrupted that thought when she walked into the office a moment later. "Did Bob like your story?"

"Yes. We have another byline on the front page of the Metro Section and another check."

"That's good, darling."

"There's more. Bob offered us some help with the *Tribune*. He said he was willing to sit down with us and help work out a plan to manage the paper. Maybe we ought to take him up on it since this will be our first attempt at managing a newspaper."

Eliza seemed genuinely excited about that news. "Wonderful. I agree with you. Let's arrange to meet with him as soon as we can." She paused, and then added, "I mean if we decide to try to run the *Tribune*."

Trying to inject something positive into the day, I said, "Well, as Bob put it, with my journalistic skills and my pretty wife's good sense we could make a go of it."

That had the desired effect of bringing a small smile to Eliza's lips. "If Bob thinks we can do it, I guess we stand a chance."

A little before noon Eliza prepared a light lunch of baloney sandwiches. Neither of us was particularly hungry. We ate the sandwiches purely for sustenance. After the sandwiches we sat at the kitchen table holding hands for a while.

"It's going to be all right, kiddo. The people who attend the service were your father's friends. They will not be there to make judgements."

Eliza looked up at me. "I know that. Still, I am also sure some people will be there just because they are curious about what was going on between Father and me. They will be the ones making judgements."

"Eliza, do those people really matter to us? They can make their judgements and it won't matter one iota. I know it is hard for you to accept that, but it is true. Your friends—like Mabel and the people you worked with at the library—honestly care about you because you are a good person. They are the ones who matter."

That broke the dam and released a flood of tears. "Oh, Lester."

I walked around the table and put my hands on her shoulders. I knew there was nothing I could say to make her feel any better, so I just stood there until Eliza got to her feet and leaned into my arms.

As her sobs gradually quieted, she asked, "What time is it, darling?"

I looked at my new Gruen wristwatch and said, "At the tone it will be twelve-forty-four p. m. Gruen watch time and I love you with all my heart."

That earned me another small smile before she said, "I guess we need to change and drive to the church."

I wore my only suit, which was a fortunate shade of dark gray, and a black tie. Eliza wore her dark blue skirt and a matching blazer-style jacket over a white blouse. When she judged our attire sufficiently solemn for the occasion, we set out for the All-Saints-by-the-Sea Episcopal Church on Eucalyptus Lane.

We got to the church at one-thirty and were met at the door by Mister McDermott. He led us into the sanctuary, a large rectangular room with graceful arched wooden beams supporting its peaked ceiling. The space was mostly lit by stained glass windows lining both longitudinal walls. The light coming through their leaded designs glowed with vivid reds, blues, and golds.

Soft strains of *Nearer, My God, to Thee* were coming from an organ on the right side of the altar. The middle-aged woman playing the instrument was dressed in a black robe. Light from arrays of candles illuminating the altar occasionally flashed in the lenses of her glasses.

At the front of the sanctuary on our side of a low railing stood Frederick Hamm's open casket. Resting atop a blue and gold cloth-draped bier, the casket was made of a highly polished dark wood and was lined with white satin. Within the coffin, Frederick Hamm's head rested on small white pillow.

I understand that the intention of the mortician is to make the deceased look as if he or she is merely sleeping, but that was not the impression that struck me. To my eyes, Frederick Hamm's complexion appeared pale and waxy, very unlike my memory of the man when I saw him last standing at the front door of my cottage. I decided then and there that, when my time came, I wanted a closed casket so those who knew me would remember me as I was in life.

While she said nothing, I guessed Eliza's reaction was similar to mine. She stood there no more than a few seconds, and then stepped back down to the floor of the sanctuary.

Gesturing toward a small curtained niche at the left end of the altar, Mister McDermott said, "We arranged this seating area for family members. You can see through the gauze curtain on the altar side, but the curtain facing the sanctuary is opaque for privacy. This way please."

We began to follow him to the enclosure, but after just a few steps, Eliza stopped. Mister McDermott sensed this and turned with a questioning look.

"Mister McDermott, I would prefer to sit in the front pew."

If Eliza's request puzzled him, Mister McDermott never let it show. He simply reversed course and led us to the end of the front pew on the left side of the central aisle. Eliza looked at me and I gave her a nod. Then she slid into the pew and I sat next to her.

McDermott said, "It is customary for the congregation to file past the casket and out of the church by way of the side aisles at the conclusion of the service. I will come and lead you out of the sanctuary as the procession begins."

Eliza shook her head. "No, Mister McDermott. I would prefer

to forgo the viewing and lead the congregation out by way of the center aisle. I understand that is not customary, but I think it would be much better for this occasion."

Suddenly I realized what Eliza was up to. She did not want her father's friends to see him as he now looked. Eliza felt so strongly about this she was willing to make herself the center of attention by leading the procession from the sanctuary. I squeezed her hand as a gesture of my understanding.

Mister McDermott simply said, "As you wish, Missus Kinney."

When McDermott was out of earshot, Eliza whispered, "I'm sorry, darling, but I just couldn't . . . ."

"I understand and agree."

Giving me a small smile, Eliza whispered, "Thank you darling."

We had not been there long when I heard the hushed sounds people make when they arrive for such an occasion. I sensed someone standing in the aisle next to me and looked up. Mabel Stafford was there with Louis Arquette from the *Tribune*.

Eliza looked up and said, "Mabel, thank you for being here. Come sit with us."

I stood to allow Mabel and Louis to sidle past and sit on the other side of Eliza. Louis shook my hand as he passed. Mabel and Eliza hugged each other.

As the organist began *Abide with Me*, I sensed the sanctuary filling up and turned to look back over my shoulder. The crowd was so large the ushers were asking people already seated to make more room by sliding closer together in the pews. Most of the faces were unknown to me, but I did recognize a few of the attendees. Among those I knew were Clarence Storche, editor of the *Santa Barbara Post-Dispatch*, Edwin Ingraham, and Danny Sullivan. I was somewhat surprised to see Sergeant Sullivan there.

Finally the organ music faded away and a gray-haired man in a white robe stepped up to a lectern to the left of the altar and identified himself as the Reverend Doctor Weld. He welcomed everyone and the service began.

After scriptures were read, eulogies were spoken by three of Frederick Hamm's contemporaries, the only one of whom I recognized was Oswald Peters, Manager of County National Bank & Trust Company—the same man who brought federal charges against the man in the casket. I glanced at Eliza and she shook her head in disgust at Peters' nerve.

The service eventually concluded with a recital of the doxology, after which the organist launched into a somewhat grand version of *Onward Christian Soldiers*. The priest walked down to the central aisle and stopped next to our pew, offering his hand to Eliza. I stepped out of the way so Eliza could pass and the Reverend Doctor Weld escorted Eliza out of the sanctuary. I followed them and the ushers herded the rest of the multitude behind us.

When we reached the front steps of the church and fresh air, Eliza thanked the priest for a lovely service and quickly stepped to my side, grabbing my hand as she did so. After that she stood there gamely thanking folks for coming to the service. In a few instances Eliza made a point of introducing me to people as her husband.

One of the last out the door was *Tribune* photographer Joe O'Conner. He got a hug and, "Thank you for being here, Uncle Joe."

As things wound down people gathered into small groups in front of the church for conversations. Mabel and Eliza were talking quietly and I simply stood to one side with my arms folded trying to look inconspicuous.

A split second later the tranquil scene turned to chaos. Somewhere behind me a woman screamed. I spun around and came face-to-face with my worst nightmare. An unshaven and bedraggled Armando Delgado stood twenty feet away glaring at me with the eye that did not have a black patch over it. In his hand was a large revolver. It was pointed directly at my chest.

Delgado screeched, "Now you will die!"

I had an idea to charge him and grab the gun, but he gave me no opportunity for such heroics. He immediately pulled the trigger and I instantly felt the solid impact of the bullet hitting my chest. As I went down I heard two more shots.

Surprisingly I felt no pain, but everything around me was growing hazy and dim. The only face I could see clearly was Eliza's. She was kneeling over me cradling my head and screaming something I could not understand. Then everything went dark and I felt sad that I did not have time to tell Eliza I loved her and that I wanted the casket closed at my funeral.

THIRTY-SEVEN

Friday - September 28, 1928

Some curious thoughts were drifting by me in my black void of nothingness. One of them had all the earmarks of a relevant question: Can dead people think?

I attempted the use of logic to resolve this conundrum. Point: So far as I knew, a brain is required for thought. Point: A person's brain is part of their body, so if a body dies, the brain is also kaput. Conclusion: Dead people cannot think.

This conclusion left me in another quandary. I thought I was thinking. Ergo, if I was indeed thinking, it might be possible that I was not as dead as I thought I was. That cheerful proposition was surely worthy of further investigation, but how does one determine whether or not one is dead?

Perhaps the answer to that question could be derived by opening my eyes. If I could see anything with my eyes open, perhaps I was not dead.

I never realized eyelids were so weighty, but they must be very heavy because opening my eyes was an undertaking requiring considerable effort. I ultimately prevailed and the first knowledge I gained was that I could see—a positive outcome. What could I see? Things around me were somewhat fuzzy, but I eventually succeeded in separating some details from the haze.

I was inside a dimly lit room with walls, a window, a ceiling, and presumably a floor. Though I could not see it, by definition rooms were required to have floors. Thus far my eye opening experiment had expanded my horizons significantly, so I tried drawing another conclusion based on circumstantial evidence. I was lying on something soft with white sheets. What is soft and has white sheets? The only thing I could think of fitting that description is a bed. Therefore, the room I was in had a bed.

A movement somewhere to the left drew my attention. I slowly moved my gaze in that direction. Doing so showed me that the movement attracting my attention was Eliza turning the page of a newspaper. Now things were getting exciting. The room I was in also contained my wife!

What now? Perhaps I should share my newly acquired knowledge about life and death with Eliza. It might be important for her to know that I was not dead. Yes, I should tell Eliza I am alive, and something else. What else? I should also tell her I love her because I missed out on the opportunity to do that when . . . when what? Well, maybe she would remember when I missed that opportunity.

Taking a deep breath, I said, "Eliza, I am not dead and I love you."

The sound of my own voice surprised me. It was scratchy and hoarse.

The sound of my voice also surprised Eliza. She dropped the newspaper and jumped out of her chair. Then she was leaning over me and taking my hand in hers. "Oh, Lester, I love you, too!"

Since she did not mention it, I wondered if she understood the first part of my pronouncement, so I repeated it. "I am not dead."

With a big smile that lit up the dim room, she said, "I am so happy to hear that, darling! I have been very worried about you."

I smiled back at her. At least I think I smiled back at her. I was still not quite sure I was really doing things I thought I was doing.

"Just lay still, darling. I need to call the nurse. I have instructions to let them know the minute you wake up."

"Nurse? This is a hospital? Big Sisters?"

"No, darling. This is Cottage Hospital in Santa Barbara."

"Oh. Panties?"

I wondered why I said that. It seemed like a stupid thing to say, but Eliza thought it was hilarious. "No panties this time, darling. Now, sit tight for just a second."

I sat tight because any alternative activity required entirely too much effort. Apparently I sat tight for quite some time. When I looked again, the room was lighter and a gray-haired fellow in a suit had joined us.

"Good morning, Mister Kinney. I am Doctor Hadley. We met a few days ago, although I doubt if you remember the occasion. I am the surgeon who patched you up after the shooting."

It seemed my thoughts were forming with less difficulty now. "Shooting? Yes. I remember I was shot by Armando Delgado at the Episcopal Church."

"Yes you were. It is a good sign that you remember the incident. Sometimes patients who suffer severe trauma experience short-term memory loss. What else do you remember?

Do you remember this lovely young lady?"

I turned my gaze toward Eliza. "Yes, Doctor. That is the beautiful woman I had the good sense to marry."

Hadley smiled. "You did in deed, Mister Kinney. Do you recall why you were at the Episcopal Church the day you were shot?"

The answer to that question seemed to arrive in my head very quickly. "I do. We were there for the funeral of Eliza's father, Frederick Hamm."

"Good. It seems your mind is functioning quite well. Now, for the more difficult part. How do you feel physically?"

I gave that question several moments of thought. The answer at which I arrived did not seem adequate, but I gave it anyway. "Honestly, Doctor . . . ah . . . ."

Eliza filled in the blank in my head. "Doctor Hadley, darling."

"Yes, Doctor Hadley. Honestly, I don't feel much of anything. There seems to be some tenderness in my upper chest, but not much else."

Hadley nodded in a positive way. "We can thank the morphine for your lack of pain, however, we must soon begin reducing the narcotic dosages to avoid dependency. In the meantime, a reduction in pain helps the healing process."

Not quite sure I really wanted to know the answer, I asked a question that occurred to me. "Exactly what parts of me are healing?"

"The bullet hit a pulmonary vein and nicked a few lesser arteries."

"That sounds serious."

"It is very serious, Mister Kinney. If you had arrived here any later than you did, we could not have saved you. As it was, we had only minutes to perform resuscitation, diagnose the injury, and repair the damage."

"Then, Doctor Hadley, thank you for saving my life. How long have I been here?"

"You arrived Monday afternoon. Today is Friday."

Five days struck me as a long time to be dead. No. Pay attention, Lester. You were not dead, you just proved that. Okay, five days is a long time to . . . to be whatever I had been. I was getting confused again, so I asked another question. Questions sometimes unconfused matters.

"What happens now, doctor?"

"I think it would be wise for you to get out of bed and move around some, just for short periods of time and certainly nothing strenuous at first. We will gradually increase the duration and strenuousness of activity as we go.

"As I said, we will be reducing the morphine dosage you are receiving, so you may begin experiencing some pain in your chest. Also, as we reduce the morphine dosage and the effects of what's in your system wear off, you should be able to think more clearly. Beyond those things, we just need to keep an eye on you for another week to ten days. If things continue to go well, we might send you home then. Overall, you should be back to your normal level of activity in a month or so."

I was absorbing his prognosis and simply nodded in reply. Doctor Hadley said, "Mister Kinney, out of curiosity, what do you do for a living?"

I knew the answer to that question without having to think about it. "I am a newspaper reporter."

"I see. I did not realize journalism is so dangerous. Judging by the recent scars on your neck, this is not the first time someone has shot you. It might be wise for you to pursue a less risky career before your luck runs out."

I thought about telling the doctor the same guy had shot me both times, but an explanation seemed like more work than it was worth, so I simply nodded again.

"All right, Mister Kinney. We'll try you out on a little solid food for dinner tonight. Tomorrow morning a physical therapy nurse will help you get a little exercise. I will stop in to see you again tomorrow afternoon."

He headed for the door and I said, "Thank you, Doctor Hadley."

As the door closed behind him, Eliza came over to hold my hand again and give me a kiss on the cheek. She had a big smile on her face. "Oh, Lester, it's so good to have you back with me. Doctor Hadley said you would survive, but you were unconscious so long, I was getting scared. I am very glad to hear such a good prognosis."

"Me, too. I am afraid my eyelids are drooping again. If I doze off, please do not take it personally."

"I won't, darling."

Something that was nagging at the back of my mind finally worked its way to the front. "Eliza, what happened to Delgado? Did he get away again?"

Shaking her head, Eliza's expression turned stern. "No, darling, Armando Delgado is dead and gone forever."

I felt an incredible sense of relief. At the same time I thought of several additional questions I wanted to ask about my assailant, but the morphine beat me to the punch.

Saturday - September 29, 1928

Saturday morning I ate a hearty breakfast of apple juice and a soft boiled egg in its shell. Fortunately, Eliza was there to give me instruction on eating a soft boiled egg in its shell. I could not recall ever seeing one before.

While we were performing the breakfast ritual, I noticed something pinned to Eliza's blouse. "You are wearing your typewriter pin. Are we working?"

"We are working on getting you well. I have worn my pin every day you've been here. It brought us good luck in the past, and I thought we could use a little more luck now."

"Thank you. Your pin's magical powers seem to be having the desired effect."

Then, as Doctor Hadley promised, a physical therapy nurse arrived in my world. She sent Eliza out for a while and proceeded to coax me out of the bed. Having accomplished that much mostly on my own, I was marched around the room. Even leaning on the nurse, I was exhausted by the time I completed one circuit of the small room. Despite my exhaustion, the physical therapy nurse congratulated me on my accomplishment. I suspected her praise was more morale building in nature than a result of outstanding performance.

When the nurse left, Eliza returned with a visitor in tow. It was Mabel. I thought it was good to see Mabel. Actually, it was good to see anyone. Eliza and Mabel took up stations on either side of my bed and I got more exercise looking back and forth from one to the other. It was sort of like watching a tennis match.

Mabel said, "Lester, you certainly look much better than you did when I last saw you. I was certain we had lost you. Thank goodness Eliza kept a cool head and got you here in time."

"Oh," I replied, "She's becoming quite expert at that. This is the second time Eliza saved my life."

Eliza said, "And I certainly hope it is the last time I am called on to perform that chore. It is not something I particularly enjoy. How did your exercise session go?"

"I was barely able to walk one lap around the room before I was exhausted, but the nurse gave me high marks."

"Well, darling, the doctor specifically said nothing too strenuous at first. Remember, you haven't walked in nearly a week and you are recovering from a major operation."

Nodding, I decided to change the subject. "Mabel, how are things going at the *Tribune*?"

With a big smile, Mabel said, "We received some exciting news yesterday. The paper officially has a new owner now, or I should say two new owners. The entire staff cheered when they heard that."

I looked at Eliza for the details. "Yes, darling, Mister Ingraham filed the paperwork on Thursday, and when you woke up yesterday I decided it was unfair to keep everyone wondering what was going to happen, so I called Louis Arquette and told him what was going on. I asked him to pass the news on about the paper and about the improvement in your condition. I also asked him to continue as managing editor until you got well enough to take over."

"I imagine Louis was thrilled about that."

Mabel spoke up. "Actually, he really was thrilled. Louis much prefers reporting to editing. He told me he would be happy to let you take over, and the sooner the better."

The conversation continued more or less along those lines for a while, but I began missing parts of it by dozing off. At one point I woke up and found Mabel replaced by a hospital worker bearing a lunch tray.

Eliza noticed my eyes open and said, "Lunch time darling. Shall I crank your bed up to a sitting position?"

"Yes please. I guess I wasn't a very good host to our guest. I hope Mabel knows I appreciate her coming to see me even if I fell asleep in the middle of her visit."

"Don't worry about that. She understands." Then, removing the domed metal warming cover from my lunch, Eliza added, "Let's see what delicious delicacies you have for lunch."

My delicious lunch delicacies consisted of a pile of brown rice topped with miniscule pieces of boiled chicken. The tray also included half of a banana and a tiny bowl of something white called yogurt. Eliza explained it was a dairy product made from curdled milk. Surprisingly, I devoured my entire lunch and enjoyed every bite, including the curdled milk.

After lunch, my regular nurse showed up to check my vital signs. She measured my blood pressure, checked my pulse, and took my temperature. When done, she pronounced me on the mend and asked if I was up to another visitor. I told her that after such a healthy lunch, I was up to anything.

She left without seeing the humor in my comment, and a few

moments later, my room door opened. My visitor was none other than Sergeant Danny Sullivan.

"Okay to come in?"

Eliza seemed quite pleased to see him. "Of course, Danny, come on in."

Danny? Eliza was on a first name basis with the guy. I can't say that turn of events thrilled me.

Wearing plain clothes that indicated he was off duty, Sullivan strolled into my room. "Hello, Eliza, Lester. How is our patient?"

Glaring at the cop, I said, "The patient is fine and wonders what the hell you are doing here."

Taking my hand, Eliza quickly said, "Darling, that's no way to talk to a man who saved your life. If it wasn't for the Sergeant's quick thinking, Armando could have shot you several more times. That would have been the end for certain."

Feeling quite sheepish, I just said, "Oh."

Sullivan said, "That's okay, Lester. I understand how you feel, but it would please me a lot if we could shake hands and bury the hatchet. Believe it or not, I like you."

Offering Sullivan my hand, I said, "That would please me, too."

We shook hands and Sullivan said, "I'm glad you finally woke up. I was concerned. Actually everyone who knows you was concerned. You may not know it, but a lot of people think you are an all right guy."

Thinking things were getting entirely too chummy, I decided to get some answers to questions that had been on my mind off and on since I regained consciousness. "Sergeant, will you please tell me exactly what happened outside the church that day? I only recall being shot. After that I went out like a light."

Sullivan glanced at Eliza and she gave him a small nod, apparently indicating that I could handle hearing whatever he had to tell me.

"Well, I arrived at the Episcopal Church that afternoon half expecting trouble. I don't know exactly why I felt that way—call it cop instinct, but I wore my revolver in a shoulder holster. I felt silly as heck with that thing on, that is until Delgado showed up.

"After the service my sense there was going to be trouble got stronger, so I just stood not too far from where you were and kept my eyes open. Suddenly that one-eyed lunatic came running around the corner of the church with a revolver in his hand. I got my pistol out, but before I could say or do anything he shot you at point blank range. I saw you fall and Delgado was lining up for another shot, so I shot him twice. From the way he went down, I'm sure he was dead before he hit the ground.

"After that Eliza was kneeling over you and yelling for someone to call an ambulance. I made sure one was on its way, and then called the office to let them in on what happened. They dispatched a couple of officers and called the coroner, fortunately for Delgado, not for you. That's pretty much what happened."

"That helps a lot. Now what little I remember of that afternoon makes sense. I heard two shots after I went down, but I figured it was Delgado shooting at me. It was you shooting him."

"That it was."

"Thank you for saving my hide."

He grinned. "All in a day's work. Actually, I am receiving a commendation for gallantry from Mayor Finley Monday, so anytime you need saving from lunatic gunmen, just holler."

Holding my hand, Eliza said, "Thank you, but I can do quite well without any further encounters with lunatic gunmen."

Sullivan left when Doctor Hadley arrived a little later to look me over. Eliza stayed.

The doctor checked my chart and nodded in what I took to be a positive way. After that he looked into my eyes and listened to my chest with his stethoscope. After each of those steps he nodded again.

I asked, "Does the fact that you are nodding a lot mean I'm doing okay?"

"It means exactly that, Mister Kinney. Your pulse is strong and your chest sounds good. Also, I understand your first physical therapy session went well. That gets another nod."

"I was rather disappointed in the physical therapy session. I felt weak as a kitten the whole time."

"Mister Kinney, forgive me for saying so, but you are darned lucky to be alive, let alone getting out of bed and walking around the room. As I thought I indicated yesterday, we are approaching your recovery one step at a time. The healing process will take some time. Just be patient and continue giving therapy your best effort and you will begin to notice the improvement."

"I apologize, doctor. I will try my best to do as you say, but I wish you had some patient patience pills."

That struck his funny bone, something I would have bet he did not have. Doctor Hadley laughed heartily. "There are times when I wish I had those too. Especially when I deal with impatient patients." In a less jovial tone he added, "Just so you know, I am off tomorrow, so I'll see you on Monday."

On that cheerful note, the good doctor left and Eliza sat gently on the edge of my bed. "Darling, I sensed that it upset you when I called Sergeant Sullivan by his first name."

"I was a little upset. I understand better now."

"There is more you should know. Danny and his officers gave me twenty-four hour protection for several days after you were shot. I would look out the front window at night and see one of them standing near our front porch keeping an eye on things. They even gave me an escort to and from the hospital when I came to be with you. I'm sure Danny didn't have to do all that. I think it was his way of showing respect for your bravery throughout this entire ordeal."

Eliza took a deep breath. "And if you were feeling a little jealous, that's understandable, but I hope you know without any doubt that I will never give you a reason to be concerned about my love for you."

"I do, Eliza. I guess that was just the morphine and my innate dislike of policemen talking."

Sunday - September 30, 1928

Eliza warned me she would be a little late Sunday morning because she wanted to attend church. That surprised me just a little. It was the first time since I've known her that she attended church services or even talked about attending them. Still, I figured we both had good reasons to thank The Man Upstairs.

When Eliza arrived I was enjoying a lunch of baked salmon that tasted fresh, brown rice, half of an avocado, four saltine crackers, and lime Jello. I promise no one will ever hear me complain about the food at Cottage Hospital.

Looking at my tray, Eliza said, "Gosh that looks good. If I hadn't eaten lunch at the cottage, I'd sneak a few bites."

"The salmon even tastes fresh. I don't know how they managed that."

"As long as you have to be here anyway, it's good they're treating you well. How did your physical therapy session go this morning?"

"I talked the nurse into letting me do two laps around the room, but I was very nearly on my hands and knees by the time. . . ."

I was interrupted by a knock on the door. Eliza said, "Come in."

The door swung in a ways and Bob Carlson's face appeared in

the opening. "Am I interrupting any crucial medical treatment?"

"Just my daily dose of morale boosting from Eliza. Come on in, Bob. I'm very happy to see you."

Bob walked in and Eliza gave him a sisterly hug. "Thanks for coming, Bob."

"Yes, thanks for coming, but how did you escape from the *Examiner*, climb down the fire escape?"

Chuckling, Bob replied, "Darn near. When Eliza told me you were awake, I had to come and see for myself. You woke up just in time. If you had not, I was going to pour some *Examiner* coffee down that tube in your arm."

"That would have done it!"

"My thought exactly."

"Bob, I'm sorry I've been out of touch, but I will have a red hot feature for you when I can get my hands on a typewriter."

Carlson looked at Eliza. "Hear that? I think we've made a real journalist out of Lester. He can't wait to see his next byline."

Feigning irritation, Eliza glared at me. "Listen, mister, you work for the *Tribune* now. No more giving scoops to the competition!"

Bob said, "Oh, oh. Sounds as if I'm losing the best stringer I ever had."

I sighed an exaggerated sigh. "I'm afraid so, Bob. The boss is laying down the law."

"As she should. So how soon can we get together for some strategy sessions on making the *Tribune* the best danged daily west of the Mississippi?"

"The doctor says I'm stuck here for at least another week. After that, I might talk Eliza into driving me down to the big city so we can meet."

Eliza quickly said, "Only if you keep up with your physical therapy and the doctor approves."

I squeezed her hand. "You heard the boss, Bob. We'll get there as soon as possible."

Bob looked thoughtful. "You know, I've got some vacation time saved up, actually a lot of vacation time. I might enjoy spending some of it in Santa Barbara."

With excitement in her voice, Eliza said, "That would be wonderful if you could, Bob."

"Yes, we might even arrange first class accommodations for you. In fact we can get you a room at the Montecito Inn. Eliza knows the owner personally."

"The Montecito Inn? Isn't that Chaplin's hotel?"

Eliza frowned. "Yes, and I'm not letting that louse within arm's reach of me."

Bob grinned. "Oh, oh. It sounds like there might be a story there."

I said, "There is, Bob, but I'm not sure Eliza will let us tell it."

Eliza said, "I might if you run the story with a photo of me slapping that louse's face."

We kidded for another half an hour or so before Bob said he needed to start back. He made Eliza promise to let him know when he should schedule his Santa Barbara vacation, and then he headed back to Los Angeles.

Eliza said, "I really like him. He is a good friend."

"I could not agree more."

"Darling, you may not know how good a friend he really is. I have no idea how he heard about you being shot because I did not think to call him Monday night, but he called me the next night and he has called every night since to find out how you are. Moreover, he told me if there was anything I needed, all I had to do was tell him. I think he really meant it."

"He meant it. If Bob Carlson says it, he means it."

Eliza brushed my forehead with her fingers. "You look a little tired, darling. Would you like to take a nap?"

"I am feeling awfully drowsy. I'm also starting to feel more pain. Not real bad, but I can tell they've begun lowering my doses of morphine. Still, I don't want to sleep while you are here."

"I'm not going anywhere, darling. Go ahead and get some rest. I'll be right here in the chair."

"Eliza, I love you."

"I love you, too, Lester. I can hardly wait for you to come home."

EPILOGUE

Monday – December 31, 1928

Our garden court cottage still did not have a mirror large enough to see much more than the black bowtie I was attempting to straighten, but I figured if Eliza could manage to look spectacular without the benefit of a full-length mirror, I had no complaint coming.

The occasion for donning our formal attire was the Mayor's New Year's Eve Ball at the new Santa Barbara Biltmore Hotel. As owners of the city's leading newspaper, we were invited.

When the invitation arrived, I thought it would be a good opportunity for us to mark the end of what for us had been a bittersweet year. Looking back on 1928, I counted nearly as many sad moments as happy ones, but in the overall scheme of things, the good outweighed the bad and we had reason to celebrate. With that in mind I asked Eliza if, in honor of the occasion, she would like to purchase a new evening dress to replace the beaded silver-gray gown she wore to Estelle Abernathy's reception back in September.

She put on her coy look and said, "Thank you for thinking of it, darling, but I think I'll wear the gown I have. I don't believe I could ever find anything to top it. Besides, I have some rather fond memories attached to that frock."

As I walked into the bedroom Eliza struck what could only be described as a sexy flapper pose and said, "What do you think, mister? Am I snazzy enough to appear at the fancy dress ball on the arm of a big-time newspaper editor?"

I whistled my approval. "Heck, with you looking like that, nobody is going to notice the big-time newspaper editor."

Eliza leaned against me and planted a kiss on my lips. "Good. I don't want those society dames getting any ideas about my man."

I felt a little tingle of thrill hearing her say "my man." "Don't worry, kiddo. It takes two to tango and I'm not interested in any society dames but the one who will be on my arm."

Eliza gave me another quick kiss. "Right answer, darling.

Right answer."

A few minutes later I opened the passenger door of Frederick Hamm's blue Buick sedan and helped Eliza into the car. By the time I got in the other side, she had slid over to the center of the large front seat to sit next to me.

Starting the engine, I chuckled. "We must look like a couple of kids on our first date."

"I could sit way over there and look proper if you prefer."

"Don't you move an inch. What do I care what people say?"

"Say, you are just full of good answers tonight, darling. I think I'll keep you."

The new Biltmore Hotel is situated on lavish grounds at the beach a few blocks south of the Montecito Inn. The place was huge and classy as all get out. I appreciate my reliable old Chevrolet, but I was glad we had transportation more appropriate to the venue for this occasion. I'm sure the valet to whom we surrendered the Buick at the hotel's main entrance shared my feelings on that subject.

The Biltmore's swanky lobby was decked out with an overabundance of festive holiday trimmings, and so were most of those inside it. There were even a few top hats in evidence. These were, of course, on the heads of the community's elder statesmen. Like me, most of the younger guests were bare headed.

The women were attired in an amazing array of the finest gowns Santa Barbara has to offer. Still, not one of them caused heads to turn as consistently as Eliza. She sparkled as brightly as the silver angel atop the Biltmore's giant Christmas tree, and that sparkle owed as much to Eliza's natural beauty as it did to her gown. She was the essence of grace and poise. I was right. Very few of those milling about in the lobby took notice of the big-time newspaper editor on whose arm Eliza arrived.

We found our way to the grand ballroom entrance where a fellow looked at our invitation. He consulted a list and almost jumped to attention. "Good evening Mister and Missus Kinney. Please follow me."

He led us to a table at the front of the room just below the dais on which city big shots and honored guests were being seated. I wondered if Estelle Abernathy had been seated on that dais in years past.

As Eliza was seated facing the dais and I slid into the chair next to her, I said quietly, "Wow, this is some shindig."

"It sure is. I haven't seen this many of our leading citizens since father's funeral."

Almost as if on cue, attorney Edwin Ingraham and a pleasant looking woman I soon learned was his wife, Bessie, were seated next to Eliza. A moment later a waiter arrived to fill our champagne flutes from a green bottle of S. Martinelli's sparkling cider. I was wondering if everyone attending the gala event was drinking non-alcoholic beverages when I caught the flash of a silver hip flask at another table.

Ingraham raised his glass and said, "I am taking the honor of making the first toast of the evening. To Eliza and Lester, may the new year bring you the success you so justly deserve."

Eliza smiled demurely and I said, "Thank you, Edwin, but I am obligated to point out that what success comes our way will be a direct result of your legal knowledge."

"Nonsense, young man. It was your knowledge of things nautical that saved the day."

Next, the Reverend Doctor George Weld was shown to our table. He was the Episcopalian minister who presided at Frederick Hamm's funeral. Weld occupied the seat to my left.

The sixth and final seat at our table was filled by Eliza's favorite louse, none other than the famous Charles Chaplin. I wondered what stroke of irony resulted in Chaplin being seated at our table.

Everyone greeted the film actor warmly, except Eliza. Predictably, her gracious smile conveyed all the warmth of the iceberg that sank the Titanic.

Leaning close to Eliza's ear, I whispered, "Don't worry, kiddo, if he makes one move toward that cute fanny of yours, I will defend your honor to the death."

Eliza gave me a disapproving look and muttered, "Swell."

Soon thereafter dinner was served. The Biltmore's chef did the hotel proud with a four course feast featuring tender slices of prime rib roast and a dessert of brandied peaches. If anyone left the ball hungry, they only had themselves to blame.

With the serving of the peaches, Mayor Theodore Finley stood and tapped a champagne flute with his spoon to get the crowd's attention. He then welcomed everyone and introduced the dignitaries on the dais.

With those chores out of the way, Mayor Finley moved on to the next piece of business on his agenda. "As I am sure you all remember, we take advantage of this gala gathering each year to announce the name of Santa Barbara's Man of the Year. Our Man of the Year is selected by members of the city council in recognition of community service and outstanding personal accomplishment.

"For 1928 our Man of the Year is a relative newcomer to Santa Barbara, but in the short time he's been here, this young fellow has made his presence known in large ways. As a journalist, he exposed shameful events that cast dark shadows on the integrity of our fair city. In doing so our Man of the Year also exposed himself to great risks. He, in fact, was twice seriously injured in his pursuit of truth and justice."

I was not paying full attention to the mayor's speechifying, but when I realized about whom he was speaking, I was surprised to say the least. I expected Santa Barbara's city fathers would be eager to bury Estelle Abernathy's misdeeds deep in the past. Instead they were spotlighting them for all to see, and I was to be the source of that illumination.

"So please join me in honoring a true American hero, Mister Lester Kinney. Come on up here, Lester."

I looked at Eliza in bewilderment. She said, "I think he means you, darling. Better go up there and get your award."

As I stood the room burst into applause that continued the entire time it took me to mount the dais and walk to the speaker's podium. When I got there Mayor Finley shook my hand and held the pose while photographers, including at least one in my employ, flashed and snapped.

When the flashing ended, the mayor read the inscription on a large, handsome plaque, and then he handed it to me. "We are all in your debt, Mister Kinney, and we are proud to call you 'neighbor.'"

I accepted the plaque and gave it the admiring look expected of me while the photographers did more snapping and flashing. All the while I was wondering what the heck I was going to say by way of an acceptance speech for an honor I was not sure I truly deserved. I glanced down at Eliza and suddenly the solution to my dilemma was clear to me.

Holding my arms up for quiet, I cleared my throat and said, "First, I want to express my gratitude to the members of the city council for selecting me as the recipient of this prestigious recognition. I am honored.

"I am, however, also obligated to share this honor with a man whose dedication and personal sacrifices to the City of Santa Barbara go back much further and were far greater than mine—a man you all knew to be honorable and a leading citizen of this community. I speak of the late Frederick Hamm, without whom none of my accomplishments would have been possible."

At first there was complete and utter silence in the room. Then, after what seemed like an eternity, a few people began to clap. A moment later the entire grand ballroom exploded into applause again, only this time everyone in the room stood to honor Frederick Hamm. I glanced down at Eliza again. Despite the tears in her eyes, she was smiling proudly.

Still standing next to me, Mayor Finley was also smiling. I shook his hand again and carried my plaque back to our table. As I took my place next to Eliza, she stood on tiptoes and gave me a kiss right there in front of God and everybody. With that the applause was renewed with even greater enthusiasm.

I whispered in Eliza's ear. "You knew about this, didn't you?"

Grinning, she replied, "I might have had an inkling about something special coming your way."

When the room was finally quiet again, Mayor Finley made a few remarks about the state of the city and announced that the Anson Weeks orchestra was about to provide music for our dancing pleasure. When the music began a moment later Eliza and I found ourselves surrounded by a mob of folks who congratulated me on winning the award and on my acceptance speech.

When the wave of congratulatory handshakes ebbed, I escorted Eliza to the dance floor. Weeks' orchestra was playing a popular ballad, *What a Difference a Day Makes.*

As we danced, Eliza asked, "Have I mentioned lately that I am married to the greatest guy in the world?"

I cocked my head to one side as if contemplating my answer to her question. "No, I don't believe so, at least not in the last thirty seconds."

"Well, I am. Including Father in your acceptance speech was a kind and generous thing to do. It was also unexpected. I could tell the people around me were moved by your words. Thank you, darling."

"I meant what I said."

"That was obvious. What made your words especially meaningful to me is that I know how Father treated you the last time you saw him. That you are able to forgive him is what makes you a true hero in my eyes."

Smiling, I said, "But I got the best part of the deal."

"I don't understand, darling."

"How could I not forgive a man who ultimately gave me the most precious thing in his life, and now in my life? You."

"Oh, Lester," was all Eliza said.

We danced our way through another tune, and then while Eliza visited the powder room I returned to our table. There I was approached by Eliza's least favorite louse. "Lester, may I have a word with you?"

I stood, and preferring to keep the conversation on a more formal level, I said, "I suppose so, Mister Chaplin."

"Listen, old man, I committed an unfortunate faux pas that night at Estelle Abernathy's party. Please tell me how I can make it up to Missus Kinney."

I looked him squarely in the eyes for a few seconds, and then said, "You cannot, Mister Chaplin. Your unfortunate faux pas is also unforgiveable."

Chaplin's mouth opened as if he intended to say something. He then clamped his mouth shut and walked away without another word.

Eliza witnessed the end of my encounter with Chaplin as she returned to our table. "What was that all about, darling? Chaplin looked as if you stole his lollipop."

"He wanted to know how he could gain your forgiveness for his 'unfortunate faux pas' at Estelle's party."

"Oh?"

"Yes. I told him his unfortunate faux pas was also unforgiveable."

"Did you now?"

"I did."

"Bravo, darling!"

A few minutes later I handed a valet the claim ticket for our Buick. After helping Eliza in the passenger door, I placed my Man of the Year plaque on the rear seat and slid behind the steering wheel. Leaving the Biltmore Hotel, I turned west on Cabrillo Boulevard and continued along the coast past Stearns Wharf, where Cabrillo becomes Shoreline Drive.

By this time, Eliza figured out where I was headed. "You can't fool me, mister. I know where you're going."

"Do you object?"

"Not at all, if you think it's all right for an old married couple to park and pet."

"I won't tell if you don't."

A few minutes later Eliza's head was resting on my shoulder, just as it was the first time we parked on the bluff overlooking the ocean. She said, "Thank you for bringing us here, darling. It's the perfect way to end a lovely evening."

"If I am really fortunate, this lovely evening will not end here."

Feigning shock, Eliza said, "Oh my! Just exactly what do you mean by that, mister?"

I kissed her a long and intense kiss, after which, she gasped, "Oh. That's what you mean."

"It seems appropriate that we finish the evening the way we both wanted it to end the first time we came here."

"Yes, darling, it does, but before we do that, there is something I must tell you."

I looked at her face. "Oh? A confession, perhaps?"

"In a way. Actually, it's more like a disappointment."

Surprised, I said, "Disappointment? What could you possibly find disappointing tonight?"

"Well, I was just thinking how sad it is that Father will never meet his grandchild."

It took a moment for what she was telling me to sink into my thick skull. "I . . . ah . . . wait a minute. What grandchild?"

Eliza took my hand and gently placed it on her stomach. "This one, darling."

"Really? I'm going to be a daddy?"

"Unless Doctor Wilson is sorely mistaken, yes darling, you are going to be a daddy."

"Wow! When did that . . . I mean . . . how soon?"

"Doctor Wilson says the blessed event is scheduled for next summer—he estimates the middle of July. That means it must have happened right after you got home from the hospital. If I had to guess, probably your first night home. We were both particularly . . . amorous that night."

"With good reason. My faded blue shirt never looked as good as it did that night."

"It never felt better than it did that night."

Puzzled, I said, "My shirt?"

Grinning, Eliza said, "Not exactly your shirt, darling."

"Gosh. We have a lot to do by summer. We need a new place to live with more room and . . . ."

"I've already started one of my famous lists. Tell me darling, would you prefer a son or a daughter?"

"I've never really thought about it, but I think maybe a daughter. With you as her mom, she would be the most beautiful kid in town. Golly, this is wonderful news!"

"I think so, too, and we are going to find out if you really meant what you said in Carlsbad."

"Huh? What did I say in Carlsbad?"

"You said the only thing that would make me more beautiful

was the blush of motherhood."

"That I did, and you will soon discover that prediction could not have been more accurate."

There was a tear in her eye as she whispered, "Yes, mister, I am definitely keeping you."

THE END

MEET H. P. OLIVER

H. P. Oliver began his career with a degree in journalism from San Jose State University and spent the next twenty-some years writing award-winning entertainment and educational media. Now he applies his creativity and imagination to writing historical mysteries.

About mystery writing, Oliver says, "To be truly engrossing, a mystery needs a little meat on its bones—something more than just figuring out who did the evil deed. Taking a story back in time or even basing it on actual historical events is a great way to endow a good yarn with even more color and depth. Historical periods and locations give the writer an opportunity to take most readers where they've never been before."

H. P. Oliver lives in northern California and spends much of his time working on projects throughout the western states. In addition to his love of history, Oliver's interests range from vintage film to restoring classic cars.

For information about H. P. Oliver's books, including synopses, previews, video trailers, and purchase links, visit his fan site at www.HPOliver.com, where you will also find illustrated history articles and other fascinating features. Plan to stay a while.

BOOKS BY H. P. OLIVER

◆ CLASSIC MYSTERIES IN HISTORY ◆

THE TRUTH BE TOLD
(E-Book)

AND THE ANGELS SING
(E-Book)

SILENTS!
(E-Book & Paperback)

WINGING IT
(E-Book & Paperback)

GOODNIGHT, SAN FRANCISCO
(E-Book & Paperback)

SO LONG, L A
(E-Book & Paperback)

◆ JOHNNY SPICER CAPERS ◆

JOHNNY SPICER: THE FIRST CAPERS
(E-Book)

PACIFICA
(E-Book & Paperback)

REVOLVER
(E-Book & Paperback)

TEMBO
(E-Book & Paperback)

S. N. A. F. U.
(E-Book & Paperback)

H. P. Oliver's books are available at Amazon.com

www.ingramcontent.com/pod-product-compliance
Lightning Source LLC
Chambersburg PA
CBHW062010170626
46813CB00001B/101